Marcia Brady Tucker

Sketch-book of British birds

Marcia Brady Tucker

Sketch-book of British birds

ISBN/EAN: 9783742848789

Manufactured in Europe, USA, Canada, Australia, Japa

Cover: Foto ©Andreas Hilbeck / pixelio.de

Manufactured and distributed by brebook publishing software
(www.brebook.com)

Marcia Brady Tucker

Sketch-book of British birds

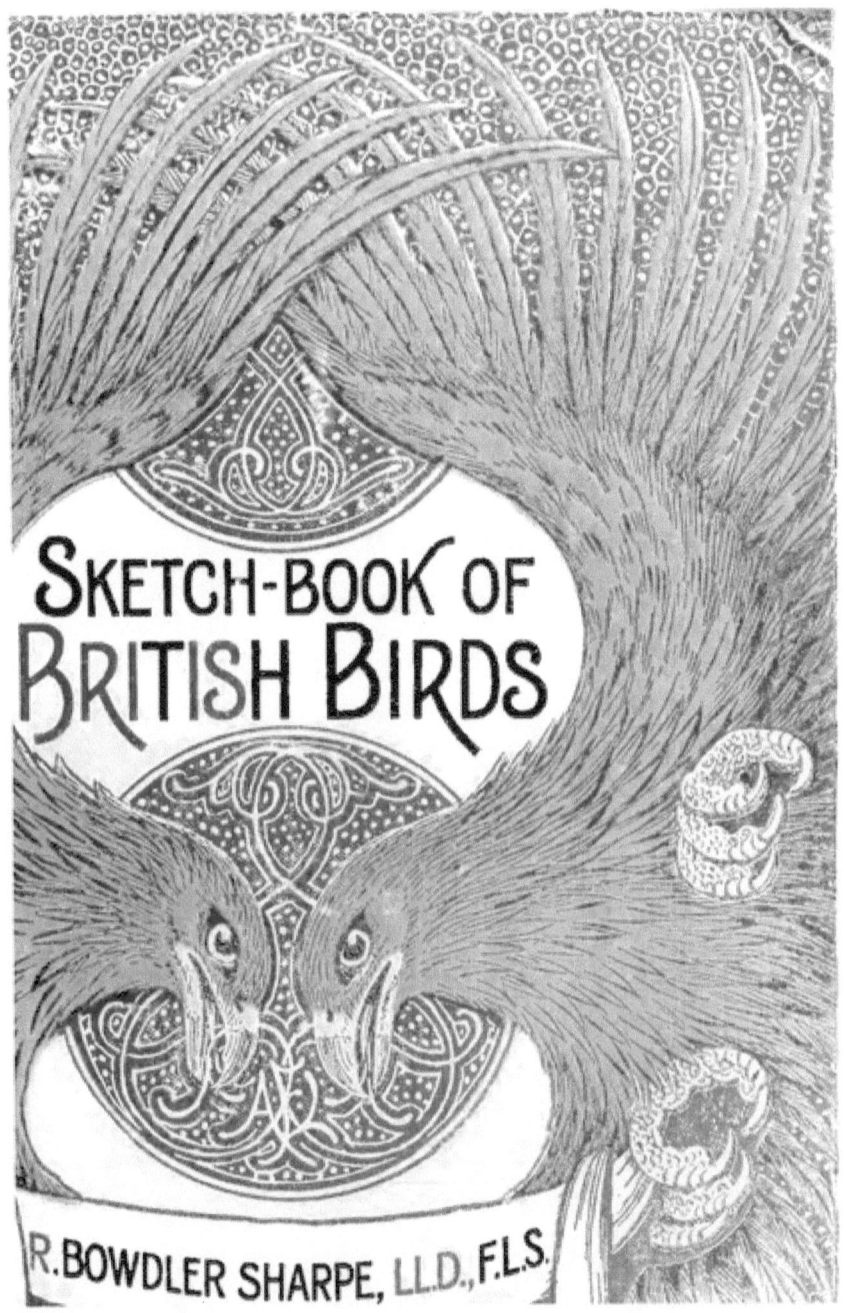

SKETCH-BOOK OF
BRITISH BIRDS

R. BOWDLER SHARPE, LL.D., F.L.S.

THE SONG THRUSH.

SKETCH-BOOK

OF

BRITISH BIRDS.

BY

R. BOWDLER SHARPE, LL.D., F.L.S., ETC.

Assistant Keeper, Sub-Department of Vertebrata, British Museum.

THE PEREGRINE FALCON.

WITH COLOURED ILLUSTRATIONS

BY

A. F. AND C. LYDON.

London:
SOCIETY FOR PROMOTING CHRISTIAN KNOWLEDGE.
NORTHUMBERLAND AVENUE, W.C.; 43, QUEEN VICTORIA STREET. E.C.
BRIGHTON: 129, NORTH STREET.
NEW YORK: E. & J. B. YOUNG & CO.
1898.

PUBLISHED UNDER THE DIRECTION OF THE GENERAL
LITERATURE COMMITTEE.

Printed by BIDDLE & COUCHMAN, 22, Southwark Bridge Road, London, S.E.

PREFACE.

THIS little work will, I trust, be found useful as a Sketch-book of the Birds of Great Britain. Its limits have not allowed of my attempting a full history of the species, and I have but added a few notes as a running commentary on the little pictures which Messrs. A. F. and C. Lydon have provided.

The Systematic Index is, I believe, the most complete record of the birds in the 'British List' yet published. It contains the two latest additions to the British Avifauna, *Herbivocula schwarzi* and *Munia atricapilla*, and brings the total number of species to 445.

R. BOWDLER SHARPE

CHISWICK,

October 31st, 1898.

THE BLACKBIRD.   THE REDWING.   THE MISTLE THRUSH.   THE THRUSH.

INTRODUCTION.

THE Orders of the Class *Aves* are thirty-four in number, and of these twenty-two are represented in the 'British List.' Such is the term applied to the roll of species which have occurred, or which are supposed to have occurred, within the area of the British Islands. The birds which ought to be considered as actually British are those which *nest* with us, as the breeding-place is, after all, the real home of a bird; but there are also the regular migrants to be considered, *viz.*—the species which pass to and fro in spring and autumn—and finally, the occasional or accidental visitors. The claims of many of the species included under the last two headings are often so slight, that the birds can hardly be considered worthy of a place in the 'British List' at all, but in the present work every species has been mentioned, so that the evidence of these stray occurrences may be taken for what it is worth.

The total number of British Birds is now believed to be 445, divided as follows :—

	SPECIES		SPECIES
Passeriformes (Perching Birds) ...	156	*Lariformes* (Gulls) ...	32
Piciformes (Woodpeckers) ...	7	*Alciformes* (Auks) ...	8
Cuculiformes (Cuckoo-like Birds) ...	4	*Procellariiformes* (Petrels) ...	17
Coraciiformes (Roller-like Birds) ...	14	*Colymbiformes* (Divers) ...	4
Strigiformes (Owls) ...	11	*Podicipediformes* (Grebes) ...	6
Accipitriformes (Birds of Prey) ...	31	*Ralliformes* (Rails) ...	10
Pelecaniformes (Pelican-like Birds) ...	4	*Columbiformes* (Pigeons) ...	6
Phœnicopteriformes (Flamingoes) ...	1	*Pterocletiformes* (Sand-Grouse) ...	1
Anseriformes (Duck-like Birds) ...	48	*Galliformes* (Game-Birds) ...	8
Ardeiformes (Heron-like Birds) ...	14	*Turniciformes* (Hemipodes) ...	1
Gruiformes (Cranes) ...	2		
Charadriiformes (Plover-like Birds) ...	60		445

Of these four hundred and forty-five species, there are doubtless several that have no real claim to be considered British at all. The evidence of the capture of many of the specimens is not convincing, and many species are included in the British Avifauna on untrustworthy data. They have been, however, on the British list for so many years that any attempt to shake the authenticity of their occurrence by a single author may be resented. It is to be hoped that an authoritative list of British Birds may be published by the British Ornithologists' Union or by the B. O. Club.

The difficulty of arranging and tabulating the various species which have been recorded as 'British,' is much greater than any one who had not essayed the task would believe, and it is scarcely possible that any two Ornithologists will entirely agree on the subject. I have, therefore, ventured, entirely on my own authority, to place before my readers, a synopsis of the British species as chronicled up to the present time, and I have assigned to them what I believe to be their constituent worth with regard to their membership of the British Avifauna, so that there is room for ample discussion on the subject. I propose to arrange the British Birds under the following heads :—

I.—SPECIES TO BE REJECTED (3).

The evidence in the cases of *Melanocorypha calandra, Pycnonotus capensis* and *Turnix sylvatica,* seems to be utterly untrustworthy, and the species should be dropped out of all future lists of British Birds. The occurrence of the Orphean Warbler is also not satisfactorily proven, but as several Warblers from the south have undoubtedly reached Britain, it is as well to leave *Sylvia orphens* in the list for the present. There are several other species, like Ross's Gull, the Swallow-tailed Kite, Purple Martin, etc., which are included on evidence quite as slender.

The Polish Swan (*Cygnus immutabilis*), is considered to be a domestic variety of *C. olor.*

II.—SPECIES WHICH HAVE PROBABLY ESCAPED FROM CONFINEMENT (14).

1 *Agelæus phœniceus.* 2 *Scolecophagus carolinus.* 3 *Sturnella magna.* 4 *Serinus canaria* (Wild Canary). 5 *Munia atricapilla.* 6 *Bernicla canadensis.* 7 *Æx sponsa.* 8 *Chenalopex ægyptiaca.* 9 *Cairina moschata.* 10 *Chionis alba.* 11 *Porphyrio cœruleus.* 12 *Porphyrio porphyrio.* 13 *Cygnus buccinator.* 14. *C. americanus.*

That some of the above occurrences are those of escaped birds, no reasonable doubt can be felt; but in the case of the three species of the North American Hang-nests, it is quite possible that they were migrants blown out of their course to the eastward, and, if this be conceded, they can be reckoned with the 'Occasional Visitors from the West' mentioned below. On the other hand, some of the latter, such as *Turdus migratorius, and Ectopistes migratoria* might be added to the category of those species which have, in all probability, escaped from confinement.

III.—INDIGENOUS SPECIES (138.)

1 *Trypanocorax frugilegus.* 2 *Corvus corax.* 3 *Corone corone.* 4 *C. cornix.* 5 *Colœus monedula.* 6 *Garrulus glandarius.* 7 *Pica pica.* 8 *Graculus graculus.* 9 *Sturnus vulgaris.* 10 *Ligurinus chloris.* 11 *Coccothraustes coccothraustes.* 12 *Fringilla cœlebs.* 13 *Chrysomitris spinus.* 14 *Carduelis carduelis.* 15 *Cannabina flavirostris.* 16 *C. cannabina.* 17 *C. rufescens.* 18 *Passer domesticus.* 19 *Passer montanus.* 20 *Loxia curvirostra.* 21 *Pyrrhula europæa.* 22 *Emberiza schœniclus.* 23 *E. citrinella.* 24 *E. cirlus.* 25 *Miliaria miliaria.* 26 *Alauda arvensis.* 27 *Lullula arborea.* 28 *Motacilla lugubris.* 29 *M. melanope.* 30 *Anthus pratensis.* 31 *A. obscurus.* 32 *Certhia familiaris.* 33 *Sitta cæsia.* 34 *Parus major.* 35 *P. cœruleus.* 36 *P. britannicus.* 37 *P. dresseri.* 38 *P. salicarius.* 39 *Lophophanes cristatus.* 40 *Ægithalus rosgans.* 41 *Calamophilus biarmicus.* 42 *Regulus regulus.* 43 *Melizophilus undatus.* 44 *Merula merula.* 45 *Turdus musicus.* 46 *T. viscivorus.* 47 *Erithacus rubecula.* 48 *Pratincola rubicola.* 49 *Tharrhaleus modularis.* 50 *Cinclus aquaticus.* 51 *Anorthura troglodytes.* 52 *A. hirtensis.* 53 *Gecinus viridis.* 54 *Dendrocopus major.* 55 *D. minor.* 56 *Alcedo ispida.* 57 *Asio otus.* 58 *A. accipitrinus.* 59 *Syrnium aluco.* 60 *Strix flammea.* 61 *Pandion haliaetus.* 62 *Circus cyaneus.* 63 *C. æruginosus.* 64 *Accipiter nisus.* 65 *Buteo buteo.* 66 *Aquila chrysaetus.* 67 *Haliaetus albicilla.* 68 *Milvus milvus.* 69 *Falco peregrinus.* 70 *Cerchneis tinnunculus.* 71 *Phalacrocorax carbo.* 72 *P. graculus.* 73 *Dysporus bassanus.* 74 *Anser anser.* 75 *Cygnus olor.* 76 *Tadorna tadorna.* 77 *Spatula clypeata.* 78 *Anas boscas.* 79 *Chaulelasmus streperus.* 80 *Mareca penelope.* 81 *Nettion crecca.* 82 *Nyroca ferina.* 83 *Fuligula fuligula.* 84 *Somateria mollissima.* 85 *Œdemia nigra.* 86 *Merganser merganser.* 87 *M. serrator.* 88 *Ardea cinerea.* 89 [*Botaurus stellaris*]. 90 [*Otis tarda*]. 91 *Œdicnemus œdicnemus.*

92 *Charadrius pluvialis.* 93 *Ægialitis hiaticola.* 94 *Vanellus vanellus.* 95 *Hæmatopus ostralegus.* 96 *Numenius arquatus.* 97 *N. phæopus.* 98 *Totanus calidris.* 99 *Glottis nebularius.* 100 *Pelidna alpina.* 101 *Gallinago gallinago.* 102 *Scolopax rusticula.* 103 *Phalaropus hyperboreus.* 104 *Larus ridibundus.* 105 *L. marinus.* 106 *L. fuscus.* 107 *L. argentatus.* 108 *L. canus.* 109 *Rissa tridactyla.* 110 *Megalestris catarrhactes.* 111 *Stercorarius crepidatus.* 112 *Alca torda.* 113 *[Plautus impennis].* 114 *Uria troile.* 115 *U. ringvia.* 116 *Cepphus grylle.* 117 *Fratercula arctica.* 118 *Procellaria pelagica.* 119 *Oceanodroma leucorrhoa.* 120 *Fulmarus glacialis.* 121 *Puffinus puffinus.* 122 *Colymbus arcticus.* 123 *C. septentrionalis.* 124 *Lophaethyia cristata.* 125 *Podiceps fluviatilis.* 126 *Rallus aquaticus.* 127 *Gallinula chloropus.* 128 *Fulica atra.* 129 *Columba palumbus.* 130 *C. œnas.* 131 *C. livia.* 132 *Lagopus scoticus.* 133 *L. mutus.* 134 *Lyrurus tetrix.* 135 *Tetrao urogallus.* 136 *Caccabis rufa.* 137 *Perdix perdix.* 137 *Phasianus colchicus.*

IV.—VISITORS FROM THE SOUTH.

REGULAR VISITORS (70).

The following may be considered as regular visitors. They can be divided into two categories—those which breed, or have bred, in the British Islands, and those which have not been known for certain to do so. To the latter category belong 12 species as follows:—

1 *Emberiza hortulana.* 2 *Merops apiaster.* 3 *Strepsilas interpres.* 4 *Squatarola helvetica.* 5 *Limosa lapponica.* 6 *Totanus fuscus.* 7 *Helodromas ochropus.* 8 *Calidris arenaria.* 9 *Limonites minuta.* 10 *L. temmincki.* 11 *Ancylochilus subarquatus.* 12 *Tringa canutus.*

The following 58 species breed regularly within our area, or have been known to do so at some time or other. Many species have been banished from their northern nesting-places by the drainage of the fens, or by the march of civilisation:—

1 *Oriolus galbula.* 2 *Motacilla alba.* 3 *M. campestris.* 4 *M. flava.* 5 *Anthus trivialis.* 6 *Lanius collyrio.* 7 *Sylvia sylvia.* 8 *S. curruca.* 9 *S. atricapilla.* 10 *S. simplex.* 11 *Phylloscopus sibilatrix.* 12 *P. trochilus.* 13 *P. minor.* 14 *Acrocephalus phragmitis.* 15 *A. streperus.* 16 *A. palustris.* 17 *Locustella nævia.* 18 *[L. luscinioides.]* 19 *Merula torquata.* 20 *Dandias luscinia.* 21 *Ruticilla phœnicurus.* 22 *Saxicola œnanthe.* 23 *Pratincola rubetra.* 24 *Muscicapa grisola.* 25 *Ficedula atricapilla.* 26 *Chelidon urbica.* 27 *Clivicola riparia.* 28 *Hirundo rustica.* 29 *Iynx torquilla.* 30 *Cuculus canorus.* 31 *Apus apus.* 32 *Caprimulgus europæus.* 33 *Upupa epops.* 34 *Circus pygargus.* 35 *Pernis apivorus.* 36 *Falco subbuteo.* 37 *F. æsalon.* 38 *Querquedula querquedula.* 39 *Platalea leucorodia.* 40 *[Grus grus].* 41 *Eudromias morinellus.* 42 *Ægialitis alexandrina.* 43 *[Recurvirostra avocetta].* 44 *[Limosa limosa].* 45 *Tringoides hypoleucus.* 46 *Rhyacophilus glareola.* 47 *[Pavoncella pugnax].* 48 *[Hydrochelidon nigra].* 48 *Sterna fluviatilis.* 50 *S. macrura.* 51 *S. dougalli.* 52 *S. cantiaca.* 53 *S. minuta.* 54 *Crex crex.* 55 *Porzana porzana.* 56 *P. intermedia.* 57 *Turtur turtur.* 58 *Coturnix coturnix.*

OCCASIONAL OR ACCIDENTAL VISITORS (69).

1 *Pyrrhocorax pyrrhocorax.* 2 *Serinus serinus.* 3 *Calandrella brachydactyla.* 4 *Galerita cristata.* 5 *Tichodroma muraria.* 6 *Lanius minor.* 7 *L. pomeranus.* 8 *Sylvia subalpina.* 9 *S. orphea.* 10 *Aedon galactodes.* 11 *Hypolais hypolais.* 12 *H. polyglotto.* 13 *Acrocephalus aquaticus.* 14 *A. turdoides.* 14 *Monticola saxatilis.* 16 *Saxicola isabellina.* 17 *S. stapazina.* 18 *S. deserti.* 19 *Accentor collaris.* 20 *Coccystes glandarius.* 21 *Apus melba.* 22 *Caprimulgus ruficollis.* 23 *Coracias garrulus.* 24 *C. abyssinicus.* 25 *Scops scops.* 26 *Carine noctua.* 27 *Gyps fulvus.* 28 *Neophron percnopterus.* 29 *Buteo desertorum.* 30 *Milvus migrans.* 31 *Elanus cœruleus.* 32 *Cerchneis cenchris.* 33 *C. vespertina.* 34 *Phœnicopterus roseus.* 35 *Phoyx purpurea.* 36 *Herodias alba.* 37 *Garzetta garzetta.* 38 *Nycticorax nycticorax.* 39 *Ardeola ralloides.* 40 *Bubulcus lucidus.* 41 *Ardetta minuta.* 42 *Ciconia ciconia.* 43 *Plegadis falcinellus.* 44 *Anthropoides virgo.* 45 *Tetrax*

tetrax. 46 *Cursorius gallicus.* 47 *Glareola pratincola.* 48 *Ægialitis dubia.* 49 *Himantopus himantopus.* 50 *Totanus stagnatilis.* 51 *Hydrochelidon hybrida.* 52 *H. leucoptera.* 53 *Gelochelidon anglica.* 54 *Hydroprogne caspia.* 55 *Sterna anæstheta.* 56 *S. fuliginosa.* 57 *Anous stolidus.* 58 *Larus melanocephalus.* 59 *Oceanodroma castro.* 60 *Pelagrodroma marina.* 61 *Daption capensis.* 62 *Puffinus yelkouanus.* 63 *P. obscurus.* 64 *P. assimilis.* 65 *P. grisens.* 66 *Œstrelata brevipes.* 67 *Bulweria bulweri.* 68 *Diomedea melanophrys.* 69 *Prostapus nigricollis.*

V.—VISITORS FROM THE EAST.
REGULAR VISITORS (5).

1 *Anthus campestris.* 2 *A. spipoletta.* 3 *Sylvia nisoria.* 4 *Ruticilla titys.* 5 *Larus minutus.*

ACCIDENTAL OR OCCASIONAL VISITORS (38).

1 *Nucifraga macrorhyncha.* 2 *Pastor roseus.* 3 *Carpodacus erythrinus.* 4 *Emberiza melanocephala.* 5 *E. pusilla.* 6 *E. rustica.* 7 *E. cioides.* 8 *Melanocorypha sibirica.* 9 *Anthus richardi.* 10. *Regulus ignicapillus.* 11 *Phylloscopus viridanus.* 12 *P. superciliosus.* 13 *P. proregulus.* 14 *Herbivocula schwarzi.* 15 *Oreocichla varia.* 16 *Geocichla sibirica.* 17 *Merula atrigularis.* 18 *Siphia parva.* 19 *Caprimulgus isabellinus.* 20 *Chætura caudacuta.* 21 *Merops philippinus.* 22 *Coracias indicus.* 23 *Aquila maculata.* 24 *Bernicla ruficollis.* 25 *Casarca casarca.* 26 *Netta rufina.* 27 *Nyroca nyroca.* 28 *Ciconia nigra.* 29 *Houbara macqueenii.* 30 *Charadrius dominicus.* 31 *Ochthodromus asiaticus.* 32 *Chettusia gregaria.* 33 *Heteropygia acuminata.* 34 *Larus ichthyaetus.* 35 *Lophæthyia griseigena.* 36 *Zapornia parva.* 37 *Turtur orientalis.* 38 *Syrrhaptes paradoxus.*

VI.—VISITORS FROM THE NORTH (35).
REGULAR VISITORS.

1. *Fringilla montifringilla.* 2 *Cannabina linaria.* 3 *Plectrophenax nivalis.* 4 *Calcarius lapponicus.* 5 *Otocorys alpestris.* 6 *Anthus rupestris.* 7 *Lanius excubitor.* 8 *Ampelis garrulus.* 9 *Turdus iliacus.* 10 *T. pilaris.* 11 *Cyanecula suecica.* 12 *Anser fabalis.* 13 *A. albifrons.* 14 *A. brachyrhynchus.* 15 *Branta leucopsis.* 16 *B. bernicla.* 17 *Cygnus musicus.* 18 *C. bewicki.* 19 *Dafila acuta.* 20 *Fuligula marila.* 21 *Clangula clangula.* 22 *Harelda glacialis.* 23 *Arquatella maritima.* 24 *Gallinago major.* 25 *Limnocryptes gallinula.* '26 *Crymophilus fulicarius.* 27 *Larus hyperboreus.* 28 *L. leucopterus.* 29 *Pagophila eburnea.* 30 *Stercorarius pomatorhinus.* 31 *S. parasiticus.* 32 *Alle alle.* 33 *Colymbus glacialis.* 34 *C. adamsi.* 35 *Dytes auritus.*

OCCASIONAL OR ACCIDENTAL VISITORS (29).

1 *Cannabina holboelli.* 2 *C. exilipes.* 3 *Loxia bifasciata.* 4 *Pyrrhula pyrrhula.* 5 *Pinicola enucleator.* 6 *Anthus cervinus.* 7 *Parus ater.* 8 *Ægithalus caudatus.* 9 *Lanius sibiricus.* 10 *Cinclus cinclus.* 11 *Picus martius.* 12 *Bubo bubo.* 13 *Nyctea nyctea.* 14 *Surnia ulula.* 15 *Nyctala tengmalmi.* 16 *Astur palumbarius.* 17 *Archibuteo lagopus.* 18 *Hierofalco candicans.* 19 *H. islandicus.* 20 *H. gyrfalco.* 21 *Cosmonetta histrionica.* 22 *Somateria spectabilis.* 23 *Heniconetta stelleri.* 24 *Œdemia fusca.* 25 *Mergus albellus.* 26 *Limicola platyrhyncha.* 27 *Nema sabinii.* 28 *Rodostethia rosea.* 29 *Uria bruennichi.*

VII.—VISITORS FROM THE WEST.
REGULAR VISITORS (1).

1 *Puffinus gravis.*

OCCASIONAL VISITORS (43).

1 *Cannabina rostrata.* 2 *C. hornemanni.* 3 *Loxia leucoptera.* 4 *Regulus calendula.* 5 *Turdus migratorius.* 6 *Progne purpurea.* 7 *Dendrocopus villosus.* 8 *D. pubescens.* 9 *Coccyzus americanus.* 10 *C. erythrophthalmus.* 11 *Ceryle alcyon.* 12 *Surnia funerea.* 13 *Astur atricapillus.* 14 *Buteo borealis.* 15 *B. lineatus.* 16 *Elanoides furcatus.* 17 *Plotus anhinga.* 18 *Chen hyperboreus.* 19 *Mareca americana.* 20 *Nettion carolinense.* 21 *Querquedula discors.* 22 *Charitonetta albeola.* 23 *Œdemia perspicillata.* 24 *Lophodytes cucullatus.* 25 *Botaurus lentiginosus.* 26 *Oxyechus vociferus.* 27 *Numenius borealis.* 28 *Macrorhamphus griseus.* 29 *Totanus flavipes.* 30 *Helodromas solitarius.* 31 *Tringoides macularius.* 32 *Bartramia longicauda.* 33 *Tringites subruficollis.* 34 *Limonites minutilla.* 35 *Heteropygia maculata.* 36 *H. fuscicollis.* 37 *Steganopus tricolor.* 38 *Larus philadelphia.* 39 *Oceanitis oceanica.* 40 *Œstrelata hæsitata.* 41 *Podilymbus podiceps.* 42 *Porzana carolina.* 43 *Ectopistes migratoria.*

I can quite imagine that considerable exception will be taken by many Ornithologists to the arrangement of the above list, but, as Dr. Sclater pointed out at a recent meeting of the British Ornithologists' Club, the flight of any American species to the shores of Great Britain is not really greater than the bird would take in its ordinary flight to its winter home. It would require, therefore, but an adverse wind to drive it to Britain instead of to its ordinary winter home in Central or South America.

I fully expect that a difference of opinion on many points in the above synopsis will be felt amongst Ornithologists, especially amongst those who cling to the traditions of the recognised ' British List.' The different categories under which the species should be arranged are not easy to define, and exception may be taken to the headings under which I have placed some of them. Thus, for instance, the Alpine Chough (*Pyrrhocorax pyrrhocorax*) might reasonably be considered to be one of those species which have escaped from confinement. *Coracias abyssinicus* might with reason be relegated to the list of spurious British species, and so on.

Again, the Little Bunting (*Emberiza pusilla*) might be supposed to be a visitor from the North instead of from the East, but in each case I have had in my mind the winter home of the species, and its probable line of migration.

All the questions respecting the status of every species in the List of British Birds could easily be settled by a committee of expert ornithologists, and if each bird was considered under its English name, some unanimity might be expected. Opinions differ so widely as to the proper scientific names of our British Birds, that it is useful sometimes to have an independent opinion on the subject, and such I have endeavoured to express in the present work.

R. B. S.

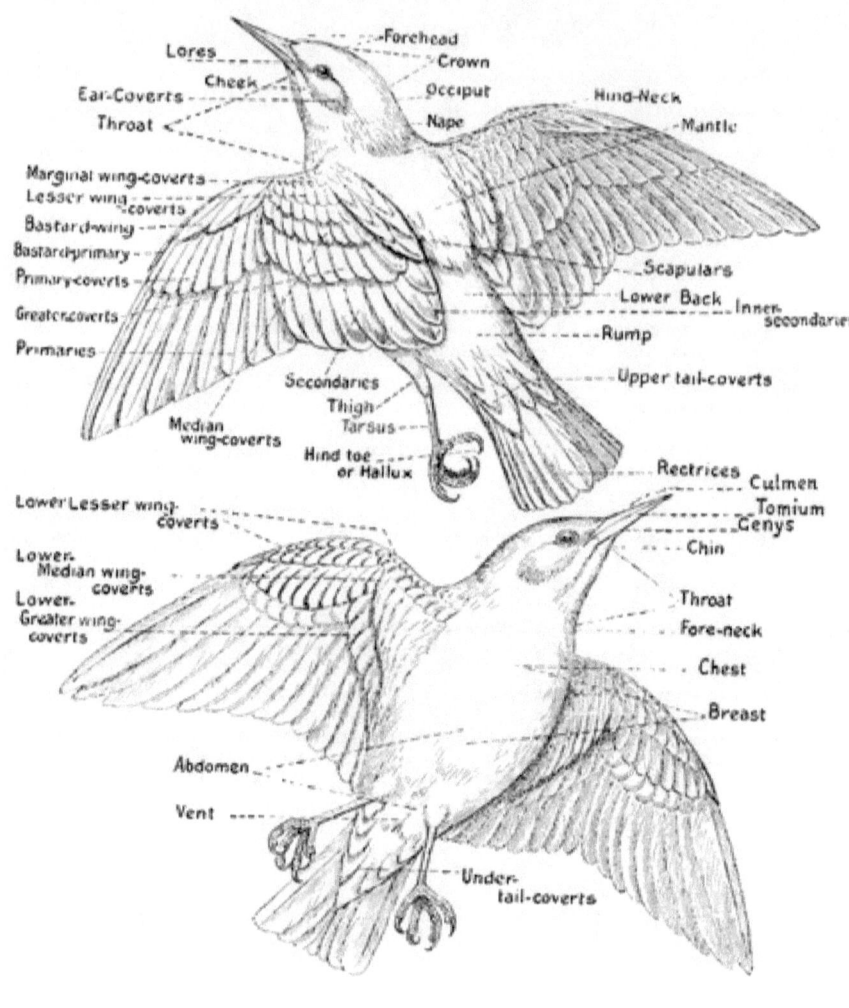

DIAGRAM OF A STARLING,
DEFINING THE TERMINOLOGY OF A BIRD.

SYSTEMATIC INDEX.

ERRATA.

———

Page 15, line 2, read "This is."

Page 47, line 14 from bottom, for "National" read "Natural."

Page 146, line 10 from top, for "*Nyroca nyroca*" read "*Nyroca ferina*."

BRITISH BIRDS.

PERCHING BIRDS. Order PASSERIFORMES.

THE first ORDER of Birds, the *Passeriformes*, contains a larger number of species than any of the others, and we find that quite a third of the British species belong to the Perching Birds. The characters by which they are distinguished from the members of other Orders are not so easily explained as might be imagined by any one who compares in his mind a Rook or a Canary with a Duck or an Owl; for although the external differences between the various Orders of Birds may be obvious enough, the characters for their recognition are deep-seated and often anatomical. Thus the principal feature which distinguishes a Passerine, or Perching, Bird is to be found in the form of the palatine bones, where the vomer is truncated in front, and is not connected with the maxillo-palatines. The arrangement of the tendons of the foot is also peculiar and is characteristic of the Order. As regards external form, the Perching Birds present us with every possible variation -- strong bills, weak bills, hooked bills, flat bills, wings, powerful, weak, pointed, rounded, and so on through every character. Those characters which are of service in classifying the larger birds, such as Hawks, Ducks, or even Wading Birds, fail us when we wish to define the Order *Passeriformes*, nor are the nesting-habits or the colour of the eggs of much assistance. It may indeed be said that the classification of the *Passeriformes* has not yet been thoroughly mastered, and considerable modifications in our present systems may be expected.

THE CROWS.
Family
CORVIDÆ.

There appears to be a concensus of opinion in the present day that the Crows ought to form the leading Family of the Perching Birds. As long ago as 1877 I commenced the 'Catalogue' of the *Passeriformes* in the British Museum with the Family *Corvidæ*, nor have I seen any reason to deviate from this arrangement, while the high position of the Crows and their perfect structure had already been insisted upon by such masters in anatomy as Macgillivray and W. K. Parker.

The Crows are more remarkable for strength than beauty, for the majority of them are black, relieved only by a purplish or green gloss on the plumage, and even this adornment is perceptible only at close quarters. Our Raven and Carrion-Crow are typical examples of this sombre family, but the Hooded Crow is a handsomer bird, with drab-coloured mantle and breast. The Magpies and Jays redeem the family *Corvidæ* from the stigma of dingy colouring, and even some of the Ravens have their black dress relieved by a white collar, as is seen in the thick-billed Ravens (*Corvultur*) of Africa.

THE ROOK.
(*Trypanocorax*
frugilegus.)

This is the most gregarious of all the Crows we have in Great Britain, and usually builds in colonies, known as 'Rookeries.' The nest is substantially and even artistically built of twigs, with a large deep cup in the centre, lined with roots and moss. It is generally placed at a considerable height from the ground, and is a comfortable dwelling enough for the young. So firmly built is the nest that it withstands a great deal of rough weather, and is not often dislodged by a gale, although the young birds are sometimes blown out. When the latter are full grown, they differ from the parent birds in being more dingy, as they have not the beautiful gloss on the plumage which makes the old Rook quite a beautiful bird, when looked at closely. Young Rooks too have the base of the bill and the fore part of the cheeks feathered, so that they much resemble Carrion Crows, but may be distinguished from the latter by their longer and more slender bill, and by the bases of the body feathers being grey, not white. The eggs are like those of typical Crows, being from three to five in number, spotted and blotched with greenish brown on a bluish green ground. From the number of grubs and wire-worms which the Rooks consume, they must be considered as most useful birds to the farmer, though they are desperate hands at harrying a walnut tree in the autumn, and they likewise devour a considerable number of birds' eggs in the spring, particularly those of the Sky-lark when it builds in exposed country. Even in the Zoological Gardens strict watch has to be kept on the nests of the birds in the open paddocks, as the Rooks soon find out the nests of Cranes, Bustards, Geese and Swans, and carry off the eggs.

In an article recently published in the *Contemporary Review*, Mr. Phil.

Robinson, that most delightful of observers of the habits of birds, discourses on the 'First Nest of a Rookery'; and he mentions several facts which seem to me to have been unnoticed before, one of the most important of which is that a second hen bird, having no nest and eggs of her own, was allowed to take part in the incubation of the eggs of a lawful mother.

1 THE ROOK.   2 THE RAVEN.   3—THE JACKDAW.
4 -THE HOODED CROW.   5 -THE CARRION CROW.   6—THE CHOUGH.

THE RAVEN.
(*Corvus corax.*)

The Raven is the largest of the European Crows, and is found in North America as well as in the northern parts of the Old World. The species has been so persecuted on account of the supposed depredations it commits, that it has deserted many of its old breeding-haunts, and now nests but seldom in inland counties, though its eyrie is still to be found on several of our rocky coasts. It breeds quite early in the year, and eggs are to be found in the beginning of March or at the end of February. They are large editions of the eggs of the Rook and Carrion Crow, and are sometimes so small that they can scarcely be distinguished from those of the latter bird. From its size the Raven is able to make

1*

considerable havoc among the sheep farms, as it attacks wounded or sickly sheep, as well as fawns, and, in fact, will eat everything from a rat to a chicken, while it also feeds on carrion.

THE
CARRION-CROW.
(Corone corone.)

This is a much smaller bird than the Raven, and has a somewhat differently shaped wing. In habits it is very like a Raven, but is of course not so powerful a bird, and like that species, it is generally seen in pairs, though occasionally it is said to assemble in flocks. The eggs resemble those of other Crows, all of which have a family likeness. The Carrion-Crow is less common in the South of England than it is in Scotland and Wales, and it often mates with a Hooded Crow, producing a curious hybrid which shows the saddle-back and light-coloured breast of the latter bird, though these pale portions of the body are always more or less intermixed with black smudges and spots.

THE
HOODED CROW.
(Corone cornix.)

This Crow, often called the ‘ Royston ’ or ‘ Danish ’ Crow, is better known as a migrant than as a resident of Great Britain, though the species also breeds with us in certain districts. To the eastern counties come numbers of Hooded Crows in the autumn from Scandinavia and Russia, when they distribute themselves over the Midlands, though the bulk remain near the coasts. In Norway they are by no means uncommon in summer, and harry the nests of the Willow-Grouse as they do those of our Red Grouse on the northern moors. One which I brought up from the nest in 1896 proved to be the most amusing and, at the same time, the most mischievous of pets. His affection was at all times embarrassing to its object, and was demonstrated by tweaks, pinches, and digs at one’s head, or attempts to bite a piece out of one’s ear. This individual was never caged, and would absent himself from home for half the day, but he never failed to appear the moment we came back from our day’s fishing, and would fly out half-a-mile to welcome us.

Some ornithologists disagree with the Crows being placed at the head of the Perching Birds, and argue that the Thrushes and Warblers should have this place of honour, on account of their wonderful development of singing powers. No one seems to have credited a Crow with any such a faculty, but my Hooded Crow would sit for an hour at a time, croaking forth his melody, which really constituted a by no means despicable effort at a song. It was only when he fancied himself quite unobserved that he gave vent to his feelings, and he would fly up to his perch in a garden house, and thence proceed to utter the most extraordinary succession of notes it is possible to imagine. He certainly fancied himself immensely, for he raised his crest and puffed out all the feathers of his throat, and was evidently of the opinion that the Thrushes and Blackbirds could do nothing equal to his own song. The nest and eggs of the Hooded Crow resemble those of the Carrion Crow.

THE JACKDAW.
(Colœus monedula.)

The Jackdaw is the smallest of the true Crows in Great Britain, and differs from them in its nesting place, which is almost invariably in a building or in the hole of a tree. It is also to a certain extent gregarious like the Rook, many couples nesting in the same vicinity, and in the autumn small flocks of Jackdaws may be observed in migration. Nesting as it does under cover, the structure which it makes is a slovenly affair, wanting the neatness and substantiality of the Crows' nest. The eggs, too, are different from those of the latter birds, being paler and much less plentifully marked.

THE NUTCRACKER.

THE SIBERIAN NUTCRACKER.
(Nucifraga macrorhyncha.)

It would seem from the recent observations of Mr. Ernst Hartert (Nov. Zool. IV., pp. 131-136) that ornithologists have been in error in supposing that the Nutcracker which occasionally visits England is the Scandinavian species, the true *N. caryocatactes* of Linnæus. There appear to be four races which have been confounded under the latter heading, viz.:— *N. caryocatactes* from Scandinavia and the Russian Baltic Provinces, *N. relicta* from the Alps and mountains of Central Europe, *N. macrorhyncha* from Siberia, and *N. japonica* from Japan. The Siberian form apparently migrates, whereas the others are stationary, and it is this Siberian bird which invades Europe at certain periods, coming in large numbers, like Pallas' Sand-Grouse and the Waxwing (*Ampelis garrulus*). At rare intervals the Nutcracker visits England. It is a most unmistakeable kind of Crow, having a long thin bill, more slender than that of a Rook, while the upper plumage is varied with triangular spots of white. In their native home these birds are quite early breeders, nesting in March in the pine forests of Europe and Asia. Like other Crows, the Nutcracker is almost omnivorous.

1 THE JAY.   2 THE MAGPIE.

THE JAY.
(Garrulus glandarius.)

The Jay divides with the Magpie the palm of being the handsomest of our British *Corvidæ*, and, though it does not possess the iridescent tints of the latter bird, the beauty of the blue and black barred feathers on the wing is unsurpassed by any of our native birds. Unfortunately the Jay, despite his beauty, has few friends, for he is an unmerciful pilferer of the eggs and young of Game birds, and is waged war upon in consequence.

Luckily for himself, the Jay is gifted with an uncommon degree of artfulness, and its presence is generally only detected by its harsh note of alarm from some thick covert. It has also a strong partiality for fruit and will commit havoc in the early morning on rows of peas, should the kitchen-garden be in the proximity of a wood. At certain times of the year the Jay devours a large quantity of grubs, and a good acorn year is sure to attract a number of the birds to the oak trees. The nest is a tolerably neat cup of twigs and roots, lined with finer rootlets, and the eggs, sometimes as many as six in number, are olive brown or clay colour, finely dotted with pale brown, so minutely that the eggs appear to be sometimes quite uniform in colour.

THE MAGPIE.
(Pica pica.)

A resident species in most parts of the British Islands, but absent in some districts of Scotland, and now rare in many of the southern and midland counties of England, where it was formerly not uncommon. The bright colours of the wings, the long tail, and the conspicuous white shoulder-patch are features which easily distinguish the Magpie from all the other British Crows, and its chattering cry is also quite different from the harsh croaking notes of the other species. The generic character by which it may be told from the other members of the family which are found in Great Britain is the long tail, and another peculiarity is seen in the attenuated first primary-quill of the wing, which is narrowest towards the end, while the quick flapping of the wings is also different from the ordinary powerful flight of other Crows. The pilfering habits of the Magpie and its egg-destroying propensities render it obnoxious to farmers and game-keepers, who ignore the fact that it is a bird which devours a large number of injurious insects and grubs. In other countries of Europe, such as Norway, for example, the bird is not persecuted and becomes comparatively tame, three and four individuals being often seen in company. The nest is an artistic structure of twigs and is generally domed, and the eggs are sometimes as many as seven in number, of a light greenish colour, mottled or spotted with brown or greenish brown.

THE CHOUGH.
(Graculus graculus.)

This bird is easily recognised by its black plumage and bright red bill. The nostrils are differently placed to those of the true Crows, being situated lower down in the bill, nearer to the cutting edge of the mandible than to the ridge. Its former inland habitats in Great Britain now know the Chough no more, but it is found still on many of the rocky coasts of Wales and Ireland, and on some of the Western Islands of Scotland. It breeds in caves or in holes of cliffs, where it builds a nest of sticks and heather-stems, lined with wool and hair. The eggs are much lighter than those of any other British Crow, being nearly white with brown spots.

THE ALPINE CHOUGH.
(Pyrrhocorax pyrrhocorax.)

The Alpine Chough is distinguished from the Red-billed Chough by its shorter and yellow bill, and by having the base of the cheeks bare, and not feathered, as in the foregoing species. It is an inhabitant of the mountains of Southern Europe, whence it extends through the

Alpine regions to Central Asia and Northern China. One specimen has been recorded from England, having been obtained in Oxfordshire, but the bird may probably have been an individual which had escaped from confinement.

THE STARLINGS.
Family STURNIDÆ.

THE ALPINE CHOUGH.

THE COMMON STARLING (*Sturnus vulgaris*). Our Starling is the typical representative of a family of birds which is widely distributed over the old world. They are allied to the Crows in many respects, and, like the latter birds, they walk, instead of hopping, like Thrushes or Finches. They further differ from Crows in having a distinct winter dress, when their bright plumage becomes obscured by whitish tips to the feathers, which fall off as spring approaches, and leave the burnished colour of the Starling in full perfection. The bill, too, loses its dull colour, and becomes bright yellow. No one, to see a Starling on a lawn, would guess that the bird which appears

to be entirely of a dull black, is really shot with iridescent and metallic shades of bronze and green and purple. In full summer plumage, it is indeed a beautiful bird, and one which does an immense amount of good in the destruction of grubs and wire-worms. In the neighbourhood of towns Starlings are a common feature during the winter until the early summer, rearing their young under the roofs of houses, or in holes in trees, or old buildings, but, as soon as the young are able to take care of themselves, they disappear for some weeks, and do not reappear until October, visiting, no doubt, the fruit gardens in the country, where they often commit great havoc. The nest is a rough structure of grasses and straws, and has generally a peculiar odour, as is the case with hole-breeding Crows,

THE STARLING.

THE ROSE-COLOURED STARLING.

like the Jackdaw. The eggs, often as many as seven, are of a delicate pale blue or bluish white.

The typical Starling (*S. vulgaris*) has a green head as well as green cheeks and throat, but a large number of the specimens procured in Great Britain, particularly on the east coast, have a good deal of purple on the head and throat, while the ear-coverts remain green. This is probably owing to the crossing of *S. vulgaris* with the Purple-headed Siberian Starling (*Sturnus menzbieri*).

THE ROSE-COLOURED STARLING (*Pastor roseus*). This is one of the most brightly coloured members of the family, being a remarkably handsome bird. It is only an occasional visitor to Great Britain, its breeding home being in South-eastern Europe, and its winter home in India, where it occurs in vast numbers. It builds its nest in holes of walls or rocks, and is gregarious during the nesting-season as well as in winter. The eggs are whitish or pale grey.

THE ORIOLES.
Family
ORIOLIDÆ.

THE GOLDEN ORIOLE (*Oriolus galbula*). But for the destruction which the brilliant plumage of the Oriole invites, there can be little doubt that the species would nest in England, as scarcely any spring passes without the bird being observed in our southern counties, and it breeds not uncommonly on the opposite side of the Channel. The nest is quite peculiar, being suspended between a fork at the end of a branch, generally of an oak-tree. It is a slender structure, made of strips of bark, which are wound round the branch to which the nest is attached. The eggs, four or five in number, are quite unmistakable, being white, spotted with black and chocolate brown. The winter home of the species is in Africa, and at this season of the year it is found as far south as the Cape Colony.

THE GOLDEN ORIOLE.

THE RED-WINGED HANG-NEST.　　THE MEADOW LARK.

THE HANG-NESTS.
Family
ICTERIDÆ.

THE RED-WINGED HANG-NEST (*Agelæus phœniceus*) is an American bird, of which some dozen specimens have been recorded as British. Like the two following species, it is a member of the truly American family *Icteridæ*, though generally called the 'Red-Winged *Starling*.' Whether the birds which have been captured in Great Britain are really wild individuals which have flown across the Atlantic, or whether they have escaped from confinement, it is difficult always to decide, but in any case the species can never be considered anything but a very irregular visitor to Britain. Like our own Starlings, the *Agelæus* seems to feed its young on insects, of which it devours a vast quantity, but at the same time it does considerable damage to corn and rice. The nests are generally placed in swampy localities in bunches of reeds or in small bushes at no great height from the ground. The eggs are bluish green, of a different type to those of our Starling, as they are spotted with black, brown, or purple.

THE RUSTY BLACK HANG-NEST (*Scolecophagus carolinus*) is said to have occurred once in Great Britain, and is included in the British List on even slenderer grounds than the foregoing American species, which it much resembles in its mode of nidification. The eggs also are blue, spotted with brown or grey.

THE MEADOW LARK (*Sturnella magna*) has been procured three times in Great Britain.

THE RUSTY BLACK HANG-NEST
(Male and Female).

THE GREENFINCH.

It is a ground-loving species, and in North America it is considered to be a most useful bird, as it feeds upon insects and worms, and does but little damage to crops. Its nest is placed on the ground and has a dome of grass, so that it is generally well concealed. The eggs are pale greenish white with brown or grey spots and blotches.

THE FINCHES.
Family
FRINGILLIDÆ.

THE GREENFINCH (*Ligurinus chloris*). The Finches are numerously represented as a family in Great Britain, and we have a good many resident species, of which the Greenfinch is one of the best known. The bright colours are confined to the male, the hen bird, as is usual in this family, being much more dingily coloured than her mate. The Greenfinch is found all over Europe, and as far east as Central Asia, and a considerable migration takes place to the British Islands, the birds which arrive from the Continent being generally of a brighter and purer colour than our own resident birds. Like most Finches, the Greenfinch feeds its young upon insects, but in the autumn and winter it consorts with others of its kind and feeds principally on grain, visiting the fallow-fields and the stock-yards for this purpose. The young, when brought up from the nest, are easily tamed, and make amusing little pets, but they are dangerous denizens of an aviary, as their powerful bills inflict pecks upon their weaker companions which have generally a fatal result. The nest is often a rather large structure, not very carefully constructed, and built of moss with a few twigs or roots outside, and lined with horsehair. The eggs are four to six in number, and are bluish-white with blackish spots or lines.

THE HAWFINCH (*Coccothraustes coccothraustes*).

THE HAWFINCH

is the largest of the British Finches, and is a very powerful bird. For some years past its range in Great Britain has been evidently increasing, and it now breeds in some of our midland counties where it was formerly quite unknown. Notwithstanding its large size, the Hawfinch is never very easy to observe, and often a glimpse of the white on the wings and tail is all that is seen of the bird as it disappears with a wonderfully rapid flight. This species does considerable damage to peas, of which the young birds will devour a large quantity, and stone fruit is also a favourite food of the Hawfinch, which strips off the fruit in order to get at the stone and devour the kernel. The nest is made of twigs and lined with roots and hair, and there is an external net-work of small twigs imparting rather a pretty appearance to some of the nests.

THE CHAFFINCH.

THE CHAFFINCH. (*Fringilla cœlebs.*) With the exception, perhaps, of the Greenfinch, the Chaffinch is our commonest Finch, and it not only nests everywhere throughout the British Islands, but is also plentiful in winter, when a considerable immigration to our shores takes place. The Chaffinch is a very pretty bird, and if it were a denizen of some tropical country, its beauty would be thought still more of than is the case in Europe. As with the generality of Finches, the female is different from the male, and not nearly so bright in colour.

The nest of the Chaffinch is a beautiful little structure, being cup-shaped, and made of moss, with a few twigs, lined with horsehair, feathers and down. It is placed in the fork of a branch of a tree, and the outside of the nest is covered with lichens and cobwebs, which cause the nest to resemble the bark of the tree to which it is attached, so that it is often difficult to discover. The eggs are from four to six in number, and vary considerably, being sometimes pale blue without any spots. Typical eggs, however, have more or less of a pinkish shade, and show a few blotches or scribblings of black or reddish brown.

THE BRAMBLING (*Fringilla montifringilla*). Although similar in form to the Chaffinch, building a nest and laying eggs like those of the last-named bird, the Brambling is very

THE BRAMBLING OR MOUNTAIN FINCH.

THE SISKIN.

different in colour, and is easily distinguished by its white rump, black head, and orange breast. This is as the bird appears in summer, for in winter all the feathers have paler edges, which obscure the bright plumage which lies underneath, and the female is always duller in colour than the male. The Brambling is a winter visitor to Britain, and it is sometimes seen in large numbers, frequenting the beech woods during the day, feeding on the beech-mast, and betaking itself in the evening to the evergreen woods to roost. It nests in Scandinavia and throughout the northern part of the Old World, and is a familiar feature of bird life in Norway in the valleys, but still more so on the fjelds. There nearly every hill has its pair of Bramblings, which frequent the birch woods and build their nest in one of the taller trees. The nest is not at all easy to find, but its vicinity can generally be discovered by following up the note of the male, for the Brambling has a curious habit of sitting on the top of a tree and uttering a continuous note, more like that of a Bunting than a Finch. It is, in fact, something like the call of the Yellow Bunting, but has no inflection at the end, and is, of course, much more powerful. When giving vent to this note, the Brambling raises his crest and throws his head back, and is apparently engaged in uttering defiance to the Brambling which occupies the next hill, for the bird appears to be oblivious of everything except his challenge, and allows a spectator to approach within a few yards. When thus engaged the bird looks very handsome, his black head and orange breast being puffed out to their full extent.

THE SISKIN (*Chrysomitris spinus*). This pretty little Finch is a great favourite with lovers of birds, on account of the facility with which it can be tamed. It nests in the pine-woods in parts of Scotland and Ireland, and is also found breeding over the whole of Northern Europe, and Northern Asia as far as Japan, so that its range

THE GOLDFINCH.

is very similar to that of the Brambling. In winter it goes south from its breeding places, and is then found, in small parties, frequenting the alders, and often consorting with Redpolls and Goldfinches. Sometimes flocks of Siskins, consisting of twenty or thirty individuals, may be noticed on the alders, all busily engaged in obtaining the seeds, and hanging on to the twigs in every conceivable position. So intent are the birds on their task that a note is seldom uttered, and I have many times waited for several minutes under an alder into which I had seen a flock of Siskins pass, before I could discover the little birds, which are generally seen feeding close together at the end of the slender twigs. The nest of the Siskin resembles that of the Goldfinch in size and in material, and the eggs are very similar to those of the latter bird ; it is generally placed at a good height in a fir-tree, and is difficult to find.

The Goldfinch (*Carduelis carduelis*). This bird, like its relation the Siskin, has a more pointed bill than the Chaffinch and the Brambling, and is of much more slender build than those birds : otherwise, however, it is very difficult to distinguish the different characteristics of these Finches, which are very similar in structure to each other, and are told more by their style of coloration than by any other well-marked character. It is, in fact, very interesting to notice how a certain pattern of colour runs through a genus of Finches. Thus the Siskins are nearly all greenish birds with black heads and throats and yellow bands on the wings, so that this coloration is characteristic not only of our European species, but of the majority of the species of Siskins which are spread over the New World. So, with the Goldfinches, the only species known are recognisable at a glance by their crimson face and the patch of gold on their wings. In form and in habits the Goldfinch is most like the Siskin, and the call-note of both these species, and also that of the Redpolls, is much the same, and sounds like the word *eaglet*. The food of the Goldfinch consists of the seeds of the alder trees and those of plants, and it is very fond of thistle-seeds. The nest is a pretty little structure, smaller than that of the Chaffinch, but built on the same plan of concealment by means of the lichens and cob-webs with which it is covered. It is built in an evergreen bush, or in a fruit tree, and is often placed at the very end of an outlying branch of an oak or birch-tree, when it is often quite inaccessible. The eggs are like small editions of those of a Greenfinch or Linnet.

THE TWITE.

The Twite (*Cannabina flavirostris*). Just as the Goldfinches and the Siskins have a characteristic style of colouring, so have the Linnet group of Finches, viz.—a red rump and a red cap and breast generally the three combined. The principal exception to this rule is the Twite or Mountain-Linnet, which has no red on the

THE BROWN LINNET.

breast and no red cap, the head being coloured like the back. It is also easily recognised by its *yellow bill.* The Twite is a resident bird with us, but breeds only on the moorlands of certain parts of Ireland, Scotland, and the northern counties of England, as far south as some of the Midlands. In winter it migrates southwards and is seen in flocks of considerable size near the coasts, where the birds feed on seeds of aquatic plants, and keep up a continued and musical twittering as they feed. The call-note resembles that of a Redpoll or Siskin, being a somewhat harsh '*eaglet.*' The nest is cup-shaped and made of moss with a few heather twigs and is lined with rootlets or feathers and down. The eggs are from four to six in number, and are of the usual Linnet type, being light blue with red or purple spots and lines.

THE BROWN LINNET (*Cannabina cannabina*) is easily recognised from its allies by the crimson forehead and breast of the male, but more especially by the white on the upper tail-coverts and tail-feathers, which are edged with white. The young birds have the breast spotted with brown, and in winter the plumage of the adults is concealed by broad brown margins to the feathers, which gain their full beauty in spring by the abrasion and falling off of these brown edgings.

The Linnet is found breeding over the greater part of the British Islands, and in winter and spring considerable accessions to the number of our resident birds take place by the immigration of birds from the Continent; these individuals are generally brighter in colour than our resident birds. The food of the Linnet consists almost entirely of seeds of some kind, and the birds distribute themselves over the stubbles and fallow ground in the autumn, when I have seen large flocks of them, in September, in the coast-lands in the south of England. The nest is a neat cup, made of moss with a few twigs, and lined with horse-hair. It is generally to be looked for in gorse or heather, and the eggs are from four to six in number, bluish with spots and streaks of purplish-brown.

THE LESSER REDPOLL (*Cannabina rufescens*). This is a smaller bird than the Linnet or the Twite, and is brown, with a crimson cap, breast, and rump. It is exclusively a species of Western Europe, and nests in nearly every part of the United Kingdom, excepting the south-western counties of England; in the south of England it appears to be spreading, as it nests not unfrequently now in Middlesex, Surrey and Kent. On the Continent it nests in France, Belgium, Holland, and Western Germany, as well as in the Alps of Italy, Savoy, and Styria. In

winter a large southward
migration takes place, but
the species does not seem to
reach the countries of the
Mediterranean basin.

THE MEALY REDPOLL.   THE LESSER REDPOLL.

In its ways the Lesser
Redpoll, whether free or in
captivity, is a most engaging
little bird, and in confinement it makes the tamest of
pets and can be taught to do
a number of tricks. It will
even nest in an aviary, a pair
which Mr. Lort Phillips took to Norway this year (1897) building their nest in a
pine branch placed in a cage on his verandah, and rearing four young. In the winter
in the Thames Valley the Lesser Redpoll frequents the alders in company with the
Siskins, and is very similar to these birds in its habits, collecting in flocks or small
parties and feeding on the seeds of the birch and alder. The call-note is also '*cuglet*,'
like that of the Siskin and Twite. The nest is a compact little cup-shaped structure of
moss and grass-stems, lined with hair and vegetable down and a few feathers.

THE MEALY REDPOLL (*Cannabina linaria*). A larger bird than the
Lesser Redpoll, and easily told by its white rump, which is streaked with
dark brown; the bill and feet are also much stouter than in the Lesser Redpoll. It is a
winter visitor to the British Islands, arriving in some numbers on our eastern and
north-eastern coasts. Its breeding-range extends across Northern Europe and Siberia,
and in Norway I have found it breeding on the fjelds near the limit of the birch-growth,
at a height of about 3500 feet, but the nesting-habits certainly vary according to the
season, as in 1896 scarcely a Mealy Redpoll was noticed during the whole summer
until the end of July, when the sorrel and plantain seeds were ripe, and then numbers of
the birds descended from the higher mountains and frequented the meadows of the upper

HOLBOELL'S REDPOLL.

valleys. In the present year (1897), on the
contrary, the species was quite common all
over the birch-region and bred in the neighbourhood of every saeter. The nests were
only discovered when the young were far
advanced, and this may account for their
very untidy and slovenly appearance, for
they by no means recalled the pretty little
nests of the ordinary Redpoll. The eggs
are five or six in number, and resemble
those of the Linnet, but are much
smaller.

COUES' REDPOLL.

HOLBOELL'S REDPOLL. (*Cannabina holbælli*). This a large form of Mealy Redpoll with a much stouter bill. Two specimens have been obtained in England, near Norwich, in January. They were formerly in the collection of Mr. John Gould, and are now in the British Museum. The habitat of this species is Scandinavia and Eastern Siberia, so that it can only be considered a rare and occasional visitor to this country.

THE LARGE-BILLED MEALY REDPOLL (*Cannabina rostrata*). This form differs from the preceding one in having a larger and more obtuse bill, and in being very coarsely striped on the flanks. It inhabits Greenland and Eastern North America, and I have recently seen two specimens shot in Achill Island, on the West Coast of Ireland, by Mr. J. Sheridan.

COUES' REDPOLL (*Cannabina exilipes*) is an inhabitant of Arctic America, as well as the Northern part of the Old World, from Northern Scandinavia across Siberia. It is very similar to the Mealy Redpoll, but is easily distinguished from that species by its unstreaked white rump. I know of four specimens having been captured in England, viz.: three in Yorkshire and one near Tring, in Hertfordshire. It doubtless occurs more frequently than is suspected, and is confounded with the ordinary Mealy Redpoll.

THE GREENLAND REDPOLL (*Cannabina hornemanni*) is another big race of Redpoll, resembling *C. exilipes*, but differing in its larger size, and having a wing of 3·2—3·4 inches, instead of 3 inches, as in Coues' Redpoll. Its home is in Iceland, Greenland, and Eastern North America, and it has only occurred once in England, a specimen having been shot in Durham in April, 1855.

THE HOUSE-SPARROW (*Passer domesticus*). In the common Sparrow we have perhaps the most abundant species of bird in the world, and there is no doubt that it is a species which needs little encouragement, as it takes up its abode in every kind of situation where cultivation provides it with a living, and not only drives away more useful species, but is in many places an absolute pest. Against the damage which the Sparrow unquestionably does to grain crops, must be recorded the fact that, like most Finches, it feeds its young largely upon insects, and, I have seen one shot with the crop absolutely crammed with the Bean Aphis. Nevertheless, the general verdict of those countries into which the Sparrow has been introduced, seems to be that it is a pest, as it ousts the

THE SPARROW.

insectivorous species and is undeserving of protection. In this country it certainly drives away and persecutes many useful birds, and it flourishes to such an extent that I am informed by Mr. Ashton Jones, our Chief Messenger, that any Warbler or other bird which happens to visit our gardens in the Natural History Museum, is at once attacked by the Sparrows and either driven off, or killed instantly.

The House-Sparrow is found throughout the greater part of Europe and Asia, as far as Lake Baikal, though the individuals from Asia are certainly smaller and brighter in plumage than those of our own islands. In the South of Europe the Spanish Sparrow, and in Italy *Passer italiæ*, replace our domestic species.

The sexes differ greatly in colour, and the male Sparrow, when not disfigured by the smoke of towns, is really quite a handsome little bird. Like most Finches, he gains his summer plumage by the abrasion of the brown edges to the feathers with which he is clothed in winter, and as these tips fall off, his spring dress, which is hidden beneath, becomes apparent. White varieties of the House-Sparrow are not uncommon, and a pair of birds which frequented our gardens at the Natural History Museum a few years ago, were noticeable for their white wing-feathers, and this peculiarity was reproduced in their young ones. To this day a few birds with a more or less marked degree of albinism may be seen in the vicinity, but the white-winged birds seem to have gradually died out. The nest of the common Sparrow is to be found in all kinds of situations, and the way in which it chokes up water-pipes with its untidy structure of grass and straw, is well known to and dreaded by the dwellers in our suburbs. Where the hole of a roof or a barn is not available, the Sparrow often builds its nest in ivy or even on a tree apart, while in the Natural History Museum may be seen a curious example of the bird's choice, a pair having sought the shelter of a large fungus on old Putney Bridge, under which they placed their nest.

THE TREE-SPARROW.
(*Passer montanus.*)

The present species is quite different in appearance from the House-Sparrow, being not only a smaller bird, but distinguished by its chocolate-coloured pate. The sexes are alike in colour, and the note is not nearly so harsh as that of the Common Sparrow. In the British Islands the Tree-Sparrow is always more or less local in its habitat, and is principally an inhabitant of the Eastern Counties in England and Scotland. In Ireland it breeds on the coast of Dublin and is increasing in numbers.

In the autumn the Tree-Sparrow consorts with the House-Sparrow in the stubble-fields, and retires to roost with it in the evergreens or ivy-covered trees, where the clamour of Sparrows in the evening is so noticeable a

THE TREE SPARROW.

2

THE SERIN FINCH.

feature in our country districts. It is a curious fact in distribution that whereas in Western Europe the House-Sparrow is the bird of the cities and villages, and the Tree-Sparrow is the species of the country, as the eastern range of the two birds is reached, it is the Tree-Sparrow which becomes the dominant one and replaces the House-Sparrow as the familiar species of the towns and gardens. The nest is a rough structure of straw, like that of other Sparrows, and is situated in holes of barns or rocks, but it is more frequently placed in pollard willows. The eggs are more thickly marked than those of the House-Sparrow, which they otherwise closely resemble.

THE SERIN FINCH.
(Serinus serinus.)

Is a Canary, and is so like the wild Canary of Madeira, from which the ordinary yellow cage-bird is derived, that there is practically no difference between the two birds, except that the Serin is decidedly the smaller of the two. It is an inhabitant of Southern and Central Europe, and is apparently extending its range northward, as frequent notices of its breeding in localities hitherto unrecorded appear in the German periodicals. It extends as far north as Denmark, and occasionally wanders to the British Islands, some eight individuals having been captured in England during the season of spring or autumn migration. The song of the Serin Finch or 'Zeizig,' as it is called in Germany, is quite unmistakable, as I can state from my own observations in the Frankfort Zoological Gardens, where I was first introduced to the bird, by the well-known naturalist, Ernst Hartert. The habits of the Serin are those of the Siskin, excepting that the former is a more lively bird, and is much more often seen, as it sings from the top of a tree or mounts into the air. The eggs resemble those of the Linnet, but are smaller.

Many Wild Canaries (*Serinus canaria*) have been caught in England, and I have had several brought to me at the British Museum; but whether they are really individuals which have been brought alive from the Canary Islands and have escaped, or whether they are ordinary yellow Canaries which have got out of their cages and taken to the woods and flourished, it is impossible to say. Those brought to me have shewn no signs of captivity, but a few seasons of freedom would probably result in the reversion of the yellow bird of our aviaries to the plumage of the ancestral stock—the Wild Canary.

THE SCARLET BULLFINCH. (*Carpodacus erythrinus.*) This pretty Finch has only been captured twice in England, once near Brighton, and once near Hampstead. I have seen both specimens, and could detect no sign of their having been kept in confinement, nor is the species a frequent cage-bird in this country. Its home is in Northern Russia and in Siberia, but it breeds also in Eastern Prussia, and it has occurred during the season of migration in Heligoland, in Southern Sweden, and in France, so that there is nothing extraordinary in its occasional occurrence in Great Britain. Although popularly spoken of as a 'Bullfinch,' the present species is more like a stoutly-built Canary in form, but has scarlet as the predominating colour instead of yellow. As will be seen by the accompanying figures, there is consider-able difference in the colour of the sexes, the female being a very sober-plumaged individual. The nest is

THE SCARLET BULLFINCH.

built in swampy localities, and is placed in the fork of a willow-bush or some other low tree, or amongst climbing-plants. It is a carefully made, but slenderly built cup, and is more like that of a Warbler than that of a Finch. The eggs are four or five in number, of a beautiful blue, with well-marked spots of black and purplish or reddish brown.

THE CROSSBILL (*Loxia curvirostra*). The pretty legend connected with the blood-stained breast and the crossed bill of this bird has been immortalized by Longfellow, but the same story of the attempted rescue of the Saviour from the Cross has been told of the Robin and other birds with red breasts, which were bidden to 'bear in token of this moment, marks of blood and holy rood.' The

THE CROSSBILL.

curious way in which the two mandibles of the beak cross each other at the tips is found, I believe, in but one other genus of birds, the little Hawaian form *Loxops*. A remarkable fact is that this peculiar conformation is not found in the young birds, which have a bill more like that of ordinary Finches, but as the birds advance to maturity, the crossing of the mandibles becomes a feature. The colour of the male is red, of a pale vermilion or scarlet tint, but after moulting in confinement, the red tints give place to yellow, and it is said that even in a wild state Crossbills become yellower with age. I have, however, seen no evidence of this peculiarity in the specimens which have come under my notice in the British Museum, and I believe that the red plumage is a sign of a very old bird. The female is always duller in colour and is olive-yellow where her mate is tinged with red. Young birds have streaks, both above and below, these streaks being more distinct on the under-surface of the body, which is whitish.

The Crossbill nests rarely in England, where it occurs principally in winter, but it is found breeding in the pine districts, both of Scotland and Ireland. It is likewise distributed over the pine regions of both hemispheres, and is represented as far south as Mexico in the New World, and the Himalayas and the island of Luzon in the Old. The so-called ' Parrot ' Crossbill (*Loxia pytiopsittacus*) is a strong-billed form inhabiting Scandinavia and occasionally occurring in Great Britain, and it has been said that the larger-billed Crossbills feed on the seeds of the Scotch Fir, whereas the smaller-billed ordinary Crossbills feed on berries or pine-seeds, which do not require such strength of bill to attack. The nest is built early in the year, and has a net-work of twigs outside it, as in the nest of the Bullfinch. It is cup-shaped and made of moss and grass, lined with a little wool. The eggs are four or five in number, stone-coloured to pale blue, with dark spots or lines of purplish brown.

THE TWO-BARRED CROSSBILL (*Loxia bifasciata*). This species is easily recognised by the double bar of white on the wing, formed by the tips to the median and greater wing-coverts. It is an inhabitant of Northern Russia and Siberia, and occasional stragglers visit Central and Western Europe, so that the species turns up in Great Britain at intervals, and sometimes in considerable numbers. Its habits are the same as those of the Common Crossbill, and the nest is similarly made, but is rather smaller, and the eggs are said to be darker.

THE TWO-BARRED CROSSBILL.

THE BULLFINCH.

THE AMERICAN TWO-BARRED CROSSBILL. (*Loxia leucoptera*) is said to have occurred in the British Islands. It is scarcely to be distinguished from the European form, but it is rather more crimson in tint, and has the scapulars blacker.

THE BULLFINCH.
(*Pyrrhula europæa.*) Is a resident bird in nearly every portion of the British Islands, frequenting woods and gardens, and in the spring-time doing great damage to the latter by eating the buds of the fruit-trees. The Bullfinch is a very shy bird and is more often heard than seen, but when darting from one tree to another it may generally be recognised by the white on the rump, which is conspicuous in flight. The form of the Bullfinch is quite characteristic, the bullet head and conical bill being unlike those of any other European Finch, and these peculiarities distinguish Bullfinches from all parts of Northern Europe and Asia; in most cases the male has a scarlet breast and the female a grey or brown one, but there are certain species in which both sexes are grey and no scarlet is seen on the male. The nest is a very neat one, made of twigs and lined with fine rootlets and ornamented on the outside by a fringe of scattered twigs which add to the beauty of its appearance. The eggs are four or six in number, of a clear blue with distinct spots and blotches of purplish brown.

THE GREATER BULLFINCH.
(*Pyrrhula pyrrhula.*) This is a large race of our Common Bullfinch, inhabiting Northern Europe and Siberia, which has occurred at least three times in England, and probably more often. Two were shot on the Yorkshire coast and one in Norfolk, so that the bird may be considered an accidental visitor to our east coast. It is not only a larger bird than our ordinary species, but it is brighter in colour and the red of the breast is purer and clearer than in *P. europæa*. Its habits are the same as those of the latter bird.

THE GREATER BULLFINCH.

THE PINE FINCH.

THE PINE FINCH (*Pinicola enucleator*). This fine bird is an accidental visitor to Great Britain, and it is only occasionally that the species wanders from its native pine-woods in the North of Europe and Asia to Central Europe. It is one of those species known as 'circumpolar,' occurring near the Arctic Circle in both the Old and New Worlds, and nesting only in these high latitudes.

In form the Pine Finch is very like a Bullfinch, and has the same thick-set head and bill, but it has not the black head of the latter bird. The sexes differ totally in colour, the female Pine Finch being grey with only a little yellow in the plumage, whereas the male has a fine rosy or crimson colour. In winter the Pine Finches assemble in flocks, which pair off for the summer. The food of the bird consists of seeds of pine, fir cones and berries. The nest is like that of the Bullfinch to a certain extent. It is, however, larger and is very neatly made of twigs and grasses, with a few rootlets and fine grass-stems in the lining. The outside net-work of lichen-covered pine-twigs is very pretty, and is constructed in the same style as that of the Bullfinch, but the twigs are rather closely and firmly intertwined. The eggs are greenish blue with tiny spots and larger blotches of brown, distributed over their surface, the stronger markings being chiefly at the larger end of the egg.

THE BUNTINGS. *Sub-Family* EMBERIZINÆ. The bill in this sub-family of birds is generally more acute than in the Finches or the Grosbeaks, and the angle of the 'genys,' as the outline of the lower edge of the under mandible is called, is much more marked. Some Buntings have a distinct gap in the bill, the mandibles not meeting along their whole line, while in many species a round knob is found in the roof of the palate, which has been supposed to be of use to the birds in crushing up the grain on which so many of them feed.

THE REED BUNTING (*Emberiza schœniclus*). This species is widely distributed throughout Great Britain, and is found in many situations near water, frequenting the sides of rivers, brooks or ponds. The female, which is much browner and

THE REED BUNTING.

duller in colour than the male, is not so often seen, but the latter is often a conspicuous object by the river-side, as he sits on the top of a reed or bush and utters his twittering call-note ; his black and white head and neck render him easily recognisable. The nest is generally found in marshy ground in a clump of rushes or in a bush where the surrounding plants help

THE LITTLE BUNTING.

to conceal it. I have, however, taken a nest at some little height above the ground in a bush, and in Norway I have twice found a nest at some distance from water, built upon the ground under the roots of a small birch tree. In each case the young were well advanced before the nest was discovered, so well was the latter concealed, though placed within a few feet of a well-frequented path. I was led to suspect the presence of a nest in both instances through the action of the parent-birds, who pretended to be wounded and were nearly caught by the hand, as they fluttered along the ground, trying to draw me away from the vicinity of the nest. The eggs are boldly marked, being of a stone-brown colour with very distinct writing-lines and spots of black.

THE LITTLE BUNTING. (*Emberiza pusilla.*) Only one occurrence of this Bunting has as yet been recorded in England, a specimen having been captured near Brighton in November, 1864. As, however, the species visit Heligoland during the autumn migration, and has occurred occasionally in Holland, it may be expected to occur more frequently in Great Britain than has been hitherto supposed. It is a smaller bird than the Reed Bunting, but has the sides of the body striped with

THE BLACK HEADED BUNTING.
THE RUSTIC BUNTING.

black as in that bird. It is, moreover, easily distinguished by the chestnut colour on the ear-coverts and throat.

In its native home in Siberia, the Little Bunting is said to be remarkably tame, but in its winter home in India and Burma, where it assembles in flocks after the manner of other Buntings, it is very shy in its habits. The nests found by Mr. Seebohm on the Yenesei River were simply holes made in the dead leaves, moss, and grass, and lined with dead grass or reindeer-hair. The eggs are like those of the Corn Bunting, but are smaller.

THE RUSTIC BUNTING (*Emberiza*

rustica). Some three or four occurrences of this Bunting have been recorded, examples having been obtained near Brighton, near London, and in Yorkshire. The species is more rufous in colour than either of the preceding birds, and distinguished from both of them by the chestnut streaks on the flanks, while the lesser wing-coverts are chestnut, and there is a band of chestnut across the fore-neck. In the female the lesser wing-coverts are brown, and there is no rufous on the head and throat. The Rustic Bunting is a Siberian bird, and breeds as far westward as Archangel and Finland, up to almost 64° or 65° N. Lat. It is said to possess a rich and melodious song, and its alarm-note to resemble that of the Redwing. Its habits are like those of the Reed Bunting, and its home is in the marshy pine-woods of Northern Europe. Properly identified nests and eggs of this species are desiderata in most of our Museums.

THE BLACK-HEADED
BUNTING.
(*Emberiza melanocephala.*)

This richly-coloured bird is an Oriental species, whose migrations appear to be due east and west, instead of north and south, as is the case with most migratory birds. Although it is more gaudily coloured than is the case with most Buntings, which, as a rule, are remarkable for a sober plumage, the observations of naturalists tend to shew that it is a true Bunting in its habits. The breeding home of the species extends from the Riviera to Greece and Turkey, and thence to Central Asia, while it winters in North-Western India in enormous numbers, leaving its European breeding-quarters very early in the year, and disappearing at the end of July or the beginning of August.

Three specimens of the Black-headed Bunting have been recorded in the British Islands, the species having occurred in Sussex, Nottinghamshire, and near Dunfermline, in Scotland ; so that it may be reckoned as an occasional visitor to our shores. The nest is a somewhat bulky structure, and is placed on the ground or in some low bush, or amongst the vines and other trailing plants. Near Constantinople, Seebohm found it principally amongst the rows of peas and beans. The eggs are four or five in number, and are of a different type from those of most European Buntings, being of a pale greenish blue colour, with brown spots and grey underlying markings.

1—THE YELLOW BUNTING.   2—THE CIRL BUNTING.
3—THE ORTOLAN BUNTING.

THE YELLOW BUNTING.
(Emberiza citrinella.)

Our commonest Bunting, generally called the 'Yellow Hammer,' or, more correctly, the Yellow ' Ammer,' the name being, no doubt, derived from the German name of ' Ammer,' a Bunting. In many parts of England it is known as the ' Writing Lark,' from the scribblings which are the chief feature of the Yellow Bunting's egg. The last-mentioned species, *E. melanocephala*, which is even more brilliantly coloured than our Yellow Bunting, is easily recognised by its black head and by the absence of any streaks on the flanks, whereas the Yellow Bunting has the centre of the crown yellow, and has very distinct blackish streaks on the flanks: the breast and sides of the body also are light chestnut. It is universally distributed throughout the British Islands, and receives a large addition to its numbers in the autumn. The breeding-range of the Yellow Bunting extends throughout Northern Europe and Eastern Siberia as far as the River Ob, and in winter it visits Southern Europe and Central Asia.

The nest of *E. citrinella* is a neat structure of grass and bents, usually placed on the ground and well concealed, but occasionally to be found in a low bush. The eggs vary from four to six in number, and are of a stone-grey or pinkish-grey colour, with spots and scribblings of grey and purplish brown.

THE CIRL BUNTING.
(Emberiza cirlus.)

In appearance and also in habits the Cirl Bunting is very similar to the Yellow Bunting, with which it is often confused. The male, however, can always be distinguished from *E. citrinella* by the black throat, and the olive-green rump and lower back, these parts being streaked with dusky black. The female Cirl Bunting is more difficult to tell from the same sex of the Yellow Bunting, but it may be distinguished by the greenish grey colour of the lesser wing-coverts, which contrast with the colour of the back.

Instead of being universally distributed throughout the British Islands, like the Yellow Bunting, the present species is decidedly local, and is not known to nest to the north of our Midland counties. In the South of England, though still local in its distribution, the Cirl Bunting is generally met with, but from its retiring habits and from its resemblance to the Yellow Bunting, it is a species which escapes general observation. To anyone acquainted with the voice of the Cirl Bunting, which has a different intonation to that of *E. citrinella*, and lacks the final ascending note of the latter species, it is not difficult to discover *E. cirlus* in the South of England, where, as late as May, small flocks may be found, composed of birds in full breeding plumage, while in the autumn small parties, composed of young and old birds, may be noticed; from which it would appear that the Cirl Bunting never associates in autumn and winter with Chaffinches and other kindred species in the stubble-fields and farmyards, but keeps to small family parties of its own kind. Such, at least, has been my own experience. The nest is sometimes placed on the ground, but is more often built in bushes, at a height of a few feet from the ground. The eggs are four or five in number, but are rather lighter than those of the Yellow Bunting, with rather more distinct scribblings and lines than in the eggs of the latter species.

THE ORTOLAN BUNTING. (*Emberiza hortulana*). This species, which is easily distinguished by its red bill from the two preceding species, is to be recognised by the absence of stripes on the flanks, by its cinnamon-coloured breast and olive-yellow throat. The hen bird is paler in colour and has dark brown streaks on the fore-neck and lower throat.

Considering the wide range of the Ortolan, it is strange that it has not been noticed more often in the British Islands, but it is doubtless overlooked or mistaken for one of the allied species of Buntings. It must be considered a rare but regular visitor to Great Britain. The species is spread over the greater part of Europe in the summer, and extends in Asia as far as the valley of the Irtisch, and it winters in Central Asia and probably in North-eastern Africa as well. Mr. Seebohm says that the Ortolan is not shy in its nature, and has much the same habits as our Yellow Bunting, sitting on the top of a tree and uttering a song like that of the last-named bird, but without the curious ending which is characteristic of *A. citrinella*. The nest is built on the ground, and the eggs are from four to six in number, differing in appearance from those of the other British Buntings, and being most like those of the Reed Bunting, but clearer and paler in colour, and having black spots instead of streaks and lines.

THE SIBERIAN MEADOW BUNTING (*Emberiza cioides*) has once been noticed in England, a specimen having been obtained at Flamborough, in Yorkshire, in October, 1887. It is a Siberian species, shewing no yellow on the under parts, with a chestnut lower back and rump, and the crown of the head and ear-coverts chestnut in the male. In the female the head is dark brown in the centre, with lateral bands of chestnut.

THE CORN BUNTING (*Miliaria miliaria*). This species is very like a Lark in appearance, being of a sober brown colour, with a tail longer than the wing, and the inner secondary-quills so long that they nearly equal the primaries in length, as

THE SIBERIAN MEADOW BUNTING.

is the case with the Wagtails and Pipits. Although somewhat local in its habitat, the Corn Bunting is distributed over the whole of the British Islands. It is a species of the Western Palæarctic Region, not breeding outside European limits, nor extending very far north, but being found in winter as far east as the Persian Gulf. In Great Britain it is commonly observed in summer, when it sits on some telegraph wire by the side of the road, or on the top of a tree or hedge, and utters its somewhat monotonous and long-drawn-out trill, which resembles that

THE CORN BUNTING.   THE LAPLAND BUNTING.

of the Yellow Ammer, but is more powerful, and ends without the high note which distinguishes the song of the last-named bird. In the autumn the species is somewhat gregarious and collects in small flocks. The nest is a carelessly-built structure of bents, grass, or rootlets, with a scanty lining of fine grasses or hairs, and is placed on the ground. The eggs are four or five in number, rather handsome, stone-grey or purplish brown, with large spots, lines and scribblings of purplish black.

THE SNOW BUNTING (*Plectrophenax nivalis*). This is a by no means uncommon winter visitor to our shores, coming from the Arctic Regions. It is an inhabitant of the Northern territories of both the old and new Worlds, and also ascends the mountains in the lower latitude of its range; thus it is known to breed in the North of Scotland high up on the hills. In winter, when it visits Great Britain, the Snow Bunting is found in flocks along our sea-coasts, but is sometimes driven far inland by stress of weather. The plumage of the male in summer is white and black, the wings and tail being for the most part black like the mantle. The female is duller in colour and is never so black as the male. In winter both old and young birds are suffused with rufous, both above and below, and the black of the nesting plumage is entirely obscured by margins of this colour. In spring the birds do not moult, but gain their full coloration by the shedding of these pale tips to the feathers. Where the Snow Bunting breeds in the rocks, the nest is placed in a hole under shelter, and when built on the ground the structure seems to be the same, being composed of grasses, twigs, and moss, and lined with hair and feathers. The eggs are from five to eight in number,

THE SNOW BUNTING.

varying in colour from stone-grey to greenish white, with spots or streaks of purplish black, and faint blotches of violet or lilac-grey.

THE LAPLAND BUNTING. *(Calcarius lapponicus).*   This is a handsome bird, remarkable for the length of the claw on the hind-toe, whence it is often called the Lapland Long-spur or Long-spurred Bunting. The adult male is easily recognised by its black crown, throat, and sides of face, followed by a broad collar of bright chestnut which surrounds the hind neck and the sides of the neck ; the under-surface of the body is creamy white, the flanks being streaked with black. The adult female has the head and neck like the back and lacks the black crown and chestnut collar. In both sexes there is a conspicuous buff eyebrow, and a broad line of white from the eyebrow down the sides of the neck to the sides of the upper breast. This white marking is evident even in the winter dress, when the whole of the plumage is obscured by sandy buff edges, which fall off in the spring and leave the summer plumage in its full beauty. In habits the Lapland Bunting presents few features of difference from those of the Snow Bunting, and it also collects in flocks like that species. The home of the Lapland Bunting is on the tundra or barren grounds of the Arctic portions of both hemispheres, and the nest is placed on the ground in tussocks on the marshy tundra; it is made of dry grass and roots and is plentifully lined with feathers. The eggs are four to six in number, and are of a dark olive-brown or stone-brown, streaked and spotted with purplish brown.

THE LARKS. *Family ALAUDIDÆ.*   The Larks may be recognised from other Passerine Birds by having both aspects of the tarsus scutellated.

THE SHORE-LARK (*Otocorys alpestris*). A visitor to Great Britain in late autumn and winter, and sometimes noticed on its return journey in spring. The species is the sole British representative of a genus of

THE SHORE LARK.

Larks which is distributed over Northern Europe, and Northern and Central Asia, but is much more plentiful in the New World, where not only our own Shore Lark is found in the Arctic Regions, but many other races of these Horned Larks occur, extending even into the mountains of the South American Continent as far as Colombia.

The Shore-Lark is an Arctic species, breeding in the high north beyond the limit of forest-growth both in Europe and America. It is essentially a ground bird, and according to Seebohm's observations, even sings on the ground, as do several of the Larks. On the other hand, it will frequently mount into the air to sing. The nest is on the ground and is of the usual Lark-like pattern, a loosely-made structure of dry grass and stalks, with a lining of hair or willow-down. The eggs are from three to five in number, brown, with spots of darker brown, generally collected round the larger end.

THE WHITE-WINGED LARK.

The Shore-Lark is recognised by the tufts of black feathers, forming horns, on each side of the hinder part of the crown. The general colour is ashy vinous, and the eyebrow and forehead are yellow, followed by a broad band of black across the crown.

THE CALANDRA LARK. (*Melanocorypha calandra*). The occurrence of the Calandra Lark, which is a South European species, in England is doubtful, and is generally discredited, though the species appears in most lists of so-called British Larks. The pointed wing and stout bill distinguish it from the rest of our British Larks.

THE WHITE-WINGED LARK (*Melanocorypha sibirica*) is a smaller species than the true Calandra Lark, and is to be easily told by its rusty-red lesser wing-coverts, which form a distinct shoulder-patch, and by the white secondary-quills, which are very conspicuous, especially when the bird is flying. It has been observed once only in Great Britain, a specimen having been obtained near Brighton, in November, 1867. On the Continent it has been noticed in Belgium and Northern Italy, and also in the Island of Heligoland, but it can only be reckoned as a very rare and occasional visitor to Western and Southern Europe. The home of the species is in Central Asia and Southern Russia, whence it wanders westward to Poland and Galicia, and still further into Western Europe. In its habits the White-winged Lark resembles our Sky-Lark, mounting into the air and singing, and assembling in flocks in the autumn. The nest is built on the ground, under the covering of a tuft of grass or small bush, and is constructed of grass. The eggs are four or five in number, of the usual Lark-like character, being white or greenish white, with numerous brown spots and grey underlying spots and markings.

THE SKY-LARK (*Alauda arvensis*). This familiar species would seem scarcely to require any detailed description, as it is well known to all of us as a companion of our walks or as a frequent cage-bird. It may be known, however, from the other British species, by its very diminutive first primary, which is so small that it is distinguished with difficulty, and in reality looks like one of the primary-coverts. The

THE SKY-LARK.

hind-claw, moreover, is long and straight. The resident Sky-Lark of the British Islands is a rufous bird, and the birds which visit us on migration, often called 'Northern Larks,' or 'Scotch Larks,' are decidedly larger than our ordinary Sky-Lark, and are darker and greyer in colour. In all the members of this family it must be borne in mind that the females are, as a rule, smaller than the males.

Our Sky-Lark inhabits the greater part of Europe and breeds even beyond the Arctic Circle. Several races, more or less recognisable from our own bird, represent the true *Alauda arvensis* in Southern Europe and in temperate Asia, and though it is quite certain that two forms are found in Great Britain, their constant inter-breeding renders it very difficult to separate them. Like our Starlings, which undoubtedly intermarry with the migrants from the Continent, the large Northern Larks also find British mates, and it becomes more and more difficult every year to distinguish our rufous resident form from the winter visitor which overruns all Great Britain. That our Sky-Lark is a migrant in vast hordes can be proved by anyone who visits the Island of Heligoland in autumn, when, on a favourable night, the quantity of Larks which fly over the little sea-girt rock is almost incredible. Gätke speaks of 15,000 Larks having been captured in a single night on Heligoland and estimates that this only represented the capture of one individual in every 10,000 which passed over the island. The nest of the Sky-Lark is built on the ground, and is a simple structure of grass, but is generally well concealed. The eggs are from three to five in number, and are so thickly speckled with brown that the greenish white ground colour is obscured, the brown spots being mingled with the underlying grey ones. Very frequently the dark spots are congregated at the larger end of the egg, and often form a ring.

The SHORT-TOED LARK (*Calandrella brachy-dactyla*). This is a diminutive Sky-Lark in appearance, and has the first primary-quill rudimentary; it may, however, be easily recognised by its curved hind-claw. Unlike the Sky-Larks, in the genus *Calandrella* the sexes do not differ much in size. The Short-toed Lark is a bird of Southern Europe, and is only of accidental occurrence in Central Europe and Great Britain, where it has occurred on some eight occasions.

THE SHORT-TOED LARK.

It is of a tame disposition, and is entirely a ground-loving species, and an inhabitant of sandy districts. In habits and nesting it much resembles the Sky-Lark, but the song is not so vigorous as in the last-named species, though it also mounts into the air to sing. In winter, the Short-toed Larks congregate in large flocks. The nest is placed on the ground, and is made of dry grass, with a lining of vegetable down and fine hair. The eggs are four or five in number, the ground colour being whitish, but in some instances obscured by a mass of tiny brown dots, while in others the pale ground colour is less obscured by brown spots and markings, which, when present, are confined to the larger end of the egg.

THE CRESTED LARK.

THE CRESTED LARK (*Galerita cristata*) is only a rare visitor to Great Britain, having occurred some half-dozen times, and it is somewhat remarkable that it should not have been more often noticed, as it is by no means uncommon in the adjoining countries of the Continent. Many more instances of its occurence have been reported to me, but on enquiry I have always found the evidence to be inconclusive, as it is the Sky-Lark which has been observed by my correspondents. The latter bird has a very full crest of feathers, which it often erects, and hence the bird is mistaken for a Crested Lark. The crest of the last-named species is, however, of a different form to that of the Sky-Lark, being long and pointed, projecting from among the feathers on the back of the head. Another difference between the two species consists in the greater development of the first primary in the Crested Lark, which is very distinctly indicated. The species is generally distributed over Europe, and is represented by closely allied forms in Northern Africa, India, China, and Central Asia. It rises only a little way from the ground when singing, and does not soar high into the air like the Sky-Lark, nor does it collect into flocks in the autumn. Otherwise its habits are similar to those of other Larks, and it is especially fond of dusting itself in sandy roads. The nest is generally placed on the ground, and the eggs are rather paler than those of the Sky-Lark.

THE WOOD-LARK (*Lullula arborea*) is a small species, with a well-developed first primary, and although of a generally rufous coloration like the Sky-Lark, it is easily distinguished from that species by the broad band of buffy white which encircles the head, and by the blackish patch on the wing, formed by the black primary-coverts. The crest-feathers are rounded and full.

THE WOOD-LARK.

The Wood-Lark is a local bird in all the three kingdoms, being decidedly rarer towards the north, and scarcely known from Scotland. It frequents woodlands and loves to perch on trees, whence it takes short flights into the air, descending with the wings half-closed like a Tree-Pipit, for which the Wood-Lark is often mistaken. The song is very sweet. The nest is placed on the ground, and is rather more neatly constructed than that of the Sky-Lark, and the eggs are much lighter in appearance than those of the latter bird, being white, with numerous reddish brown dots and underlying grey spots.

THE
WAGTAILS AND PIPITS.
Family
MOTACILLIDÆ.

In some respects these birds resemble the Warblers (*Sylviidæ*), but they possess one character which shews a direct resemblance to the Larks, viz., the shape of the wing, in which the inner secondaries are lengthened, so as to nearly equal the primary-quills in extent. They are also ground-loving birds, walking or running like the Larks, and not hopping like Finches or Thrushes.

THE WHITE WAGTAIL.
THE PIED WAGTAIL.

THE PIED WAGTAIL (*Motacilla lugubris*). This is one of our most elegant little birds, and is familiarly known as the 'Dish-washer' in many parts of England, and in France it is called the 'Lavandière' or 'Washer-woman.' It has a graceful way of vibrating the tail, especially when it first alights on the ground, a peculiarity also observable in the Pipits. The male Pied Wagtail is black above, but the female never seems to acquire a perfectly black back, this being dusky grey, more or less mixed with black, even in the breeding season. In winter the throat is white, with a black band across the fore-neck, and instead of a perfectly black head, the forehead is white, with only the hind part of the head black. Young birds in their first winter may be told by the yellowish tinge on the face; otherwise they resemble the old birds in their winter plumage.

Great Britain is the home of the Pied Wagtail, as it breeds scarcely anywhere else, and is a species peculiar to Western Europe. It has been found nesting in the North West of France, and occasionally in Holland. It remains in England during the winter, though a certain number migrate, but the winter range extends only through Western Europe to France, Spain and Morocco.

The nest is a simple structure of grass or moss, neatly lined with hair or wool, built in the hole of a wall or bank, or on the stems of ivy. The eggs are five or six in number, pale, sprinkled with purplish brown dots on a whitish ground.

THE WHITE WAGTAIL. (*Motacilla alba*). This species is similar in form and markings to the ordinary Pied Wagtail, but is easily distinguished by its uniform grey back, instead of the black back of the last-mentioned species. It is a widely spread form, ranging from Western Europe across Siberia to the Valley of the Yenesei, and wintering in India and in Western and North-eastern Africa.

On the Continent the White Wagtail is a very common bird, and it probably occurs more frequently in England than is generally supposed, and it has been certainly identified as nesting occasionally. It ranges far to the north in Europe, and in northern Norway it is certainly one of the most interesting of the birds, and is remarkable for its tameness. The 'Linel,' as it is called, is to be seen in the vicinity of every 'saeter' or dairy-farm in the mountains, and each year that I have visited Norway, these pretty birds have been my constant companions, building their nests on beams in the hay-barns, or in holes in the roofs of the houses. A pair, which were more than usually tame, and frequented Mr. Lort Phillips' house on the Alfheim Lake, reared their young in a barn in perfect confidence, and when the nestlings were able to support themselves, the parents brought them down to the lake, where they would run about the verandah or settle down on the boats within a few feet of us. No sooner were they started in life than the old female laid a second set of eggs in the same nest and reared a second brood. The short summer in Norway probably accounted for the lack of time necessary for the building of a second nest. The latter is inartistically constructed, and resembles that of the Pied Wagtail of Britain. The eggs are five or six in number (in the second nest above-mentioned there were only four eggs), and are generally lighter than those of *M. lugubris*.

THE GREY WAGTAIL. (*Motacilla melanope.*) This species is intermediate between the ordinary Pied Wagtails and the Yellow Wagtails which follow. It has a very long tail, with bright yellow under tail-coverts, which are very conspicuous in both old and young birds. It is light blue-grey above with a black throat in summer, this being absent in the winter plumage. Young birds can always be told by the fawn-coloured eyebrow, and the tint of the same colour which pervades the throat and fore-neck. During the nesting season, the Grey Wagtail is decidedly a local bird in Great Britain, but it is universally spread over Europe and Northern Asia, though always affecting its own peculiar haunts. It loves rocky places, and builds its nest by the side of mountain streams, though in the South of England it may be found in other situations, under the shadow of a sluice-gate in water-meadows, or in the ivy against an old building, but always close to water. The nest is like that of other Wagtails, but is lined with cow's hair, generally white. The eggs vary from five to seven in number, and are rather more uniform in tint than those of other *Motacillidæ*, being sometimes of an olive tint or bluish-white, with only a little rufous mottling.

THE YELLOW WAGTAIL. (*Motacilla campestris.*) This species is often known as Ray's Wagtail, and is of a beautiful canary-yellow on the head and underparts, the back being olive-yellow. It is a smaller bird than the preceding species, and has a shorter tail. The female is duller in colour than the male, and has the head of the same greenish-yellow colour as the back, so that the bright yellow forehead is not visible. The winter plumage is also similar, but the under parts are brighter yellow, and there is a tinge of saffron colour on the breast; the eyebrow is well marked and of a bright yellow. The breeding range of the Yellow Wagtail is very similar to that of our Pied Wagtail, as its principal nesting place is in the British Islands, and it is almost entirely a bird of Western Europe. It goes, however, much further south for its winter home, wintering in West Africa, while many find their way along the east coast of Africa as far as the Zambezi and the Transvaal. As, however, there seems to be a second colony of the Yellow Wagtail in Southern Russia and Central Asia, it is probable that the birds from this area, choosing the

THE GREY WAGTAIL.
THE YELLOW WAGTAIL.

THE BLUE-HEADED WAGTAIL.

east coast route, find their way into South-eastern Africa. In habits the present species differs considerably from its relatives, being mostly gregarious, except in the nesting-season. On their arrival in Great Britain the Yellow Wagtails frequent commons and pasture-lands in small parties, and are very fond of feeding in the neighbourhood of cattle, running about the feet of the latter and feeding on flies. In the autumn they collect in large numbers in the reed-beds near the shores of our south coast, and hundreds roost in these places, before their autumn migration. The nest is placed on the ground, generally under some shelter, and is made of grass and rootlets, and lined with hair or feathers. The eggs are from four to six in number, and vary in colour and markings more than do those of the other species of Wagtails.

THE BLUE-HEADED WAGTAIL (*Motacilla flava*). Is of the same size and general appearance as the Yellow Wagtail, but distinguished by its blue-grey head and broad white eyebrow. The females and young birds can, however, scarcely be told from those of Ray's Wagtail. *M. flava* is an accidental visitor to Great Britain, but has been known to breed in Northumberland, and pro-bably occurs more

THE MEADOW-PIPIT.   THE TREE-PIPIT.

frequently than is supposed. Like its relative, *M. campestris*, it winters both in Western and South-eastern Africa, but it otherwise enjoys a much wider range, extending across Siberia to the Pacific, and wintering as far south as the Moluccas and in the peninsula of India. In habits and its mode of nidification it does not differ from those of the Yellow Wagtail.

THE TREE-PIPIT. (*Anthus trivialis.*) This is a very elegant little bird, in appearance like a Lark, but more trim and brighter looking. All the Pipits have a more or less Lark-like plumage, being brown streaked with black, and paler underneath, with blackish streaks on the breast. The Tree-Pipit is distinguished from the Meadow-Pipit and the other British species by its curved hind claw; it is also much less of a ground bird than the other Pipits.

The present species breeds over the greater part of Europe, as far as the Valley of the Yenesei, but it only nests on the mountains of Southern Europe. Its winter home is in Northern and North-eastern Africa, and in Western India. It is locally distributed throughout England, but becomes gradually rarer in Scotland, and is scarcely known in Ireland. The Tree-Pipit may often be observed on the outskirts of woods and plantations, flying up from the trees and bushes into the air, and descending spirally to its perch or to the ground, and singing melodiously all the while. Its food consists chiefly of insects, and it also frequents the neighbourhood of cattle on the pastures, to catch flies like the Wagtails, and it has the same dipping motion of the tail as in the latter birds. The nest is a simple structure of dried grass or rootlets, with a lining of fine grass or horsehair, and is always placed on the ground. The eggs are from four to seven in number, and vary

3°

from purplish or pinkish-red to olive-grey, with sometimes tiny dots and sometimes bolder spots and blotches of reddish brown and purplish-grey.

THE MEADOW-PIPIT. *(Anthus pratensis.)* The present species is rather a smaller bird than the Tree-Pipit, is not so bright in colour, and may always be told by its straight hind-claw, which exceeds the length of the hind toe itself. It is found everywhere throughout Great Britain, and is resident with us, though a considerable number migrate. There is some difference in size observable among our British Meadow-Pipits, and the ones from the south coast seem to constitute a smaller race than those from more upland localities. It must also be noted that in Pipits, as in Larks, the females are always smaller than the males. The range of the Meadow-Pipit extends over the greater part of Europe and reaches east as far as the Valley of the Ob. Its winter home is in the Mediterranean countries and Northern Africa.

It is generally a ground-loving bird, but in the mountains of Norway, at 3,500 feet, where it is exceedingly common, I have found it more like a Tree-Pipit in habits, perching on the birch trees, and soaring high into the air like a Sky-Lark, singing the while very sweetly. I shot one or two birds after they had perched on the trees to make sure that they were not Tree-Pipits. Its food consists almost entirely of insects, which it seeks on the ground. The nest is always built on the latter, and is generally sheltered ; it is a neat little cup of grass with a little moss and lined with fine grass or hair. The eggs are from four to six in number, and are somewhat browner and more uniform in appearance than those of the Tree-Pipit, being brown, more or less clouded with minute spots and markings of brown and purplish-grey.

THE RED-THROATED PIPIT (*Anthus cervinus*). This is a kind of Meadow-Pipit, very similar to *Anthus pratensis*, and only distinguishable in the winter plumage by the streaks on the rump, this part of the back being uniform in the Meadow-Pipit. Three undoubted specimens of the Red-throated Pipit have been taken within the British Islands, so that the species may be considered to be an occasional visitant, but it may occur more often than is suspected, as its plumage in winter is so very similar to that of *Anthus pratensis*. In the summer dress, of course, the uniform vinous red throat and breast easily distinguish the species. In the female the red colour is confined to the throat, and does not extend to the chest.

RED-THROATED PIPIT.   RICHARD'S PIPIT.

The range of the Red-throated Pipit is more eastern than that of the Meadow-Pipit, as it breeds from Northern Scandinavia to Eastern Siberia and Kamtchatka, beyond the limits of forest growth, wintering in China and Burma, and the Malayan Islands, as well as in Persia and North-eastern Africa, as far as Machakos in British East Africa.

It is an inhabitant of the swampy districts of the north, breeding in June, and making a nest of dry grass, placed under a tussocky ridge in the bogs, according to Mr. Seebohm. In habits it resembles the Meadow-Pipit, as might be expected, and the eggs are similar in colour and variation to those of the last-named bird.

RICHARD'S PIPIT.
(Anthus richardi.)
This is a large species, with a very strong hind claw, equal to the hind toe in length, or even exceeding the latter. The male measures 7½ inches in length, and the wing is 3·95 : the female, which is smaller, having a wing of 3½ inches. It is very much like a Lark in appearance, but has no dark streaks on the flanks, and the pale portion of the outer tail-feather is white. All Pipits have the outer tail-feathers of two colours, and the extent of the pale marking forms a distinctive character in many of the species, as will be seen below.

Richard's Pipit seems to be a regular autumnal visitor to Western Europe. It has been met with in England several times at this season of the year. Its breeding home is in Siberia, from the Valley of the Yenesei and Central Asia to Mongolia, and it is a frequent winter visitor to China and the Indian Peninsula. It is a grass-loving species and is seldom seen in its northern haunts during the breeding season, except when it rises into the air to sing. In its winter quarters in India and Ceylon, it is a shy bird, as it is also in its northern habitat, but it resembles a Lark in its fondness for cattle pastures, and like the last-named bird, it is fond of dusting itself in a sandy road.

The eggs are from four to six in number, the ground-colour being greenish-white, nearly hidden by spots of greenish-brown and grey. Some eggs are browner in tint than others.

THE TAWNY PIPIT.

THE TAWNY PIPIT (*Anthus campestris*). A rare winter visitor from the Continent to the southern coasts of England, several specimens having been captured near Brighton. The home of the species is in Central and Southern Europe, where it inhabits the sandy districts, as far east as Central Asia, extending even to Eastern Siberia. The winter home is in Senegambia, North-east Africa, and the plains of North-western India.

THE WATER-PIPIT.

The Tawny Pipit is easily distinguished, when adult, by its uniform plain-coloured under-surface of buffy white, without any streaks on the breast. These streaks are present in young birds, but are very indistinctly indicated. The outer tail-feather is almost entirely white, and has a white shaft, with a brown edging to the inner web; the next feather has a brown shaft, and is blackish-brown, but the outer web is light buff and this pale colour extends obliquely across the inner web to the tip. The sides of the face are whitish, with a well-marked moustachial streak of dusky brown. The flanks are uniform, and the wing-coverts have broad margins of pale sandy colour.

In its habits the Tawny Pipit is very Lark-like, soaring into the air for a little distance and singing. The nest is placed on the ground, concealed under a tuft of grass or a clod of earth, and is simply made of dry grass, lined with fine roots or horsehair. The eggs are from four to six in number, very pale, being white with numerous dots of black and grey.

THE WATER-PIPIT (*Anthus spipoletta*). A rare visitor, some half-dozen specimens having been procured in England and Wales, on the spring and autumn migrations. Adult birds, with their uniform vinous-coloured breasts and also in their striped winter plumage, might be mistaken for Rock-Pipits, but they may always be distinguished by the white pattern on the outer tail-feathers, this light portion being always smoky brown in the Rock-Pipit. The Meadow-Pipit has the end of the last tail-feather but one white, whereas in the Tawny Pipit it is brown. The latter is moreover, a larger bird than *Anthus pratensis*. The streaks on the flanks will always distinguish the latter from the Tawny Pipit.

The Water-Pipit, or, as Seebohm calls it, the Alpine Pipit, is an inhabitant of the mountains of Central and Southern Europe, extending to Central Asia and Baluchistan. It is found nesting beyond the limits of forest-growth, and resembles the Meadow-Pipit in habits, and soars into the air to utter its song. The nest is always on the ground, and is made of dry grass and moss, lined with rootlets, hair, or wool. The eggs are four or five in number, dull white, closely mottled or spotted with purplish-brown.

THE ROCK-PIPIT (*Anthus obscurus*). This is also, like the Pied Wagtail, a

THE ROCK-PIPIT.

species of Western Europe, nesting in the British Islands, and, according to Mr. Howard Saunders, on the opposite shores of Northern France. In Northern Europe its place is taken by the Scandinavian Rock-Pipit, *Anthus rupestris*. The species can always be told by the smoky brown tint of the light portion of the outer tail-feathers, which distinguishes it from all other British Pipits. Although, in my opinion, the Scandinavian Rock-Pipit is easily recognisable in its summer plumage from our own *A. obscurus*, at other times of the year the young and winter birds are indistinguishable.

The Rock-Pipit is an inhabitant of our wilder coasts, and does not frequent the more open portions during the breeding season, though it occurs in winter on our southern coast-line. In habits it closely resembles the Meadow-Pipit, and its food is similar. During the breeding season the male flies up into the air to sing, and warbles sweetly as it descends spirally with outspread wings. The nest is a rough structure of dead grass with shore-plants intermixed, and lined with moss or hair according to the facilities with which the bird can obtain these materials. It is placed generally close to the shore, but not unfrequently on a cliff at some height. The eggs are four or five in number, rather dark in tint as a rule, the brown mottlings obscuring the greyish-white ground colour.

THE SCANDINAVIAN ROCK-PIPIT (*Anthus rupes-tris*). As already remarked, there is no obvious difference between this species and the ordinary Rock-Pipit in the winter plumage or in that of the young birds, but in the summer dress the two species are quite recognisable, the

THE SCANDINAVIAN ROCK-PIPIT.

vinous breast of the Scandinavian form being a distinct feature. In this respect it is allied to the Water-Pipit, but is easily separated from that species by the tint of the light pattern on the outer tail-feather, which is smoky brown instead of being white as in *A. spipoletta*.

The present species is an autumnal migrant to the eastern and southern coasts of England, returning eastwards in spring, and moulting on the journey, as is the habit of Pipits, which have a spring as well as an autumnal moult. Thus, the individuals procured near Brighton in spring, generally shew traces of the change to the uniform vinous breast from the preceding winter plumage with its striped breast. The Scandinavian Rock-Pipit, in fact, follows the same line of western migration as the Black Redstart (*Ruticilla titys*), in the British Islands. In summer it is distributed along the rocky shores of Scandinavia and the Baltic Sea, as far as the White Sea. The habits and nesting are similar to those of our own Rock-Pipit, and the eggs are indistinguishable from those of the last-named species.

THE CREEPERS.
Family
CERTHIID.E.

The Creepers are truly insectivorous birds and expert climbers on rocks and trees, feeding on tiny insects which they discover in such situations. The family is almost entirely a northern one, being distributed over the temperate portions of the Old and New Worlds, ranging in the west to Central America, and in the east to the Himalayas, being sparsely replaced by allied genera in the Indian Peninsula, Africa and Australia. The true Creepers have a stiffened and pointed tail like that of the Woodpeckers, but there are many soft-tailed species, just as there are the soft-tailed Wrynecks (*Iynx*), amongst the Woodpeckers. One of the most conspicuous of the soft-tailed Creepers is the following :—

THE WALL-CREEPER.

THE WALL-CREEPER (*Tichodroma muraria*). This bird has occurred in Norfolk and in Lancashire, while a third has been recently recorded from Sussex. Mr. Howard Saunders has pointed out that the species occasionally visits Normandy, so that its occurrence in the British Islands may now and then be expected. It is a bird easily recognisable on account of the crimson in the wings. As in other Creepers, the bill is long, slender, and curved. The general colour of the Wall-Creeper is a delicate blue-grey, and the wings and tail are black, with a conspicuous white spot on the outer primaries, very much in evidence when the bird is flying; the tail is likewise tipped with white spots. In summer the throat is black, but in winter it is white.

The Wall-Creeper inhabits the mountain ranges of Southern Europe, North-east Africa, Central Asia, and the Himalayas as far as China. It has a peculiar flight, like that of a Butterfly, and climbs up rocks and buildings with a sidling crab-like motion, flicking its wings open rapidly, and exhibiting their beautiful crimson colour with every movement. The nest is placed in crevices of rocks, and is made of moss and grass, with a mass of hair, wool and feathers compacted together, and is lined with wool and hair. The eggs are from three to five in number, pure white, sparsely spotted with tiny black or reddish-brown dots.

THE TREE-CREEPER (*Certhia familiaris*). This is a small bird with a curved bill and a peculiar tail, the feathers of which are stiffened and pointed, serving the same purpose as the rigid tail of the Woodpeckers, as the bird climbs up the trunk of a tree or runs along the branches. The Tree-Creeper of Great Britain has been separated as a distinct race by Mr. Ridgway, and called *Certhia britannica*, and

Mr. Hartert in his recent review of the species, also considers it to be different from the Continental form, and names it *Certhia familiaris britannica* (Novt. Zool. iv., p. 139). He says that it differs from the form of Western Europe (*C. brachydactyla*), in having the orange-tawny colour of the rump more extended and slightly more orange, the whole aspect of the upper surface being more rufous, the beak also averaging decidedly shorter, the hind-claw longer. Thus, in the opinion of the two above-mentioned observers, the British Creeper is a form peculiar to our islands, like our Coal-Tit and Long-Tailed Tit.

The Creeper is not a very easy bird to observe, as it is small, and not readily seen. It flies down to the bottom of a tree-trunk and climbs to the top with a rapidly jerking motion of the body, generally keeping itself well out of sight on the other side of the tree, and feeding on minute insects as it goes. The single hissing note, when once comprehended, is not easily mistaken, and seems to come from all points of the compass. Competent observers have assured me that the Creeper has a song, but I have never heard this myself in England, though on the Continent I have heard a Creeper sing as loudly as a Tit. The nest is placed under shelter below the eaves of a shed or in the hole of a tree, or behind a crevice of bark on the latter. It is generally an untidy structure of small roots and moss, with strips of inside bark and dead wood. The eggs are from four to six in number, very similar to those of Tits, being white or pinky-white, with rufous or blackish spots.

THE TREE-CREEPER.
THE NUTHATCH.

THE NUTHATCHES.
Family
SITTIDÆ.

THE NUTHATCH (*Sitta cæsia*) is our only representative of a family which is widely distributed over the northern parts of the Old and New Worlds. The members of it may be said to have the plumage of a Tit with the habits of a Creeper, but instead of the long curved bill of the latter birds, the Nuthatches have a powerful wedge-shaped bill, more like that of a Woodpecker, though they have not the extensile tongue of the last-named bird, nor do they possess a spiny tail. The Nuthatch is principally an English bird, being pretty generally distributed, but becoming rarer towards Scotland, and being unknown in Ireland. On the Continent it is found westwards of the Peninsula of Jutland, through Central and Southern Europe, east to Asia Minor and Palestine. The favourite haunt of the Nuthatch is in the large trees of a well-timbered park, and

1—THE GREAT TIT.   2—THE CRESTED TIT.   3—THE COAL TIT.   4   THE MARSH TIT.
          5—THE BEARDED TIT.   6—THE BLUE TIT.

here its presence may be detected by its note, ' too-ee, too-ee,' many times repeated,
or by the sound of its hammering on the bark, the blows which it gives being
remarkably powerful for so small a bird.   It runs round the branches like a Creeper,
prising off the bark to get at the ants and small insects, and often runs on the
under side of a bough or comes along the trunk for a short distance head-downwards.
The nest is a very rough structure of a few grasses or dead leaves, and is placed in
the hole of a wall or of a tree, in the latter case the entrance being plastered up.
The eggs are from four to eight in number, white, with rufous spots and grey underlying dots.

THE TITS.
Family
PARIDÆ.
These birds are found in nearly every part of the globe, excepting
the Australian Region and South America from Mexico southwards.
They are, however, more numerous in the northern countries of both
hemispheres, and several species occur in Great Britain.   They are
birds of small size, but have a stout conical bill, with the base covered with feathers.

THE GREAT TIT (*Parus major*).   This is the largest British species, and is
distinguished by its black head, breast, and abdomen, the black on the latter
parts forming a broad streak, which is less evident in the female than in the male.
There is a patch of white on the nape as in the Coal Tit, but the large size and
yellow colouring on the under-surface of the Great Tit, easily serve to distinguish
the two species.

The ' Ox-eye,' as this bird is frequently called, is a very active little creature,
and is always in evidence in woods and gardens in the spring, when its lively

song is sure to attract attention. In winter it frequents the woods in company with other Tits, Creepers, and Nuthatches, and is always distinguished from its relatives by its larger size and more powerful note. As a nest-builder it is one of the most industrious of birds, for it will fill a box or an inverted flower pot of large size with moss, and sometimes two or three nests will be found in the same bed of moss, as if the bird inhabited the place for year after year and occupied a fresh nest each season. The eggs are from five to nine in number, white, with red and grey (underlying) spots.

THE BLUE TIT.
(*Parus cœruleus.*)

This is by far the most plentiful of the British Tits. It is smaller than the Great Tit, and is easily distinguished by its blue crown, pale green back, blue tail and wing-coverts, white cheeks and eyebrow, and yellow under-surface. The Blue Tit is found everywhere throughout the United Kingdom, and large numbers migrate every year from the Continent, where it is also everywhere distributed, but its range does not extend beyond the Ural mountains.

Though chiefly subsisting on insect food, the Blue Tit does considerable damage in the spring of the year by devouring the buds of fruit-trees, and is as much persecuted as the Bullfinch at this season. At other times, however, it is so entirely an insect-feeder that great good must be done by these active little birds, though again in the fruit-season it does some damage by pecking holes in the pears and other fruit. At the same time the number of insects caught by the Blue Tits ought to be taken into consideration, when their family consists of perhaps eight little ones. The nest of the Blue Tit is always in the hole of a tree or a wall, and the entrance is sometimes so tiny that it is difficult to believe that even a Blue Tit can squeeze through the aperture. Here in a rough nest of moss and grass, but comfortably lined with feathers, the young are reared, and fed entirely on insects. The eggs, from five to twelve in number, are white, sprinkled with tiny dots of reddish.

THE COAL TIT (*Parus britannicus*). This is entirely a British species, and differs from the Coal Tit of the Continent in having an olive-brown back, instead of a blue-grey one. Our Coal Tit has a white patch on the nape, in which respect it resembles the Great Tit, and, like the latter, it has a black head and white cheeks, but it is a very much smaller bird, has no yellow on the under-parts, and entirely lacks the black band down the centre of the breast and abdomen. It is also a bird of somewhat different habits, as far as two species of Tits can differ in habits. It is much more shy than the Great Tit, and except in winter, when it joins the roving parties of Tits and Creepers, is not easy of observation. Its plain coloration protects it as well as its small size, but where it occurs it is an interesting little species to watch, though it is by no means so noisy as the Blue or Great Tits. I was very much interested in watching a pair which were

THE COAL TIT

nesting last summer (1897) in Froyle Park, in Hampshire, where my friend, Captain Sawbridge, would on no account allow any of the birds to be disturbed. The Coal Tits were particularly tame, and I soon found their nesting-place in a tiny hole in the wall which formed the terrace between the garden and the park. While standing quite still under an elm tree, the little birds flew from the stable-yard into the branches not two feet above my head, with a feather or some other nesting material in their bill, and after making sure that all was safe, they descended, and hovered in the air for a second or two in front of the hole, into which they disappeared with their prize. This was not the only pair of Coal Tits nesting in this same old wall. The species also often selects a hole in a tree for its nest, and lays from six to eight or nine eggs, white, with dots of light and dark rufous, generally clustering round the larger end of the egg.

THE EUROPEAN COAL TIT (*Parus ater*). Occasional individuals of the Continental form appear to visit our eastern coasts in autumn. They may be recognised from our British Coal Tit by their blue-grey back, and in winter plumage, when the olive-brown back of the British form is very pronounced, the two races are recognised at a glance, but in summer, when the olive-brown edges to the feathers of our British bird become abraded, and the general aspect becomes grey. I admit that the two races are difficult to distinguish. The European Coal Tit is found throughout Europe and Northern Asia. Its habits are similar to those of our British Coal Tit.

THE BRITISH MARSH-TIT. (*Parus dresseri.*) The exact range of the different species of Marsh Tits in the Palæarctic Region, that is, in Europe and Northern Asia, is a very difficult problem to solve, and it is far from being settled at the present time. Compared with the Marsh-Tit of the Continent, the true *Parus palustris*, the British representative shews certain differences which point to its recognition as a distinct insular form. It is a much darker bird, with a more marked buffish-brown rump and browner flanks. Though generally considered to be a marsh bird, from its popular name, our Marsh-Tit is by no means entirely a frequenter of the willows and water meadows, but on the contrary, is found, in winter at least, far away from such localities, in parks and woodlands, in company with companies of other Tits and kindred wanderers, feeding on insects, and even frequenting the neighbourhood of houses. It is to be told by its brown back, glossy blue-black crown, whitish face and under parts, isabelline-buff sides and flanks, and black throat.

The nest is almost always in the hole of a tree, and sometimes the bird digs out its own nesting-place, being armed with a powerful little pick-axe of a bill, like all Tits, and knowing well where to attack a rotten part of a tree, generally a willow, wherein to place its nest. The latter is rather more carefully built than is usual with the *Paridæ*, and is made of moss and wool and hair. The eggs are from five to eight in number, white, with rufous spots, either scattered all over the egg, or collected at the larger end.

THE CONTINENTAL MARSH-TIT (*Parus salicarius*). This is supposed to be a separate race of our ordinary Marsh Tit, and Mr. Hartert (Bull. Brit. Orn. Club. vii., p. iv.), gives the differences as follows:—The crown is less glossy and more of a brownish black, the flanks are strongly marked with rufous, and the proportions of the bill, wings and tail are slightly different. The call-note also is not the same, and its habitat is confined to dark, shadowy and swampy places. The same form is said by Mr. Kleinschmidt, who first drew Mr. Hartert's attention to the occurrence of *P. salicarius* in England, to be found in Germany.

THE CRESTED TIT (*Lophophanes cristatus*). Members of the genus *Lophophanes* are distinguished by their pointed crest, which forms an evident tuft. The genus is more strongly represented in the New World than in the Old, but there are a few species in the Himalaya Mountains. Otherwise the Crested Tit of Great Britain is the characteristic Palæarctic representative of the genus, and is found over the greater part of Western Europe, wherever pine-forests occur, extending east to the Volga, but not occurring in Greece or Italy below the line of the Alps.

The species is distinguished by its sober olive-brown colour, white face, black throat joining the black of the nape, and long crest of black, white-edged feathers, the crown itself being black. It is at the present time only found within a certain limited area in Scotland, but has occurred in many of the English counties and in Ireland. The Crested Tit seems to be everywhere a bird of the pine-forests, where it searches for its insect food after the manner of a Creeper, and, according to Mr. Seebohm, it never comes down to the ground, like other Tits sometimes do. The nest is roughly made of dry grass and moss, and is placed in the hole of a tree or in the foundations of Crow's, Magpie's, or even Squirrel's nests. The eggs are from four to seven in number, white, with very distinct spots of red and purplish-red.

THE BRITISH LONG-TAILED TIT (*Ægithalus vagans*). The members of this genus have a very long tail, which exceeds the wing in length, thus differing from all the other British *Paridæ*. The nest of the Long-Tailed Tits, too, is quite different from those of the rest of the family, being a moss-built, domed structure, placed in the open, and not in the hole of a wall or tree.

Our Long-tailed Tit may almost be considered a peculiar British species. Like the Coal Tit, it is easily recognisable from its Continental representative, as it has only the centre of the crown white, with a broad lateral stripe of black on each side of it,

THE WHITE-HEADED LONG-TAILED TIT
THE BRITISH LONG-TAILED TIT

whereas the true *Æ. caudata* of Linnæus inhabits Northern Europe and has a pure white head. It is distributed over the greater part of the British Islands, becoming rarer towards the northern parts, and it is said to range over France into Northern Italy, and east into the Rhine Provinces, but the actual distribution of the species is not exactly known at present.

In spring these pretty little birds build their nest of moss and lichen, warmly coated inside with a mass of feathers, in a hedge or furze-bush, sometimes in a tree at a considerable height from the ground. The nest is often to be found quite early in the year, before the leaves have grown on the trees, and it is frequently placed in quite exposed situations. The eggs are white, with scarcely perceptible reddish dots, and are from six to ten in number, or even more. This numerous family is snugly housed in the mossy nest, and is brooded over at night by both parents, so that the long tails of the latter can be seen resting against the hind wall of the nest, and they are even said to protrude sometimes through the opening. In the autumn, family parties are formed, consisting of old and young birds, which fly about the woods hunting for their insect food, and following one another in regular procession from tree to tree.

THE WHITE-HEADED LONG-TAILED TIT. (*Ægithalus caudatus.*)

This is the common species of Scandinavia and Northern Europe, visiting Central Europe in winter, at which season it occasionally migrates to the British Isles. In its adult plumage it is easily told by its pure white head, but the young of this and our British Long-Tailed Tit cannot be told apart, both having a dull white crown with a dusky band on each side, and, curiously enough, a longer tail than the old birds. In habits, nest, and colour of eggs, the White-Headed Long-Tailed Tit does not differ in any way from our insular species.

THE BEARDED TIT. (*Panurus biarmicus.*)

This is not a true Tit at all, and ought perhaps to be called by its other name of the Bearded Reedling. In plumage, mode of nesting, and colour of the eggs it is so different, that many naturalists have referred it to the Buntings rather than to the Tits. My own opinion is that it belongs to neither group, but is really a Timeline bird, akin to the Reed-birds of the tropical east, such as *Paradoxornis*, to which it assimilates in style of plumage and in habits.

The old male is easily to be told by its cinnamon-red colour, its pearly-grey head, and by its broad black moustachial streak on each side of the cheeks. The female is duller in colour, has no black moustache, and the head is brown like the back. The young differ remarkably from both parents, being more tawny, and have a black patch in the centre of the back and a black stripe along either side of the crown. Though doubtless of wider distribution formerly in England than it is at the present time, the Bearded Tit is now almost confined to a few districts in the Norfolk and Suffolk Broads. On the Continent it occurs in marshy localities from Holland, France, and Spain, eastwards to Central Asia.

It is a bird of retired and skulking habits, and it lives entirely in the reed-beds, where it feeds on insects and tiny mollusca, as well as on the seeds of the reeds themselves. The nest is placed low down in a clump of rushes, and is rather a deeply made structure of flat grass, lined with down. The eggs are from four to seven in number, white, with dots and streaks of dark brown.

THE
GOLD-CRESTS.
Family
REGULIDÆ.

The Gold-Crests are among the smallest of known birds, and are found only in the temperate portions of the Old and New Worlds, occurring as far south as the Himalayas in the former, and in Central America in the latter. They have all a beautiful crown of orange, yellow, or red, more or less concealed by the lateral feathers of the head.

THE COMMON GOLD-CREST (*Regulus regulus*). This is the resident species in Great Britain, and is found everywhere, excepting in the northern islands of Scotland, while a large migration from Northern Europe occurs annually, and a corresponding wave of returning migrants is often noticed in spring. How such a tiny and fragile little bird accomplishes these long distances of flight is one of the puzzles of nature, and the migration is often performed in daylight, as I have seen myself in Heligoland, while that it travels also by night is shewn by its appearance in numbers at the lighthouses, and also by a curious instance which occurred at the end of October, 1897, when a gentleman

THE FIRE-CREST.   THE GOLD-CREST

brought to the National History Museum a live Gold-Crest, which had flown at ten o'clock on the preceding night into the top-most carriage of the gigantic wheel at the Earl's Court Exhibition. It was by watching this interesting little captive that I was enabled to see that the orange crest is not displayed as a rule, but is kept concealed by the feathers on each side of the crown.

The nest is made of green moss, lined with feathers, and is slung, hammock-like, under the branch of a fir or yew, and the young, when fully fledged, sit in a row on some adjoining fruit tree, being fed in turn by the industrious little parent birds, and the clamour made by the nestlings is something quite remarkable. The eggs are from five to eight in number, creamy white or isabelline in colour, usually with a distinct zone of reddish-brown around the larger end of the egg.

THE FIRE-CREST (*Regulus ignicapillus*). This species is an inhabitant of Central and Southern Europe, extending as far north as the Baltic Provinces, but not nesting in Scandinavia. It is only a winter visitant to Great Britain, and never comes over in such large hordes as the Gold-Crest, although I noticed it as a migrant on Heligoland in larger numbers than the last-named bird. The golden-orange crown, richer in colour than that of the ordinary Gold-Crest, with the black band on each side of the crown, and the conspicuous white eyebrow, distinguish the Fire-Crest from the Gold-Crest at a glance. The habits and mode of nesting are similar in the two species. The eggs, from five to ten in number, are more rufous than those of the Gold-Crest and are almost chocolate in colour, either sprinkled with reddish dots or with a ring of the latter round the larger end of the egg.

THE RUBY-CREST (*Regulus calendula*) of North America has been supposed to have occurred in Scotland; a specimen from Loch Lomond, said to have been shot by Dr. Dewar, in 1852, being in the British Museum.

THE SHRIKES.
Family
LANIIDÆ.

This is a wide-spread family of birds, and is represented even in Australia, but not in South America. The members of the family which occur within British limits are all true *Laniidæ*, and do not belong to the aberrant groups which are found in tropical countries.

THE LESSER GREY SHRIKE (*Lanius minor*). This species visits Central and Southern Europe in summer, extending to Persia and Central Asia and wintering in Africa. It is one of the 'Grey' section of the genus *Lanius*, and can be recognised at any age by its short first primary-quill. The adult birds have a broad black band on the forehead, and a beautiful rosy blush over the breast. The species has occurred at least four times in England, as an occasional visitor both in autumn and spring. Its food consists principally of insects, which it is said to impale on thorns after the manner of its kind, but, according to Seebohm, it will also devour fruit in the shape of figs, cherries, and mulberries. The nest is a rough structure of moss and twigs, lined with wool, and the eggs, from four to seven in number are white, or greenish-white, with markings of brown and purplish-grey.

THE LESSER GREY SHRIKE.

THE GREAT GREY SHRIKE (*Lanius excubitor*). This large species is a regular winter visitor to Great Britain, and comes to us from Scandinavia, where the bird is a summer visitor only. In Central Europe it is a resident species.

This species, like the next, is told from the other British Butcher-birds by its large size and grey colouring above, with the base of the forehead and a small eyebrow white, contrasting with the black lores and ear-coverts: the wings and tail

1 The Great Grey Shrike.   2 -The Red-backed Shrike.   3—The Woodchat Shrike.

are black, with white ends to most of the feathers, the outer tail-feathers being broadly tipped with white. On the wing are two conspicuous patches of white, the first formed by the white base of the primaries, and the other by the white base to the outer secondaries. Young birds are shaded with brown, both above and on the breast, the under surface of the body being barred with brown margins to the feathers.

The two species of Great Grey Shrike are very conspicuous birds wherever they occur, from their habit of selecting the top of a bush or small tree from which to take a good survey of the surrounding ground. They devour all kinds of food, insects, frogs, lizards, and mice being eaten in summer, but in winter mice and small birds form their prey. The Shrikes have a very strongly hooked bill like that of a Hawk, and they are called 'Butcher-birds,' from their habit of impaling their prey on thorns, and here, in the Shrike's 'larder,' as it is called, may often be found hanging the remains of the bodies of his victims.

The nest is a somewhat rough structure of twigs, grass and moss, and the eggs, from five to seven in number, are greenish-white or brownish-white, with spots of olive or greenish-brown.

PALLAS'S GREAT GREY SHRIKE (*Lanius sibiricus*). This is another winter visitor, coming from Siberia and Northern Russia, where it breeds. In habits and form it exactly resembles the foregoing species, from which it differs in only having one white wing-patch instead of two, the inner secondaries being entirely back.

PALLAS'S GREAT GREY SHRIKE.

4

THE RED-BACKED SHRIKE.
(*Lanius collurio.*)

This is the common Butcher-bird of our islands, visiting us regularly in summer, and nesting over the greater part of England, but becoming rarer towards the north, and not breeding in Scotland; it has only once been recorded from Ireland. It is generally distributed over Europe as far east as Central Asia, and it winters along the Persian Gulf and in East and South Africa.

Although a much smaller bird than the three Grey Shrikes, the present species has much the same habits as its larger relatives, and impales insects and mice and small birds on the thorns which constitute its store-house. It is fond of frequenting dells and over-grown gravel pits, or commons where there are plenty of scattered clumps of bushes, and it may often be seen on the telegraph-wires, swooping down from this perch on the insects which fly below. The nest is an untidy structure of moss and roots, lined with grass and hair. The eggs are from four to six in number, of two kinds, a reddish and a white type, with rufous spots in the one and olive or greenish-brown spots in the latter.

The Red-backed Shrike is distinguished by its blue-grey head and chestnut back, and pinkish under-surface. The female is duller in colour and is reddish-brown with a brown head, while there are crescentic bars of brown on the sides of the body and breast.

THE WOODCHAT.
(*Lanius pomeranus.*)

This Shrike is of about the same size as the preceding species, but is easily to be told by its coloration, the back being black, with white shoulders and rump, the head and neck chestnut, with a broad frontal band of black, and the sides of the face also black. The Woodchat is a common summer visitor to the greater part of Europe, but has only occurred a few times in England, though it has been said to nest in the Isle of Wight. The eastern range of the species extends to the Caucasus and Western Persia, and it winters in North-eastern Africa and Senegambia. Like other Shrikes, the Woodchat takes up its perch in some conspicuous position on a bush or tree, from which it sallies forth after its insect prey, and its white breast renders it easily seen. It has a gentle and not unmusical song. The nest is more carefully built than is usually the case with Butcher-birds, and is placed in the fork of a tree, without any attempt to conceal it, beyond the fact that the materials of which it is composed resemble the bark of the tree in which it is placed. The eggs are from four to six in number, and are subject to the same variation as the eggs of the Red-backed Shrike.

THE WAX-WINGS.
Family
AMPELIDÆ.

Of these birds, easily distinguishable by the curious tips to the secondary quills, which look like little tags of sealing-wax dropped on the ends of the feathers, there are three species found in the Northern parts of the Old and New Worlds. In the latter the commonest species is the Cedar-bird (*Impelis cedrorum*), but the European Wax-wing also occurs in Arctic North America.

THE WAX-WING.

THE WAX-WING (*Ampelis garrulus*). The plumage of this bird is singularly delicate in tint, being of a drab-brown colour above, becoming grey towards the rump and upper tail-coverts; the quills are black, with white tips and some yellow near the end of the outer web. There is a very full crest on the head, of the same colour as the back; the throat is black and the under tail-coverts chestnut, contrasting with the greyish-drab colour of the under surface.

The Wax-wing visits us nearly every winter, and sometimes invades Great Britain in large numbers. It breeds in the high north of Europe and America, and wanders south in winter, when it has been found in most countries of Europe. Its food in summer time consists of insects, but in winter it feeds on various kinds of berries, and large numbers of these birds are shot for the market in Russia. The nest is a large but well-built structure, made of twigs and moss with a lining of feathers. The eggs are from five to seven in number, of a lilac-grey colour with spots of black or blackish-brown.

THE WARBLERS.
Family
SYLVIIDÆ.

This is one of the representative families of birds of the Old World, where it is represented by a number of species, mostly migratory, but some stationary. The Warblers differ from the Thrushes in having the young plain-coloured like the old birds, and not spotted as in the *Turdidæ*. The latter, likewise, go through but a single moult, whereas the Warblers moult twice in the year, once in autumn before migration, and again in the spring before they return to their breeding-haunts.

THE BARRED WARBLER (*Sylvia nisoria*). A rare and accidental visitor, of which some nine specimens have been recorded, eight

THE BARRED WARBLER.

4*

from England and one from Ireland. The most recent occurrence was on the 27th of August, 1897, when the Rev. H. H. Slater shot an adult female of this Warbler on the coast of Norfolk, and as the bird had evidently bred during the past season, he thinks that the species may yet be found nesting in the eastern counties of England. From Central Europe to Central Asia the Barred Warbler is a nesting bird, and it reaches Denmark and Southern Sweden, but does not breed apparently west of the Rhine. It winters in North-eastern Africa and along the Persian Gulf.

In habits the Barred Warbler resembles our Whitethroats, and is a very shy and skulking bird. It builds a more substantial nest than the last-named birds, of dried grass-stalks and roots mixed with plants, thistle-down and wool, and neatly lined with horse-hair and fine roots. The eggs are from four to six in number, creamy-

THE WHITETHROAT.
THE LESSER WHITETHROAT.

white or light olive, slightly spotted with greenish-brown, the spots being often so faintly indicated as to appear almost obsolete.

The Barred Warbler is a little larger than the Whitethroat and is of a greyish-brown colour above, greyish-white below, with cross-bars of grey. The young are more uniform brown, with the breast and sides of the body ochreous-buff, and there are no bars on the under-surface.

THE WHITETHROAT (*Sylvia sylvia*). This species is more rufous than the Barred Warbler or the Lesser Whitethroat, and has pale chestnut edges to the wing-coverts and quills. Another character by which even the young birds can be distinguished as well as the old, is by the small size of the first or little 'bastard' quill, which never reaches beyond the end of the primary-coverts. The colour of the male Whitethroat is greyish-brown and the head is ashy-grey, contrasting with the back. The tail is darker and has the outer feathers edged with white while the chestnut edges to the wing-feathers are very conspicuous; the under-surface is white, with a pinkish shade on the breast. The female is browner than the male and is whiter underneath, with the pink shade less evident. In winter this pink shade entirely disappears, and the head is also brown like the back. The young birds are browner than the adults, with brown heads and a tint of sandy-buff colour over the lower throat, breast and side of the body.

The Whitethroat is a shy little bird and creeps about in search of its insect food in the thick hedges, especially those encumbered with a side-growth of nettles and brambles. Occasionally the male bird mounts into the air, utters a pretty little song and descends with a quivering flight to its former place of retreat. After their first arrival in spring, the Whitethroats may be noticed in the gardens and orchards, where they often appear on the tops of the hedges with the feathers of the crown and throat distended, making their heads look double their actual size, and they will often come so close that their pale-coloured little eye can be seen distinctly.

The Whitethroat is called ' Nettle Creeper ' and ' Hay Chat ' in different districts of England, and is found everywhere in summer, but becomes rarer in the North of Scotland, where it is not known to breed. It is generally distributed throughout Europe in summer and winters in Africa. The nest is made of grass-stems and is so slightly constructed that it can be seen through. The eggs are from four to six in number, the ground colour being white, spotted with olive-brown and violet-grey.

THE SUB-ALPINE WARBLER.
(Sylvia sub-alpina.)

A single occurrence of this pretty little Warbler has been noted in Britain, a specimen having been procured on S. Kilda, of all places, on the 13th of June, 1894, by Mr. J. S. Elliot, who thought that it was a Dartford Warbler at the time he captured it. The species inhabits the Mediterranean countries, and is easily distinguished from the Whitethroats by its chestnut chin and breast. In habits it much resembles the last-named birds.

THE SUB-ALPINE WARBLER.

THE LESSER WHITETHROAT.
(Sylvia curruca.)

As its name implies, this is a smaller bird than the common Whitethroat, and has the bastard-primary longer than the primary-coverts. It is pale ashy-brown, with a lighter slaty-grey crown, contrasting with the back; the under surface is pure white, with a tint of pink on the fore-neck and breast, less distinct on the sides of the body. It is a little browner in winter and the young birds are washed with brown below, with a great deal of white on the outer tail-feather, which has an oblique black mark across the inner web.

The present species is a summer visitor to Great Britain, but does not nest in Ireland and only sparingly in the south of Scotland. It breeds throughout Central and Western Europe, and winters in the Mediterranean countries and Northern Africa. In habits it is a very shy bird, and seeks for its food in hedgerows, where the foliage is dense, but it is also sometimes found in trees, engaged in searching the leaves diligently for insects. Like the common Whitethroat and other Warblers, it utters a scolding ' churr,' when disturbed, or when its nest is approached. The latter is somewhat similar to that of the Common Whitethroat, but is rather more coarsely made, consisting of grass-stems, bound together with spiders'-webs, and lined with fine rootlets and horse-hair. The eggs are from four to six in number, white, with spots of light brown or greenish-brown and violet-grey, while a frequent feature is the distribution of black spots over the greater part of the egg.

THE ORPHEAN
WARBLER.
(*Sylvia orpheus*).

This species is larger than any of the preceding ones, with a wing three inches in length. Its black head might render it liable to be mistaken for the Black-cap, but the latter bird has the throat ashy-grey, whereas in the Orphean Warbler it is white. The general colour of the upper surface is slaty-grey, the tail black, tipped with white, increasing in extent towards the outer feathers, which are white on the entire outer web; cheeks, throat, and under parts white, with the sides of the breast and flanks ashy-grey, tinged with pink and becoming browner on the lower flanks; the

1. THE GARDEN-WARBLER.   2—THE ORPHEAN WARBLER.   3 —THE BLACKCAP.

iris is pale yellow. The female is browner than the male, and the cap is lighter, and more dusky black; the young birds are also browner than the adults, and have the fore-neck and chest rosy buff, inclining to vinous on the sides of the body.

The Orphean Warbler is supposed to have occurred twice in England, once in Yorkshire and once near Hampstead, but considerable doubt attaches to both records. It is a species of Southern Europe, and is common in Spain and the South of France. Naturalists who have heard this bird sing state that its melody is nothing remarkable, and Lord Lilford says that he is puzzled to know why the name of 'Orpheus' should have been bestowed on the species. The nest is placed in the branch of a tree at from five to twenty feet above the ground, and is somewhat deep, composed of dry grass and stalks, with finer grass inside, the lining consisting of down of the thistle or cotton grass. The eggs are four or five in number, white, spotted with olive-brown or black, and with blotches of violet-grey.

THE BLACKCAP (*Sylvia atricapilla*). This beautiful songster is distributed over the greater part of England, Wales and Ireland in summer, but does not nest beyond the south of Scotland, occurring in the northern parts of the latter kingdom on the autumn migration. It extends throughout Europe in summer, as far east as the Caucasus and Persia, and winters in North East Africa and Senegambia.

The Blackcap's song is considered by many observers to equal that of the Nightingale, and it certainly sings in a more sustained manner. The male takes his share in hatching out the eggs, and my experience in the South of England is that he is more often seen brooding than his red-capped mate, and the birds sit so close that they are easy of observation. The nest is an extremely slight affair, made of dry grass with a little moss, a few cobwebs, and sparsely lined with horse-hair. It is placed in small bushes, such as wild-growing privet or brambles, sometimes among the slender twigs of a small tree or among the dense 'growers' at the foot of an old elm, where the accumulation of dead leaves helps to conceal it. The eggs are from four to six in number, olive-brown or white, or salmon-pink in ground colour, varying both in tint and markings to a remarkable degree, the spots and blotches being olive-brown or grey or reddish-brown, with occasional black spots.

THE GARDEN-WARBLER. (*Sylvia simplex.*) This plain-plumaged little bird is also a beautiful songster, and it much resembles the Blackcap in habits. It is, however, very simply coloured, being olive-brown above, with the head of the same tint as the back, and the wings and tail also resembling the latter. The under parts are ochreous-buff, with the centre of the breast and abdomen greyish-white, and the under wing-coverts and axillaries orange-buff. This last character will generally distinguish the species. Young and old birds, after the autumn moult, are more russet brown and not so olive as in the breeding plumage. The Garden-Warbler is a summer visitor to Europe, extending to Western Siberia, and it winters in South Africa. It is found over the greater part of England, and nests in Southern Scotland, but becomes less frequent in our northern districts, and is rare and local in Ireland.

The food of the species consists almost entirely of insects, but in the autumn it frequents elder bushes along with the Blackcaps, and feeds on the berries. As a rule it is a shy and retiring bird, and its song is only heard from the depths of the thickets which it loves to frequent. Like the Blackcap, it makes a slight and artless nest of dry grass and a few rootlets, with a little moss and a lining of horsehair. Sometimes the nest is suspended in nettles, like a Whitethroat's, but at other times it is built in the thin twigs of a blackberry or elder bush. The eggs are from four to six in number, and resemble greatly those of the Blackcap, though the markings are, as a rule, somewhat coarser.

THE DARTFORD WARBLER (*Melizophilus undatus*). The present species is a dark-coloured kind of Whitethroat with a longer tail than in these birds, the tail exceeding the wing in length. The general colour is a dark slaty-grey, the under surface

THE DARTFORD WARBLER.

vinous chestnut, with the abdomen white. It is an inhabitant of heath-land, nesting in the furze districts of the South of England, extending, so it is said, into the Midlands. Its Continental home is confined to Western Europe, viz., France, Spain, and Italy, nesting on the mountains in South-western Europe, and descending to the low country in winter.

The note of the Dartford Warbler resembles the syllables *pit-it-chou*, and the French name for the species is *Pitchou*. Like other Warblers, it has a harsh scolding note when disturbed or when its nest is approached. In the districts which it frequents it is always very shy and skulking in its habits, but the male is sometimes to be seen on the top of a furze-bush for a second or two, whence it takes its flight to another, only pausing occasionally to utter a little song from the top of the bush. The nest is rather neatly constructed and deep, made of fine grass-stems, with a little moss and wool, and scantily lined with horsehair. The eggs are from four to five in number. They are greenish-white, with numerous spots of greenish-brown and grey sprinkled all over the egg.

THE RUFOUS WARBLER (*Aedon galactodes*). This Mediterranean species is found in Spain and North Africa, and has occurred three times in England, once near Brighton, and twice in Devonshire. It is uniform cinnamon-rufous in colour above; the outer tail-feathers broadly tipped with white, and before this white tip is a broad band of black. There is a distinct eyebrow of a creamy-buff colour, and a faint moustache of dusky brown. The under surface

THE GREAT REED-WARBLER (*p*. 63)
THE RUFOUS WARBLER.

of the body is sandy buff, whiter on the throat, breast and abdomen, with a wash of cinnamon on the sides of the body.

In Algeria and the countries where the Rufous Warbler nests, it is a lively bird, though quick of observation, and retiring to concealment on finding that its movements are being watched. It has a habit of flirting its tail, the white-tipped feathers of which render it somewhat conspicuous. The nest is usually placed in the fork of a tree, made of dead tamarisk shoots or such-like material and lined with feathers with usually a piece of snake's skin added! The eggs, from three to five in number, are of a dull white, streaked and spotted with reddish-brown, and violet-grey, especially near the larger end.

THE WOOD-WARBLER (*Phylloscopus sibilator*). This is the largest of the Willow-Wrens or Leaf-Warblers (*Phylloscopi*), which come to the British Islands in summer. It is a beautiful little bird, and its ways are so graceful and butterfly-like, that anyone who has once seen the species in life in our woods in spring, is not likely to forget it. Just when the leaves are coming into life, when the woods and plantations shew their greenest tints, the Wood-Warbler makes its appearance, the males preceding the females by some days. When the latter arrive, the nest is actively prepared on the ground beneath the budding trees, and the male can be heard singing at intervals of a few moments from the boughs above the selected spot. The nest is built on the ground, and is partially domed, the structure being of grass lined with horse-hair, but not with feathers, like the nests of our other Willow-Warblers. The eggs are from five to seven in number, white, with very distinct spots and blotches

THE WOOD-WARBLER.
THE WILLOW-WARBLER.

of purplish-brown and violet-grey, generally collected round the larger end of the egg.

The Wood-Warbler is not only distinguished from its relatives by its large size, but is yellowish-green above, and has a clear yellow eyebrow. The breast and abdomen are white, and the first or bastard-primary does not reach to the end of the primary-coverts, while the second primary quill exceeds the fifth in length. It breeds in nearly every part of Great Britain and is generally distributed throughout Europe in the summer, but does not nest in some of the more northern districts. It winters in Western and North-eastern Africa.

THE WILLOW-WARBLER (*Phylloscopus trochilus*). This is a more dull-coloured species than the Wood-Warbler, and may be told at any age by the wing-formula, the second primary being intermediate in length between the fifth and sixth, while the third and fourth are the longest. It has a more pointed wing than the Chiffchaff, as might be expected in a bird which migrates so much further south than the latter bird. In addition to this different wing-formula, the Willow-Warbler can always be distinguished from the Chiffchaff by its paler legs.

The Willow-Warbler is a summer visitor and breeds in nearly every portion of the British Islands, its breeding range extending over the greater part of Europe to the high north, and as far east as the Valley of the Yenesei. In winter it is found throughout Africa, from the oases of the Sahara to the forests of West Africa, and throughout the eastern portion of the Continent down to the Cape Colony itself.

The nest is placed on the ground, and is made to look like the surroundings of dead leaves among which it is built. It is composed of dry stems of grass with a little moss, and is somewhat scantily lined with feathers. The eggs are from five to eight in number, white, with reddish dots, occasionally with more distinct spots, dots, or streaks, generally collected towards the larger end of the egg.

THE CHIFFCHAFF.

THE CHIFFCHAFF (*Phylloscopus minor*). This little Warbler is smaller than the Willow-Wren, is duller in colour, and has blackish legs. The wing-formula is also different, the wing being more rounded, with the second primary equal in length to the sixth. These characters will serve to tell the two species at all ages, even in the young plumage, which is always much more yellow in immature *Phylloscopi* than it is in the adult birds. The Chiffchaff arrives in England in March, and its feeble song and vociferous call-note are heard long before either of its near relations have reached our shores. It inhabits the whole of the United Kingdom during summer, but is rarer and more locally distributed than the Willow-Warbler. It does not extend its winter range nearly so far to the south as the latter bird, and even stays in the South of England in mild winters. It ranges in summer throughout Europe, but does not reach so far north as the Willow-Warbler, breeding only on the higher mountains in the Mediterranean countries, nor does it cross the Ural Mountains, being replaced in the east by the Siberian Chiffchaff (*P. tristis*). The winter range does not extend beyond North Africa and Abyssinia. Its habits are like those of the other Willow-Warblers, but it is a more retiring bird and is more often heard than seen. The

THE GREENISH WILLOW-WARBLER.

nest is placed close to the ground, and is composed of dry grass, sometimes half-domed, and is lined with feathers. Occasionally the nest is to be found at a height of some few feet from the ground. The eggs are from five to seven in number, white, with well-marked spots of chocolate or reddish-brown, inclining to purplish-brown or black, with underlying spots of violet-grey.

THE GREENISH
WILLOW-WARBLER.
(Phylloscopus viridanus.)

This species has only once been obtained in Great Britain, a single individual having been shot on the Lincolnshire coast by Mr. G. H. Caton Haigh, on the 5th of September, 1896. It is an Asiatic species, breeding in the mountains of Central Asia and the Himalayas, and also in Europe in North East Russia and the Ural Mountains. It has been noticed on three occasions in Heligoland, and so there is nothing very surprising in its occasional wandering to Great Britain.

In appearance the species is very like our Willow-Warbler, but is greener on the upper surface and is distinguished by the yellowish-white tips to the greater wing-coverts, which form a distinct wing-bar. The under parts are pale greenish-yellow, with the axillaries and under wing-coverts pale yellow. In its breeding home this little Warbler is said to frequent willow-bushes and the tall steppe-grass. By some observers its song has been recorded as feeble, but by others it is stated to have a very powerful song. The nest is placed on the ground and is domed, but the eggs are as yet unknown.

THE YELLOW-BROWED
WILLOW-WARBLER.
(Phylloscopus superciliosus.)

Although a frequent visitor to the island of Heligoland, this small Warbler is of rare occurrence in Great Britain, where less than a dozen specimens have hitherto been recorded, though it has been met with in different parts of the United Kingdom. It nests throughout Siberia, and its winter home is in China, Borneo and India.

It is a tiny species, scarcely larger than a Gold-crest, olive green in colour, with an indistinct line of yellow down the centre of the crown, and shewing a double wing-band of yellow, caused by the yellow tips to the median and greater wing-coverts. It has, moreover, a distinct pale

THE YELLOW-BROWED
WILLOW-WARBLER.

PALLAS'S WILLOW-WARBLER.

**PALLAS'S
WILLOW-WARBLER.**
(Phylloscopus proregulus.)

yellow eyebrow, and the under surface of the body is ashy whitish, with a few streaks of yellow on the breast, and the flanks are greenish, washed with yellow.

In Siberia the present species was found by Seebohm frequenting the pine-forests, where it was very common. The nest was made of dry grass and moss, and lined with reindeer hair, and resembled that of the British Willow-Warbler, being half domed. The eggs are white, spotted with reddish-brown, more plentifully towards the larger end.

This species inhabits South-eastern Siberia as well as the Himalaya Mountains, and occurs in winter in the Burmese provinces and Southern China, visiting South-eastern Russia in the autumn migration. It resembles the preceding species, but has a yellow rump, which is in strong contrast to its greenish back. It has the same pale streak down the crown and the double wing-bar as in *P. superciliosus.* Although its presence has twice been detected in Heligoland, it has been noticed but once in England, a specimen having been shot near Clay, in Norfolk, on the 31st of October, 1896. Like the Yellow-browed Warbler, the present species frequents the pine-woods, and places its nest, which is slightly domed, on the branch of a tree near the stem of the latter, the outside of the nest being covered with moss and lichen, so as to resemble the colour of the branch on which it is placed. The eggs are five in number, white, richly spotted with dark brownish-red, the spots collecting towards the larger end.

**THE COMMON
TREE-WARBLER.**
(Hypolais hypolais.)

The Tree-Warblers are somewhat intermediate between the Willow-Warblers and the Reed-Warblers. They have a more flattened bill than the *Phylloscopi,* and on each side of the gape are three weak rictal bristles. The two species which concern us are clear yellow underneath, and this character, along with the shape of the bill, with its yellow under mandible, is sufficient to distinguish both the British Tree-Warblers from the members of the allied genus *Phylloscopus,* while the pattern of the eggs is quite different.

The Common Tree-Warbler has been noticed in England apparently about eight times, and

THE COMMON TREE-WARBLER.

nearly always in summer. It is curious that a bird which is not rare in Holland, Belgium, and North-eastern France in the nesting-season, should not occur more frequently within the British Islands. The species is found throughout Northern Europe, as far as the birch-region extends, and winters in South Africa. Although spoken of in many works on British Ornithology as the ' melodious ' Willow-Warbler, Seebohm and other observers have failed to find any particularly striking melody in its song, which is described as partaking of imitations of the notes of other birds mixed together, from which the species has probably acquired the name of ' Mocking-bird ' in Germany. The food consists principally of insects, but it feeds on a variety of fruit in the autumn. The nest is placed in the fork of a small tree, and is made of dry grass, with wool and lichen and thistle-down intermixed, and lined with finer roots, grass-stems and horse-hair. The eggs are from four to six in number, of a characteristic pinkish stone-colour, sprinkled or spotted with black dots.

THE WESTERN TREE-WARBLER. (*Hypolais polyglotta*.) Some years ago Mr. Howard Saunders assured me of his belief that the present species occasionally nested in England, as he had seen an egg obtained by a schoolboy at Lancing in Sussex, which could only have been that of *H. polyglotta*. The bird also had been obtained, but the specimen was spoilt in the skinning. More recently an individual has been actually procured, as recorded by Mr. N. F. Ticehurst. It was shot near Burwash, in Sussex, on the 30th of April. The species probably occurs more often than has been supposed. *H. polyglotta* is very similar to *H. icterina*, but is smaller, and has a large bastard primary, and the second quill is shorter than the fifth. It inhabits Western Europe, being found in Spain and Portugal and Central France, and is also found in Algeria and Tunis, passing to Senegambia in winter.

THE AQUATIC WARBLER. (*Acrocephalus aquaticus*.) This species belongs to the group of Sedge and Reed-Warblers, which have the bill somewhat flattened, with well-developed rictal bristles. The bastard primary is very small and does not reach to the ends of the primary-coverts, though it is slightly longer in birds of one year.

The Aquatic Warbler is a small species which breeds in Central Europe, including Italy, Sicily and Sardinia, and extends eastwards to the Ural mountains and Southern Russia, wintering in Northern Africa. It has occurred only three times in England, as far as has been recorded hitherto, once in Leicestershire, once in Sussex, and once in Kent,

THE AQUATIC WARBLER.

near Dover. In appearance the Aquatic Warbler is very like the Sedge-Warbler, but has a pale streak down the centre of the crown with a black band on either side. It is more of a reed-haunting species than the Sedge-Warblers, and it differs considerably from that species in its choice of a nesting-place. The nest is made of grass and lined with horse-hair. It is never suspended in reeds but is built near the ground among the sedge or stalks of water plants. The eggs exactly resemble those of the Sedge-Warbler, and are four or five in number.

THE
SEDGE-WARBLER.
(*Acrocephalus
phragmitis.*)

The present species is distinguished from the Aquatic Warbler by the absence of the pale streak along the crown of the head, this resembling the back, the whole upper surface being russet brown streaked with black, the rump and upper tail-coverts being more uniform rufous. It has a very distinct eyebrow, which can always be seen in the living bird. Young birds resemble the

THE SEDGE-WARBLER.

adults, but have the under surface more yellow, and shew a few triangular dusky brown spots on the fore-neck. The Sedge-Warbler is a smaller bird than the Reed-Warbler or the Marsh-Warbler, which are uniform on the upper surface and therefore easily recognisable. The species winters in South Africa and apparently migrates back to Europe by the Great Lakes and the Nile Valley route, arriving at its breeding quarters in April or early in May. From Turkestan to Central and Northern Europe the species nests freely in the vicinity of water, but is sometimes found building at some distance from the latter. The nest is made of dry grass-stems and dead water-plants, scantily lined with hair and pieces of vegetable down; it is placed on a platform of dead reeds or on a branch overhanging the water, sometimes being on the ground itself. The eggs are from four to six in number, of an olive-brown or stone-grey tint, being entirely clouded with specks of these colours, which hide the greenish-white ground-colour of the egg; there is nearly always a blackish line near the larger end of the egg.

The Sedge-Warbler has a powerful but not musical song, which is heard from the depths of its retreat in the rushes or bushes, especially in the evening, and a stone thrown into its sleeping haunts, even after darkness has set in, will cause it to babble.

THE GREAT REED-WARBLER. (*Acrocephalus turdoides.*) The large size of this species easily distinguishes it from all the other British species of river Warblers, as it is more than seven inches in length. The general colour of the plumage is brown, a little more rufescent on the lower back and rump ; the sides of the face are greyish and there is a distinct white eyebrow. The under surface is white, with a tinge of tawny-buff on the breast and sides of the body, and the under wing-coverts, axillaries, and lining of the quills are of a pronounced tawny-buff colour. Young birds and adults killed in autumn and winter are decidedly more buff below. To Great Britain the species is only a rare and occasional visitor, but throughout the greater part of Europe, excepting the north, the Great Reed-Warbler breeds plentifully in the marshes, as far east as Turkestan, and it winters in Africa, having been procured on the upper Congo and as far south as the Transvaal. The song is harsh but powerful, and like other species of the genus, the male bird often ascends to the top of a reed, singing lustily as it climbs up. The nest is a compactly made structure, suspended between reeds, and is a round and deep cup formed of dead reeds with a little moss or leaves of water-plants intermingled, and lined inside with grass-stems and the flowers of the reed. The eggs are from four to six in number, greenish-blue or greenish-white in colour, blotched and spotted with greenish or reddish-brown, generally collecting near the larger end of the egg.

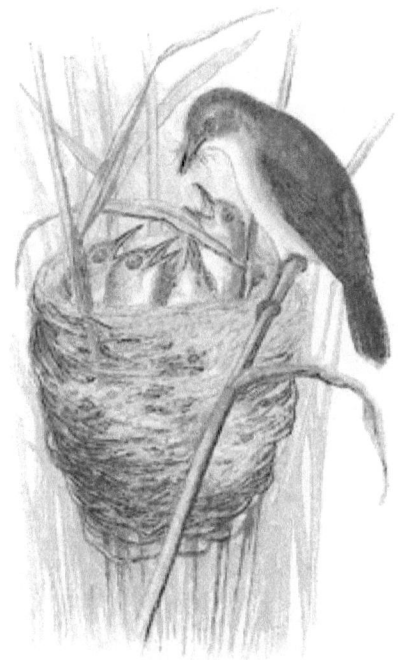

THE REED-WARBLER. (*Acrocephalus streperus.*) This Warbler, often called the Reed-'Wren,' is a sober coloured little brown bird, which visits the southern and central portions of England in summer,

THE REED-WARBLER.

but becomes rarer towards the south-western and northern portions of its range, and is not yet known to have occurred for certain in Scotland or in Ireland. Its breeding-area is spread over the greater part of Europe, below the line of the Baltic Provinces and Southern Sweden, as far east as Turkestan ; it winters along the Persian Gulf and in the Mediterranean.

The Reed-Warbler builds in many of the swamps and ditches of the south of England, its nest being suspended between reeds, but it is not uncommonly found in willow-trees and bushes by the side of the rivers. It is a noisy little songster, its notes resembling those of the Sedge-Warbler, and the song is to be heard after darkness has set in. It is, like the rest of the Reed-Warblers, a shy and retiring bird, and is more often heard than seen, excepting before the autumn migration, when family parties consisting of the old and young birds are often to be noticed on the alders and willows, by the river's edge, before they migrate to their southern home. The nest is cup-shaped, made of dry grass with a little wool and thistle-down, and the eggs are from four to six in number, the ground-colour being greenish or greyish-white, with pronounced mottlings and spots of greenish-brown and violet-grey, often forming a ring round the larger end of the egg.

THE
MARSH-WARBLER.
(*Acrocephalus palustris.*)

This species is very similar to the Reed-Warbler, and resembles it in form and in the proportion of the quills, the bastard-primary not exceeding the primary-coverts in length, but with the second primary longer than the fifth. The Marsh-Warbler is very difficult to tell from the Reed-Warbler, and the only characters of importance are the greenish-olive-brown colour of the back, the paler and more sulphur-coloured (less rufous) tint of the buff on the under surface of the body, and the paler colour of the legs. Nevertheless it is advisable to submit any supposed Marsh-Warblers for the opinion of an expert, as many of the specimens certified in ornithological works to be Marsh-Warblers have turned out, after all, to be only Reed-Warblers.

On the Continent the Marsh-Warbler is a thoroughly recognised species, distinguished not only by its different colour and its song, but by its nesting-habits, and that the species comes to Great Britain every summer

THE MARSH-WARBLER.

THE GRASSHOPPER-WARBLER.

is beyond doubt, the nests and eggs having been taken on several occasions. The Marsh-Warbler has almost identically the same breeding-range as the Reed-Warbler, and winters in Africa, going, however, much further to the south than *A. streperus*, and occurring in South-eastern Africa. It is said to have a far superior song to that of the Reed-Warbler, and to frequent trees and bushes, rather than the river-side or the marshes. The nest is placed in bushes, often far away from water, and the eggs are white with greenish brown spots and blotches, with some purplish black spots always in evidence, while the underlying spots of purplish or violet-grey are always strongly indicated.

THE GRASSHOPPER-WARBLER.
(Locustella nævia.)

This dull-coloured little Warbler is a summer visitor to Great Britain, but is one of the most difficult to observe, as it is an inveterate skulker, and even when its presence is betrayed by its note, the latter is so ventriloquial that the finding of the nest is not an easy problem to solve. The Grasshopper-Warbler is to be distinguished by its olive-brown upper surface, striped with blackish, and by its very graduated tail, in which the outer tail-feathers are very much shorter than the centre ones, while the under tail-coverts are exceptionally long, buffy white in colour, with dark centres. Its nest is always difficult to find and is generally placed on or close to the ground, as a rule closely concealed and approached by a 'run' or narrow passage like that of a mouse. Its song is unmistakable when once heard, and is like a long-continued note of a grasshopper, but is of course much more powerful, and has a curious ventriloquial effect, seeming to come from one point of the compass after another. The eggs are from four to seven in number, and are easily recognisable, as their general tone is pinkish, sprinkled all over with reddish-brown and grey dots.

SAVI'S WARBLER.
(Locustella luscinioides.)

This species used to nest regularly in the fen districts of England, but has not been known to do so for many years past. It is of the same shape as the Grasshopper-Warbler, but is not spotted on the back, which is uniform like that of the Reed-

5

Warblers. Savi's Warbler, however, is of
a much darker brown colour than any of
the last-named birds, and may be distinguished by the vinous brown colour
of the sides of the body. It is an
inhabitant of the marshy districts of
central and southern Europe, as far east
as central Asia, but is only found in
certain favourite haunts, and is everywhere very local. The song is described
as a monotonous whirr, and is heard all
day from the reed-beds frequented by the
species, which may be seen climbing up
the reeds in pursuit of its insect-food.

SAVI'S WARBLER.

The nest is made of dead rushes and flags, with a little moss, but with no lining
beyond a few twisted reeds: it is a well-made and rather deep cup, and is
placed in a tuft of spiky grass or on a platform of broken reeds. The eggs
are from four to six in number, the ground-colour being brownish-white, with
numerous spots of light brown and violet-grey, generally collecting round the
larger end of the egg.

THE THRUSHES.
Family
TURDIDÆ.

This family of birds is closely allied to the preceding
one, but the front aspect of the tarsus is never divided
by scales or cross-lines, being smooth throughout. All
the Thrushes have spotted young ones, and they only
moult once in the year, in the autumn, but do not have a second moult in
the spring like the Warblers.

WHITE'S
THRUSH.
(Oreocichla varia.)

This species, named in honour of Gilbert White of
Selborne, is an inhabitant of Eastern Siberia and winters in China and the Philippine Islands. On its
migration it not unfrequently wanders into Europe, and
has occurred in most of the countries on the Continent, and has been met
with many times in Heligoland, whilst at least a dozen British captures
have been recorded. It is an unmistakable species, having the upper surface
profusely spangled with golden-buff spots, and black crescent-shaped spots on
the fore-neck, breast and sides of the body; on the under side of the wing
there is a very conspicuous patch of white, forming a pale lining across the
base of the quills.

In habits, White's Thrush appears to be a shy and skulking species, feeding
on the ground in damp places and among dead leaves under trees, but little has
been recorded of its ways, and it is doubtful whether the nest and eggs are
really authentically known.

THE SIBERIAN
GROUND-THRUSH.
(*Geocichla sibirica.*)

As its name implies this is an inhabitant of Siberia, where it breeds in the valleys of the Lena and Yenesei Rivers. A specimen in the British Museum was presented by Mr. Frederic Bond, and was said to have been killed in Surrey, near Guildford. A second occurrence in the Isle of Wight has also been surmised, and as the species migrates from its Siberian home as far as the Malayan countries, and has occurred in many places on the continent of Europe, there is nothing to be wondered at in its occasional capture in England.

In Siberia it is a very shy bird during the breeding season, and, though not uncommon, it is a very difficult species to observe, as it keeps to the woods and searches for food upon the ground among the dead leaves. Mr. H. L. Popham noticed this Thrush, remarkable for its dark grey colour and conspicuous white eyebrow, during his expedition to the Yenesei, and says that it was often heard to make a few rich notes from the top of a tree, but was extremely wary. The eggs, which he found in the Yenesei valley, were pale blue, with distinct spots of reddish-brown.

1 - WHITE'S THRUSH.   2—THE BLACK-THROATED OUZEL (*p.* 69).   3—THE ROCK THRUSH (*p.* 75.)
4 - THE GOLD-VENTED BULBUL. (*p.* 83).   5—THE SIBERIAN THRUSH.   6 - THE AMERICAN ROBIN (*p.* 72).

THE BLACKBIRD.

THE
BLACKBIRD.
(*Merula
merula.*)

The Blackbirds and Thrushes have not the large white wing-patch on the inner side of the wing which distinguishes the members of the genera *Oreocichla* and *Geocichla*. In the genus *Merula* the sexes are different in colour, whereas in the true Thrushes the male and female are alike. The male Blackbird is distinguished by its bright yellow bill, this being dark brown or blackish in the female, although in very old birds it has a tendency to become yellow. It is a species found everywhere in the British Islands and extends throughout Europe, but does not range far north in Russia.

This familiar species is too well known to require much notice of its habits. It is found inhabiting every variety of situation, and is a denizen of our parks and gardens, and is very common in the neighbourhood of London. Like other Thrushes its food consists largely of worms and insects, and it devours a great quantity of fruit, when the latter is unprotected. The nest is a large and well-built structure of twigs and moss, grass and mud, and finally lined with fine grass. The eggs are from four to six in number, and vary considerably in colour, from greenish blue thickly spotted with reddish brown to blue with only a small proportion of reddish dots.

THE
RING-OUZEL.
(*Merula
torquata.*)

In this species the colour of the sexes does not differ to the same extent as in the Blackbird, but both male and female are black, with a broad white gorget, which is very conspicuous when the bird flies ; in the hen-bird, however, this gorget is slightly overshadowed with brown, and the feathers of the under parts are edged with whitish,

THE RING-OUZEL.

otherwise the general plumage of the bird is black. The Ring-Ouzel is a summer visitor to Northern Europe, and nests in the mountainous parts of Great Britain and in Scandinavia. In habits it much resembles the Blackbird, but prefers the open moorland and the rocky districts. In Norway I have found it nesting at 3500 feet, and inhabiting the scattered birch-woods, visiting the adjacent grass-land to pick up its food. It is always very shy. The nest is similar to that of a Blackbird, but is placed on the ground or close to the latter, though it is sometimes found in the hole of a bank or wall. The eggs are generally four in number and much resemble those of the Blackbird.

THE BLACK-THROATED OUZEL.
(*Merula atrigularis.*)

This species (*see p.* 67) is a much paler bird than the two preceeding, and is of a light olive-brown colour, with the face, throat and chest black; the axillaries and under wing-coverts are rich chestnut, and the bill is blackish brown, not yellow. The female has the face and throat white, spotted with black on the cheeks, sides of throat and fore-neck; the breast and the sides of the body are ashy-brown, with dusky brown streaks. The Black-throated Ouzel has only been obtained once in England, a young male having been shot near Lewes in December, 1868. It has occurred on several occasions on the continent of Europe. It breeds in Siberia, in the valley of the Yenesei, and also in central Asia, and is very common in winter throughout the Himalayas, in the higher portion of which chain it is also supposed to nest. The species is said by Seebohm to be very wary in its habits, but he found it to be a noisy and active bird, frequenting the neighbourhood of villages in the Yenesei valley. The nest is not yet described, but the eggs are said to be similar to those of the Blackbird.

THE REDWING.
(*Turdus iliacus.*)

This is one of the true Thrushes, in which the male and female are alike in plumage, and the species is easily recognised by its distinct white eye-brow, and by the vinous chestnut colour of the axillaries and under wing-coverts, a feature which is very much in evidence when the bird flies. By this red colour of the under sur-face of the wing the species is easily told from the Song-Thrush, which has the wing-coverts golden buff below, and so there should not be any difficulty in recognizing the two

THE REDWING.

birds apart, though they are otherwise very much alike in size and general appearance. The Redwing is a common winter visitor to every part of Great Britain and at that season of the year is distributed over the greater portion of Central and Southern Europe. It breeds from Iceland and Scandinavia to the valley of the Yenesei in Siberia, and is, in northern Norway at least, a difficult species to observe during the nesting-season. In 1896 I could not see anything of the Redwing at 3500 feet in Sundalen, but in 1897 the young were observed in many parts of the birch-forests, and I caught several. During the period of incubation the birds were very silent, and the song of the male was not often heard, but when the young were hatched both parents were very vociferous, when the neighbourhood of their nest was approached, and came quite close when they perceived their young ones to be in danger. The nest is like that of the Blackbird and Ring-Ouzel, but is smaller, and is neatly constructed of grass, moss, and mud, lined with finer grass. The eggs are from four to six in number, bluish-green with reddish spots and blotches, and are distinguished by their small size. The Redwing suffers greatly in severe winter weather, and numbers perish during a prolonged frost.

THE
SONG-THRUSH.
(*Turdus musicus.*)

The Song-Thrush (*see Frontispiece*) is one of the smaller species of *Turdidæ* and is the most plentiful of all the Thrushes of Great Britain, being distinguished by its golden-buff wing-lining. It breeds everywhere throughout our islands, and a considerable number migrate south in winter, when thousands are caught during passage on the continent. It nests throughout the greater part of Europe to the Yenesei, but in southern Europe is only found breeding in the mountains.

The beauty of the Thrush's song renders the bird an universal favourite, excepting with those who cannot brook the inroads it makes upon fruit-gardens at certain times of the year. It nests very early in the year, if the season be mild, and the eggs are among the most beautiful of any of our British birds, being of a clear blue with black or purplish-brown spots. The nest is remarkable for the way in which the cavity is lined with powdered wood, said to be moulded by the bodies of the birds, until it presents a perfectly smooth surface; it thus differs in plan and finish from the nest of the Blackbird. Besides devouring a great number of worms, the Song-Thrush feeds largely on snails, the *débris* of which can often be found in the places where the birds have broken them against a stone.

THE
MISTLE-THRUSH.
(*Turdus viscivorus.*)

This is the largest of our resident Thrushes, and is a very handsome species, with a number of boldly marked fan-shaped spots of black on the under surface of the body. The axillaries and under wing-coverts of the Mistle-Thrush are white, and this character will generally serve to distinguish the species on the wing, as the Song-Thrush and Redwing, which alone among the British Thrushes could be mistaken for it, always show in flight the golden-buff or chestnut colour of their

THE MISTLE-THRUSH.

under wing-coverts. It is somewhat remarkable that a delicate bird, like the Mistle-Thrush, for, despite its bravado, which gains for it the name of the 'Storm-cock,' it succumbs to a hard season almost as quickly as the Redwing, should be gradually extending its range in Great Britain, notwithstanding the checks which some of our severe winters have imposed upon it. On the continent of Europe it is generally distributed, and it is found as far east as Lake Baikal, while it also breeds in the mountains of Central Asia and in the higher ranges of the Himalayas. Excepting in the breeding-season, when the Mistle-Thrush makes its nest very early in the year and is, as a rule, easily discovered by its clamourous protest against intrusion upon its chosen domain, the bird is a shy and timid species, but in stormy weather it mounts to the top of a tree, and shouts its melody, which is vastly inferior to that of the Song-Thrush. The nest is of the usual Thrush-like type and is placed in the bough of a small elm or in an evergreen bush, but the most beautiful examples of the bird's architecture are to be seen when the nest is built in an old lichen-covered fruit-tree, when the outside of the nest is also covered with lichen so as to assimilate to its surroundings. The eggs are four or five in number, and are distinguished by the stone grey or clay ground-colour, with markings of reddish brown, and under-lying spots of light brown or dull grey.

THE FIELDFARE. (*Turdus pilaris*.) This is the handsomest of the European Thrushes, and is a winter visitor to Great Britain. It has white axillaries and under wing-coverts, like the Mistle-Thrush, but far more distinct, and this white is a conspicuous feature as the bird sits up in the sunshine or flies through the wintry air. It is found breeding throughout northern Europe, and in central Russia and eastern

THE FIELDFARE.

Prussia, extending to central Siberia, and wintering to the southward in the rest of Europe and North Africa, as well as in Central Asia and North-western India.

The Fieldfare is a conspicuous bird with a chestnut-brown back and grey head and rump; the throat and breast are ochreous-buff, with black streaks on the former and black spots on the latter. In Great Britain it is only found in winter, and in mild seasons is the very shyest of birds, frequenting the open country, but in severe times it has to subsist on berries and is then driven in by stress of weather to parks and gardens, where their hard lot makes the poor birds comparatively tame. In many parts of its northern breeding-range the Fieldfare is a gregarious species and nests in company, but not invariably. I have found them in colonies up to 2000 feet in Norway, but at 3000 feet they are often found in isolated birch-woods, two and three pairs together within a small area. A few couples nest in the upper regions at about 3500 feet, generally selecting a belated pine-tree in which to build. The vociferous chatter which distinguishes the note of the Fieldfare in England in winter is also heard in the colonies which breed in Norway, and the nest can generally be discovered without difficulty from the anxious cries of the parents. Some of the situations chosen by the birds are almost absurd in their prominence, the nest being placed in an isolated tree, or on the top of a hedge, passed a dozen times a day within a yard by every inhabitant of the farm, and in 1897 I actually found a nest on the exposed window-ledge of an inhabited dairy-farm high up in the mountains. The nest resembles that of the Blackbird, and the eggs, from four to six in number, are bluish-green with rufous or chestnut markings.

THE AMERICAN THRUSH. (*Turdus migratorius.*) This species (*see p.* 67) often called the Migratory Thrush, and in the New World known as the American 'Robin' on account of the similarity of its red breast to that of our European Robin, has been twice procured in Great Britain, once near Dover and a second time near Dublin; whether these individuals had escaped from confinement is uncertain, but the species is common in North America, and may occasionally wander eastward to our shores.

THE COMMON NIGHTINGALE. (*Daulias luscinia.*) The Nightingale is a somewhat sober-plumaged bird, but its song is one of the most beautiful in the world. Thus it proves the fact, that our little warblers excel in song if not in the brilliancy of their plumage, whereas tropical species, of extreme splendour as regards their colour, are not remarkable for their voice, and generally possess no song at all. The spotted plumage of the young proves the Nightingale to be a member of the family *Turdidæ*, and not to be a Warbler as is often suggested. It is only a summer visitor to England, and scarcely extends beyond the midland counties nor westward beyond Devonshire and the eastern counties of Wales. Its winter home appears to be in West Africa, and its summer range on the continent of

THE COMMON NIGHTINGALE.

Europe comprises the greater part of Central and Southern Europe, but it is not found in the north.

Arriving about the middle of April, the males precede the females by at least a week, and even in the early days of May the males may be heard in the copses of the south of England, four or five singing at one time, showing that thus early in the year the birds have not yet separated for their breeding-quarters. When the nesting-place is selected, no bird can be more difficult of observation, for it frequents the most secluded thickets and hedge-rows, and is very seldom seen, though the liquid notes of the male may be heard throughout the day and often far into the night. The nest is a ragged affair, of dead leaves, principally oak-leaves, and lined with grasses or a little horse-hair. The eggs are from four to six in number, of an olive-brown or olive-green colour, with sometimes a little clouding of olive-brown dots round the larger end.

THE REDBREAST. (*Erithacus rubecula.*) The Robin is such a familiar bird that any detailed description of its plumage or its habits seems to be unnecessary in a little treatise like the present. It is a common bird throughout the greater part of the British Islands, but a good many Robins leave us in the Autumn, when old and young birds, the latter mostly moulting from the spotted-dress into the adult red-breasted plumage, may be seen and heard among the orchards and plantations on our southern coasts, where

THE REDBREAST.

they halt for a little time before commencing their migrations The Robin is found everywhere throughout the British Islands, and is likewise distributed throughout Europe, migrating in autumn to the Mediterranean countries in considerable numbers, and as far east as Persia.

The nest is made of dead leaves and moss lined with rootlets and hair, and is often placed on the ground in a bank, and is concealed by the surrounding herbage ; but all sorts of places are chosen by the bird, the hole of a tree or wall, the inside of a tin or kettle, or an old hat hung up as a scarecrow. The eggs are from five to eight in number, white, more or less thickly spotted with rufous, while sometimes they are spotless blue or white.

THE RED-SPOTTED BLUE-THROAT.
(Cyanecula suecica.)

This pretty species occurs with us only on migration, and is much more frequently observed in the autumn than in the spring, though it has been known to occur at the last-named season of the year ; it has chiefly been noticed on our eastern coasts. On the continent it breeds in the high north and extends to Kamtchatka and even to Alaska in North West America. It is also found in Central Asia, and its winter home is in North East Africa, India and the Burmese Provinces.

In Norway I have observed this species breeding every year at 3500 feet in the birch-woods, and always in the vicinity of swampy ground, though I never could discover the actual nest. A young bird which I caught in 1897 was a curiously striped little creature, unlike the young of the Robins

THE RED-SPOTTED BLUE-THROAT.

or Redbreasts, and he carried his tail at an angle to his back, and stood very high on his legs, having the aspect more of a Chat than a Robin. In a few days he became so tame that he would fly out of his cage when called by his mistress, and sit on her finger and take meal-worms from her hand ; and this, although the room door stood open to the garden, and he could have flown away at any time. The parent birds hovered round the house for a few days, and even came down to the door of the room, calling to their youngster to accompany them, but he seemed to be quite contented with his lot.

The Blue-throat is a very handsome little bird, with a chestnut tail, which is black for the terminal half. The upper surface is brown, but the principal feature of the species is the cobalt blue of the throat, which has also a conspicuous spot of chestnut. There is a black and white collar across the chest, while the breast is chestnut, the abdomen white. The female has no blue on the throat. The nest resembles that of a Robin and is placed on the ground and well-concealed.

The eggs are olive-brown or bluish-green, clouded with reddish dots, and resemble some of the eggs of the Nightingale.

THE
ROCK-THRUSH.
(*Monticola saxatilis.*)

The Rock-Thrush (*see p. 67*) has a red tail like the Redstarts, and the male and female are very different in colour, the male being slaty-black, with the centre of the back white. The head and throat are greyish-blue, with the rest of the under surface of the body orange-chestnut. The female is ashy-brown mottled with pale margins to the feathers, and the throat is white, mottled with dark brown edges; the breast and sides of the body are golden buff with dusky brown edges to the feathers. It is a species of Central and Southern Europe, extending to Central Asia and Mongolia and wintering in East Africa and in North-western India. It has been shot once in England, in Hertfordshire, in May, 1843. It has a fine song and resembles a Redstart in its ways, the nest being placed in the hole of a rock or wall, and is like that of a Chat or Redstart. The eggs are four or five in number, of a bright blue colour, with sometimes a few brown specks.

THE REDSTART.
(*Ruticilla
phoenicurus.*)

The red tail of this bird makes it rather a conspicuous species, as the bird has a way of flirting its tail up and down and spreading it out. It is a summer visitor to Great Britain, and breeds in all three kingdoms. Its breeding-range extends throughout the greater part of Europe, north to the Arctic Circle, and east to the Yenesei. It winters in West

THE REDSTART.
THE BLACK REDSTART.

Africa as well as in North-east Africa and along the Persian Gulf. The male is recognised by its slaty grey back, white forehead, black face and throat, and orange-chestnut breast. The female is more of an ashy brown colour above, and has the sides of the face brown, the throat dull white like the abdomen, the fore-neck, breast and flanks sandy-brown, and the under wing-coverts and axillaries yellowish-buff. The winter plumage is more grey, but the summer dress can be detected below the grey margins of the winter plumage, for it is gained by the shedding of the latter, as the grey becomes abraded and the edgings disappear as spring advances. The young are spotted with ochreous-buff, and resemble the young of the Robin.

The male Redstart is the first to arrive in its nesting-quarters, before the female, and is then often in evidence, but during the breeding season the bird is decidedly shy, and it is only before the autumn migration that the species is freely noticed. Then in such places as the New Forest and other woods of our southern counties, the Redstart is often to be seen on the side of the coppices flying out into the air after some insect, after the manner of a Flycatcher, but easily recognisable by its red tail. The nest is placed in the hole of a tree or a wood stack, or in the hole of a building, the entrance to the latter being often so narrow that even a child's hand cannot be inserted. The eggs are pale blue and from five to six in number.

THE BLACK REDSTART.
(Ruticilla titys.)

This species visits us regularly in winter, journeying from east to west along the south coast of England and returning by the same route in spring. It is also known as a winter visitor to Scotland and Ireland. On the continent it is confined to the Western and Central districts of Europe and does not extend beyond Southern Norway and Sweden. The Black Redstart is slaty grey, the rump and upper tail-coverts being orange-chestnut like the tail; there is no white band on the crown, the forehead being black at its base, like the face, throat and breast; the abdomen whitish, and the flanks slaty-grey, turning to cinnamon on the lower flanks and under tail-coverts. The female is slaty-brown, the under surface being also of this colour but paler than the back, and the under wing-coverts and axillaries resemble the breast in colour. Instead of being a frequenter of woods like the Common Redstart, the present species seeks the neighbourhood of houses, and resembles the Robin in its habits. The nest is built in holes of buildings, and the eggs, from four to six in number, are white, with occasionally a faint greenish tinge.

THE WHEATEAR.
(Saxicola œnanthe.)

This Chat is to be observed plentifully on our coasts during the autumn migration, when it is preparing for its flight towards its winter home in Africa. It is also found in the latter season from the shores of the Persian Gulf to North-western India. In summer the Wheatear is not only found throughout Northern Europe and Northern Asia, but even extends to Greenland, where it has been observed up to 80° N. Lat. The male is slaty blue, with a conspicuous white rump, the tail also is white with a broad band of black at the end; the forehead and eyebrow are white, and the sides of the face black, the throat and breast pale tawny-buff, and the rest of the under parts creamy white; the axillaries are white and the under wing-coverts black. The female is browner than the male, and the under surface is pale sandy-buff. In autumn the plumage of both old and young birds is like that of the female, but is rather more rufescent.

The Wheatear nests in a variety of situations, on the sea-shore in the south of England, under a tussock on the downs and moors, or in the stony crevices of the mountains of Norway beyond the limits of forest-growth. The nest is very simply made of grass with some moss and rootlets, and is lined with hair or a few feathers;

THE WHEATEAR.

it is generally well concealed. The eggs are from four to seven in number, greenish blue or greenish white, with sometimes a few purplish-brown spots round the larger end.

THE ISABELLINE WHEATEAR. *(Saxicola isabellina.)* This is a large Chat of very pale and sombre colour, which might be mistaken for a female or young of the Common Wheatear, but may always be distinguished by its longer leg, the tarsus measuring 1·2 inch instead of 1·05 as in the common species. The sexes are alike in colour, being of an earthy-brown, more or less ashy, and the under surface is light isabelline-rufous, becoming sandy-white on the throat and abdomen; the axillaries and under wing-coverts are creamy-white.

THE BLACK-THROATED WHEATEAR.   THE ISABELLINE WHEATEAR.

The Isabelline Wheatear is an inhabitant of the desert countries from Mongolia to Arabia and Eastern Africa, and has once been obtained in England, near Allonby in Cumberland, in November, 1887. The bird is said by Mr. Danford to frequent barren grounds, bushy hill-sides and even fir-woods, and to rise into the air and sing. The nest is placed in burrows and resembles that of the Common Wheatear, the eggs being pale greenish blue with occasionally some faintly indicated spots of brown.

THE
BLACK-THROATED
WHEATEAR.
(*Saxicola stapazina.*)

This Chat, which is an inhabitant of Algeria, Spain, and the South of France, has once occurred near Bury, in Lancashire, in May, 1875. It is sandy-rufous in colour, with a white rump, black wings and black under wing-coverts. The latter character will distinguish the female of the Black-throated Wheatear from the hen of *Saxicola œnanthe*. The habits of the species are like those of the other members of the genus, excepting that it frequents rocky localities and builds its nest in the grass under the shelter of a rock or a stone. The eggs are light blue in colour, sprinkled with reddish dots.

THE DESERT-
WHEATEAR.
(*Saxicola deserti.*)

As its name portends, this little Chat comes from the Sahara and other desert countries, ranging from North Africa to Egypt and Palestine, and thence to Central Asia. It has been noticed three times in Heligoland and twice in Great Britain, viz.:—near Alloa in Scotland, in November, 1880; and again near Holderness on the 17th of October, 1885. It is a small species, of a bright sandy rufous colour, with the lower rump and upper tail-coverts white, and the wings black, showing a large white patch formed of the inner median and greater coverts; the tail is black, with the concealed basal third white; the head is sandy rufous like the back, but the sides of the face and throat are black, and there is a distinct white eyebrow; the under surface of the body is sandy rufous, but the abdomen and centre of the breast are whiter; the under wing-coverts are white and the axillaries are black tipped with white. The female has no black on the face or throat, and the under wing-coverts and axillaries are white, with dusky bases. It can be told from the hens of the other Wheatears by the less extent of white on the tail, this being confined

THE DESERT-WHEATEAR.

to the basal third. In habits and in the choice of a nesting-place it resembles the other species, and the eggs are greenish blue with reddish brown spots.

THE WHINCHAT.
(*Pratincola rubetra.*)

This little bird is a summer visitor to Great Britain, arriving early in May from its winter home in West Africa and North-east Africa. It nests in all parts of Great Britain, but is more local and rarer in some counties than in others. Its nesting range extends east to the Ural Mountains, and it even reaches beyond the Arctic Circle. In the South of Europe it is mostly found on migration and breeds only in the mountains. The Whinchat belongs to a little group of birds peculiar to the Old World, having broader bills and more abundant rictal bristles, in which respect they resemble the Flycatchers, and are like the latter birds in their habits. The general aspect of the male Whinchat is rufous, with a white wing-patch, formed of the white inner median and greater wing coverts; the tail-feathers are white with a broad band of brown on their terminal third; the sides of the face are black, surmounted by a broad white eyebrow; the cheeks and chin are white and this extends on to the side of the neck, skirting the cinnamon-rufous colour of the throat and breast, the rest of the under surface of the body being sandy buff. The female is not so brightly coloured as the male, the sides of the face being browner, and the rufous on the throat and breast not so bright. The flight of the Whinchat is very rapid, as it flits from one furze bush to another, and perches invariably on the topmost bough. It frequents commons and the slopes of rough hills and downs, and the nest is well concealed, being generally placed in the grass under a bush, and approached by a run or small tunnel. In the mountains of Norway it nests on the high fjelds, choosing the thickets of rough bushes and small birch-trees which may be found on the edges of some of the swamps and generally in the vicinity of the hay-fields, where there is an abundance of insect food. The hen bird is very seldom seen and it is only by driving her off the nest that the latter is usually discovered. The eggs are greenish-blue, with minute specks of reddish-brown.

THE STONECHAT.
(*Pratincola rubicola.*)

Though of similar habits to the Whinchat, the Stonechat is a much darker bird and can be distinguished by its black head and the white patch on the

THE WHINCHAT.   THE STONECHAT.

neck, both of which are very conspicuous as the bird sits on the top of a furze bush or low hedge. The tail, when spread in flight, does not show the amount of white which is so evident in the Whinchat. Although found in most parts of Great Britain in summer, the Stonechat is everywhere a local bird, and a few remain with us during the winter, but the greater number migrate. It is a local bird throughout Europe, as it is in Great Britain, and it does not extend nearly so far north as the Whinchat, while its eastern range is bounded by the Ural Mountains, or perhaps a little further to the eastward, its place being taken in Siberia by a different species, *Pratincola maura.* Our Stonechat is a much more plentiful species in Southern Europe than it is in the more northern parts of the continent, and breeds throughout the Mediterranean countries, wintering in North-east Africa and Senegambia.

The species is very similar in its habits to the foregoing species, but frequents the more open country. Its nest is quite as hard to find, and as equally well concealed. The eggs are pale bluish-green, but the reddish-brown spots are larger and more distinct than those of the Winchat, and the spots generally form a zone round the larger end of the egg.

THE
HEDGE-SPARROW.
(*Tharrhalcus
modularis.*)
Excepting in the extreme north of Scotland and the Orkneys, Shetlands, and the Hebrides, the Hedge-Sparrow is universally distributed throughout the British Islands, and is almost as familiar a pensioner in our gardens as the Robin.

Its lively little song is heard throughout the spring and summer, and it is one of the first birds to commence to sing when winter is barely over. The nest is a beautiful structure, composed principally of moss, and the eggs are of a clear greenish-blue, with no spots of any kind. Although the Accentors have spotted young, they differ from the rest of the Thrushes in having scales on the tarsus, and in their general aspect they are much more like Robins. They are to a great extent migratory, but have a much more rounded wing than the majority of the *Turdidæ*, to which family they really belong, and the rounded wing merely shews that they are less migratory than their relatives with pointed wings. Nevertheless numbers of our Hedge-Sparrows leave us in the autumn and cross the channel. With the exception of Southern Europe, where the species only nests in the mountains, the Hedge-Sparrow is generally distributed during the breeding season throughout Europe as far

THE HEDGE-SPARROW.

THE ALPINE ACCENTOR.

as the Ural Mountains. The plain colouring of the species, its brown back, striped with black, and slaty grey under surface have doubtless suggested its resemblance to a Sparrow, but here the resemblance ends, for the Sparrow is a Finch, and the Accentor is a sort of dwarf Thrush, with spotted young.

THE
ALPINE ACCENTOR.
(*Accentor collaris.*)

This species is only an occasional visitor to Great Britain, but nearly a dozen authentic records of its occurrence have been published. It is a mountain-loving bird, quite different in its habits from our garden-frequenting Hedge-Sparrow, from which it differs moreover in its more pointed wing. The Alpine Accentor is an inhabitant of the mountains of Southern Europe from Spain to the Caucasus and Northern Persia, and it is also found in the mountains of other parts of Central Europe, breeding on the higher ground and wintering in the lower valleys. The nest is placed on the ground under the shelter of a bush, and the eggs are greenish blue.

THE DIPPER.
(*Cinclus aquaticus.*)

This interesting bird is only found in the mountainous districts of Central and South-western England, and in similiar localities in Wales and Ireland, but it is met with throughout Scotland, near rocky streams and rivers. It is an unmistakable species, appearing, at first sight, to be quite black as it stands on a stone in the middle of a torrent or perches on the banks of a brook, but its white throat and chest are soon plainly observable. Below this white chest, the breast is rufous and the sides of the body are slaty-grey. The sexes are alike, but the young birds are mottled with black edges to the grey feathers of the upper surface, and with dusky margins to the white plumage of the lower parts.

The Dipper is an

THE DIPPER.

6

interesting bird to watch, as it flies with rapid beats of its wings, much after the manner of a Kingfisher, and settles down on a stone, from which it deliberately walks into the water and disappears beneath the surface, seeking for its food at the bottom of the stream. It is accused of devouring trout-ova, but its principal food consists of caddis-worms, water-beetles and small shells. The nest of the Dipper is a domed structure, with the entrance-hole rather low down, made of moss which assimilates to the surroundings of the rocky-hole or bank in which the nest is placed, and hence it is never easy to find. Inside this dome of moss the real nest is placed, and this consists of grass, slender twigs and leaves, closely compacted together. The eggs are pure white, but without any gloss, so that they cannot be mistaken for the eggs of the Kingfisher.

THE BLACK-BELLIED DIPPER.
(Cinclus cinclus.)

The Dippers of the Old World are divided into several races, which inhabit certain mountainous areas of the continents of Europe and Asia. Our Common Dipper, for instance, is only found in Great Britain, France and Germany, Holland and Belgium, and in the Alps and the Pyrenees its place is taken by a paler form, *Cinclus albicollis.* In Scandinavia occurs the Black-bellied Dipper, which differs from our own species in having a chocolate-brown or blackish breast, instead of a rufous one. Occasionally the Scandinavian form appears to cross the sea, as it has been met with in our eastern counties. In habits as well as in its nest and eggs there is no difference between *C. cinclus* and *C. aquaticus.* I have found the Dipper in Norway nesting by the side of a roaring torrent, and perching on the rocks in the midst of the foam. The close-set plumage of the bird, however, seems to be impervious to wet, as might be gathered from the way in which it is able to remain under water. The young birds on leaving the nest, keep to the rocks by the side of the stream and are assiduously fed by their parents.

THE WREN.
(Anorthura troglodytes.)

This tiny little bird is found all over Great Britain, and is resident with us throughout the year, though our eastern coasts are visited by a considerable number of individuals during the autumn migration. It seems curious that such a small bird should brave the North Sea, but it is not more wonderful than is the

THE BLACK-BELLIED DIPPER.

case of the Gold-Crest. As in the Dippers, which are also allied to the true Wrens, there are no rictal bristles at the base of the bill, as in the Thrushes and Warblers. They have too a remarkably rounded wing, which fits to the form of the body, and resembles that of the Bush-babblers (*Timeliidæ*). For the size of the bird, the volume of song which the Wren pours out is extraordinary. It is generally an inhabitant of dense hedges and undergrowth, and is not often seen at any height in the trees. The tail is often carried at right angles to the back. The nest is a large one, composed principally of moss and leaves, and is placed in the stems of ivy against a large

THE WREN.

elm tree, or in the trellis-work of a summer-house or garden-building, and in all sorts of queer places. The eggs are four or six in number, sometimes nine. They are white with reddish-brown spots and tiny dots of the same colour.

THE S. KILDA WREN. (*Anorthura hirtensis.*) The Wrens which inhabit the outlying islands of Scotland appear to be somewhat larger than those of the mainland. Thus birds from the Shetlands are bigger than the ordinary run of British individuals, and this is especially the case with the S. Kilda Wrens, which exceed *A. troglodytes* in size and approach the larger Wren of the Faroes *A. borealis*). The absence of trees on S. Kilda makes this Wren an inhabitant of the rocks, and it may be this rougher mode of life which has developed its more robust form and stronger legs. It sings as vigorously as the Common Wren, and builds a similar kind of nest, which it places in the holes of walls or under the shelter of a bush. The eggs are like those of *A. troglodytes*, but are larger and more boldly marked.

THE BULBULS. *Family* PYCNONOTIDÆ. This is a tropical family of birds, plentifully represented in Africa, India and China, but not a Palæarctic group at all. In fact the only species which comes within European limits is the Dusky Bulbul (*Pycnonotus barbatus*) which is found in North-western Africa (Algeria and Marocco). If any Bulbul occurred in Great Britain, it might have been expected to be this species, whose habitat is the nearest to our shores, but the so-called 'Gold-vented Thrush' of the old British Lists is *Pycnonotus capensis* (*see page* 67), a species confined to the Cape Colony and not in any degree migratory. The specimen said to have been shot near Waterford, in January, 1848, by Dr. Burkitt must have been therefore an escaped individual. It is a brown bird with yellow under tail-coverts, and is one of the species which should be expunged from the list of British Birds.

THE
FLYCATCHERS
Family
MUSCICAPIDÆ.

The Flycatchers have distinctly spotted young, and hence they show their alliance with the Thrushes. Many of them, however, though not moulting entirely in the spring as the Warblers do, gain their summer plumage by a change of feather without moult, therein differing from the majority of the *Turdidæ*. The Flycatchers are essentially 'snappers,' and catch their insect prey on the wing, returning to their original perch from whence they sally forth again. The bill is much flatter than in the Thrushes and is furnished with very distinct rictal bristles.

THE COMMON
FLYCATCHER.
(Muscicapa grisola.)

This little bird arrives in Great Britain after the bulk of the summer migrants, as if it timed its arrival when the warm weather might be expected to have set in in our uncertain climate, so that it is hardly to be expected before the early part of May. It then spreads over the whole of Great Britain and migrates south in autumn, after the moult is completed, to Western and Southern Africa. The breeding-range of the species extends to the Yenesei valley in Siberia, and the eastern examples apparently winter in Persia and North-western India.

The colour of the Common or 'Spotted' Flycatcher, as it is often called, is a plain brown, with the under surface white, except for a tinge of isabelline-brown on the breast and sides of the body, which are streaked with

1- THE COMMON FLYCATCHER.
2- THE PIED FLYCATCHER.

dark brown. It frequents every kind of situation where its insect food is assured, and is to be found in parks, orchards, and gardens, even in the suburbs and parks of London, where it may be seen sitting on railings or the lower branches of trees, from which vantage it sails out after any passing insect, which it secures, and again takes up its former position. In the case of large flies, which are often captured, the hard portions of the bodies are thrown up by the birds in the shape of pellets, which form small iridescent particles on the ground near the nest. The young birds, in spotted plumage, generally take up their seats, side by side, on a rail or lawn-tennis net in the autumn, and are assiduously fed by the parent birds till the moult is complete and they are strong enough to perform their long southern journey.

The nest is an artless structure of dry grass with a lining of horse-hair, but it is skilfully decorated outside with cobwebs and lichens so as to assimilate to the surroundings of the bark of the tree, in a crevice of which it is generally placed, but, like the Robin, the Flycatcher is a confiding bird, and often builds its nest on the trellis-work against a house or conservatory. The eggs are from four to six in number, and are buffy-white or greenish-white, spotted and blotched with reddish-brown, with grey underlying markings.

THE PIED
FLYCATCHER.
(Ficedula atricapilla.)

One great difference which separates the present species from the common Flycatcher is the contrast in the colour of the sexes, the male being black, with the under-surface white, a white patch on the wing, and the outer tail-feathers also white for the most part. The female is brown with the tips of the greater wing-coverts white, the upper tail-coverts and tail black, excepting the outer feathers, which are, to a great extent, white : the sides of the face and under parts are pale ochreous brown, shading off into white on the abdomen and under tail-coverts.

The breeding-range of the Pied Flycatcher extends throughout Europe, and it breeds up to 69° in Scandinavia. To Great Britain it is a visitor in summer, and is decidedly local, nesting in the northern counties of England and Wales, as well as in Scotland. In Norway it builds its nest under the eaves of the farm-houses, and in the boxes which are often put up for its accommodation ; at other times it nests in the hole of a tree or wall. It resembles our Common Flycatcher in general habits, but in some respects reminds one of a Chat in its ways ; like the last-named species it feeds principally on flies and other small insects, but also devours berries in the autumn. The nest has no pretensions to architecture and is composed of grass and leaves with a little moss and a few feathers. The eggs are quite different from the red-spotted ones of the majority of Flycatchers, being of a pale blue colour and varying from four to eight in number. They are smaller than those of the Hedge-Sparrow and more brittle, while the position of the nest should always render any doubt as to the authenticity of the eggs of the two species impossible.

THE
RED-BREASTED
FLYCATCHER.
(Siphia parva.)

This is a little bird, not unlike a Robin in appearance, as it has a red breast, bordered from the forehead down the sides of the neck with light bluish grey. It can, however, be easily recognised by its ashy-brown colour and blackish tail-feathers, which have the basal two-thirds *white*. The female is browner than the male, and does not show the grey on the forehead or sides of the neck,

THE RED-BREASTED FLYCATCHER.

while the throat and chest are yellowish-buff. It is a bird of Eastern Europe, nesting in the Baltic Provinces and in Russia, and migrating to North-western India and South-eastern Europe. It has, however, been obtained on migration in many parts of Central Europe, and has been captured in Great Britain on some half dozen occasions. The nest is placed in the hole of a tree, and is made of moss, lined with hair and fine grass. The eggs are from five to seven in number, and resemble those of the Robin or Common Flycatcher, but are less strongly marked.

THE HOUSE-MARTIN.

THE SWALLOW.

In habits the species resembles *M. grisola*, but it also has many of the ways of a Tit, and the note resembles the ‘pink’ of the Chaffinch, though it is more subdued and uttered more quickly.

THE SWALLOWS.
Family
HIRUNDINIDÆ.

Because of their rapid flight and general resemblance, the Swallows and Swifts were formerly classed together, and the wide-gaping mouths of these aerial insect-hunters makes them apparently near akin. Now, however, we know from their anatomy and osteology that the two forms are widely separate, the Swallows being Passerine Birds, highly modified Flycatchers in fact, while the Swifts are Picarian and are the allies, somewhat distant perhaps, of the Goat-suckers and the Humming-Birds. Nevertheless the Swallows, Passerine though they be, are decidedly aberrant, and not only differ from Flycatchers in having nine visible primaries instead of ten, but they differ from all other Perching Birds in having the spinal feather-tract not continuous from the head to the back, but forked. They are perfectly cosmopolitan in their range, and extend even beyond the Arctic Circle in summer.

THE
HOUSE-MARTIN.
(Chelidon urbica.)

The distinguising character of the House-Martins, which are entirely birds of the Old World, is the feathering of the feet. Our British species, which is common everywhere in summer, is easily distinguished on the wing by the broad white band which is conspicuous across the lower back, as the bird flies. The rest of the upper surface is blue black, and the under surface pure white, with the tail black and only slightly forked. This is the species which frequents the suburbs of our large cities, and builds a clay nest under the shelter of the eaves of our houses. The House-Martin arrives about the middle of April from its winter quarters in Africa, and is common all over Europe, nesting in colonies in the north in the scattered farm houses. The nest is composed of small nodules of sand and mud, impressed with the saliva of the birds, and forming a compact and feather-lined home, with a narrow opening at the top, through which the head of the sitting female is often seen peeping out to take food from its industrious mate, while later on the small heads of the young ones may be observed projecting and even

clamouring for the insects brought to the nest by the parent birds. The eggs are glossy white and from four to six in number.

THE
SAND-MARTIN.
(*Clivicola riparia.*)

The little Bank Martin is the first of the Swallows to arrive in Great Britain, making its appearance early in April. It is the smallest of the British Swallows,

THE PURPLE MARTIN.   THE SAND MARTIN.

and is of a plain brown colour, white underneath, with a brown collar across the fore-neck. It nests throughout Europe and Northern Asia, and is also found on the continent of North America, wintering in the Old World in Africa and India, and in Central and Southern America. It is found everywhere in summer throughout Great Britain, nesting in colonies in sand-banks and railway-cuttings, the holes in which are excavated to a considerable depth by the birds them-selves. There, at the end of the tunnel, a scanty nest of grass is prepared with a few feathers for the lining, and four or five pure white eggs are laid. In flight and in general habits the Sand-Martin resembles our other British Swallows, but is more frequently seen flying over water than the other two species. In the autumn vast hordes of Sand-Martins congregate to roost in the reed-beds of our southern rivers and in the swamps near the sea-coast, and flocks of them may be seen in the autumn sunning themselves on the sand spits of our tidal harbours before commencing their migration.

THE CHIMNEY-SWALLOW.
(Hirundo rustica.)

The Chimney-Swallow is easily recognised by its long forked tail and rufous forehead and throat, which contrast with the purplish-blue back and light under-surface of the bird. The Swallow moults in its winter quarters, while it is away from Europe, and on its return to this country the plumage is beautiful, and the male bird often looks quite rufous underneath as it turns in the sunlight. The old female is generally whiter below, and the young have shorter tails than the adult. They can, however, always be distinguished by their blue backs from the Sand-Martin; and by their unfeathered toes, and by the absence of the white band on the rump from the House-Martin.

Our Swallow winters in Africa and in India, and is found during the breeding-season throughout Europe and Western Siberia, even to the far north, as it has been seen on Jan Mayen, and Mr. F. G. Jackson tells me that he once saw one on Franz Josef Land. The nest is usually placed on a beam inside a shed, and is made chiefly of mud, with a little grass and straw, and is lined with feathers and dry grass. Unlike the two species of Martin, both of which lay white eggs, the Swallow's eggs are white with reddish or purplish brown spots.

PICINE AND CUCKOO-LIKE BIRDS.—*Orders PICIFORMES and COCCYGES.*

THE characters which separate the *Piciformes* from the *Passeriformes* are anatomical and need only be referred to here, as the Woodpeckers, which are the only Picine family occurring in Great Britain, are so easily recognised that external characters are sufficient for the reader to determine them. First of all there is the scansorial (climbing) or zygodactyle (yoke-footed) feature of the toes, which are arranged in pairs, two turned forwards and two backwards. The tongue is extensile, and capable of being projected to a considerable distance by means of its muscles, and the hyoid cornua are curved backwards over the skull.

THE GREEN WOODPECKER.
(Gecinus viridis.)

In this species, as in all the other members of the sub-family *Picinæ*, the tail is stiffened and remarkable for its spiny shafts, which are pressed against the tree as the bird climbs or clings to the trunk. The general colour is green, yellow below, and with the rump bright yellow, which colour shows very distinctly when the bird is flying. The male has a red head and a broad red moustache, the latter being replaced by a black band in the female, which otherwise resembles the male. It is a species of the southern and midland counties of England, becoming gradually scarcer towards the north, and to Scotland and Ireland it is only a rare visitor. It is found throughout the greater part of Europe. The food of the Green Woodpecker consists largely of ants and it may often be seen digging among the ant-hills. The note is a noisy cackling laugh, which can be heard at a considerable distance. It is a shy bird, and generally commences work on the trunk of a tree opposite to the spectator and makes its way to the top, occasionally putting its head round to see

1—THE GREEN WOODPECKER.   2—THE GREAT BLACK WOODPECKER.
3 THE GREAT SPOTTED WOODPECKER.
4—THE HAIRY WOODPECKER.   5—THE LESSER SPOTTED WOODPECKER.

that there is no danger approaching. There is no nest, but the eggs, which are pure white and from four to seven in number, are laid on the chips of wood at the bottom of a hole which is excavated by the birds themselves.

THE GREAT
BLACK
WOODPECKER.
(*Picus martius.*)

Although this large species has been recorded as having occurred in several places in Great Britain, but one instance of its capture can be considered authentic beyond any doubt. A specimen was shot near Otley, in Yorkshire, in the presence of Colonel Dawson, on the 8th of September, 1897, and is vouched for by the latter gentleman; but the probability is that it was one of the individuals let loose from the Lilford Aviaries a short time previously. The Great Black Woodpecker is one of the most unlikely birds in the world to migrate from its home in the pine forests of Scandinavia. It is an unmistakable species, being black all over, with the top of the head red in the male, black in the female, which has a patch of red on the occiput.

THE GREAT SPOTTED WOODPECKER. (*Dendrocopus major.*) The genus *Dendrocopus* contains the Pied Woodpeckers, of which two species are resident in the British Islands, while two are accidental visitors. *D. major* is the largest of the four, and may be recognised by having the back and rump black, with the wings and tail chequered with black and white. The crown and nape are black in the male, with a scarlet patch on the occiput, while the adult female has the head entirely black, without the red occipital patch. The young birds of both sexes, however, have an entirely red crown. In England and Wales the present species occurs, but is always local, and in the north of England it becomes gradually rarer, and is not known to breed either in Scotland or Ireland. It is found throughout the greater part of Europe and Northern Asia, and sometimes migrates in considerable numbers, as I have myself witnessed in Heligoland. Like other Woodpeckers, *D. major* is decidedly a shy bird, and is more often heard than seen. It has a curious habit of drumming on a slender branch of a tree, the sexes apparently using this method of signalling instead of a call-note. The food of this species consists of insects which it obtains by hammering on the bark and forcing pieces off, but it also feeds on nuts, fruit and berries. The eggs are white, and from five to seven or eight in number, and are deposited on the chips at the bottom of a hole hewn out by the birds in a hollow tree.

THE HAIRY WOODPECKER. (*Dendrocopus villosus.*) The British Museum possesses a specimen of the Hairy Woodpecker, obtained near Whitby in 1849, and presented by the late Mr. Frederic Bond. Another specimen of this North American species is said to have been procured in Yorkshire about a hundred years ago. Its home is in North America, where it is found from the Eastern States to the Rocky Mountains. It is distinguished from *D. major* by the white stripe down its back, but, like that species, it has a black crown with a scarlet band on the occiput, the latter being absent in the female, while the young birds have all the feathers of the crown tipped with orange-red. Its habits are similar to those of its allies.

THE DOWNY WOODPECKER. (*Dendrocopus pubescens.*) This is a small American species, which is found from Alaska to Florida, and has occurred in France and also once in Dorsetshire in 1836. It has a white stripe down the back like *D. villosus*, but is of the size of *D. minor* and has a black head with a red band on the occiput, this band being absent in the female.

THE LESSER
SPOTTED
WOODPECKER.
(*Dendrocopus minor.*)

The present species is the smallest of our British Woodpeckers, and has the scapulars and lower back barred with black and white, the under surface being brownish with narrow streaks of black on the sides of the body. The crown is crimson, mottled with white spots and dusky bases to the feathers. The female differs in having the crown black, without any crimson, the forehead being of a buffy white colour. The young birds have only the centre of the crown crimson. The range of the Lesser Spotted Woodpecker is nearly the same as that of *D. major* in the British Islands, and it extends into the South of Scotland, but it is only an occasional visitor to Ireland. It is found throughout the greater part of Europe and ranges into Eastern Siberia.

The habits of this little species more resemble those of the Nuthatch than those of its ally, the Great Spotted Woodpecker. It is found in orchards and parks, and nests in poplars as well as in fruit-trees, and can often be seen climbing on the lower branches of the larger elms, or clinging to the small twigs, looking not unlike a Tit or Nuthatch. The eggs vary from five to eight in number, and are white : they are deposited on the touch-wood at the bottom of the hole, but no attempt at a nest is made.

THE WRYNECK.
(*Iynx torquilla.*)

The appearance of the Wryneck is quite different from that of the other Woodpeckers found in Britain, for its plumage is a brightly mottled brown, with rufous and black vermiculations. That it is a member of the great family of Woodpeckers is seen by the zygodactyle formation of the feet, and it has the same extensile tongue as the latter birds, from which, however, it differs in having a soft tail of rounded feathers, instead of the sharply pointed stiffened tail-feathers of the true Woodpeckers.

The genus *Iynx* contains a few species, all confined to the Old World, the majority of the Wrynecks being found in Africa. Our British bird has a wide range, extending in summer from Great Britain to Japan, and wintering in Northern Africa, India and China. It is often called the 'Cuckoo's Mate,' from the fact that the date of its arrival coincides with that of the Cuckoo, but in the neighbourhood of London I have generally noticed it to be a little later in coming than the last-named bird. Like the Woodpeckers, it lays perfectly white eggs, in the hole of a tree, and makes no nest.

It is of a tame disposition and often takes advantage of any nest-box put up

THE WRYNECK.

for its accommodation, while I have known a Wryneck to sit in the lower boughs of a poplar tree in my garden and answer the children imitating its call for a quarter of an hour together. The note is very peculiar and sounds like the syllables '*pee-pee-pee*' often reiterated.

THE CUCKOOS.
Sub-Order CUCULI.

Like the preceeding birds, the Cuckoos have a zygodactyle or scansorial foot, with the toes arranged two in front and two behind, but the disposition of the tendons is different and resembles that of the Game-birds. They have only ten tail feathers.

The Cuckoos are the only European representatives of the Order *Coccyges*, which contains a large number of Cuckoo-like birds, as well as the Plantain-eaters (*Musophagi*) of Africa.

THE COMMON CUCKOO.
(Cuculus canorus.)

In a little sketch of the Birds of Great Britain, such as this book alone pretends to be, there is not space to enter at length into the history of a species like the Cuckoo, the study of which is among the most interesting problems of Bird life. In appearance the Cuckoo is very like a Sparrow-Hawk, and it has a similar flight, so that when it appears in the open, the small birds mob both the Cuckoo and the Hawk in the same manner, whether from hatred towards the former on account of its parasitic habits, or from fear of the latter as a natural enemy, it is hard to decide. Independently of the grey colour of the upper surface and the barred under parts which complete the resemblance between the Cuckoo and the Sparrow-Hawk, there is yet another peculiar feature in common between the two, viz.: the lengthened thigh-feathers which are found in both, and render the Cuckoo still more remarkably like the Sparrow-Hawk in appearance.

The female Cuckoo resembles the male, but is a little smaller, and has generally some rufous on the chest, and this colour is very conspicuous in life, and generally serves to distinguish the hen bird when flying. There is also a curious rufous phase of plumage, called the 'hepatic phase,' which occurs in both sexes, but is more commonly met with on the Continent than in the British Islands. The young birds are quite different from the adults, being dark brown or blackish, mottled with rufous and white, and with a distinct white spot at the back of the neck. The tail shows rufous bars and the under surface of the body is buffy white, barred across with blackish-brown bars.

As is well known, the

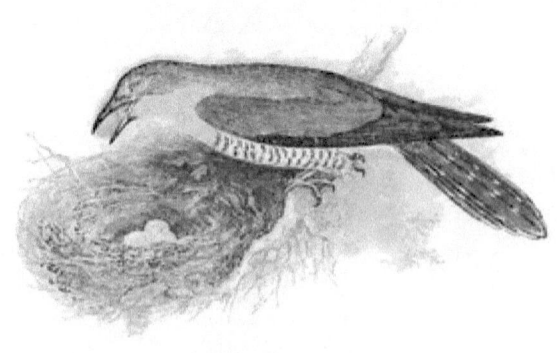

THE COMMON CUCKOO.

Cuckoo does not make a nest of its own, but places its egg in those of other birds, leaving the latter to hatch it out along with their own rightful offspring. Then when all the young birds are hatched together, the young Cuckoo disposes of the occupants of the nest by tilting them over the side, so that they perish while the Cuckoo endures, and receives for the rest of the summer the unremitting care and attention of its two foster parents. The eggs of the Cuckoo vary *ad infinitum*. Some are brown, others are grey, with or without darker brown mottling, some are quite pale, others whitish with dark brown spots, while some are even clear blue; they are remarkable for their small size, considering the bulk of the bird which lays them, and this doubtless renders the deception practised on the foster-mother more easy of accomplishment, as the Cuckoo's egg so little exceeds that of the rightful owner of the nest.

The food of the Cuckoo consists almost entirely of insects, and the fact that it robs other birds of their eggs has been noted by some recent observers, but when the bird has been shot with an egg in its mouth, there can be no doubt that it is often the Cuckoo's own egg which it was carrying at the time to some nest it intended to victimise. That the Cuckoo lays its egg on the ground and then carries it in its bill to the nest selected for its deposition seems to be a well-established fact.

The range of the Cuckoo extends over Europe and Siberia, and it winters in Western and Southern Africa as well as the Indian Peninsula. It is a common bird in Northern Europe in the summer, and in Northern Norway I have heard the birds calling abundantly in June, while doubtless the number of Meadow Pipits' nests on the moors afford ample opportunity for the exercise of its parasitic habits.

THE
GREAT SPOTTED
CUCKOO.
(*Coccystes glandarius.*)

The present species occasionally strays to Great Britain, having been captured on two occasions, once in Ireland, and once in Northumberland. It has occurred in many places in Central Europe, but its breeding-home is in the Mediterranean countries, where it nests in Southern Spain and Northern Africa. In winter it betakes itself to Western Africa and even reaches to the Cape Colony. Like our Common Cuckoo, its southern relative is parasitic in its nesting habits, and it deposits its eggs in the nests of Crows and Magpies, some-

THE GREAT SPOTTED CUCKOO.

British Birds.

THE BLACK-BILLED CUCKOO.   THE YELLOW-BILLED CUCKOO.

times four Cuckoo's eggs being found with six of the eggs of the last-named bird. Lord Lilford even gives an instance of his meeting with a nest which contained eight eggs of the Great Spotted Cuckoo and five of a Magpie.

This species is easily recognised by its pointed crest, grey colour and buffy throat and neck, as well as by the white-tipped quills and upper tail-coverts. The young bird for the most part has the quills chestnut, the forehead blackish, and the throat more rufous.

THE
YELLOW-BILLED
CUCKOO.
(*Coccyzus americanus.*)

The two American species which have visited Europe at rare intervals are much plainer in colour than our own birds and have no bars on the plumage, which is of an olive brown colour. They both make nests of their own and lay green or bluish eggs. In the bringing-up of the young they are said to be most affectionate, and differ in this trait entirely from their European representatives.

The Yellow-billed Cuckoo is distinguished by the orange-yellow colour of the lower mandible. It has been met with in Belgium and in Italy, and has occurred twice in Ireland, once in Wales, and once on Lundy Island. Its home is in Eastern North America, and it also breeds in the West Indies.

THE
BLACK-BILLED
CUCKOO.
(*Coccyzus
erythrophthalmus.*)

This species and *C. americanus* may be recognised by the white tips of the tail-feathers, preceded by a sub-terminal band of black, but the Black-billed Cuckoo is further distinguished by the absence of the chestnut lining to the quills. It is an inhabitant of North America, and has been once observed in Ireland, near Belfast. A specimen has also been captured in Italy, near Lucca.

THE PICARIAN BIRDS.—*Order CORACIFORMES.*

THESE birds may be distinguished from the Passerine Birds by the different arrangement of the tendons of the foot. External characters are less easy to find for their separation, but, as a rule, they nest in holes, and lay white eggs, though the Goatsuckers are an exception, as these lay mottled eggs in the open on the ground and the young are covered with down, whereas the rest of the *Picariæ* have the young hatched naked.

THE SWIFTS.
Sub-Order CYPSELI.

Generally these birds have been classed along with the Swallows, which they resemble only in external appearance, having the same long wings and feeding on insects in the open air. This resemblance, however, is merely superficial, for the Swallows and Swifts belong really to different Orders of birds, the former having twelve tail-feathers, and the latter only ten, and the proportions of the wing-bones, the shape of the breast-bone, and the formation of the toes are also different in the two groups.

THE WHITE-BELLIED SWIFT.
(Apus melba.)

This is a large bird, measuring eight-and-a-half inches in length, and distinguished by its white under-surface, varied only by a brown band across the chest and by the brown on the sides of the body. The home of the species is in Southern and Central Europe east to the Himalayas, and it winters in Northern Africa and in the Indian Peninsula. It has occurred about twenty times in Great Britain, but has not been noticed in Scotland as yet. The nest is a rough structure of earth and rubbish such as leaves, paper and feathers, gathered by the birds themselves on the wing, as their short feet and long wings prevent their rising from the ground, should they be so unfortunate as to be driven to the latter; this is sometimes the case when they first arrive and the weather happens to turn cold, so that the birds become numbed. They are, however, able to cling to rocks with the greatest ease by means of their grasping toes. The eggs are two in number, rarely more, and are pure white.

THE WHITE-BELLIED SWIFT.

THE
COMMON SWIFT.
(Apus apus.)

Although the Swift may often be seen hawking for insects in the air or over a river, in company with Swallows or Martins, it requires but a short acquaintance with its appearance and mode of flight to distinguish it from the latter birds. Not only does it appear to be perfectly black, for the white on the throat is seldom seen during flight, but its long wings and much more vigorous method of propelling itself through the air are in contrast to the graceful and more leisurely flight of the Swallows. The tail is slightly forked, but this is not often observed, for the bird generally carries the tail closed as it dashes through the air. In the evening Swifts

THE COMMON SWIFT.

become more active, though they may often be seen flying in full sunshine, but, as night approaches, they often assemble in small parties and dash round the houses or old towers in which their nests are built. The latter are of the roughest material, composed of wool and a few straws and feathers, and cemented together by the bird's saliva. They are generally found under the roofs of houses, or in old spouts on buildings, such places being accessible to the birds by reason of the fall which is available for them to take to flight immediately they leave their nesting-place, as they are unable to rise from the ground; the nesting-materials are therefore collected on the wing. The eggs are two or three in number, and are pure white.

The Common Swift is found throughout Europe and the British Islands in summer, and winters in South Africa.

THE NEEDLE-TAILED SWIFT.

THE
NEEDLE-TAILED
SWIFT.
(Chætura caudacuta.)

For a member of the family of Swifts, which are generally black or dull-coloured, the present species is rather a handsome bird and is of large size, measuring eight inches in length. It is recognised by the spiny shafts of the tail-feathers, which project beyond the feather itself. The colour is brown, with a gloss of green or steel-blue on the black wings and tail, and the throat is conspicuously white. The bird breeds in Central and Eastern Siberia, and winters in Australia. It has been procured in England on two occasions, once near Colchester, and again near Ringwood in Hampshire. It nests in the mountains, and resembles the other Swifts in its habits, but is of course a much more powerful bird, and one of the fastest fliers in existence. It is often seen in large flocks on migration.

THE NIGHTJARS.
Sub-Order
CAPRIMULGI.

Like the Swifts, the Nightjars have a very wide gape, but the latter is also equipped with some very strong bristles, the use of which is still doubtful. They have been associated by many writers with the Owls, probably on account of their soft and Owl-like plumage, and also because, like the *Striges*, they have the habit of coming out in the gloaming to seek for their food. There is, however, scarcely any relationship to be traced between them and the Owls, and the nearest allies of the Nightjars among our British birds are certainly the Swifts, but even here there are differences between the two groups. Between the harsh body-feathering of the Swifts and the soft mottled plumage of the Nightjars, there is a striking divergence, and the latter birds mostly lay distinctly marbled eggs on the ground, without an attempt at a nest, and have, moreover, downy young, whereas the Swifts lay white eggs under the shelter of a roof or other substantial covering and the young are hatched naked.

The true Nightjars (*Caprimulgidæ*) are of nearly wide-world distribution, and are represented in Great Britain by a single species which visits our islands regularly in summer, while two other species are occasional visitors. The true Nightjars, or 'Goat-suckers' as they are often familiarly called, have a pectinated middle claw: that is to say, the edge of it is toothed like a comb.

THE COMMON
NIGHTJAR.
(Caprimulgus europæus.)

Our Nightjar is found over the greater part of Europe in summer, and extends into Western Siberia, its winter home being in South Africa. Its densely mottled plumage is impossible to describe in detail, but it can be distinguished from the other European Goat-suckers by the absence of the rufous collar, and by having a white spot on the inner web of the three outer primary quills, and by the large white spot at the end of the tail-feathers. These white spots are represented in the female by spots of ochreous buff.

The Nightjar is crepuscular in its habits, that is to say, it is a bird of the twilight, and it is only when disturbed that it ventures to fly in the day-time. In the evening its unmistakable churring note is heard in heathy districts or near open forest-land, and this peculiar note is generally uttered when the bird is sitting lengthwise along a branch; for, unlike most birds, the Nightjar never perches on a branch transversely, but always *along* the surface of the latter. Its food consists entirely of moths and other insects, and when rising from the ground, or when

THE COMMON NIGHTJAR (*p.* 97).   THE ISABELLINE NIGHTJAR.

sailing high in the air across a valley, it has a curious habit of striking its wings together above its back, producing quite an audible clap. No nest is made by the bird, and the eggs, two in number, are laid on the bare ground. They are elliptical in shape, with both ends equally rounded, and are marbled with brown and violet-grey spots and lines.

THE ISABELLINE NIGHTJAR. (*Caprimulgus isabellinus.*) This is a very pale-coloured species, and is distinguished by the notches of white on the inner webs of the primaries, which do not have the large white spot so conspicuous in *C. europœus*. One specimen of this Nightjar has been obtained in England, viz., in Nottinghamshire, on the 23rd of June, 1883. Its home is in the deserts of Northern Africa, whence it extends into Central Asia.

THE RED-NECKED NIGHTJAR. (*Caprimulgus ruficollis.*) A single specimen of this Nightjar has been obtained at Killingworth, on the 6th of October, 1856. It is a slightly larger bird than the Common Nightjar, but has a large white spot on the inner web of the primaries, as in that species, from which it is distinguished by the broad rufous collar on the hind neck. Another difference between the two species lies in the fact that in *C. ruficollis*, the female, as well as the male, has the large white spots on the inner webs of the primaries. These spots are found only in the male of *C. europœus*.

THE BEE-EATERS. *Sub-Order MEROPES.* The external form of the Bee-Eaters

THE RED-NECKED NIGHTJAR.

readily serves to distinguish them from other Picarian birds. Their long curved bill and flat foot, with the toes joined together for some distance, and their ten tail-feathers, the two central ones of which are generally elongated, are well pronounced characters, and in addition to these they have the fore part of the breast-bone perforated, so that the feet of the coracoid bones meet together through the opening. This curious arrangement is found in Hoopoes, Hornbills and Game-birds.

THE BEE-EATER.

THE COMMON
BEE-EATER.
(*Merops apiaster.*)

This brightly-plumaged bird visits Europe in summer and extends through the Mediterranean countries, eastwards to Central Asia and to Cashmere. In winter it betakes itself by the east coast of Africa down to the Cape Colony, and is said to breed a second time in its winter quarters. The food of the Bee-eater consists entirely of insects, and in Southern Spain the bird is said to earn the hatred of the peasantry from the slaughter it creates among the bees. There is no nest, but the birds tunnel for a long way into sandy banks, and deposit their five or six white eggs in a chamber at the end of this tunnel.

THE BLUE-TAILED
BEE-EATER.
(*Merops philippinus*).

This Indian species is said by the late John Hancock to have been shot at Seaton Carew, in Northumberland, in August, 1862. Its home is in India and Southern China, whence it extends through the Burmese countries and the Malayan Peninsula to the Philippines, Java, Borneo, and Celebes. In habits it resembles the Common Bee-eater, and lays four or five glossy pure white eggs at the end of a hole without any nest. The species may be distinguished from *M. apiaster* by its green upper surface and blue tail.

THE HOOPOES.
Sub-order UPUPÆ.

These are most unmistakable birds, remarkable for their enormously developed crests, variegated wings, and desert-coloured sandy plumage: they have also a peculiarly long and curved slender bill. They have the same perforation of the fore part of the breast-bone as the Bee-eaters, but

THE BLUE-TAILED BEE-EATER.

THE HOOPOE.

the sternum can be distinguished from that of the last-named bird by its having only two notches, instead of four, at the posterior end, while both aspects of the tarsus are scaled across, as in the Larks.

The COMMON HOOPOE (*Upupa epops*) is an inhabitant, in summer, of the whole of temperate Europe and Asia to Northern China and Japan, and it winters in Southern China and the Indian Peninsula, North-eastern Africa, and Senegambia. It occurs in the British Islands regularly every spring, and has undoubtedly nested with us. There can indeed be no doubt that the Hoopoe would breed regularly in our southern counties, were it unmolested, but unfortunately it is such a conspicuous bird that any unfortunate individual that comes over to our shores is certain to be shot at once. In places where the Hoopoe is not interfered with it becomes wonderfully tame during the nesting-season, and will come down into gardens after its food, which appears to consist entirely of insects and worms. The nest is always in the hole of a tree, and the eggs are from five to seven, of a stone-grey or greenish olive colour without any distinct spots.

THE KINGFISHERS.
Sub-Order
HALCYONES.

Kingfishers are found all over the world, and they are divided into two great groups : those which feed almost exclusively on fish, and those whose food consists mainly of insects, crustacea, etc., rather than of fish. The former group is generally known by the long and pointed bill and shorter tail, and to this group belongs our British Bird. There are many anatomical and osteological characters by which Kingfishers may be distinguished from other Picarian Birds, but there is no need to enter upon them in a little book like the present, as the form and colour of the birds renders them easily recognisable.

THE COMMON KINGFISHER (*Alcedo*

THE KINGFISHER.

ispida) is certainly the most brilliant of our birds as regards plumage, and though not much can be said for the beauty of its form, there is no more charming sight on our rivers than that of a Kingfisher speeding along with the sun shining on his plumage. The bird progresses through the air in a straight line, with the bill out-pointed and the wings vigorously beaten, so that the bright blue back is very conspicuous, while, when the bird turns in its flight, the chestnut of the under parts is also perceptible. As it flies it utters an occasional shrill and unmusical note. The food of the Kingfisher consists almost entirely of fish, though small crustaceans and insects are also sometimes eaten. A hole is tunnelled out by the birds themselves in a sandy bank, and at the end of this tunnel the eggs are laid in a kind of chamber. The eggs are pure white, from five to seven in number, and are at first laid on the bare floor of the chamber, but they gradually get surrounded by the débris of fish-bones and the castings thrown up by the old birds.

THE BELTED KINGFISHER.
(Ceryle alcyon.)

This North American species is said to have been shot in Ireland on two occasions, viz. :— in October and November, 1845. It differs from our Common Kingfisher in being much larger, and in having quite a long tail. Whereas in *Alcedo ispida* the only difference between the male and female is in the red base to the lower mandible of the female, in the genus *Ceryle* the males differ from the female in colour, and the former has one grey band across the breast, while the female has a grey, as well as a rufous band on the lower parts. The habits of the Belted Kingfisher do not differ from those of our own Kingfisher.

THE BELTED KINGFISHER.

THE ROLLERS.
Sub-Order
CORACI.E.

Although in many characters, both osteological and external, the Rollers have strong affinities with the Kingfishers and Bee-eaters, especially in the way in which the toes are united together, they have a very peculiar and Crow-like bill, quite different from the slender and pointed bills of the other groups. They are an old-world group of birds and are spread over the greater part of the Eastern Hemisphere.

THE COMMON ROLLER.
(Coracias garrulus.)

This splendidly plumaged bird is only an occasional visitor to Britain, but it has been recorded more than a hundred times. Its bright colour renders it easily recognisable, and it has a curious habit of tumbling in the air, whence it gets its name of 'Roller.' It has a harsh note like that of a Crow, and lays its four or six white eggs in the hole of a tree or building, and sometimes excavates holes for itself in a bank. There is generally no attempt at a nest, but sometimes a few twigs or stems of grass are collected as an apology for one.

The Roller winters in Eastern and Southern Africa, and, more sparingly, in North-western India. It arrives in its breeding-home in April, and is found throughout Central and Southern Europe, nesting as far north as Southern Sweden, and as far east as Cashmere.

THE ABYSSINIAN ROLLER.
(*Coracias abyssinicus.*)

Two specimens of this purely African species are said to have been shot in Scotland, in 1857. It is a most unlikely bird to occur away from its African home, and one would almost think that some mistake must have taken place in the identification. The Abyssinian Roller is an exact counterpart of *Coracias garrulus*, excepting that the outer tail-feather on each side is prolonged into a long black 'streamer.' Its home is in Senegambia and Abyssinia.

THE COMMON ROLLER.

THE INDIAN ROLLER.
(*Coracias indicus.*)

A single specimen was shot near Louth in Lincolnshire, on the 27th of October, 1883, and was at first supposed to be an example of the Common Roller. It has since been identified by Mr. Cordeaux as the Indian species, which differs from *C. garrulus* in the colour of the under parts, as can be seen by the figures of the two birds. The Indian Roller is, as its name implies, an inhabitant of the Indian Peninsula, but it extends westward into Asia Minor.

THE INDIAN ROLLER.　　　THE ABYSSINIAN ROLLER.

THE OWLS.—*Order STRIGIFORMES.*

In the preceding pages I have discussed all the birds of the orders *Passeriformes,* *Pici, Coccyges, and Picariæ* which are found in Great Britain. These are the *Insessores* of the older authors. I now come to the groups of the larger and more conspicuous birds, the British species of which I shall pass in review. The Owls are considered by some modern ornithologists not to be true Birds of Prey like Eagles and Hawks, but to constitute a totally distinct group, not very far removed from the Parrots. I cannot, however, agree to this proposition at all, for, allowing that the Owls are somewhat aberrant in structure, they so closely resemble other Birds of Prey in their habits and method of capturing their food that they must be held to be part of the great Accipitrine group, being connected with the Eagles and Falcons, etc., by the intermediate form *Pandion* which contains the Ospreys only. The Owls are remarkable for having a reversible outer toe, that is to say, this toe can be turned either backwards or forwards at will. As a rule the plumage is very soft and downy, and the flight noiseless, as befits a nocturnal bird setting forth to capture mice and other unwary animals in the gloaming. Some of the day-flying species, however, such as the Hawk-Owls and the Snowy Owls, have a more close-set and harsher plumage. The ear-openings of the Owl are always a feature in the different genera and vary to a great extent, being sometimes shut in by an operculum, while in many cases the bony orifices are not symmetrical on both sides of the head, and differ in shape. There are two great families of Owls, the *Bubonidæ* and the *Strigidæ,* which are at once distinguished by the form of the 'merry-thought' or furcula, which is free in the former, but is united to the sternum in the *Strigidæ,* of which the Barn Owl is our only British representative, all the other species of Owls belonging to the *Bubonidæ.*

THE EAGLE-OWL. *(Bubo bubo.)* This is a magnificent bird measuring two-and-a-half or three feet in length, and remarkable for its dark colour and strongly mottled plumage. It is scarcely possible to give a description of an Owl's plumage in detail, as there are so many wavy lines and mottlings, but the Eagle-Owl is easily recognised by its large size, enormous ear-tufts of feathers, and by its densely feathered toes. It is only a rare and accidental visitor to Great Britain, and is more often seen here in captivity than in a wild state. Its range extends throughout Europe and Northern Asia to Eastern Siberia.

As might be imagined in so powerful a bird, the Eagle-Owl is capable of destroying a considerable quantity of game, as it takes not only Rabbits and Hares, but Grouse and Pheasants, while it also captures other wild birds, such as Crows. The nest often consists of nothing more than the pellets cast up by the birds and the bones of animals. It is often placed on the ground or on a rock, more rarely in the hole of a tree. The eggs are white, rather rough in texture, and measure more than two inches in length.

THE SMALL TUFTED OWL. *(Scops scops.)* This is a *Bubo* in miniature, with the same elongated ear tufts, but only seven and a half inches in length. The general aspect of the plumage is grey, and the vermiculations and pencillings on the plumage are very fine, and not coarse as is the case with the great Eagle-Owl.

THE EAGLE-OWL.

The Small Tufted Owl, or 'Scops' Owl, as it is often called, is a rare and occasional visitor to Great Britain, and has occurred in various parts of England, Scotland, and at least three times in Ireland. It often happens, however, that specimens of the 'Scops' Owl said to have been killed in Britain turn out to be examples of South American species, palmed off on the unwary purchaser. This little Owl has a wide range thoughout Europe and Northern Asia. It is a night-flying species, and makes scarcely any nest, laying its eggs in the hole of a wall or of a tree.

THE SNOWY OWL. *(Nyctea nyctea.)* Although the fact is not generally known, the Snowy Owl has ear-tufts, as in the Eagle-Owl, but they are never very large, and are consequently difficult to detect in the plumage of the bird's head. The species is, however, easily told by its snowy-white plumage, and by its densely plumed feet, the claws being almost entirely hidden by the feathers of the toes.

THE SMALL TUFTED OWL.

THE SNOWY OWL.

The home of the Snowy Owl is in the Arctic Regions, where it is a resident, but as winter comes on a certain number appear to migrate south, and it is then that the bird visits Great Britain occasionally, occurring in Scotland nearly every year. The Snowy Owl is a day-flying species, and feeds principally on the hordes of Lemmings which make their wonderful migrations in countless numbers in northern latitudes. It also catches Hares, Grouse and Ptarmigan, as well as Duck, and is even said to feed on fish. The nest is built on the ground in the open tundra, and consists only of a little moss or lichen with a few feathers: sometimes it is only a hollow scooped out in the moss. The eggs are six or eight in number, white, and measuring over two inches in length.

THE HAWK-OWL. (*Surnia ulula.*) The 'Hawk' Owls are so-named on account of their barred plumage, which gives a slight similarity to a Hawk in appearance, and also probably on account of their habit of hunting in the daylight. They are smaller than the Snowy Owl, have no trace of ear-tufts, and have a long and wedge-shaped tail. The European species of Hawk-Owl (*S. ulula*) has certainly occurred in Great Britain, as I have seen a specimen killed in Wiltshire, and it has also been noticed in the Shetlands; but most of the specimens obtained have undoubtedly belonged to the American form, *S. funerea.*

THE HAWK-OWL.

THE AMERICAN HAWK-OWL.

The range of the Hawk-Owl extends from Northern Europe to Kamtchatka, and it occurs a little to the south of its breeding range during winter. It is a bold and fierce bird, and will attack a man who attempts to rob its nest. Its food consists of mice and lemmings, on which it preys largely, like the Snowy Owl. The bird makes no nest, but lays its white eggs (five to eight) on the wood at the bottom of a hole in a tree, their length being about one-and-a-half inches.

THE AMERICAN
HAWK-OWL.
(*Surnia funerea.*)

The American representative of *S. ulula* has occurred at least four times, twice in England, and twice in Scotland. It differs from its ally *S. ulula* in being a darker bird, with the bars on the under parts broader and more of a vinous brown. It is found throughout the Arctic regions of North America, and its habits, nest, and eggs, do not differ from those of its European ally.

THE LITTLE OWL.
(*Carine noctua.*)

This is a small species, measuring about eight inches in length, with no ear tufts, but having a well-pronounced facial disk, as have so many of the Owls. This facial disk gives them that curious rounded visage which is a principal characteristic of the *Strigiformes.* The colour of the Little Owl is brown, with a good many ovate white spots on the upper surface, while the under surface of the body is white, with brown streaks on the breast and abdomen, and a bar of brown across the fore-neck; the iris is bright yellow. It is a species which is by no means rare on the continent of Europe, and it has undoubtedly been met with as an occasional visitor to this country, but in future it will be more difficult to chronicle the Little Owl as a visitor, as several have been reared in this country in captivity and have then been allowed to fly, though up to the present time. I am not aware that any nests have been discovered in a wild state. It is found generally throughout Europe. It breeds freely in captivity, and makes an interesting little pet. The food of the Little Owl consists largely of insects, but it also catches mice and small birds.

THE LITTLE OWL.

It makes no nest to speak of and the white eggs, four to six in number, are laid at the bottom of a hole in a tree or building.

THE
LONG-EARED
OWL.
(Asio otus.)

All the 'Eared' Owls, as they are called, and the 'Wood' Owls belong to a separate Sub-family *Syrniinæ*, which are remarkable for their complete facial disk, and for the large operculum which shuts in the ear-openings. The Long-eared Owl has very distinct feather-tufts on the head, and these it is able to erect; the plumage is thickly mottled and lined with blackish. It looks like an Eagle Owl in miniature, but is not half the size, and on the under parts it has some very broad black streaks. It is found throughout the British Islands, nesting in the darkest recesses of the pine-woods, and it breeds throughout Europe and Northern Asia, as well as in the Himalayas. It is strictly a night-flying bird, preferring to sit during the day-time in the dark shade of the woods, generally near its nest, which is usually an old one of some Crow or Hawk. Its food consists of rats, mice, and small birds. The eggs, from four to seven in number, are white, with a slight gloss.

THE LONG-EARED OWL.

THE SHORT-EARED OWL.

THE
SHORT-EARED
OWL.
(Asio accipitrinus.)

This Owl is of about the same size as the preceding species, but is rather a stouter bird, and is to be told at once by the short feather-tufts or 'ears' on the head, and by the lighter colour of the plumage, especially underneath, where the breast is broadly streaked with brown, but there are no wavy cross-lines or vermiculations as in *A. otus*. It nests in the northern parts of England and in Scotland, and is found over the rest of the United Kingdom in winter and during migration. Its breeding home extends from Northern Europe and Siberia to Kamtchatka, and it is also found across North America. On migration it extends occasionally

THE WOOD-OWL.

as far as South Africa, and the British Museum has received a specimen from the Seychelles. The Short-eared Owl is quite at home in the daylight, and is often flushed by shooting-parties in the autumn from the turnip-fields. Its food consists almost entirely of mice, but it is also said to prey on small birds, reptiles, insects, and even fish. The eggs, from six to eight in number, are white, and are laid in a depression of the ground, there being seldom any attempt at a nest.

THE WOOD-OWL.
(*Syrnium aluco.*)

The 'Tawny' Owl, as this species is often called, is a stouter bird altogether than either the Long or Short-eared Owls, but it has the same large operculum to the ear: it is distinguished, however, at a glance by the complete absence of ear-tufts. It has two distinct phases of plumage, a rufous one and a grey, in which the markings and mottlings are the same, but the tone of colour is quite different. Many Owls and Night-jars have this peculiar double phase of plumage, which appears not to be dependent upon age, sex, or season. Nor do I think that locality or altitude have anything to do with causing this difference in plumage. Although not found in Ireland, the Wood-Owl is distributed over the greater part of England and Scotland, and is spread also over the whole of Europe. It is a wood-loving species and only comes forth at night, when its hooting note is constantly to be heard. It feeds on small mammalia, and sometimes catches young game-birds as well as rabbits. The eggs are three or four in number, white, rather glossy and about one-and-three-quarter inches in length. They are laid in a hole of a tree, or building, but have also been found in a rabbit-burrow or in the old nest of a Crow or Sparrow-hawk.

TENGMALM'S OWL.
(*Nyctala tengmalmi.*)

This is a small species, about nine-and-a-half inches in length, similar in many respects to the Wood-Owls, but having the ear-conches on each side of the skull asymmetrical, the right one being placed higher than the left, as if to enable the bird to hear towards the sky with one ear,

TENGMALM'S OWL.

and towards the ground with the other. The facial disk is very evident in Teng-malm's Owl and is pure white: there are no ear-tufts, and the toes are much more densely clothed with feathers than in the Little Owl, which is of about the same size, and it is much more distinctly spotted with white than the latter bird. The species has occurred on some sixteen occasions in various parts of England and twice in Scotland. It is an inhabitant of the mountains of Europe and Northern Asia, as well as of North America. It feeds on Lemmings and other small rodents, as well as insects. The eggs are white and from four to seven in number, and are laid in holes of trees, an old nesting-place of the Great Black Woodpecker being often thus utilized, as well as the wooden nest-boxes put up by the peasants for the Golden-Eye Duck to breed in.

THE
BARN-OWL.
(*Strix flammea.*)

The very distinct facial disk, the light orange buff colour of the upper plumage with its ashy-grey mottlings and black spots, the white or buff under surface, and the pectinated or comb-like margin of the claw on the middle toe, are all characters which serve to distinguish the Barn-Owl at a glance. Though found nesting in every part of the British Islands, it is by no means so plentiful in many parts of Europe, extending no further north than the south of Sweden and Central Russia, and being apparently absent in Greece and other parts of South-Eastern Europe. Barn-Owls, slightly varying in size and colour from our European bird, are found over the greater part of the tropical and temperate portions of the globe. The food of the species consists

THE BARN-OWL.

principally of mice and rats, of which it catches an immense number, going in pursuit of them in the twilight and during the night: it also eats small birds, but does little or no harm to game. The eggs are white, about one-and-a-half inches in length, and are placed at the bottom of a hole in a hollow tree or ruin: no nest is made, but there is generally an assemblage of pellets thrown up by the birds themselves.

THE BIRDS OF PREY.—*Order ACCIPITRIFORMES.*

In this Order are placed all the Birds of Prey which are not Owls. The eyes are in all cases placed sideways in the head, not directed forwards as are those of the last-named birds, and there are other well-marked anatomical and osteological differences between the two Orders. They are, however, connected together by the Ospreys, which constitute the Sub-order *Pandiones.* These birds combine the aspect of Sea-Eagles with the structure of Owls, and like the latter they possess a reversible outer toe.

THE OSPREY.

THE OSPREY.
(Pandion haliaëtus.)

This fine bird is preserved from extinction by being protected in a few districts in Scotland by enlightened land-owners : otherwise there can be little doubt that it would long ago have been exterminated by the greed of collectors and egg-hunters. Young birds are frequently shot on our sea-coasts and inland waters, generally during the season of autumn migration. The species may always be distinguished by its blue feet and by the spicules which cover the soles of the feet, and these little spikes must be of great assistance to the bird in the capture of large fish, at which the Osprey is an adept. The bird loves solitude, and generally only one pair is found inhabiting a district in Scotland, but on the Continent two or three nests are sometimes met with in close proximity, and in North America as many as three hundred pairs have been found breeding together. The Osprey is a bird of very fine flight, and it circles over the water in graceful curves, occasionally hovering like a Kestrel, and dropping like a stone when it perceives a fish. The nest is a huge structure of sticks, and is built on a tree or on a ruined building in an inland lake. The eggs are two or three in number and are beautifully marked with red and purple blotches on a white ground : they measure about two-and-a-half inches in length.

THE FALCONS.
Sub-order
FALCONES.

None of the members of this Sub-Order, which includes the remainder of the Birds of Prey, viz., the Vultures, the Hawks, Harriers, Buzzards, Eagles, Kites, and Falcons, have a reversible outer toe, but, like the Ospreys, all these birds have the eyes placed laterally in the head and not directed forwards : in every case likewise a more or less distinct 'cere,' the bare or wax-like base to the bill, is present. The *Falcones* may be divided into two great Families, the Vultures (*Vulturidæ*) and the Falcons (*Falconidæ*). The latter are divided into several Sub-families, the *Accipitrinæ* (Long-legged Hawks), the *Aquilinæ* (Buzzards, Eagles, and Kites) and the *Falconinæ* (Falcons).

THE EGYPTIAN SCAVENGER VULTURE.   THE GRIFFON VULTURE.

**THE GRIFFON
VULTURE.**
(Gyps fulvus.)

Although the Griffon is believed to have been seen on more than one occasion in England, the only authentic instance of its capture within the British area is that of a young bird caught by a boy on the rocks near Cork Harbour in the spring of 1843. It is a bird of the Mediterranean region and especially of Northern Africa. It makes a large nest of sticks, placed on a ledge of rock or in a cave, generally in an almost inaccessible position. A single egg is laid, never more than two, dull white, with occasionally some faint rufous markings, which are seldom very distinct.

THE EGYPTIAN SCAVENGER VULTURE. *(Neophron percnopterus.)* Two specimens of this Vulture have been killed in Britain, one in Somersetshire and one in Essex. It is an inhabitant of the Mediterranean countries, and extends as far as Central Asia in summer, while Africa forms its winter resort. The young birds are brown, with the bare face grey instead of yellow. As in other Vultures the food consists of carrion, and the nest is placed on the ledge of a rock: it is compiled of all sorts of rubbish and decaying filth, while the species is, according to Colonel Irby, ' probably the foulest feeding bird that lives.' The eggs are very handsomely coloured, being richly marked with red, on a white ground. They measure about two-and-a-half or two-and-three-quarter inches in length.

The *Accipitrinæ* Hawks comprise the Harriers and Sparrow Hawks, in both of which the tibia and tarsus are about equal in length. In the Hawks the tarsus is transversely scaled behind, in the Harriers it is reticulate; and the latter birds are further distinguished by having a ruff of feathers surrounding the face, much the same as in the Owls: this has resulted in their being associated with the latter birds in former arrangements of the *Accipitriformes*.

THE HEN-HARRIER. *(Circus cyaneus.)*

The male of this Harrier may be recognised by its blue-grey colour and pure white upper tail-coverts, as well as by the uniform white thighs and blue-grey throat and chest. The absence of rufous streaks on the breast and under surface of the body separates it

THE HEN-HARRIER.   MONTAGU'S HARRIER.   THE MARSH-HARRIER.

from Montagu's Harrier, as does also its larger size. The hen birds and young of the two species are not so easily distinguished, but the female Hen Harrier always

has a notch or indentation on the outer web of the fifth primary, this notch
not being found in Montagu's Harrier. This species no longer nests in England,
but is still found breeding in Northern Scotland and a few counties in Ireland.
Its breeding-range extends throughout Central and Northern Europe across
Siberia to Japan, and it winters in Southern Europe, the Indian Peninsula, and
China. The food of the Hen-Harrier is varied, and consists of small rodents,
lizards, frogs, insects, and also small birds, as well as their nestlings and eggs. The
nest is placed on the ground, generally in a marshy situation, and the eggs are from
four to six in number, bluish white in colour, and from one-and-three-quarters to two
inches in length.

MONTAGU'S
HARRIER.
(*Circus pygargus.*)

This is a smaller and more slightly built bird than the foregoing
species, and is recognised by the longitudinal rufous streaks on
the under parts and thighs. The wing-formula is sufficient to
distinguish the females and young birds from the corresponding
plumages of the Hen-Harrier (*see above*). The range of Montagu's Harrier is not
so extensive as that of the latter species, as it does not range so far north on the
Continent, nor does it extend into Eastern Siberia. It has bred in several counties
of England and Wales, and scarcely a year passes without its nest being found in
some part of our area, but at present it has only occurred accidentally in Ireland.
In habits the present species resembles the Hen-Harrier, and like that bird it devours
a number of eggs. The nest consists of a hollow in the ground, lined with dry
grass. The eggs are bluish-white, from four to six in number, and measure
about one-and-three-quarter inches in length.

THE
MARSH-HARRIER.
(*Circus æruginosus.*)

This is the largest of the three British species of Harrier,
and is of a much darker type of plumage than the Hen-Harrier
or Montagu's Harrier. The male is a handsome bird of a dark
rufous brown, with a grey tail, and a considerable amount
of bluish ashy on the wing-coverts and quills; the under surface is creamy buff,
streaked with brown, and the thighs and abdomen are rufous. The female is a
brown bird with a creamy buff crown, and the young birds are also brown with the
head at first uniform like the back.

Although the Marsh-Harrier still nests in certain districts in Ireland, it has
become extinct as a breeding bird in England, where it used to be not uncommon
in the fen-country. It is found thoughout Europe and as far east as Central
Asia. Its food resembles that of the Harriers already mentioned, but it is a
great egg-robber, and devours also numbers of chickens in the countries where
it is abundant. In Southern Spain it nests in colonies, and the nest is
generally placed on the ground in a reed-bed, the old nest of a Coot or Moorhen
being sometimes utilized. The eggs are from three to six in number, pale bluish
white, with scarcely any markings of pale brown: the lining in the freshly
blown egg is bluish.

8

THE GOS HAWK.

THE
GOS HAWK.
(*Astur palumbarius.*)

The Gos Hawks and Sparrow Hawks differ from the Harriers in having the hinder portion of the tarsus transversely scaled and not reticulated, and in lacking the facial ruff. The Gos Hawks are heavily built and powerful birds, with strong feet and talons and a very stout bill, whereas the Sparrow-Hawks are of a much more slender and supple build. In both groups the wings are very short and rounded, as compared with the long and pointed wings of a Falcon, and they capture much of their prey in direct pursuit through bushes and undergrowth, as well as by pouncing down or snatching unsuspecting quarry.

The Gos Hawk is believed to have bred in Scotland in former times, but is now only known as a visitor to Great Britain. Its range extends throughout Europe and Northern Asia to Japan. It feeds on hares or rabbits, which it captures with the utmost dexterity and swiftness, as well as on all kinds of game-birds, and it is often trained by Falconers for the pursuit of these. The swiftness with which it can follow the doublings of a rabbit in the open give the latter but little chance of escape. The nest is a large structure of sticks placed on some tall tree, and is added to year by year. Moss and roots form a scanty lining, but there is no attempt to line the interior of the nest with green leaves, as is done by some of the *Accipitres.* The eggs are four or five in number, bluish white, with scarcely ever any brown markings, and they measure about two-and-a-quarter to two-and-a-half inches in length.

THE AMERICAN
GOS HAWK.
(*Astur atricapillus.*)

This species has been noticed in Scotland, in Perthshire, and twice in Ireland. It very much resembles the European Gos Hawk, but has a black head, and is freckled, not barred, with black below. It is an inhabitant of North America, and resembles *A. palumbarius* in size, the male being considerably smaller than the female. Its habits and

THE AMERICAN GOS HAWK.

THE SPARROW-HAWK.

nesting are also similar to those of the European bird.

THE SPARROW-HAWK
(*Accipiter nisus*)

Differs from the Gos-Hawks in being much smaller, and in having a smaller bill and longer toes. The adult male is rufous below, and the female is barred underneath, but has a large tuft of rufous down on the flanks. It is found everywhere throughout Europe and Northern Asia, and inhabits the wooded districts of Great Britain, but is subject to constant persecution at the hands of game-keepers, and many are shot down. There is no doubt that the Sparrow-Hawk does considerable damage among the young game-birds during the hatching season, but at other times of the year it feeds on mice and rats, and also largely on small birds which it captures by surprise. It is an object of detestation to the latter, who never fail to mob one of these Hawks when it appears in the open. The nest is a somewhat bulky structure of sticks and is constructed by the birds themselves. The eggs are often very handsome, being three or four in number, greenish-white with reddish brown or chestnut markings, and some beautiful varieties are sometimes found with the red blotches collected near the larger end of the egg.

THE COMMON BUZZARD. (*Buteo buteo.*) In Buzzards the tibia is much longer than the tarsus, not equal to the latter, as in the Harriers and Short-winged Hawks. They have a stout and powerful foot and have the hinder aspect of the tarsus transversely plated, not reticulated. Although resembling an Eagle in appearance, the Buzzard is always a smaller bird, and is much more

THE COMMON BUZZARD.

8°

sluggish in its ways. Our Common Buzzard nests now only in certain districts of Wales, Scotland and Ireland, and occasionally on the northern moors of England, but constant persecution has greatly cut down its numbers, and it is not so common as it used to be. It is found in Northern and Western Europe, but does not extend very far east into Russia, and is again not plentiful in the Mediterranean countries.

The Buzzard is decidedly a useful bird, as it feeds largely on mice, frogs and reptiles, as well as occasionally on small birds. It generally builds its nest in a tree, or on ledges of rocks, or in small caves. The nest is rather roughly made of sticks, lined with smaller twigs, and with fresh green leaves. The eggs are two to four in number, white or greenish-white, and generally without spots, though occasionally there are mottlings of rufous brown.

THE DESERT BUZZARD.   THE RED-TAILED BUZZARD.

THE DESERT BUZZARD.
(Buteo desertorum.)

This may be called a rufous form of the Common Buzzard, with more rufous on the upper tail-coverts and tail, this rufous colour being distinguishable in the young birds, as well as in the old ones. It is an inhabitant of Southern Europe and Africa and has been said to have occurred three times in England, twice in Northumberland, and once in Wiltshire. In its habits, nest, and eggs it does not differ from the Common Buzzard.

THE RED-TAILED BUZZARD.
(Buteo borealis.)

A single specimen of this Buzzard is said to have been obtained in Nottinghamshire. The species is an inhabitant of North America, and is a somewhat larger bird than our Common Buzzard, and it is also distinguished from

that species by its red tail,
which has one sub-terminal
bar of black on it. There is
nothing in its habits different
from those of other species of
Buzzards.

THE RED-SHOULDERED
BUZZARD.
(*Buteo lineatus.*)

This is another North-
American species which is
supposed to have occurred
once within our limits, a
specimen having been said

THE RED-SHOULDERED BUZZARD.

to have occurred in Inverness-shire in 1863. Its home is in North America, and
even the single occurrence in Great Britain is considered to be doubtfully authentic.

THE
ROUGH-LEGGED
BUZZARD-EAGLE.
(*Archibuteo lagopus.*)

The principal difference between a Buzzard and an Eagle
exists in the different configuration of the hinder aspect of
the tarsus. In a Buzzard this is transversely scaled, while
in an Eagle it is reticulated or covered with a ' net '-like
pattern of scales. In the case of some of the true Eagles and
of the Rough-legged Buzzard-Eagle, this character is difficult to distinguish when
the entire tarsus is clothed with feathers.

The present species is intermediate between the true Buzzards and the true
Eagles, being much smaller than any of the latter and differing from them in the

THE ROUGH-LEGGED BUZZARD-EAGLE.

shape of the nostrils. The Buzzard-
Eagle has been supposed to breed
in Scotland, but no satisfactory
evidence is, as yet, forthcoming,
and the species is generally known
as an autumn visitor on migration
to all three Kingdoms, but
especially to Scotland. On the
Continent it breeds in the north,
in Scandinavia and Northern
Russia, as far as the valley of
the Lena. In many of its ways
the present species is said to resemble the Eagles, frequenting
the open country, and feeding on

rabbits and other small mammals, as well as reptiles and water-fowl. The nest is placed in trees, and is made of sticks. The eggs are three or four in number, white or greenish white, with rufous markings.

THE
GOLDEN EAGLE.
(Aquila chrysaëtus.)

The large size and feathered legs, in addition to the tawny colour on the hind neck will always serve to distinguish a Golden Eagle. In the old birds the ashy grey tail, mottled and tipped with brown, is a characteristic feature, and in the young birds the tail is white for its basal half. The species is now undoubtedly more plentiful in Scotland than it used to be, owing to the protection which has been afforded to it during recent years, but it has been exterminated in the parts of England and Wales in which it used to breed formerly. In Ireland it still breeds in a few counties. It is found throughout the mountains of Europe, Northern and Central Asia, as well as in the Himalayas, and throughout the northern parts of North America. The Golden Eagle feeds on hares and rabbits, but will also

THE GOLDEN EAGLE.

eat carrion on occasion; it is much detested by the sheep-farmers on account of the damage it causes by killing lambs and even sheep, and is often caught in traps. The nest is a large and clumsy structure of sticks and is placed on a shelf of rock or in a small natural cave. The eggs are two or three in number, white, richly marked with rufous, these markings sometimes clouding the whole egg, and while in others they are absent altogether.

THE LARGER
SPOTTED EAGLE.
(Aquila maculata.)

An accidental visitor to Great Britain, where it has occurred in England and Ireland, but it has not been met with as yet in Scotland. There are two races of Spotted-Eagle in Europe, a small one and a large one, and it is the latter which has occurred

THE LARGER SPOTTED EAGLE.

in Britain on about ten occasions. It is an inhabitant of South-eastern Europe and extends to Central Asia and even to Eastern Siberia. The Lesser Spotted Eagle (*A. pomarina*) is found in Central and Southern Europe, and it is this form which might have been expected to visit Great Britain, but has not been identified as yet within our limits.

The present species is very little larger than some of the Buzzards, and may be recognised by its uniform brown adult plumage, and by the tail, which is perfectly uniform underneath. Young birds are remarkable for the tawny spotting on the wings, whence the name of 'Spotted' Eagle is derived. Its food is also like that of a Buzzard, consisting of frogs, snakes, lizards, and insects. The nest is placed in trees in swampy forests. It is a large structure of sticks and is lined with green leaves or fresh green grass. The eggs are two in number, very rarely three, and measure about two-and-three-quarter inches in length. They are small editions of the egg of the Golden Eagle.

The Sea-Eagles are to be recognised from the Golden and Spotted-Eagles by their bare feet, and the absence of feather-

THE WHITE-TAILED SEA-EAGLE.
(*Haliaëtus albicilla.*)

ing on the tarsus. The white tail is a distinguishing character of the adult Sea-Eagle, and the young birds have a white tail mottled with brown. In most of its former breeding haunts in Great Britain, the White-tailed Eagle has become exterminated, but a few

THE WHITE-TAILED SEA-EAGLE.

pairs still nest in the North and West of Scotland and in one or two places in Ireland. Its range extends over Northern and Central Europe in suitable localities and throughout Northern Asia to Kamtchatka. In many parts of Europe, however, it is only known as an occasional visitor, as it is in England.

The food of the White-tailed Eagle consists of hares, lambs and young deer, as well as ducks, and it also eats carrion and fish. The nest is a large structure of sticks and is placed in a tree or on a rock, sometimes on the ground or in a reed-bed. The eggs are white, without markings, and are from two-and-three-quarters to three-and-a-quarter inches in length.

THE SWALLOW-TAILED KITE.
(*Elanoides furcatus.*)

This unmistakable species of Kite has been supposed to have occurred on two occasions in England, but the records are by no means satisfactory. It is an inhabitant of North America and migrates in winter to Brazil. It is said by observers to be a bird of very grand flight, and catches a good deal of its insect food on the wing.

The nest is made of sticks, and is built on a high tree. The eggs are two or three in number, white, boldly marked with reddish brown or chestnut.

THE COMMON KITE.
(*Milvus milvus.*)

This species is recognised by its rufous colour and long red tail, which is strongly forked. Although formerly common in Great Britain, there are now only a few places in Wales and Scotland where the species still breeds.

THE COMMON KITE.
THE SWALLOW-TAILED KITE.

It is found throughout the greater part of Europe and breeds in the Mediterranean countries, but does not extend so far in Russia as the Ural Mountains. Like all of its kind, the Kite is a fine bird on the wing, and is capable of soaring to a great height. Its food consists of reptiles and frogs and small birds, and it is said to be very destructive to young birds, while it will also attack wounded or sickly grouse and partridges. The nest is placed in a tree, more rarely on a rock, and is built of sticks, but is also remarkable for the assemblage of rubbish which the bird manages to collect. The eggs are two or three in number, greenish white, often unspotted, but on occasions blotched with reddish-brown.

THE BLACK KITE.
(*Milvus migrans.*)

This is a much darker bird than *M. milvus*, and is to be told by its dark brown tail, which is barred across with blackish brown. A single specimen has been obtained at Alnwick, in Northumberland, in May, 1866. It is found locally throughout the greater part of Europe, being more abundant in the south, and it extends eastwards into Central Asia; its winter home is in Africa. In habits it resembles other Kites, but is more gregarious than the preceding species, and frequents the neighbourhood of towns and villages in many parts of its range, where it feeds on all kinds of garbage. The nest is built of sticks and is profusely garnished with every sort of rubbish. The eggs vary in number from two to five; they are dull white, with red blotches, and are more strongly marked than the eggs of the Common Kite.

THE BLACK-
SHOULDERED
KITE.
(*Elanus cæruleus.*)

This is a tropical species found in Africa and India, and is a rare bird in Southern Europe. It is said to have occurred on one occasion in Co. Meath, in Ireland. It is easily recognisable by its blue-grey colour, white tail and underparts, and black wing-coverts, which form the shoulder patch from which the bird derives its name. The iris is of a bright carmine colour.

The food of this species consists of small mammals and insects, and it has a habit of hovering in the air like a Kestrel. The nest is made of sticks and is always

THE BLACK-SHOULDERED KITE.

placed in a tree. The eggs are from three to five in number, buffy white with reddish brown or chestnut markings, sometimes distributed over the whole egg, at other times collected near the larger end.

THE
HONEY-KITE.
(*Pernis apivorus.*)

This bird is generally called the Honey 'Buzzard,' but it has no relations with the genus *Buteo* and is much more nearly related to the Kites and Falcons. The plumage is of a peculiar soft texture like that of the Kites, and the feathers of the face are very close-set and dense, the plumage appearing like scales. The old Honey-

THE HONEY-KITE.

Kites may be told by their grey face, and by the three dark bands on the tail, while the young birds have the sides of the face brown, and as many as six or seven, more or less broken bars on the basal half of the tail. At one time the Honey-Kite used to breed in the New Forest and in other parts of England and Scotland, but it is now seldom observed breeding in any part of Great Britain. It is found throughout the greater part of Europe in summer, and extends to Central Siberia, its winter home being in Africa. The food of the Honey-Kite consists almost entirely of insects, but it also eats small birds and mice as well as slugs and worms. The nest is generally constructed on the old nest of some other bird, and the eggs, two or three in number, are very handsome, the white ground-colour being usually entirely hidden by the rich conglomeration of chestnut markings.

THE PEREGRINE
FALCON.
(*Falco peregrinus.*)

All the Falcons are remarkable for having the bare tarsus reticulated, both in front and behind, and for having a distinct tooth in the bill. They have also a round nostril, with a little tubercle or pedestal in the centre of it. They have pointed wings, indicative of powerful flight, and very sharp curved claws or talons. The Peregrine nests in many places throughout the United Kingdom, and is found all over the northern parts of both hemispheres in localities suited to the bird's habits, and where it can obtain a plentiful supply of food.

The female is a much larger and more powerful bird than the male, and has always been the prime favourite of Falconers for its dash and courageous bearing. There is scarcely any bird which it cannot capture in direct flight, and it feeds on wild-fowl and all kinds of game, and in the vicinity of the sea-cliffs, which it frequents, it kills numbers of Gulls and Puffins. It also strikes down Rooks, Crows, and Magpies, but the cunning way in which these latter birds manage to avoid the swoop of the Falcons, often leads to their ultimate escape.

The Peregrine generally lays its eggs on the bare rock, or under a shelving ledge, but it occasionally adopts the old nest of some other bird on a tree; the eggs are from two to four in number, they are generally very handsomely clouded and blotched with shades of rufous and chestnut, and measure about two inches in length.

THE PEREGRINE FALCON. THE GREENLAND GYR-FALCON.
THE RED-FOOTED KESTREL.

THE HOBBY

THE HOBBY.
(*Falco subbuteo.*)

This is a much smaller species than the Peregrine, and is easily recognised from that species by its rufous thighs and distinctly streaked throat and breast. It is a summer visitor to Europe, and breeds from Northern and Central Europe throughout Northern Asia to Kamtchatka, wintering in China, India and Africa. It still nests in small numbers in England every summer, and has been known to do so also in the south of Scotland, but most of the captures are those of birds on migration.

The food of the Hobby consists chiefly of insects, such as dragon-flies which it catches and devours on the wing, and it also feeds on small birds, such as Larks and Sandpipers. It generally appropriates the deserted nest of a Crow, which it sometimes repairs and re-lines.

The eggs are from three to five in number, closely mottled and sprinkled with rufous all over, so that they much resemble some eggs of the Kestrel and Merlin. They measure about an inch-and-a-half in length.

THE MERLIN.
(*Falco æsalon.*)

The Merlin is a smaller and more thick-set little Falcon than the Hobby, from which it is distinguished by its blue-grey colour and by the colour of the under surface, which is white with a rufous tinge, and streaked with black, these black stripes extending on to the thighs which are like the breast. The female is browner than the male, and is whitish underneath, streaked with dark brown; occasionally blue females are met with, which resemble the male in colour, so that, when fully mature, the sexes appear to be alike in plumage, as is the case with the Hobby.

The principal food of the little Merlin seems to be small birds such as Sandpipers, Larks, Wagtails, Pipits, etc., but it also feeds on insects, especially large moths. It frequents the open moors in Wales and the North of England, and breeds thoughout Scotland and the greater part of Ireland. It extends throughout Northern Europe and Siberia, and winters in China, Northern India and Northern Africa.

The nest is placed on the ground or on the ledge of a rock, and is merely a hole in the ground, lined with a little grass or a few bits of heather.

THE MERLIN.

The eggs are four or five in number, and are of a deep red colour, resembling those of the Hobby or Kestrel, and measuring about an inch-and-a-half in length.

THE
GREENLAND
GYR-FALCON.
(*Hierofalco
candicans.*)

Three species of Gyr-Falcon have occurred in Great Britain, and of these the White or Greenland Gyr-Falcon (*see p.* 123) is always easily recognised by its yellowish bill and by having only spots or streaks, not *bars*, on the flanks. By these features there need never be any difficulty in identifying a Greenland Falcon at any age; and throughout all its plumages it keeps up a white appearance, which is only varied with a few black spots or streaks.

This beautiful Falcon is an occasional visitor to Great Britain, and has been noticed more often in Ireland and Scotland than in England. It is generally seen in autumn and winter, and most of the individuals which visit us are young birds.

The home of the species is in Northern Greenland and Arctic America. It is a noble bird on the wing, but does not possess the fire and dash of a Peregrine, and is not so much in request with Falconers as the latter bird. In a wild state it feeds on Willow-Grouse and Ptarmigan as well as Mice and Lemmings. The eggs are laid on the bare rock, and are four in number, closely mottled and clouded with rufous or chestnut, and from two-and-a-quarter to two-and-a-half inches in length. Sometimes the bird makes use of the deserted nest of some other species.

THE ICELAND GYR-FALCON.
(Hierofalco islandicus.)

Both this and the next species have blue bills, and always have the flanks distinctly cross-barred. The head of the Iceland Gyr-Falcon is white, distinctly streaked with black, and the throat and chest are also streaked with black, while the bird is always darker in appearance than a Greenland Gyr-Falcon. The present

THE ICELAND GYR-FALCON.

species is an inhabitant of Iceland, and occasionally some individuals wander south, in winter, at which season they have been sometimes captured in Great Britain.

Like the Greenland Falcon, the Iceland representative of the Gyr-Falcons feeds largely on Ptarmigan, and also captures Plovers, Guillemots and Ducks. In mediaeval times the species was highly esteemed by Falconers, but at the present day it is not so much in vogue, for the same reason as the Greenland Falcon. The nest of a Raven is often chosen by the bird, and sometimes a nest is built on the ledge of a cliff. The eggs are four in number, closely clouded with rufous, and are about two-and-a-quarter to two-and-a-half inches in length.

THE GREY GYR-FALCON.

THE GREY GYR-FALCON.
(Hierofalco gyrfalco.)

This species has probably occurred more often in Great Britain than has been supposed, and has doubtless been mistaken for the Iceland Gyr-Falcon. It may always be distinguished from the latter species, when adult, by its uniform dark head. The young of the two birds are precisely alike and possess no character by which they can be told apart. When fully adult the Grey Gyr-Falcon bears great resemblance to a Peregrine Falcon, but the latter has the tail darker towards the end, whereas in the Gyr-Falcon it is of the same grey shade throughout. The toes in the latter bird have also different proportions, the outer and inner toes being about equal in length, as in the Kestrels, whereas in the Peregrine the outer toe is decidedly longer than the inner one.

A young bird of the Grey Gyr-Falcon was shot in Suffolk in October, 1867, and an adult bird from Sussex is in Mr. Borrer's collection. The home of the species reaches from Scandinavia across Siberia to Arctic America. The nest is built on trees or on ledges of rocks, and the eggs are four in number, either entirely clouded with light reddish-brown or having a reddish-white ground blotched and spotted with rufous.

THE COMMON KESTREL. (*Cerchneis tinnunculus*). Like the Gyr-Falcons, the Kestrels have rather weak feet, the outer and inner toes being equal in length, but the wings are longer and more pointed than in those birds, and resemble those of the true Falcons. The male Kestrel may be told by its blue-grey head and tail, the latter having a black band before the end. The female is entirely rufous above, banded with black, this being also the colour of the tail; the head is streaked with black. Young birds resemble

THE COMMON KESTREL.

the old female. The Common Kestrel, or 'Windhover,' is found everywhere in the British Islands, nesting in woods in the interior and in cliffs on the sea-shore. It is also found over the greater part of Europe in summer, and extends to Siberia, passing the winter months in Africa and India, but being resident in the Himalayas. As a rule the food of the Kestrel consists of mice and insects, and it is only when hard-pressed for food for its young that it resorts to the killing of small birds; it is, on the whole, a most useful species. It generally adopts the old nest of some other bird in a tree, and when breeding in cliffs appears to make no nest at all. The eggs vary from three to seven in number, and they are generally clouded with rufous and chestnut all over, though occasionally eggs are found in which the ground-colour is white and the rufous blotches are confined to the larger end. The length is about one-and-a-half inches.

THE LESSER KESTREL.
(Cerchneis cenchris.)

The male of this bird differs from that of the Common Kestrel not only in its smaller size, but by the absence of black spots on the back, and it may also be told by its whitish claws. This latter character also determines the female from the hen of the Common Kestrel.

The present species is common in Southern Europe in summer, and extends to Southern Russia and Central Asia, wintering in South Africa, whither it goes in large flocks with other small Falcons in pursuit of the locust-swarms. It has been met with in Yorkshire, in the Scilly Islands, and near Dover, in England, and in Co. Dublin in Ireland. It is more entirely an insect-feeder than the Common Kestrel, but otherwise resembles that species in its habits. It breeds in large colonies in the South of Europe, in holes of ruins and in church-towers, or in holes in the ground. No nest is made, and the eggs, four to seven in number, resemble those of the Common Kestrel, but are smaller and paler rufous, inclining more to a cinnamon tint; they do not exceed one-and-a-half inches in length, and are generally not more than one-and-a-quarter inches.

THE RED-FOOTED KESTREL.
(Cerchneis vespertina.)

This pretty little Kestrel has been obtained more than twenty times in Great Britain, and has occurred in various counties from Cornwall to Northumberland. Three examples have been recorded from Scotland, and one from Ireland. It is an inhabitant of South-eastern Europe, and occurs from Hungary to the Volga and thence to the Valley of the Yenesei. In winter it visits Africa, passing down the Nile Valley to South-western Africa. The male of the Red-footed Kestrel is easily distinguished by its grey plumage and rufous thighs, but the female is quite different from the male, and more resembles a Hobby in appearance, being grey banded with black above, with the head rufous. The under surface of the body is also rufous. The young birds resemble the old females, but have rufous margins to the feathers of the upper surface.

In habits the present species resembles the other small Kestrels, and feeds entirely on insects. It builds no nest but adapts the old nest of a Rook or some other bird to its wants, and breeds in companies. The eggs are like those of the Common Kestrel, but are more of a yellowish red colour and are smaller, the length being from one-and-a-quarter to one-and-a-half inches.

THE LESSER KESTREL.

THE PELICAN-LIKE BIRDS.—*Order* PELECANIFORMES.

THESE birds are also known as *Steganopodes*, and are remarkable for having the hind toe joined to the others by a web. The order includes the Pelicans, Cormorants, Gannets, Frigate-Birds, and Tropic-Birds. A Wild Pelican is said to have been shot at Horsey Fen in 1663, but is believed to have been an escaped bird. In ancient times Pelicans certainly used to inhabit England, as their remains have been found in the fen-lands.

THE CORMORANTS.
Sub-order
PHALACROCORACES.

These birds have a sharply hooked bill, and are further distinguished by their black plumage from their allies, the Gannets.

The COMMON CORMORANT (*Phalacrocorax carbo*). Although, when seen in flight, and at a distance, the Cormorant appears to be perfectly black, on closer examination it will be found that there is a good deal of metallic gloss on the bird's plumage, the general colour of the upper surface being glossy blue-black, while the wings are bronzy-brown, with black edges to the feathers. In the breeding season appears a crest of glossy blue-black plumes, and a patch of white on the sides of the lower flanks, while the head, neck, and lower throat are covered with a dense mass of filamentous white plumes. These ornamental plumes begin to make their appearance at the end of January, and are fully developed by the end of February; but they do not last long and are completely shed by the middle of May, though the white flank-plumes are retained for some time longer. It should be noted that the Cormorant has fourteen tail-feathers which will always serve to distinguish the young birds in their brown plumage from those of the Shag, which has only twelve tail-feathers, and is a smaller bird.

The Cormorant breeds on the rocky cliffs and islands in most parts of the coasts of England, excepting on the east and south, where there are not so many places suitable to the bird's habits, but in Scotland and Ireland it nests not only on the rocky coasts, but in some inland districts on trees. It is found nearly everywhere in the Old World, and along the Atlantic Coast of North America.

Though rather an awkward bird on land, the Cormorant is a splendid swimmer and catches large quantities of fish; it has the power, when swimming, of submerging its body, so that often only the head and neck are seen above the surface of the water. The nest is a roughly constructed conglomeration of old sticks and sea-weed, often lined with green leaves of some sea-plant. The eggs are two or three in number, of a chalky white, underneath which the real colour of the egg is green. They measure about two-and-a-half inches in length. The nestlings are at first naked and of a purplish black colour, but after a few days they become thickly covered with black down.

THE SHAG.
(*Phalacrocorax graculus.*)

The Shag is a smaller bird than the Cormorant, and is always to be told in the young brown plumage by its having only twelve tail-feathers. The general colour is of a bottle-green tint, and instead of the ornamental white plumes which appear in the Cormorant, the Shag only dons a crest for the breeding season, but this is soon shed.

like the white filaments in the Cormorant. It breeds on most of the rocky coasts of England, Scotland and Ireland, and is, in many places, more common than its larger ally. It is only found in Western Europe, but extends into the Mediterranean Sea.

Like the Cormorant, the Shag is a very powerful swimmer and diver, and is capable of descending to great depths. It breeds on ledges of cliffs or in caves, and makes a nest of dead sticks and sea-weed. The

THE GANNET.   THE CORMORANT.   THE SHAG.

9

eggs are like those of the Cormorant, but are smaller, seldom exceeding two-and-a-half inches in length; they have a chalky outer covering, which conceals the green colour of the egg.

THE GANNETS.
Sub-order SUL.E.

The Gannets have the same formation of the foot as in the Cormorants, but the shape of the bill is different, and they are further distinguished by several anatomical and osteological characters.

THE COMMON GANNET (*Dysporus bassanus*).   The adult bird is white, with a tinge of ochreous buff on the head and back, and the primary-quills are black. Before the adult stage of plumage is reached, however, the bird goes through several stages, and it is some years before the perfect plumage is gained.   The nestlings are at first naked and black, and they afterwards become covered with white down which lasts till the bird is of a good size.   The next plumage is brown, speckled with white, the under surface being white, mottled with grey.   After the next moult the birds become more uniformly coloured below, and the head and neck are mottled with white, which increases with successive moults until the full white plumage is attained.

The Gannet breeds in colonies, of which a few are found on our coasts, the most celebrated being the Bass Rock and Ailsa Craig.   Similar colonies exist in the Faroes, Iceland, and a few places on the Atlantic Coast of North America.   In winter the birds are found considerably to the southward of their nesting haunts. The Gannet is a bird of most powerful flight, and fishes, as it nests, in company, descending on its prey from a great height above the water, though it does not settle on the water so often as the Shags or Cormorants.   The nest is made of sea-weed and only one egg is laid, of a chalky white, which has to be removed before the blue colour of the egg can be discerned.   The length is about two-and-three-quarters to three-and-a-quarter inches.

THE FLAMINGO.

THE FLAMINGOES.

Order *PHŒNICOPTERIFORMES.*

ALTHOUGH these curious birds inhabited England in ancient times, a Flamingo is now a
bird of extreme rarity in this country, outside
of menageries. At least three instances of
the occurrence of the Common Flamingo
(*Phœnicopterus roseus*) in England are on
record, and it is probable that it occasionally
gets blown over from the South of Europe.
The Flamingo nests in Southern France and
in Spain, as well as in the neighbourhood
of the Caspian Sea; it builds a nest of mud
and lays two eggs of a chalky white, and of
about three-and-a-half inches in length.

THE SWANS, GEESE, AND DUCKS.—*Order ANSERIFORMES.*

THE aspect of these birds is so familiar that I need not specify at length the
characters which distinguish them. They may be divided into three families, viz.,
Anseridæ (Geese and Swans), *Anatidæ* (True Ducks) and *Erismaturidæ* (Diving Ducks).

THE GEESE.
Sub-family
ANSERINÆ.

This group of Swimming-Birds can be separated from the
Ducks by the absence of a lobe to the hind-toe. They are birds
of plain coloration, and do not show any metallic speculum
or wing-patch, as do most of the Ducks.

THE SNOW-GOOSE.
(Chen hyperboreus.)

The Snow-Goose, remarkable for its beautiful white plumage and black wing-feathers, is an inhabitant of the Arctic Regions of North America, but has occurred in Northern Europe. It has been noticed in Yorkshire and Cumberland, but the only birds as yet captured within British limits are a pair shot in Co. Wexford, in Ireland, in November, 1871. The nest is a mere hollow in the ground, and the eggs are five in number, of a dirty white colour, about three-and-a-quarter inches in length.

THE SNOW GOOSE.   THE CANADA GOOSE (*p.* 134).

THE GREY LAG-GOOSE.
(Anser anser.)

This Goose is to be told by the colour of the bill, which is flesh-coloured and has a white nail at the tip. The feet are also flesh-coloured, and the rump is light grey; there is no sign of white on the forehead. The Grey Lag-Goose used at one time to breed in Lincolnshire, but its nesting-area is now restricted to the North of Scotland and the Hebrides: it has not been found breeding in Ireland. It nests in Central and Northern Europe, but is known in other parts of the Western Palæarctic Region as a winter visitor only.

The present species feeds on grass and water-plants and frequents the stubble-fields to pick up grain, retiring at night-time to quiet places on the sea-shore. The nest is a large structure of dead reeds and sedge, and is lined with moss and down. The eggs are five or six in number, and are pure white when first laid, but afterwards become discoloured with the nest-stains, and appear of a dirty yellowish white colour; they measure from three-and-a-quarter to three-and-a-half inches in length.

THE WHITE FRONTED-GOOSE.
(Anser albifrons.)

This is a smaller bird than the Grey Lag-Goose, and is distinguished by its orange-coloured feet and bill, the latter having a white nail at the end; the white forehead is also a character which separates it from *Anser anser* at a glance. It is only a winter visitor to Great Britain, and is more frequently observed in Ireland than in England or Scotland, its breeding-home being in Northern Europe from Scandinavia to Central Siberia, as well as in Iceland and Greenland. In winter it is found throughout Europe and occurs at the same season in North-western India and China.

The habits of the present species do not differ from those of the Grey Lag-Goose, but Seebohm states that the note is somewhat different from that of the last-named species, and is more rapidly repeated and trumpet-like in tone. The nest is placed in a grassy hillock and consists of a hollow lined with down. The eggs vary in number from five to ten, and are of a dull yellowish-white colour; they measure from three to three-and-a-quarter inches in length.

THE BEAN-GOOSE.
(Anser fabalis.)

This species is recognisable by the colour of the bill, which has a black nail at the end of the upper mandible and an orange band across the middle of the bill. The feet are orange, and there is a distinct shade of ashy-grey on the wing-coverts.

THE WHITE-FRONTED GOOSE. THE GREY-LAG GOOSE. THE BEAN GOOSE. THE PINK-FOOTED GOOSE.

The Bean-Goose is only a winter visitor to our coasts and does not breed in Great Britain. Its nesting home is in Northern Europe from Scandinavia to the Valley of the Yenesei in Central Siberia, and in winter it is found visiting most of the countries of Europe. With the first sign of the break-up of winter the Bean-Goose appears in its breeding-grounds on the tundra of Northern Europe, and as soon as the young are hatched, the old birds commence to moult and are soon quite unable to fly. Numbers are then caught by the natives who prepare them for their winter food. A similar moult takes place with Ducks, which are for some time unable to fly and have to hide themselves for protection, until their wings are grown again. The nest consists of a slight hollow, with a little moss and is plentifully lined with the grey down of the bird. The eggs are three or four in number, creamy-white, but becoming gradually stained with buff as incubation proceeds.

THE PINK-
FOOTED GOOSE.

*(Anser
brachyrhynchus.)*

The present species is rather smaller than *A. fabalis*, which it resembles in its grey wings and rump, but it is easily distinguished by its pink feet and by the pink band on the bill. It arrives in Great Britain in the autumn and visits principally the east coast of Scotland and England : in the west of Scotland and the Hebrides it is more rare, and is almost unknown in Ireland. It is found in Iceland and Spitsbergen during the breeding-season, but very few details are known as to the nesting of the Pink-footed Goose. Numbers are to be seen near Holkham, in Norfolk, during the autumn and winter, where they are protected by the Earl of Leicester, and frequent the lake in large numbers, winging their way out to sea when the tide falls and the sand-banks become exposed. As with other Geese, the flight is performed in a ' V ' formation. The nest is said to resemble that of the Bean-Goose, and the eggs are similar in colour and shape.

THE BERNACLE
GOOSE.

(Branta leucopsis.)

The Brent Geese differ from the True Geese, the members of the fore-going genus *Anser*, in not having the serrations on the upper mandible visible from the outside of the bill. One of them, the Canada Goose (*Branta canadensis*) has for a long time held a place in the British List, but is now, by universal consent, eliminated, as the only occurrences have been those of escaped birds.

The Bernacle Goose is a handsome species, remarkable for its white-banded upper surface, and barred head and neck; the forehead is white. It is a somewhat rare visitor to Britain from the north of Europe, but very little is known of its breeding places, which are supposed to be in Iceland, Greenland and Spitsbergen.

It occurs chiefly on the western coasts of Scotland, and is seen sometimes in very large numbers, as is the case also in the north of Ireland. In winter it is found on many of the coasts of Europe, and even visits

THE BERNACLE GOOSE.   THE BRENT GOOSE.

the Mediterranean. The species feeds on grass like other Geese, and betakes itself to the sand-banks when the latter are left uncovered by the tide. The nest is unknown, but the eggs, laid in confinement, are white, and measure about two-and-three-quarters to three inches in length.

**THE
BRENT GOOSE.
(Branta bernicla.)**

In the true Brent Geese the head and neck are entirely black, and the Common Brent is recognised by the length of the upper and under tail-coverts, which generally completely hide the tail. Considerable variation takes place in the colour of the breast, which is sometimes white and sometimes blackish, but these two forms occur together in the north, and intermediate specimens are not rare, so that they cannot be considered to be different species. It is a winter visitor to Great Britain and is often seen in large flocks on the eastern coasts of England, Scotland and Ireland, being rarer on the western coasts. It nests throughout the Arctic regions from the Taimyr Peninsula to Spitsbergen and Greenland, the white-breasted form being more common in the western part of its range. It visits the coasts of Northern and Western Europe in winter, and even occurs in the Mediterranean. The Brent Goose frequents the sea-coasts, where it feeds on aquatic plants and small crustaceans and marine insects. After the nesting-season the quills are moulted and large numbers are caught in their helpless condition by the Samoyedes and stored for winter food. The nest is placed on the sloping sides of a hill and is merely a depression in the ground, covered with moss and lined with a warm bed of down. The eggs are four or five in number, creamy white in colour and measuring from two-and-three-quarters to nearly three inches in length.

**THE
RED-BREASTED
GOOSE.
(Bernicla ruficollis.)**

This is a very beautiful Goose and is of rare occurrence in Western Europe. Its red breast renders it easily recognisable. The breeding home of the species is in Siberia, in the valleys of the Ob and the Yenesei, and in winter it visits the Caspian Sea in great numbers and is found in the Mediterranean at the same season. It has occurred in many countries of Europe, and at least on eight occasions in England and Scotland. In habits it appears to resemble other Brent Geese, but is not so maritime a species as the Common

THE RED-BREASTED GOOSE.

1—THE WHOOPER SWAN.   2—BEWICK'S SWAN.   3, 4—THE MUTE SWAN.

Brent. The nests found by Mr. H. L. Popham in the Yenesei Valley were placed at the foot of a cliff and were well supplied with down. The eggs were from seven to nine in number, and of a creamy white colour.

THE SWANS.
Sub-family
CYGNINÆ.

The Swans resemble the Geese in having no lobe on the hind toe, but they are distinguished from them by having an abnormally long neck, with which they search for their food under the water. They are also remarkable for the disposition of the trachea which, in most of the species, enters the bony walls of the sternum or breast-bone.

Besides the species enumerated below, there are two North American species, *Cygnus buccinator*, the 'Trumpeter Swan,' and *Cygnus americanus*, the 'Whistling Swan,' which have been included in the British List, but on somewhat slender evidence.

THE WHOOPER
SWAN.
(*Cygnus musicus.*)

As all the Swans, when adult, are pure white, the only characters by which they can be distinguished are those of the colour of the bill, and so the Whooper is recognised by its yellow bill with a black end to it. The yellow colour extends far forward along the side of the upper mandible, beyond the opening of the nostrils, which are black, this black marking only reaching half-way towards the gape. The female is a little smaller than the male, and the cygnets are greyish brown, and have the bill dull flesh colour, black near the forehead with a band of reddish-orange across the middle; the base of the bill and the lores greenish white; the feet flesh-colour instead of black. The nestlings are covered with white down.

The adult Whooper has no knob at the base of the bill like some of the other species. The 'Wild Swan,' as it is also called, breeds in the Arctic Regions, from Iceland, through Northern Europe and Siberia, and it is only in winter that it wanders south, and is then met with on our coasts and inland waters. It arrives in its breeding haunts about the beginning of May, as soon as the ice begins to break up. It is generally seen in companies, flying in a V-shaped line, and at a great height: it is very shy and difficult of approach. The note is trumpet-like, resembling also the deep bass-notes of a trombone, sufficient, says Seebohm, to ' set your ear on edge.' The nest is a large structure, made of dead sedge and coarse grass. The eggs vary from two to seven in number; they are creamy-white in colour, with a slight gloss, the shell being granulated, while the length of the egg is about four-and-a-half inches.

BEWICK'S
SWAN.
(*Cygnus bewicki.*)

This a smaller bird than the Whooper, and, like that species, has a yellow bill, but the black marking on it is disposed differently, for it extends backwards to the gape and also beyond the line of the nostrils on its upper margin. The culmen only measures 3·8 inches, instead of 4·2. The iris is hazel in the adult birds, and lemon yellow in the young ones. The nestlings are greyish white.

To England Bewick's Swan is a rarer migrant than the Whooper, but to Scotland and the Hebrides it is a much more frequent visitor, and it visits Ireland occasionally in very large numbers. Its breeding-home is in the tundra of Northern Russia and Siberia and it also nests on the island of Kolguev. The nest is made entirely of moss, and is a large structure, but is smaller than the nest of the Whooper. The eggs are two or three in number, white like those of its larger ally, but smaller and less glossy, measuring about four inches in length.

THE
MUTE SWAN.
(Cygnus olor.)

The trachea in this species is simple and does not enter the keel of the sternum, as in the two preceding species. The adult bird is white all over, but the bill is of a reddish-orange colour, with a black tip ; the lower mandible is also black as well as the lores, base of the upper-mandible, and the nostrils : there is also a black swollen tubercle on the base of the bill, smaller in the female than in the male. The nestlings are of a dull ashy-grey, and the young birds are sooty-grey. The so-called Polish Swan (*Cygnus immutabilis*) is now considered to be merely an albino variety of the Mute Swan, due to captivity. This form has white nestlings, but when the birds are adult, no difference can be detected between them and the ordinary Mute Swan, though *C. immutabilis* has been said to have the legs and feet ashy grey. In Great Britain the present species is principally known as a domesticated bird, but occasionally examples appear to visit us from the Continent, where the Mute Swan is still met with in a wild state. It nests in South Sweden and Central Europe generally, as well as in Southern Russia, as far east as Turkestan. The food of the Mute Swan consists of water-weeds and other aquatic plants, together with small molluscs and water insects. The nest is a huge structure of dead flags and grass, and the eggs, from three to five or six in number, are greenish white : their length is about four-and-a-half inches.

THE
TRUE DUCKS.
Sub-family
ANATINÆ.

All the typical Ducks have a narrow lobe on the hind toe, and there is a metallic speculum of bright colour on the wings, by which most of the species are recognised. The males have a bony swelling on the trachea. Several species, if not every Duck, moults after the nesting-season is over, the quills even being shed, so that the bird is not able to fly. The brilliant plumage of the breeding-season is discarded, and the male puts on a sober-coloured dress like that of the female, and hides himself away in reed-beds and quiet places, until his wings have grown again. Sea-Ducks, like the Eiders, betake themselves to the open sea, where the males collect in large flocks until the moult is completed.

Besides the species enumerated below, there are several which have obtained a place in the British List, such as the Egyptian Goose (*Chenalopex ægyptiaca*), the Summer Duck (*Æx sponsa*), and the Muscovy Duck (*Cairina moschata*). These, however, are all species which are frequently kept in captivity, and the records of their capture are doubtless those of escaped birds.

THE
SHELD-DUCK.
(*Tadorna tadorna.*)

The Sheld-Ducks are easily recognised by their peculiar style of coloration, and by the fact that the sexes are alike. The shape of the bill is quite characteristic, and the birds hold an intermediate position between the Geese and the True Ducks.

THE COMMON SHELD-DUCK is a very handsome bird, and is easily told by its varied plumage, including its bright chestnut breast and chestnut inner secondaries, while the wing-speculum is metallic green. The bill is bright carmine, as is also the knob or shield at its base; this knob is not observed in the female, which is slightly duller in colour than the male. The Sheld-Duck nests in many parts of Great Britain, wherever suitable localities are found, and it is also found breeding in many Irish counties. It is also found in Northern and Western Europe, and again in South-eastern Europe, whence it extends to Central Asia and Mongolia. The nest is generally placed in the sand-dunes, into which the bird tunnels for a considerable depth, sometimes as far as twelve feet. It is found in a chamber at the end of the tunnel and is formed of the bird's white down. The eggs are from seven to twelve in number, and are dull creamy-white, with scarcely any gloss; they are about two-and-a-half inches in length.

THE SHELD-DUCK.   THE RUDDY SHELD-DUCK.

THE RUDDY
SHELD-DUCK.
(*Casarca casarca.*)

This bird differs from the Common Sheld-Duck in being of a nearly uniform tawny-chestnut colour, with a bronze-green speculum on the wing, and a black collar round the neck. This collar is wanting in the female, which is smaller and somewhat duller in colour than the male. The Ruddy Sheld-Duck is an occasional visitor to Great Britain, but sometimes arrives in large numbers, as in the summer of 1892. It is found in Europe in the Mediterranean countries, whence it extends eastwards to Central Asia and Mongolia. It breeds in holes in cliffs, often at a great height. It also nests on the ground, or in a burrow, and sometimes in the old nest of a Bird of Prey. The eggs are from nine to sixteen in number, creamy white, with very little gloss; they measure about two-and-three-quarter inches in length.

THE SHOVELLER.
(*Spatula clypeata.*)

The shape of the bill, which is flattened and widened out at the end, easily distinguishes this Duck from all other British species. The male is a handsomely coloured bird, with a green

head, a chestnut breast, and
bluish grey wing-coverts, and
green wing - speculum. The
female is very different from
the male, and is a browner bird.
The Shoveller breeds sparingly
in England and Scotland, and
in several of the Irish counties,
and is also found nesting throughout the temperate regions of Europe, Asia and North America.
It is a fresh-water species, but
in winter is found in maritime
harbours and marshes. The nest
is made of grass and lined with

THE SHOVELLER.

down, and is placed in a tussock of grass or heath. The eggs are five or six
in number, and are pale-buffish or greenish-white; they measure about two or
two-and-a-quarter inches in length.

THE MALLARD.   This well-known bird, also generally known as the Wild
(Anas boscas.)   Duck, is a fresh-water species, and is the most plentiful of all
                 the British Ducks, breeding in every part of Great Britain.
It nests throughout the temperate regions of Europe and Asia, as well as in North
America, and it comes south in winter in large numbers. The nesting-place is
variously chosen. Sometimes
many pairs will form their nests
on the ground in the high grass
near a lake, while not unfrequently the nest will be found
far away from water in the
hole of a tree, or under the
roots of some old oak or even
in a hollow where the branches
join the stem. The nest is
made of grass or rushes, sometimes of straw, and is plentifully lined with the bird's own
down. The eggs are from ten
to twelve in number, greenish
or greenish-white in colour;
their length is a little over two
inches.

THE MALLARD.

THE GADWALL.

The Gadwall has a narrower bill than the Mallard, and the
sexes are not so different in colour as in most of the Ducks.
The species is easily told by the chestnut and black patch on
the wing, the speculum of which is white, these characters
being more evident in the male than the female. The Gadwall nests in Norfolk,
but is principally known as a winter visitor to Great Britain. It nests throughout
the greater part of Europe and in Iceland, and it also extends throughout Northern
Asia to the Pacific, as well as to North America. It is a fresh-water Duck and is
shy in its habits, but sometimes congregates in large numbers on inland waters.
The nest is placed on the ground, and consists of a depression in the latter, lined
with bits of reed or grass, and with the down of the bird. The eggs are from eight to
twelve in number, and are from two to two-and-a-quarter inches in length; they are
of a buffy or creamy-white colour.

THE GADWALL.
(*Chaulelasmus
streperus.*)

THE WIGEON.
(*Mareca penelope.*)

This is a handsome Duck, very similar in form to the
Gadwall, but differing in its somewhat longer tail and in the
lamellæ of the bill being less prominent. The colour of the
bill is grey, tipped with black, and the species can always be told by its green
wing-speculum, and by the large patch of white on the wing, formed by the median
and greater wing-coverts; this is less developed in the females and young birds.
The Wigeon breeds regularly in the north of Scotland and is believed to do so
occasionally in Ireland, but it is principally known as a winter visitor to the British
Isles. The breeding-range of the Wigeon extends from Northern Europe to Eastern

Siberia and Kamtchatka, and it also nests in many localities in Central Europe. Although the species is found in flocks on inland lakes in winter, it also frequents the sea-coasts in large numbers. The nest is made in the hollow of the ground near water, and is generally well concealed in the long sedge; it is lined with grass and down from the body of the bird. The eggs are from seven to twelve in number, and are of a buffy-white or cream-colour. The length is from two to two-and-a-quarter inches.

THE AMERICAN WIGEON.
(*Mareca americana.*)

The male of this species differs from that of the Common Wigeon in having the head whitish, thickly speckled with black, and with a shade of green reaching from the eye to the hinder

THE WIGEON.   THE AMERICAN WIGEON.

nape. The female differs from the female of *M. penelope* in having the head and neck much whiter. The species breeds in Arctic America, and wanders south in winter. It has been found on one occasion with English-killed Wigeon in a London market. In habits and the construction of its nest it does not differ from our own Wigeon, and the eggs are creamy-buff, and measure a trifle over two inches.

THE COMMON TEAL.
(*Nettion crecca.*)

The small size of the Teal generally serves to distinguish the species, its length being only a trifle over a foot. The sexes are different in colour, the male being a very handsome little bird with a chestnut head and throat and green side-face, separated from the chestnut by a line of white. The Teal breeds throughout England, Scotland and Ireland, but more commonly in the north; it visits every part of Great Britain in the winter. It breeds throughout Europe in the summer, but is more common in the north, and extends across Central and Northern Asia to

the islands of the Bering
Sea. It is a fresh-water
Duck, and frequents lakes
and inland waters, though
in the winter it is found
in marshes and water-
holes near the sea-shore.
The nest is built on the
ground, near an inland
lake and is warmly lined
with down, but, like the
Wild Duck, the Teal
sometimes places its nest
at some distance from
water, and occasionally

THE COMMON TEAL.

the bird begins to nest before the snow is off the
ground. The eggs are from eight to ten in number, and vary from buffy-white or cream-colour
to greenish-white; the length is about one-and-
three-quarter inches, and does not exceed two
inches.

THE AMERICAN
TEAL.
(*Nettion carolinense.*)
This little Teal is an inhabitant of North America,
where it inhabits the British
provinces, and wanders south
in winter as far as Central America. It very
closely resembles our European species, but has
a crescentic mark of white on each side of the
neck. It has been noticed in England on three

THE AMERICAN TEAL.

occasions. In habits and
nesting it does not differ
from its European repre-
sentative. The eggs are
dull pale buff, and measure
about one-and-three-
quarter inches in length.

THE PIN-TAIL.
(*Dafila acuta.*)
The
nearly
straight
bill and the elongated tail-
feathers will generally

THE PIN-TAIL.

serve to distinguish the Pin-tail, which has also a bronzy-green speculum, bordered with black above and with white below. The speculum is present in the old female, but is of a bronzy-green tint. The bill is black, but inclines to leaden-blue on the sides of the upper mandible. The present species is believed to breed in the north of Scotland, but the fact is not yet proved, and it is known principally as a winter visitor. It is also said to have nested in Ireland, but no recent authentic instances of its doing so are known. It breeds throughout the Arctic Regions of Europe, Asia and America, and extends in winter far to the south of its nesting-range. It is a fresh-water Duck, only frequenting sea-coasts during migration. At other times it affects fresh-water lakes, rivers and swamps, where it feeds, like the Mallard, on water plants and insects, and it also visits the stubble-fields to pick up grain. The nest is generally placed at some distance from water among shrubs in dry places; it is rather deep and is lined with grass and sedges, as well as with the bird's down. The eggs are from seven to ten in number, and of a pale greenish-buff colour; they measure from two to nearly two-and-a-half inches.

THE GARGANEY.
(Querquedula querquedula.)
This is a small species of Teal which differs from the true Teal in having a soft membrane fringing the terminal portion of the upper mandible, and in its blue upper wing-coverts, in which character it resembles the Shoveller. It visits England in the spring and breeds in the eastern counties, and probably in other parts of England. In other portions of Great Britain it is only known as an occasional visitor on migration. It nests throughout the greater part of Europe and extends to Central Asia, but does not breed very far north. It is a very shy and silent species, and leaves for the south at once on the approach of the cold weather. The nest is always placed in a retired situation, often far away from water, on the ground in a corn-field or under the shelter of a bush. It is a deep depression in the ground lined with grass and leaves, and with plenty of down. The eggs are from eight to twelve in number, of a buffy-white or cream colour, and they measure about one-and-three-quarters of an inch in length.

THE BLUE-WINGED TEAL.
(Querquedula discors.)
A male of this North American species has been shot near Dumfries, and it appears to be of rare and accidental

THE GARGANEY.

THE BLUE-WINGED TEAL.

occurrence in Europe. It is similar in appearance to the Garganey, but is easily told by its brighter and more smalt-blue wing-coverts, and by the crescent-shaped white band between the eyes and the base of the bill; the crown is black and the throat and sides of the face are sooty-brown. In habits it resembles the Garganey. The eggs are pale buff, and measure about an inch-and-three-quarters in length.

THE DIVING DUCKS.
Sub-family
FULIGULINÆ.

The Diving Ducks are distinguished by having a very broad lobe to the hind toe. They are believed to have the same summer change in the males as in the true Ducks, when the ornamental breeding-dress is thrown off for a short space and the male becomes like the female.

THE RED-CRESTED POCHARD.
(Netta rufina.)

This fine species is an accidental visitor to Great Britain, having been noticed twice in England, once in Scotland, and once in Ireland. It is a most unmis-

THE TUFTED DUCK.

takable species, being distinguished by its full cinnamon-coloured crest, and white speculum on the wing; the bill in the male is brilliant crimson, and is black in the female with a good deal of reddish or orange towards the tip; in the hen bird also the speculum on the wing is greyish-white. The range of the species extends from the countries of the Mediterranean east to Central Asia, and it is very abundant in Southern Russia. In winter

THE GOLDEN-EYED DUCK.
THE RED-CRESTED POCHARD.

it is found in the Black and Caspian Seas, and occurs in large numbers in North-western India at that season of the year.

It is a fresh-water Duck and frequents open broads and lagoons, where it feeds on frogs and small fishes, shells and insects. The nest is placed close to the water, and is made of dead leaves and stems of rushes. The eggs are from seven to nine in number and, when fresh, are bright green, but fade to greenish-white: their length is about two-and-a-quarter inches.

THE POCHARD.
(Nyroca nyroca.)

The Pochard has not so broad a bill as the members of the following genus *Fuligula*, and it has not such prominent indentations on the upper mandible as in the genus *Netta*. The rufous head and the grey back, finely vermiculated with black, and the grey wing-

THE WHITE-EYED POCHARD.   THE SCAUP DUCK.   THE POCHARD.

speculum, serve to distinguish the Pochard, which also has the bill leaden-blue with a black base and tip.

The present species breeds in a few places in England and Scotland, and is said to be increasing in numbers. In Ireland it is also believed to nest, but at present positive proof of the fact is wanting. It does not breed in Northern Europe, but is found from Central and Southern Europe to Central Asia and Eastern Siberia. It is a fresh-water Duck, but is seen on the sea-coasts in winter. It feeds chiefly at night and is a fine diver. The nest is made of dead grass and sedge, and is lined with down; the eggs are from seven to ten in number, or even more; they are greenish or greenish stone-colour, and measure about two-and-a-half inches in length.

THE
WHITE-EYED
POCHARD.
(*Nyroca nyroca.*)

Like the Pochard, this species has a chestnut head and a white wing-speculum, but, when adult, is always distinguishable by its white iris, though in young birds this is brown or brownish-grey. It has occurred in different parts of England, Ireland and Scotland, but is only an irregular visitor, coming to us in winter and in spring. It breeds throughout Central and Southern Europe, as far east as Central Asia and Cashmere. The White-eyed Pochard is a fresh-water Duck and resembles the Common Pochard in its habits. It feeds on all kinds of insects and grubs, as well as water-weeds, which it obtains under the water, being a most expert diver. The nest is built on the ground, and is made of dry flags and rushes, and lined with down and a few feathers. The eggs are from nine to fourteen in number, and are of a creamy-brown colour; they measure from two to two-and-a-quarter inches in length.

THE TUFTED
SCAUP DUCK.
(*Fuligula fuligula.*)

In this species the back is uniform, and the head is very distinctly crested, while the wing-speculum is white. It nests in several places in England, Ireland and Scotland, generally on the shores of inland lakes. It likewise breeds throughout Northern Europe and extends to the Pacific Coast of Siberia, wintering in the Mediterranean countries, the Indian Peninsula and North-eastern Africa : it is also said to nest on some of the Abyssinian lakes. It is a fresh-water Duck, though many occur on the sea-coasts during the winter. Sometimes at the latter season of the year they appear in large numbers on inland lakes in company with Wigeon, and are very shy and circumspect. They feed on frogs, water-insects and leaves and stems of water-plants, and even on small fishes. The nest is placed in a tussock, or on grass-land, near the water, and is made of grass or sedge, lined with down. The eggs are from eight to twelve in number, of a stone-colour or greenish brown, and they measure about two-and-a-quarter inches in length.

THE
SCAUP DUCK.
(*Fuligula marila.*)

In this species the back is greyish-white, vermiculated all over with black lines. There is no crest, as in the Tufted Duck, but, like that species, the Scaup has a white speculum. The female is browner than the male, but has some grey specklings on the back. It has been said by Dr. Stark to breed on Loch Lomond, but otherwise it is only known as a winter visitor to Great Britain. It nests in the arctic regions of North America, as well as in Northern Europe and Asia, visiting India, China and the Mediterranean in the winter, when it also occurs as far south as the West Indies. The Scaup is an expert diver and obtains much of its food under water; it is gregarious in its habits, and generally gathers together in large flocks. The nest is placed on a sloping bank, not far from water, and is well concealed, being often built under the shadow of a bush : it is merely a hole in the ground, lined with sedge and down from the bird's body. The eggs are from six to nine in number, but as many as twelve have been found; they are of a pale greenish-grey or stone-colour, and measure about two-and-a-half inches in length.

THE
GOLDEN-EYED
DUCK.
(*Clangula clangula.*)

The Golden-eye is an unmistakable species, easily told by its black and white coloration, the white scapulars being a strongly marked feature, as also are the white wing-speculum, the orange-yellow feet, and golden-yellow iris. The female may be recognised by its white speculum, and by its brown axillaries.

It is a winter visitor to the British Islands, and has even been said to nest in Scotland, but this has not yet been confirmed. It breeds in the high north of Europe and Asia, as far south as Holstein and Eastern Prussia; it likewise occurs throughout North America. In winter it visits China, North-western India, and the Mediterranean countries, and is also found as far south as Mexico and the West Indies.

The Golden-eye is a wonderful diver, and feeds on water-plants, insects, shell-fish and even on frogs and small fish. The nest is in the hole of a tree, sometimes at a height of twelve or fifteen feet from the ground, and consists merely of the greyish-white down of the bird. The eggs are from ten to thirteen in number, of a greyish-green tint, fading to dull green or olive-green.

THE BUFFEL-HEADED DUCK.

THE BUFFEL-
HEADED DUCK.
(*Charitonetta
albeola.*)

The Buffel-head has the nostrils situated nearer to the base of the bill than in the Golden-eyes, and the style of plumage is different from that of the latter birds. The male has the feathering of the head very much developed, and the sides of the face are shot with green and steel-blue, while there is a good deal of purple on the crown of the head. The iris is dark brown. The female is much duller than the male in colour, and has a broad white patch from the ear-coverts to the sides of the neck.

The present species has occurred three times in England, and twice in Scotland, but its home is in North America, from Labrador to Alaska, whence it migrates south in winter. In habits it resembles the Golden-eye, and, like that species, nests in the hole of a tree. The eggs also resemble those of the Golden-eye, and are from six to ten in number.

THE LONG-TAILED DUCK.
(Harelda glacialis.)

This is a very handsome species of Duck, which visits us in winter, occurring most plentifully on the Scottish coasts and the Hebrides, being of less frequent occurrence in England and Ireland. It breeds throughout the arctic regions of Europe and Northern Asia, as well as in North America, coming south in winter. It is often very late in returning to its summer quarters, as I have seen a flock of birds in the Sundal Fjord, in Northern Norway, on the 13th of June. It is an extremely good diver, and the male has a remarkably musical note, which gains for it the name of the 'Organ Duck' in Alaska. The nest is a depression of the ground, and is made of grass, plentifully lined with the bird's down. The eggs are six or seven in number, of a clay brown or dull green colour, and measure from two to two-and-a-quarter inches.

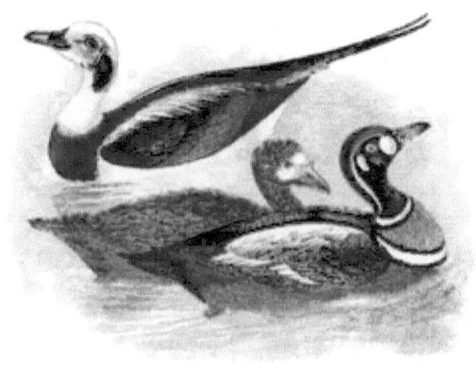

THE LONG-TAILED DUCK.
THE HARLEQUIN DUCK.

The long-tailed Duck needs no detailed description, as its pied appearance, long tail and drooping white scapulars easily distinguish it from all the other British species; the bill is orange, with a black base and black nail at the tip.

THE HARLEQUIN DUCK.
(Cosmonetta histrionica.)

This Duck is well-named the 'Harlequin,' for it possesses a very varied combination of colour, the back being slaty-blue and the sides of the body bright chestnut, with bands of black and white on the fore-neck and breast; there is a white patch on the face, also visible in the female, and the sides of the crown are chestnut. The female is a plain brown bird, and has a spot of white behind the ear-coverts, in addition to the white face.

The Harlequin Duck is an extremely rare visitor to our shores, and only three instances of its occurrence are considered to be genuine. It breeds in the high north of Europe, Asia, and North America, as well as in Greenland and Iceland. The nest is placed close to the water, and the bird frequents the vicinity of rushing streams. The nest is a depression in the ground, lined with the bird's down, which is large and dense. The eggs are from seven to ten in number, of a cream-colour, and rather glossy. They measure about two-and-a-quarter inches.

STELLER'S EIDER-DUCK. (*Henieouetta stelleri.*) This beautiful Duck has twice been shot on the east coast of England; once in Norfolk and once in Yorkshire. It is a maritime species, and breeds in the arctic regions from the north of Norway throughout Siberia to the Aleutian Islands. The male is a very handsome bird, with a white head, and a green patch on the lores and another on the nape. The wing-speculum is purple, and the chest and breast are chestnut, fading into cinnamon on the abdomen. The female is

KING EIDER-DUCK.
STELLER'S EIDER-DUCK.

very different from the male, being blackish above and below, with the head and neck rufous brown and the chest chestnut, mottled with black. The wing-speculum is purple as in the male, and the fact that the hen possesses the same speculum as the male is one of the points in which Steller's Duck differs from the other Eiders. It is a shy bird and soon deserts its nest if the latter be meddled with. The nest is a depression in the moss of the tundra, which is lined with down. The eggs are from seven to nine in number, and are of a pale greenish stone-colour; they measure about two-and-a-quarter inches in length.

THE COMMON EIDER-DUCK. (*Somateria mollissima.*) The Eiders have a bare space between the lores and the forehead, and, when adult, have sickle-shaped inner secondaries on each side of the back. The Common Eider is white, with a black head and belly, a beautiful tint of delicate pink on the chest and a patch of green behind the ear-coverts. The female is brown, mottled with black and rufous, and the young males are also at first brown like the females, and take nearly four years to gain the adult plumage. After the breeding-season the males moult their quills and don a dull dress like that of the hens, and as they are then unable to fly, they betake themselves to the open sea and associate in flocks. The species breeds along the shores of Scotland north from the Farne Islands in Northumberland, but is only a winter visitor to Ireland and the coasts of England. It nests in various places on the coasts of Norway, Denmark, the Faeroes, Iceland, and the shores of Greenland and North-eastern America, being protected in most places for the sake of the down, which is collected by the people who farm the breeding-places. It is a maritime species and is gregarious both in

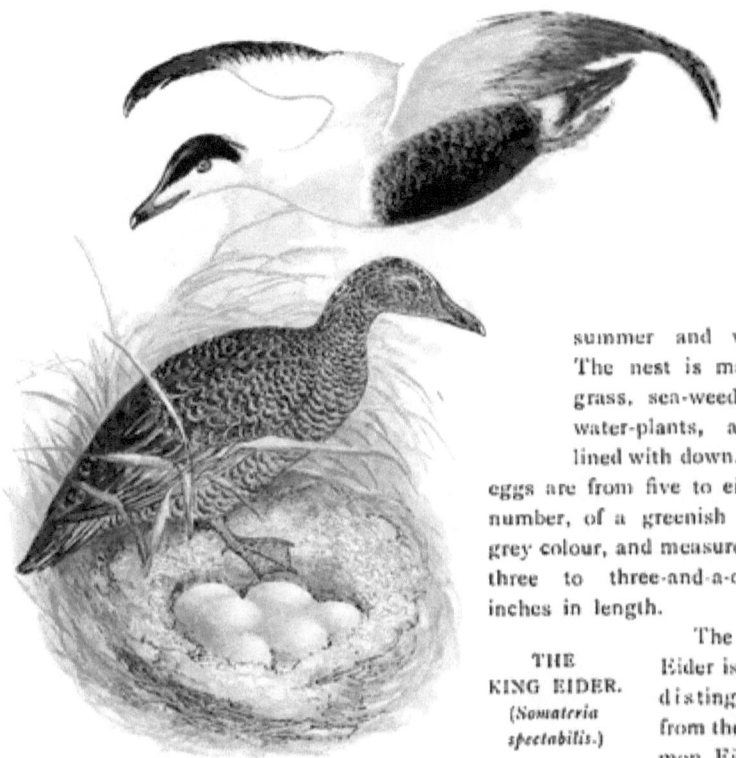

THE COMMON EIDER-DUCK.

summer and winter. The nest is made of grass, sea-weed, and water-plants, and is lined with down. The eggs are from five to eight in number, of a greenish stone-grey colour, and measure from three to three-and-a-quarter inches in length.

THE KING EIDER. (*Somateria spectabilis.*) The King Eider is easily distinguished from the Common Eider by the shape of the feathering on the forehead, which reaches forward as far as the hinder end of the nostrils. This will serve to distinguish the female birds, which otherwise resemble each other closely, except that the hen of the King Eider is more rufous than that of the Common Eider. The male has a V-shaped black mark on the throat, and has a cube of reddish orange on each side of the base of the upper mandible. The head and nape are of a delicate lavender grey, with the hind neck and mantle pure white. It breeds in Arctic America, Greenland and Northern Europe and Asia as far as Bering Sea, and occasionally visits Great Britain in winter, a few individuals having been observed at intervals off our coasts. Like the Common Eider, it is entirely a maritime Duck. The nest is a depression in the ground, lined with the bird's own down, and the eggs are of a greenish-stone colour or clay-brown, measuring two-and-a-half to two-and-three-quarter inches in length.

THE COMMON SCOTER.   THE SURF SCOTER.   THE VELVET SCOTER.

THE COMMON SCOTER.
(Œdemia nigra.)

The "Black Duck," as it is generally called, is a common winter visitor to all our coasts, and is known by its entirely black coloration, the bill having a yellow patch and a swollen knob at the base, while the iris is white. It breeds in the North of Scotland, and is said to nest occasionally in England. It also nests throughout Northern Europe and Siberia, and is only seen inland during the breeding season, when it frequents the shores of lakes; it is at other times essentially a maritime Duck. The nest consists of a hollow scraped out in the ground and lined with leaves and grass, and the bird's own down. The eggs are eight or nine in number, of a light cream-colour, and slightly glossy; they measure about two-and-a-half to two-and-three-quarter inches in length.

THE VELVET SCOTER.
(Œdemia fusca.)

This Duck is recognised from the Common Scoter by its slightly larger size, white wing-speculum, orange-yellow bill, and dull crimson or orange-red feet. It is believed that a few breed in some of the highland lochs in Scotland, but it is principally known as a winter visitor to Great Britain. Its nesting-home is from Scandinavia throughout Northern Europe and Siberia, and it visits Southern Europe, Central Asia and China in winter. It feeds principally on molluscs, which it obtains by diving. The nest is found on the shores of inland lakes and rivers, and is a mere depression in the ground, lined with grass and down. The eggs are eight or nine in number, of a creamy stone-colour, and measure two-and-three-quarters to three inches in length.

THE SURF SCOTER.
(Œdemia perspicillata.)

This is the largest of the three British Scoters, and has the bill reddish with a black spot on each side; the feet are crimson with orange-chrome on both sides of the inner toes; the iris is white. There is no white speculum on the wing, but there is a white patch on the crown and another on the back of the neck. It is a North American species, and only visits Great Britain in winter, when it is found on our western coasts as well as in other parts of western Europe. It sometimes assembles in enormous flocks, extending for ten miles in length. The nest is made of reeds, grass and water-plants, lined with down. The eggs are from five to eight in number, of a slightly greenish cream-colour, and they measure nearly two-and-a-half inches in length.

THE SMEW.
(*Mergus albellus.*)

Easily recognised by its white plumage, varied with black markings. The male has a distinct white crest. The female is a grey bird with a rufous head and neck and white under surface. The Smew breeds in Northern Europe and Siberia and visits the Mediterranean countries in winter, as well as North-

THE SMEW

western India and China. It occurs on the coasts of Great Britain in winter, but is rarer on the western side of our islands. The nest is made in a hollow tree, and consists only of the down of the bird. The eggs are seven or eight in number, of a creamy white in colour, and scarcely to be distinguished from those of the Wigeon ; they measure about two inches in length.

THE HOODED
MERGANSER.
(*Lophodytes
cucullatus.*)

This handsome Duck is an inhabitant of North America, and has only visited Great Britain on a few occasions. It has not been observed anywhere else in Europe. It is easily recognised by its striking coloration and crested head. It is a shy bird during the breeding-season and collects in flocks in the winter, like the Smew. The nest is placed in the hollow of a tree or log, and is made of dry grass, lined with grey down. The eggs are white and nearly round in shape. They are of an ivory-white, and measure two or two-and-a-quarter inches in length.

THE HOODED MERGANSER   THE GOOSANDER.

THE GOOSANDER.
(Merganser merganser.)

The Mergansers are large birds with long bills, the edges of which are 'serrated,' or have saw-like margins. The Goosander, which is the larger of the two resident British species, has no dark collar across the fore-neck, and is white underneath, with a beautiful tinge of salmon pink; the head and throat are black, as well as the crest, all these parts being glossed with green. The female is slaty-grey above with a rufous head and neck.

The Goosander breeds in the highlands of Scotland, but is elsewhere only known as a winter visitor. It nests in Central and Northern Europe and throughout Siberia. Its food consists almost entirely of fish, which it catches by diving. The nest is generally placed in the hole of a tree or cleft of a rock, while sometimes the old nest of a Crow or other bird is utilized. The nesting-place is lined with the grey down of the bird, and the eggs, eight to twelve in number, are of a creamy-buff colour and measure from two-and-a-half to nearly three inches in length.

THE RED-BREASTED MERGANSER.

THE RED-BREASTED MERGANSER.
(Merganser serrator.)

This is a smaller bird than the Goosander and is distinguished from that species by the rufous band on the fore-neck, speckled with black, as well as by the wavy bars on the sides of the body. The dark brown flanks of the Red-breasted Merganser distinguish the female of this species from the female of the Goosander. It nests in Scotland and Ireland as well as throughout the northern portions of both the Old and New Worlds, migrating south in winter. Its food consists of fish, small crustacea and shell-fish, and it is an expert diver. In winter it leaves its inland habitat, and collects in flocks. The nest is a mere hollow in the ground, lined with grass and leaves, and sometimes consists only of the bird's grey down. The eggs are from six to nine, or more, in number; they are of an olive stone-colour or creamy-buff, and measure from two-and-a-half to two-and-three-quarter inches in length.

THE HERON-LIKE BIRDS.—*Order ARDEIFORMES.*

THESE birds are remarkable for their long legs, and differ from the allied families in many anatomical characters. The Order is represented in Great Britain by the Herons and Storks. The Herons have the hind-toe on the same level as the other toes, and the middle toe has a comb-like ridge on the claw.

THE
PURPLE HERON.
(*Phoyx purpurea.*)
(*See p. 156.*)

The Purple Herons have longer toes than the other members of the family *Ardeidæ*, especially the middle toe, which is equal to the tarsus in length, and the hind-claw is particularly strong and nearly straight, with a very slight curve. The present species has frequently occurred in Great Britain, at least fifty times, only one of the occurrences having been recorded from Ireland. It is found nesting throughout the greater part of Central and Southern Europe, as well as in Africa and Central Asia. It is a shy bird and skulks among the reed-beds which form its home, instead of taking flight like other Herons. The nest is made of reeds, and is placed at no great height from the surface of the water in a reed-bed. The eggs are from three to five in number, and are of a greenish-blue colour, measuring about two or two-and-a-quarter inches in length.

THE COMMON
HERON.
(*Ardea cinerea.*)

As in the genus *Phoyx*, the tail-feathers are twelve in number in the Common Heron; the bill has saw-like edges or serrations. The grey colour, with the white crown and the long black central feathers of the throat and chest easily distinguish the species. The nestlings, which remain for a long

THE COMMON HERON.

time in the nest and are fed by the parents, are bristly little creatures, covered with greyish down, with grey filamentous plumes on the head. The Heron nests in isolated colonies all over the British Islands, generally in trees, but where these are not available, on rocks or even in scrub near the ground. It is also found nesting over the greater part of Europe and Northern Asia, as well as in Africa, India and China. The food of the Heron consists of fish and frogs. The nest is rather a large structure of sticks, brought by the male to the female, by whom the nest is built, the lining being composed of smaller twigs. The eggs are three or four in number, of a greenish-blue colour, and measure from two-and-a-quarter to two-and-a-half inches in length.

THE GREAT WHITE HERON.
(Herodias alba.)

The present species is pure white, but is distinguished from the Egrets by its much larger size. It differs from the Common Heron in having no crest, and in its beautiful dorsal train of ornamental plumes. The bill is black in summer and yellow in winter. The species has occurred about eight times in England and Scotland, but can only be considered a rare and accidental

THE LITTLE EGRET.   THE PURPLE HERON.
THE BUFF-BACKED EGRET.   THE SQUACCO HERON.   THE GREAT WHITE HERON.

visitor. It is found in Central and Southern Europe as far east as Central Asia, and it winters in Africa and India. In its habits the present species resembles other Herons, and its food consists of fish, frogs and water-insects, as well as mice and rats. The nest is built in the swamps, and is rather a large structure of sticks, lined with smaller twigs. The eggs are four in number, of a greenish-blue colour, and measure about two-and-a-half inches in length.

THE LITTLE EGRET.
(Garzetta garzetta.)
The little Egret in its full plumage differs from the Great White Heron in having a crest of drooping white plumes and some very distinct elongated plumes on the chest; the dorsal train consists of a dense mass of filamentous plumes. The bill is black both in winter and summer, but the dorsal train is lost in the winter season. It is this train of beautiful feathers which is the 'Osprey' of commerce, and every spray worn by English women in their hats and bonnets represents the murder of a pair of these elegant little birds at the nest, and the subsequent starvation of the young birds. The Little Egret inhabits Central and Southern Europe, being most plentifully met with on the Lower Danube, where it nests in communities with Night-Herons and other species. It has occurred on two occasions in England, but is one of our rarest visitors. The nest is made of sticks and reeds and is placed on low trees or bushes in the swamps. The eggs are from three to six in number, of a bluish green colour, and measure about an inch-and-a-quarter in length.

THE COMMON NIGHT-HERON.
(Nycticorax nycticorax.)
In the Night-Herons the bill is stouter than in the Egrets, and the colour is quite different The ornamental plumes consist of two or three drooping white feathers on the nape. Specimens have been shot in England, Scotland, and Ireland. It is found throughout Central and Southern Europe, and temperate Asia, as well as in Africa, breeding in colonies in the marshes. It also occurs throughout the greater part of North America. The nest is a cradle of sticks, and the eggs are two or three in number, of a pale greenish-blue colour, and measuring from one-and-three-quarters to two inches in length.

THE SQUACCO HERON.
(Ardeola ralloides.)
Although not unlike some of the smaller Bitterns in appearance, the Squaccos are true

THE COMMON NIGHT-HERON.

Herons, and have twelve tail-feathers. In the breeding plumage the upper surface is pale vinous, including the ornamental plumes of the back, and the feathers of the head and hind-neck have a black line following the margin of the feathers. At least forty occurrences of the Squacco Heron have been recorded, of which two have taken place in Scotland and three in Ireland. It is found throughout Southern Europe and Africa, breeding in company with other Herons or in colonies. The nest is built of sticks, like that of the Night-Heron, and the eggs are from four to six in number, and of a greenish-blue colour; they measure one-and-a-half to one-and-three-quarters of an inch in length.

THE
BUFF-BACKED
EGRET.
(*Bubulcus lucidus.*)

This species may be recognised by its yellow bill and by the vinous crest and dorsal train; in winter the plumage is pure white. Only one example is known to have been shot in England, in October, 1805. It inhabits the Mediterranean countries, the lower Danube and Southern Russia, as well as the greater part of Africa. It is generally known as the 'Cattle-Egret' from its habit of feeding round the cattle, and perching on their backs. It devours numbers of ticks which it picks off these animals, and feeds also on frogs and insects. The species nests in colonies in low bushes in the reed-beds, and makes a nest of sticks. The eggs are from three to five in number, and of a very pale greenish-blue colour; they measure about an inch-and-three-quarters in length.

THE LITTLE
BITTERN.
(*Ardetta minuta.*)

All the Bitterns may be told by their ten tail-feathers, and by the colour of the eggs. They are not gregarious like the small Egrets, and in the Little Bittern there is considerable difference in the colour of the sexes, the male having a greenish-black head and back, whereas in the female the upper parts are chestnut-brown, with distinct streaks on the under surface of the body. The species is believed to have bred in England in former days, but is now only known as an occasional visitor. It is an inhabitant of Central and Southern Europe, eastwards to Central Asia, and it also breeds in Scinde and Cashmere. It is a shy and skulking bird and in many of its ways resembles the Rails, threading its way through the reeds instead of taking to flight. The birds also draw themselves up and remain motionless with their bill pointing straight up in the air, so as to resemble the surrounding rushes. The nest is of sticks and reeds, and is either placed in a reed-bed or on the head of a pollard-willow. The eggs are from five to nine in number, and are white with a scarcely perceptible greenish tinge; they measure about an inch-and-a-half in length.

THE COMMON
BITTERN.
(*Botaurus stellaris.*)

The members of the genus *Botaurus* have ten tail-feathers and saw-like edges to the bill. The large size and mottled plumage of tawny-yellow and black, with the large neck frill, sufficiently distinguish the Bittern from all the other British Herons. Although it used at one time to breed in our fen-lands, the Bittern

THE LITTLE BITTERN.   THE AMERICAN BITTERN.   THE COMMON BITTERN.

is now only known as a winter visitor. It is found in the greater part of Europe and Northern Asia, frequenting swampy districts, and occurring in winter in North-eastern Africa, India, Burma, and China. It is seldom met with in companies, but is generally found solitary, or in pairs in its breeding-haunts. Its food consists of fish, small mammalia, frogs, and water insects, and it is remarkable for its booming and resonant note. The nest is made of dry rushes and is placed on the ground in the swampy habitat which it loves. The eggs are from three to five in number, of a brownish-olive colour, slightly tinted with green when fresh. They measure from two to two-and-a-half inches in length.

THE AMERICAN BITTERN. (*Botaurus lentiginosus.*) This species has a plain brown head and rufous tips to the primary-coverts and quills. The rest of the plumage is waved with buff and black as in the other members of the genus *Botaurus*. It has been many times procured in the British Islands, and seems not unfrequently to wander on migration from its home in North America. In habits it much resembles our Common Bittern, and its home is in the swamps. The nest is made of dead rushes, either on the ground or on low trees. The eggs are from four to seven in number, and are brownish-olive, measuring from an inch-and-three-quarters to two inches in length.

The Storks differ from the Herons in wanting the comb-like edge to the claw of the middle toe, and in having the hind-toe raised above the level of the others. The general colour is white, with the scapulars, greater wing-coverts and quills, black; the bill and feet are red. Although the Stork occurs commonly and breeds in Holland, it is only a rare visitor to Great Britain. It is found throughout Central and Southern Europe, as far east as Central Asia; it also breeds in suitable localities in Africa. The nest is generally placed on the roof of a house, except when an old cart-wheel or cradle is put up for the bird's accommodation; it sometimes builds its own nest in

THE WHITE STORK.

THE BLACK STORK.

a tree. The young are scantily covered with ashy-white down. The eggs are from three to five in number, of a dull white colour; they measure from two-and-a-half to nearly three inches in length.

THE
BLACK STORK.
(Ciconia nigra.)

The Black Stork occasionally visits England, but does not breed with us. It nests throughout the greater part of Europe, but is only known as a passing migrant in the south; and it is found throughout Central Asia to Mongolia, wintering in India and Africa. It has a red bill and legs like the White Stork, but is otherwise quite different in colour, being black with shades of metallic purple and green, and has the breast and abdomen white. It does not frequent the neighbourhood of houses like the White Stork, but is entirely a bird of the forests. The nest is a large structure of sticks, added to year after year, and lined with moss, generally placed in trees, but sometimes on ledges of rocks or cliffs. The eggs are from three to five in number, of a dull white and coarse texture. They measure from two-and-a-half to two-and-three-quarter inches in length.

THE
GLOSSY IBIS.
(*Plegadis falcinellus.*)

The Ibises and Spoon-bills form the Sub-order *Platalea*, and differ from the Herons and Storks in the form of the nostrils. The Glossy Ibis is only an accidental visitor to Great Britain, occurring generally in autumn and winter, but sometimes in spring. It is a common species in Southern Europe, extending to Central Asia, India and China, as well as Africa and Australia, and it even occurs

THE SPOON-BILL.   THE GLOSSY IBIS.

in the Eastern United States of North America. It is very like a Heron in habits and gathers together in companies, feeding like a Curlew on the shores of lakes and rivers, where its prey consists of frogs, worms and aquatic insects. It nests in the company of other Herons in the marshes, and builds a slight structure of sticks and reeds. The eggs are three or four in number, and are easily recognised by their dark greenish-blue colour; they measure about two inches in length, or a trifle more.

THE
SPOON-BILL.
(*Platalea leucerodia.*)

This is a quite unmistakable bird on account of its flat and spoon-shaped bill. The colour is pure white, with a tawny tinge of buff on the head and neck, and a large crest of drooping plumes, which disappears in the winter plumage. The Spoon-bill used to breed in several places in England, but is now only an occasional visitor.

11

It still nests in Holland, and in many places in Central and Southern Europe to Central Asia. The species breeds in the low-land marshes near the sea, whence it sallies out to procure its food on the mud flats; this consists of small crustacea and insects. In certain places it breeds in trees, but in marshy places the nest is composed of reeds. The eggs are four or five in number, chalky-white, with a few spots and streaks of reddish brown, and occasionally some underlying blotches of purplish-brown; they measure from a little more than two-and-a-half to three inches.

THE
COMMON CRANE.
(Grus grus.)

Cranes differ from Herons in having what is called a schizognathous or split palate, and the nasal groove extends a long way down the bill, reaching to more than half the length of the latter. The Common Crane is a dark grey bird, with a bare red crown; the inner secondaries are loose and ornamental, and form drooping plumes. The Cranes also differ from the Herons in their nestlings,

THE COMMON CRANE.   THE DEMOISELLE CRANE.

which are not hatched naked and helpless, but are covered with down, and are able to shift for themselves in a few hours. Three hundred years ago the Crane used to breed in the fen-lands of England, and its fossil remains have been found in Ireland; now it is only an occasional visitor. It breeds, however, in the marshes of the greater part of Europe, making a nest of a large size among the rushes in the swamps. The eggs are two or three in number, brown or stone-grey, with reddish spots and blotches, relieved by underlying spots of dull purplish grey; their length is from three-and-a-half to four-and-a-quarter inches. The note of the Crane is clear and trumpet-like, and, as in some of the Swans, the trachea enters the bony walls of the breast-bone and is convoluted.

THE DEMOISELLE CRANE. *(Anthropoides virgo.)* This beautiful Crane, which is an inhabitant of Southern Europe and Central Asia, has once been shot in the Orkneys, in September, 1871. It is easily recognised by its long ornamental plumes on the fore-neck, and the white whisker-like tufts of white feathers on the sides of the face.

THE GREAT BUSTARD. *(Otis tarda.)* The Bustards, though possessing many of the osteological characters which distinguish the Cranes, are very different from the latter birds in external appearance, having a mottled plumage, thickly waved with black cross-markings. The Great Bustard

MACQUEEN'S BUSTARD.   THE LITTLE BUSTARD.   THE GREAT BUSTARD.

is the largest European species, and the male has a remarkable pouch in the throat, which is capable of being distended; the sides of the throat are also furnished with some long bristly plumes like whiskers. Within the present century the Bustard has been extirpated in England as a breeding-bird, but occasional examples are obtained. It inhabits Central and Southern Europe, and is not rare in some countries, such as Poland, Hungary and Spain; it extends into Central Asia.

The food of the Great Bustard consists of small mammals and lizards, and it also eats grass, corn and peas. In the breeding season the display which the male bird makes in showing off its plumage is most extraordinary. The nesting-place is a mere hollow scraped in the ground. The eggs are two or three in number and are olive-brown, with light olive or brown spots and underlying ones of purplish-grey ; they measure about two-and-three-quarter to three-and-a-quarter inches in length.

THE LITTLE
BUSTARD.
(*Tetrax tetrax.*)

The small size of the Little Bustard renders it easy of recognition, and the black on the throat, and black and white bands on the chest at once distinguish the male. Specimens have been recorded, mostly in autumn and winter, from England, Scotland and Ireland, so that it may be considered a rare and occasional visitor. It breeds in Central and Southern Europe, as far east as Central Asia, and is sometimes seen in large flocks of a hundred birds together. The food is the same as that of the Great Bustard, and the nest is a depression in the ground, lined with a little dry grass. The eggs are three or four in number, more uniform than those of the Great Bustard, being olive-brown or olive-green, with scarcely any appearance of rufous markings or grey underlying spots. The length is about two or two-and-a-quarter inches.

MACQUEEN'S
BUSTARD.
(*Houbara
macqueenii.*)

This species of Ruffed Bustard is distinguished by the shield of soft feathery bluish-grey plumes on the crop, and by the crest of narrow erectile feathers. On each side of the neck is a ruff of stiffened plumes, white with black tips. Macqueen's Bustard breeds in the neighbourhood of the Altai Mountains and Lake Baikal in Central Asia, and visits the plains of North-western India in the winter in large numbers. It has been captured on three occasions in England. It is an inhabitant of the desert plains, where the sandy colour of its plumage affords it protection. It feeds on young corn and seeds of plants. The nest is a depression in the ground, and the eggs, two or three in number, are clay-brown or olive-brown, with faint blotches of purplish-grey and spots of dark brown. The length is about two-and-a-quarter to two-and-a-half inches.

THE
STONE-PLOVER.
(*Œdicnemus
œdicnemus.*)

This bird holds an intermediate position between the Bustards and the Plovers. Like the former birds it wants the hind-toe. The 'Thick-knee,' as this bird is often called, is not likely to be confounded with any other Plover ; for its large size and great yellow eye and sandy coloration separate it from all other British species. It inhabits the open downs of the southern and eastern counties in summer, a few remaining during the winter months. It is a shy and timid bird, and when danger approaches it drops on the ground and lies perfectly still with its neck outstretched, and the nestlings share this same instinct of protection, for when thus lying flat on the ground, the birds are almost impossible to distinguish. There is no nest, and the two eggs are laid on the bare ground, from the stones of which they with difficulty can be detected. The eggs are of a dark or light stone-colour with brown spots and blotches all over the surface, varied with underlying mottlings of pale grey.

THE STONE-PLOVER.

This rare visitor to our shores is the representative of an Old-World group of Plovers, which have a split palate and open 'schizorhinal' nostrils. The tarsus is not reticulate in front but is plated, and on the inner side of the middle claw there is a curious comb-like series of notches. The pale tawny colour of the plumage, black quills, grey head and black line along the sides of the face, are sufficient characters to tell the Courser by. It is found throughout the desert countries of Northern Africa

THE CREAM-COLOURED COURSER.

and in some of the Canary Islands, extending to Central Asia and North-western India. The nest is a slight depression in the sand, and the two eggs are scarcely to be told from the stones which surround them. The eggs are stone-colour, thickly covered all over with blackish lines and blotches, amongst which are mingled the underlying grey mott-lings; their length is from an inch-and-a-quarter to an inch-and-a-half.

THE PRATINCOLE. (*Glareola pratincola.*)

The long wings and forked tail distinguish

THE PRATINCOLE.

the Pratincoles from the Coursers, and they have much shorter legs than the last-named birds. The general colour is brown, but the throat is sandy buff followed by a collar of white and black. The Pratincole has occurred several times in England and Scotland, and once in Ireland. It nests in the countries of Southern Europe and winters in Africa. The flight is very much like that of a Swallow or a Tern, and the birds are gregarious at all times of the year, and nest in companies, sometimes of many thousands. The eggs are laid on the bare ground, and are so thickly scribbled over with black that the light ground-colour is scarcely perceptible; they measure about an inch-and-a-quarter in length.

THE GREY PLOVER.　　THE GOLDEN PLOVER.

THE GREY PLOVER. (*Squatarola helvetica.*)

Of the Plovers which put on a black breast in the summer, the Grey Plover is the largest, and it is easily distinguished by its grey plumage, mottled with black. In winter the black breast disappears, and the under surface of the body is white; the young birds are also white below, but are spangled with golden colour above, so that they resemble the adult of the Golden Plovers. From these, however, they may be always told by their black axillaries, and by the presence of the hind toe.

Although the Grey Plover arrives on our coasts in spring in full breeding dress, with its beautiful black and grey plumage fully developed, it does not nest in Great Britain, and is only known as a spring and autumn migrant, a few remaining through the winter months. It breeds in the Arctic Regions of both Hemispheres, and eggs have been obtained in Kolguev and in the Valley of the Petchora, as well as in Alaska and on the Anderson River in North America. It is a maritime Plover during the winter season, and wanders south to Africa, India and Australia, and in the New World to Brazil and Peru. The nest is simply a hollow in the moss of the tundra, and the eggs, four in number, are intermediate in colour and markings between those of the Lapwing and Golden Plover, and measure about two inches in length, or a little more.

THE GOLDEN PLOVER. (*Charadrius pluvialis.*) The Golden Plovers have no hind-toe, and may be easily recognised by the golden colour of the upper surface. The common Golden Plover is at once determined by its white axillaries, which distinguish it from the Grey Plover, both in summer and winter plumage. It breeds on the moorlands of the United Kingdom, being more plentiful in Scotland and Ireland, but it is also found nesting in the wilder districts of England and Wales. In winter it frequents the mud-flats on the coasts, as well as inland pastures. It inhabits the northern and central districts of Europe during the breeding-season, and winters in the Mediterranean countries and in Africa. The nest consists of a depression in the ground or tuft of grass, and is made of a few stems of dry grass with a little heather and moss. The colour of the eggs varies from a clay-brown to a light stone-grey, with lines and blotches of black, and underlying markings of reddish brown. The length is from an inch-and-three-quarters to two inches, or a little more.

THE LESSER GOLDEN PLOVER. (*Charadrius dominicus.*) This is smaller than the common Golden Plover, and has much more slender legs. It goes through the same changes of plumage, but can be recognised at all ages by its smoky-brown axillaries. Four examples of this small Golden Plover have been obtained in Great Britain, two in England and two in Scotland. It breeds in the high north of both Hemispheres, and in winter wanders to India, the Moluccas, and Australia, as well as to South America. In habits the species resembles *C. pluvialis*, and it makes its nest in a depression in the moss, or scantily lines

THE LESSER GOLDEN PLOVER.

it with grass and leaves. The eggs are precisely similar to those of the Golden Plover, but are rather smaller, and measure about an inch-and-three-quarters to two inches.

THE ASIATIC DOTTREL.
(Ochthodromus asiaticus.)

This species is distinguished from the Sand-Plovers (*Ægialitis*) by its much stouter bill, and by the chestnut band across the chest in the summer plumage. In winter the chest is brown, but the young birds can always be told from our ordinary Ringed Plovers by their longer legs (tarsus 1·35 inch). A specimen in summer plumage was shot in Norfolk, in May, 1890. The home of the species is in the Kirghis Steppes and Central Asia, whence it ranges into East Africa in winter. Both in its summer and winter home, it is an inhabitant of the steppes and grass-lands.

THE DOTTREL.
(Eudromias morinellus.)

This handsome little Plover is recognised by its white chest-band, black breast and abdomen, and orange-chestnut flanks. Although not so plentiful as in former years, the Dottrel is still found breeding on the moors of Cumberland and Westmoreland, and in the highlands of Scotland. It also breeds on the mountains of Scandinavia and Central Siberia as well as on the high ground of other parts of Europe. It is a wonderfully tame bird near its nest, and last summer (1897) I captured a young nestling on one of the high mountains of the Sundal Valley in Norway. The old bird did not attempt to fly away, but ran round us within a few yards, and finally led off its youngster in triumph when I let the latter go. The eggs are deposited in a hollow in the moss, and are three in number, of a greyish stone-colour, tinged with olive, and largely blotched with black, rufous, and grey; the length is a little over one-inch-and-a-quarter.

THE DOTTREL.

THE KILL-DEER DOTTREL.
(Oxyechus vociferus.)

The present species belongs to a little group of Sand-Plovers, which have a long tail, measuring

more than half the length of
the wings. The Kill-Deer
Dottrel, so called from its note,
is an inhabitant of North
America, and is said to have
been twice obtained in England.
It is recognised at once by the
cinnamon-rufous colour of the
lower back, rump and upper
tail-coverts. The nest is a
depression in the ground, lined
with grass, and the eggs are
four in number, brownish or

THE KILL-DEER DOTTREL.   THE SOCIABLE LAPWING.

cream-colour, with numerous spots of blackish-brown ; their length is about an inch-
and-a-half.

THE RINGED
SAND-PLOVER.
(*Egialitis hiaticola.*)

The true Sand-Plovers resemble the foregoing species, but
have a shorter and less conspicuous tail. The Common Ringed
Plover has a black collar across the fore-neck, brown in young
birds, a white forehead, followed by a black band across the
head, and black ear-coverts. It is found on all the coasts of Great Britain, and breeds
everywhere, being also occasionally noticed on inland waters, though here principally
on migration. It nests throughout Europe on the shores and inland lakes as far as
Central Asia, and is found in the far north on Spitsbergen and Jan Mayen. The
bird is very wary, and is difficult of approach in the autumn, when it consorts with
Dunlins and other shore birds and leads them out of danger. Both parents sham
to be wounded, when the nest is approached, in order to draw the intruder away from
their eggs or young. The eggs are pear-shaped, and are laid in a little hollow in

THE KENTISH SAND-PLOVER.
THE LITTLE RINGED SAND-PLOVER.   THE RINGED SAND-PLOVER.

the sand, and are four in number, placed point to point, as is the mode with all Plovers and Sandpipers. They very much resemble the stony surroundings amongst which they are placed, and are clay-coloured, with small black spots and lines, sometimes forming blotches; they measure an inch-and-a-quarter to an inch-and-a-half.

THE LITTLE RINGED SAND-PLOVER.
(Ægialitis dubia.)

This is a smaller bird than the Ringed Plover and resembles the latter species very closely, but can always be told by the white shaft, which is only seen on the first primary. The shafts of several of the quills are white in *Æ. hiaticola.* In the latter also the bill is orange with a black tip, whereas in *Æ. dubia* the bill is black, with only the base of the lower mandible yellow. There is also a ring of yellow round the eye.

The Little Ringed Plover has been captured in England half a dozen times, chiefly in the autumn. It is found throughout the whole of temperate Europe and Asia, and in winter visits Africa, India and the Malayan Archipelago. It is essentially an inland species, and is found on the shores of lakes and on sand-spits in the large rivers. The nest is a little cavity in the sand, and the eggs are four in number, smaller than those of the Common Ringed Plover, but similar in colour. They measure a little over an inch to an inch-and-a-quarter.

THE KENTISH SAND-PLOVER.
(Ægialitis alexandrina.)

This little species can be told by its rufous head, white forehead, and white collar round the hind-neck. There is no complete black ring on the fore-neck, but a black patch on each side of the latter. Young birds may be recognised by their black legs and by the white collar round the hind-neck.

The Kentish Plover nests on the sea-shores in the south-east of England, and occurs in other parts of the United Kingdom during migration. It is found throughout Central and Southern Europe in suitable localities, and extends to Eastern Asia, wintering in Africa, India and Australia. The present species always looks a whiter bird in life than either of the Ringed Plovers, and the nestlings are decidedly lighter in colour than those of the last-named birds. The species is not gregarious in summer, but collects in flocks in the autumn. The eggs are laid on the shingly beach, and are three, more rarely four, in number. They are very similar to those of the Ringed Plover, but have the markings more distributed over the egg. Their length is about an inch-and-a-quarter, or a little more.

THE LAPWING.
(Vanellus vanellus.)

This bird is often called the 'Peewit' from its note, or the 'Green Plover' from the colour of its plumage. It has a remarkably long crest of upturned feathers, a black throat and neck, and the upper and under tail-coverts of a light cinnamon-colour. The young birds and the adults in winter plumage have sandy-buff edgings to the feathers of the upper surface. It is found everywhere throughout the British Islands, nesting on the moors and fallow-land, and frequenting the sea-shore in large flocks in winter. It inhabits the whole of Europe and Northern Asia.

THE LAPWING.

The food of the Lapwing consists of slugs, grubs and small insects, and on the sea-shore it feeds on minute molluscs and insects, being everywhere a most useful bird and deserving of every protection. The eggs form a much appreciated article of food in the spring, and are diligently sought after. They are four in number, pear-shaped, and are laid point to point on the ground or in a slightly-constructed nest of grass in a tussock. The colour varies from dusky-olive or greenish-brown, to light clay-brown, with very distinct black blotches or spots, and underlying spots of purplish-grey; they measure about an inch-and-three-quarters in length.

THE SOCIABLE LAPWING.
(Chætusia gregaria.)
(p. 169.)

This is a species of the steppes of South-eastern Europe, and has occurred once in Great Britain, when a specimen was procured in the autumn of 1860, in Lancashire. It differs from the Common Lapwing in having no crest, and is of an ashy-brown colour, with the rump and upper tail-coverts pure white, the crown black, as also the lower breast and abdomen, with a patch of chestnut on the latter. In winter it frequents the uplands in flocks, preferring dry and sandy places. The eggs are four in number, and are very like those of the Lapwing.

THE TURNSTONE.
(Arenaria interpres.)

This little Plover has no 'dertrum' or swelling at the end of the bill, which is more wedge-shaped than is usual in the

THE TURNSTONE.

Waders, and is used by the bird for turning over stones in its search for food. The colour of the male is of a 'Harlequin' pattern, and is quite unlike that of any other Plover. The dress of the young birds and of the old ones in winter is much duller and browner. It is an autumn and spring migrant in Great Britain, but a few remain throughout the winter, and it is probable that the Turnstone may breed in the North of Scotland. It nests in Northern Europe as far south as Denmark and the shores of the Baltic, and is known to occur throughout the Arctic Regions of both the Old and New Worlds. As a rule the Turnstone keeps in pairs, but a few may be found together in the autumn on the sea-shore; it is entirely a shore-frequenting species, and is generally not very shy. It feeds on insects which it searches for under stones. The nest is placed on the ground, and is a little hollow in the latter, lined with a few dead leaves. The eggs are four in number, of a greenish-grey or clay-brown colour, with chocolate-brown and purplish-grey markings; their length is about an inch-and-a-half to an inch-and-three-quarters.

THE OYSTER-CATCHER.
(*Hæmatopus ostralegus.*)

The Oyster-Catcher has a long and narrowly compressed bill. Its plumage consists entirely of black and white, and it has pinkish legs and a ring of vermilion round the eye. It nests in certain localities in England, but more plentifully in Scotland and Ireland, along the shores of some of the rivers and even on inland lochs. It is found in similar localities all over Europe and as far east as the Valley of the Ob, while it winters in the Mediterranean and on the Caspian and

THE OYSTER-CATCHER.

Red Sea coasts. In autumn and winter it collects in large flocks, and haunts the sandy-shores left uncovered by the tide. I have kept several of these birds in confinement, but they never became very tame, and their soft toes suffered greatly when the ground became hard and frozen; they were then nearly always lame. The nest is a small hollow, lined with pieces of shells and little stones, and when in the moss or peat, the nest is generally ornamented with limpet-shells. The eggs are three in number, clay-brown to greenish-olive in colour, and lined or blotched with blackish brown or purplish-grey; the length is from a little over two inches to two-and-a-half inches.

THE AVOCET.   THE BLACK-WINGED STILT.

THE AVOCET.
(Recurvirostra avocetta.)

The 'Scooping' Avocet, as this species is sometimes called, on account of its upcurved bill, is now only an occasional visitor to British shores, but in former days it used to breed in our eastern and southern counties. It is easily told by its black and white plumage, and its slender bill. It nests in suitable places throughout Central and Southern Europe to Central Asia and Mongolia, as well as in many parts of Africa. It is still found nesting in Holland and on the shores of the Baltic.

The long bill of the Avocet is not used to probe the mud or sand, but is employed by the bird in scraping the sand from side to side. Its food consists of aquatic insects, as well as worms and small crustacea, and it often swims out on the water. The nest is a mere depression in the sand or short grass, with a few leaves or grass for a lining. The eggs are four in number and pear-shaped, of a clay-brown with a little tinge of olive, and scribbled or blotched all over with black and stone-grey markings; the length is from an inch-and-three-quarters to two inches.

THE BLACK-WINGED STILT.
(Himantopus himantopus.)

An unmistakable species is the Stilt on account of its long legs. It bears a certain amount of resemblance to the Avocet in its black and white colour, but is easily told by its straight bill. It has occurred in the southern and eastern counties of England, as well as in Ireland and Scotland, but is a very rare visitor to Great Britain. Its home is in the Mediterranean countries to Central Asia, Mongolia, and North-western India. The Stilt is not a shy bird, and is gregarious in its habits, large numbers nesting in company in marshes. The food consists largely of gnats and mosquitoes as well as of water-beetles and small shell-fish. The nest is made of small bents of grass or dead reeds. The eggs are three or four in number, very similar to those of the Avocets, and measure an inch-and-a-half to an inch-and-three-quarters in length.

THE COMMON CURLEW.

THE COMMON CURLEW.
(Numenius arquatus.)

With the Curlews we commence the study of a large group of Wading-Birds belonging to the Sub-family *Totaninæ*. They have a long bill, often curved, and the tarsus is transversely plated before and behind, though in the true Curlews the hinder aspect of the tarsus is reticulated. Both the outer and inner toe are joined to the middle one by a basal membrane.

The Curlew nests on the moor-lands of all three kingdoms, and in the autumn and winter betakes itself to the sea-shore, where it is found either singly or in small flocks on the mud-flats of tidal rivers. The female is larger than the male and has a much longer bill. In spring the streaks on the breast become broader and blacker, and the upper plumage is also much darker. In winter the Curlew visits India and Africa, and in the breeding-season it is found in Northern and Central Europe, as far east as Lake Baikal. The nest is a depression in the grass, with a slight lining of leaves or dead grass. The eggs are four in number and pear-shaped, olive-brown, with black spots and blotches, generally round the larger end of the egg. The length is from two-and-three-quarters to nearly three inches.

THE
WHIMBREL.
(*Numenius phæopus.*)

The Whimbrel is a much smaller bird than the Curlew, and the sexes are of about the same size, while the bill is only a little over three inches in length. In winter the lower back is pure white, but in summer plumage it is streaked with black, and the under surface is distinctly streaked with black as well. The Whimbrel is a summer visitor to Great Britain, though some remain over the winter, and a few breed on the moors in the North of Scotland. It nests on the tundra of Northern Europe from Scandinavia to the Petchora River, and possibly in Central Siberia. The Whimbrel resembles the Curlew in habits, and breeds on the moors, collecting in flocks in the autumn. The nest is merely a little hollow among the heather, with a lining of a few dried grasses. The eggs are like those of the Curlew, but are smaller, measuring from two to nearly two-and-a-half inches in length.

THE WHIMBREL.

THE ESKIMO
CURLEW.
(*Numenius borealis.*)

The small size of this Curlew distinguishes it from the Whimbrel, like which bird it has a pale stripe down the middle of the crown, and it has plain-coloured primary quills; the lower back and rump are like the back, and not white. It has occurred at intervals in England, Scotland and Ireland, but its native home is in North America. The nest is only a depression in the ground, with a slight lining of dry grass; the eggs are four in number, measuring about two-and-a-half inches in length, and are olive-brown, with the usual brown and grey spots and blotches seen on all Waders' eggs.

THE ESKIMO CURLEW.

THE
BAR-TAILED
GODWIT.
(*Limosa lapponica.*)

The Godwits, instead of a curved bill, have the latter slightly upturned, or nearly straight. In summer both species of Godwit are remarkable for their red breasts, which are replaced by a white breast in the winter, while the young birds have a buff tinge on the under parts.

The Bar-tailed Godwit is told at all ages by the distinct bands on the upper tail-coverts and tail. The female never has quite as much rufous colour on the breast as the male. The species is only known as a migrant in Great Britain, and it breeds in the marshes of Northern Europe from Finland to the Yenesei River, in Siberia. On their way north in spring, the birds feed on the mud-flats of our tidal harbours, and when the sea covers the latter, they retire inland to rest. In the autumn they come in small flocks and frequent the mud-flats before going south. The nest is merely a depression in the moss with a few dry leaves for a lining, and the eggs are four in number, olive or olive-brown in colour, sparsely marked with light brown and purplish grey spots and blotches. Their length is from two to two-and-a-quarter inches.

THE BLACK-TAILED GODWIT.   THE BAR-TAILED GODWIT.

**THE
BLACK-TAILED
GODWIT.**
(Limosa limosa.)

This Godwit is easily to be told from the foregoing species by the black terminal band on the tail. The rufous colour on the under surface is not so universally distributed as in the Bar-tailed Godwit, especially in the female. The Black-tailed Godwit used formerly to breed in the fen-lands of the eastern counties of England, but is now only a visitor on migration. It nests still in Central Europe, and is to be found in the breeding-season in Holland and the countries of the Baltic Sea. In habits it resembles the foregoing species, and the nest is a depression in the moss, the eggs being four in number, and resembling those of the Bar-tailed Godwit, but they are occasionally darker than those of the latter species; their length is from two to two-and-a-half inches.

THE RED BREASTED SNIPE-TATTLER. *(Macrorhamphus griscus.)*

This is essentially a Godwit in plumage, but has a different bill, somewhat widened out at the tip and pitted. The female has a slightly longer bill than the male. In winter the plumage is grey, with the under-parts white, the throat streaked, and the chest and sides of the body barred with blackish. It is a North-American species, which

THE RED-BREASTED SNIPE-TATTLER.

has occurred more than a dozen times in England, and twice in Ireland.

THE SPOTTED REDSHANK. *(Totanus fuscus.)*

Distinguished in summer by its sooty-black under-surface; and in the winter plumage, which resembles that of the other Tattlers, the Spotted Redshank may always be recognised by its white rump, and by its barred secondaries. It does not nest in the British Islands, but is only a visitor on migration. Its breeding range extends through Northern Europe and Northern Asia, and it migrates south in the autumn to India, Burma and China, as well as Southern Europe. It frequents inland marshes during the breeding season, and the shores of lakes, and it nests on hill-sides, often away from water. The nests are depressions in the ground with a few dry leaves. The eggs are of a rich green colour, when fresh, but fade to a light brown, with reddish-brown blotches and scribblings, generally collected near the larger end. They measure about an inch-and-three-quarters in length.

THE SPOTTED REDSHANK.

THE COMMON REDSHANK. *(Totanus calidris.)*

The Common Red-shank is recognised by its white rump and white inner second-aries; it has also orange legs like the Spotted Redshank. The stripes on the breast are more distinct in summer than in winter, and the upper surface is blotched with black. It breeds in marshy places throughout England, Ireland and Scot-land, and is found in localities suited to its habits throughout Europe and Central Asia as far as Mongolia. In winter it

12

THE COMMON REDSHANK.

spreads along the shores and inland waters of Africa and India, even to the Moluccas. At the nest the Redshank is one of the noisiest birds imaginable, whether it be on shingly beach or moss-covered broad, or on the shores of a lake in the mountain. The birds protest loudly against any intrusion, and will fly round and round, occasionally settling with upraised wings and tail on a rock or on the bough of a dead tree or stump. The cry is very like a shrill 'mew,' interrupted by a constant clatter of 'Kitty, Kitty,' 'Kiup,' till it becomes distracting. In the autumn, Redshanks are found either singly or in small parties on the sea-shore, and are then equally detestable for the way in which they startle every bird within shot. The nest is a depression in the ground, or in a hummock, and is generally well concealed by the surrounding grass. The eggs are four in number, pear-shaped, and rather large, measuring an inch-and-three-quarters to nearly two inches in length. The colour is clay-brown, with blackish-brown spots and blotches.

THE MARSH-GREENSHANK. (*Totanus stagnatilis.*)

This small species, which is only about nine-and-a-half inches in length, is an inhabitant of Southern Europe, extending into Central Asia and Eastern Siberia, and wintering in Africa, India and Australia. Mr. Walter Rothschild shot a bird on Tring Reservoir which he believes to have been of this species, but the specimen was unfortunately destroyed in a fire, so that the occurrence of the species in England requires confirmation.

THE MARSH-GREENSHANK.

THE
YELLOWSHANK.
(*Totanus flavipes.*)

This American species has occurred twice in England, once in Nottinghamshire and once in Cornwall. It has the lower back and rump dusky brown, and the upper tail-coverts white, banded with brown. Its yellow legs also distinguish it from the other Tattlers.

THE
GREEN-LEGGED
TATTLER.
(*Helodromas
ochropus.*)

In the genus *Helodromas* the tarsus is much shorter than in the genus *Totanus*, and only just exceeds the length of the middle toe and claw. The Green Sandpiper, as it is usually called, is told at once by its dark coloration, which is dark olive-brown, with a few tiny white spots; the rump is like the back, but the upper tail-coverts are white, as also are the

THE YELLOWSHANK.

tail-feathers, the latter having blackish bars; the under surface is white, with brown streaks on the lower throat and fore-neck; the feet are greyish-blue, tinged with green. Young birds have pale edgings of ashy-bronze to the feathers of the upper surface.

The Green Sandpiper does not breed in Great Britain, but it occurs plentifully on migration on the banks of rivers and inland waters. In the autumn it frequents the muddy ditches of tidal waters, generally in small parties of six or eight together. It breeds in Northern Europe and Siberia, and is found in winter in Africa, India and Australia. It nests in trees, generally selecting the old nest of a Thrush or other bird, but sometimes laying its eggs on the moss of an old bough. The eggs are four in number, about one-and-a-half inches in length, greenish-white or clay-colour, with reddish-brown and purplish-grey blotches and spots.

THE COMMON SUMMER-SNIPE.   THE WOOD-TATTLER.   THE GREEN-LEGGED TATTLER.

THE SOLITARY TATTLER.

THE SOLITARY TATTLER. (*Helodromas solitarius.*) Distinguished from the foregoing by having no white on the rump; the white bars on the axillaries are much broader than in the Green Sandpiper. It is a North American species, and has occurred three times within the British area, once in Scotland, on the Clyde, once in the Scilly Islands and once in Cornwall.

THE COMMON SUMMER-SNIPE. (*Tringoides hypoleucus.*) See p. 179. This little bird differs from the Tattlers in its short bill, short legs and more pointed wings, the long secondaries being nearly equal to the primaries in length. It nests on the moors of the south-west of England and in Wales, in the north of England and Scotland, and in every county in Ireland. In other parts of Great Britain it is a common migrant. It nests throughout Northern and Central Europe in suitable localities, as well as in Northern Asia, and winters in Africa, India and Australia.

At the nesting-place the 'Summer-Snipe' is very demonstrative, and makes a great fuss when its domain is invaded. A pair is to be found in Norway at about every quarter of a mile, nesting on the green banks by the rivers or on the sides of the lakes, but the nest is always hard to discover. The species is never found in large flocks, though small family parties may be seen during the autumn migration, frequenting the pasture lands near the shores of the rivers, and often feeding round the cattle, when they keep up a bobbing motion of the tail like a Wagtail. The nest is a depression in the moss, and the eggs are four in number, pear-shaped, clay-colour or greenish-white, with spots and blotches of chocolate-brown and purplish-grey.

THE SPOTTED SUMMER-SNIPE. (*Tringoides macularius.*) The winter plumage of this species is almost identical with that of our Summer-Snipe, but it may be recognised by the black sub-terminal bar on all the secondaries, none of which are entirely white as in the preceding species, and also by the colour of the bill, which is yellow for some distance along the under mandible. It is a North American species, which is believed to have occurred in Great Britain. In habits and nesting it

THE SPOTTED SUMMER-SNIPE.

resembles our Summer-Snipe from which it differs in its spotted under-parts in summer.

THE GREENSHANK. (*Glottis nebularius.*) This is the largest of the group of Tat-tlers, and has a slightly upturned bill, while there is scarcely any web between the base of the inner and middle toes. The plumage of the Greenshank is ashy-grey with whitish edges to the feathers; the lower back, rump and upper tail-coverts are pure white, as also are the tail-feathers, which have broken bars of black; the under surface of the body is pure white, with some dusky frecklings on the side of the breast, and some streaks on the sides of the neck. Young birds are tinged with brown on the upper surface and have distinct bars across the tail. The Greenshank is chiefly known as a migrant on our coasts, but a few stay through the winter. It breeds in the north of Scotland and on the islands of the west of Scotland. It also nests throughout Northern Europe and Siberia, and migrates in winter to Africa, India and Australia. It is a shy bird at all times of the year, and makes a slight nest of grass or dead leaves in a depression of the ground. The eggs are four in number, pear-shaped, and of a creamy-buff colour, with spots and blotches of blackish-chestnut and grey; they measure an inch-and-three-quarters to a little over two inches in length.

THE WOOD-TATTLER. (*Rhyacophilus glareola.*) See p. 179. In this species the bill is very short, and the legs rather long; the centre tail-feathers are not produced beyond the others, as in most of the Tattlers. It has also a peculiarly spotted plumage. It is believed to have nested in Great Britain in former days, but is now only known as a visitor, occurring every autumn on our eastern coasts, but being much rarer on the west and in Ireland. Its breeding-range extends throughout Northern Europe and Siberia, and it visits Africa, India, and the Malayan Archipelago on its winter migration.

The Wood-Tattler makes its nest in the neighbourhood of swamps, but often on the open grass-land surrounded by trees, on which the bird often perches. Mr. H. L. Popham has found it utilising the old nests of the Fieldfare in the Yenesei Valley, but its nest is generally a slight depression in the ground, lined with a few stalks and dry grass. The eggs are four in number, olive-grey or stone-colour, handsomely spotted and blotched with blackish or reddish-brown and purplish-grey; they measure about an inch-and-a-quarter to an inch-and-a-half in length.

THE RUFF.
(Pavoncella pugnax.)

This is one of the most curious of all Wading Birds, for no two males are exactly alike. On the sides of the crown is a kind of ruff or tippet, while on the breast is a large shield of plumes, and these may be of any colour or pattern, plain white or black, or barred with white, rufous, black, or cream-colour, in never ending variety. The female and the male in winter plumage, as well as the young birds, look like any ordinary Tattler.

The male is much larger than the female, which is known as the 'Reeve.' There is no white on the quills, but the axillaries are white, so that the bird in winter plumage can be easily recognised.

The Ruff used formerly to breed in our fen-lands, but is now only an occasional visitor. It nests in favoured localities in Northern Europe and Siberia, and can still be seen breeding in the marsh-lands of Northern France, Holland and Denmark. The head-dress and the pectoral frill are orna-

THE RUFF.

ments donned for the breeding-season, and the males fight for the possession of the females. The nest is a depression in a tuft of long grass, and the eggs, always well-concealed, are four in number, olive or clay-coloured, with streaks or blotches of rufous brown or black, with underlying markings of purplish-grey. The length is from about an inch-and-a-half to an inch-and-three-quarters.

BARTRAM'S TATTLER.

THE BUFF-BREASTED SANDPIPER.

BARTRAM'S TATTLER.
(Bartramia longicauda.)

In the genus *Bartramia* the bill is short and not so long as the tail, the latter being graduated, and the outer feathers much shorter than the middle ones. The general colour of the bird is tawny, mottled or barred with black. It is a North

American species, which has occurred in England and Ireland on several occasions in the autumn and winter. At this season of the year it wanders to South America, and has even been captured in Australia.

THE BUFF-BREASTED SANDPIPER.
(Tringites subruficollis.)
With the present species commences the Sub-family *Scolopacinæ*, or Snipes and Sandpipers. They are distinguished from the *Totaninæ* by having the toes cleft to the base, with no web between them. In the genus *Tringites* the bill is short, measuring less than the length of the tarsus, and the centre tail-feathers are not produced beyond the others. The Buff-breasted Sandpiper is a North American bird, which has occurred about sixteen times in the British Islands. It is a very conspicuous species by reason of the mottling on the under side of the primary-quills. (*See p.* 182.)

THE SANDERLING.

THE SANDERLING.
(Calidris arenaria.)
The Sanderling differs from all the other species of Sandpipers in the absence of the hind-toe. It is a very pretty bird, especially in summer, with the bright rufous colour of the upper parts, and its chestnut throat and breast; but in autumn it looks much whiter than any of its allies, and only the Kentish Plover presents the same appearance on the shore. The Sanderling breeds in the Arctic Regions of Siberia and North America, but very few authentic eggs have as yet been taken. In autumn and winter it is a very common bird on all our coasts, and ranges to Africa, as well as India, Australia and South America. When noticed in England, it is either consorting with Dunlins and other Waders, or it goes in flocks consisting mostly of young birds of its own species. Colonel Feilden found the nest in Grinnell Land at a height of several hundred feet above the sea; it was a depression in the centre of a recumbent plant of the Arctic Willow, and had a few dead leaves and catkins for its lining. The eggs are four in number, a little more than an inch-and-a-quarter in length, of a pale olive-brown, faintly mottled and spotted with brown and violet-grey.

THE LITTLE STINT.
(Limonites minuta.)
The Stints have a hind-toe and a very short bill, and they are all very elegant little birds, being remarkably tame in their arctic breeding-haunts, so much so that they scarcely move from their nest when it is being rifled, and Mr. Pearson tells of one that actually sat on his gun. The Little Stint belongs to the section of the genus which has the tail-feathers smoky-brown: it has blackish legs, and is distinctly of a rufous shade both in old individuals and young birds of the year, while, in winter, the old birds are ashy above and white below. To Great Britain the Little Stint is a visitor during the spring and autumn migrations, but does not breed with

us: it nests throughout the tundra of Northern Europe and Siberia. The nest is a depression in the ground, lined with a few dead leaves. The eggs only measure a little over an inch in length; they are four in number, uniform in shape, of an olive-grey or creamy-brown colour, with distinct chocolate-brown or blackish markings, and underlying spots of light grey.

THE LITTLE STINT.   THE AMERICAN STINT.   TEMMINCK'S STINT.

THE AMERICAN STINT.
(Limonites minutilla.)

This is a smaller species than our Little Stint, and has an ashy-brown fore-neck and chest, mottled with dark spots and shaft-streaks. It is a North American species, and has occurred but twice in England, once in Cornwall and once in Devonshire.

TEMMINCK'S STINT.
(Limonites temmincki.)

In this little species, which is a smaller and much greyer bird than the foregoing Stints, the outer tail-feathers are pure white. It is a migratory visitor to Great Britain, but is a rarer bird than the Little Stint. It breeds on the tundra of Northern Europe and Asia, but does not go so far south in winter, as it does not wander beyond North-eastern Africa and Senegambia, whereas the Little Stint migrates as far as South Africa. Both species visit the Indian Peninsula in winter. Seebohm says that Temminck's Stint is not so exclusively a marine bird as the Little Stint, and the male has quite a song during the breeding-season, not unlike that of a Grasshopper-Warbler. The male is said to hatch out the eggs, which are four in number, rather smaller than those of *T. minuta*, and with the markings less distinct. They measure a little more than an inch in length, but do not reach an inch-and-a-quarter. The nest is a depression in the ground, with a little dry grass for lining, and several are often seen in close proximity.

THE PECTORAL SANDPIPER.
(Heteropygia maculata.)

In the genus *Heteropygia*, the general appearance of the birds is like that of the Dunlins, but the bill is shorter than the tarsus, and the latter is longer than the middle toe and claw, in which respect they differ from the Stints. This Sandpiper is a North American species, and on migration occurs throughout

THE PECTORAL SANDPIPER.

South America. It has been met with in Great Britain on at least twenty-five occasions, and is to be told by the broad band across the breast, the brown legs and dark upper tail-coverts. During the breeding-season the male has a habit of inflating his throat till it hangs down like a kind of dewlap. The nest is built in the grass in a high and dry situation, and the eggs are four in number, pear-shaped, stone-grey, with spots, blotches, and tiny dots of blackish brown and pale grey.

THE SHARP-TAILED PECTORAL SANDPIPER.
(Heteropygia acuminata.)

This species is very like the Pectoral Sandpiper, but has not such a wide breast-band, which is also not so well-defined, while the flanks are plentifully streaked with dusky black. Its home is in North-eastern Siberia, and it migrates in winter to Alaska, Japan, China, and as far south as Australia. It has twice occurred in Norfolk.

THE SHARP-TAILED PECTORAL SANDPIPER.

BONAPARTE'S SANDPIPER.

BONAPARTE'S SANDPIPER.
(Heteropygia fuscicollis.)

This is very like a small Dunlin in appearance, but is distinguished by its shorter bill, which is not longer than the tarsus. The upper tail-coverts are white, and this character suffices to separate Bonaparte's Sandpiper at all ages. It is a common North American species, but has been found accidently in Great Britain about a dozen times. It has occurred as far east as Franz Josef Land, where Mr. F. G. Jackson obtained it.

THE PURPLE SANDPIPER.
(Arquatella maritima.)

The bill is longer than the tarsus in this species, and the latter is not equal to the length of the middle toe. The thigh is feathered right down to the bend of the tarsus. The Purple Sandpiper may nest on the hills of the Shetlands and the moors

THE PURPLE SANDPIPER.

of Northern Scotland, but no authentic instances of its nesting within British limits are known. It breeds, however, in the Arctic Regions of Europe and North-eastern America, and has recently been found nesting in Franz Josef Land by the Jackson-Harmsworth Expedition. It is easily recognised by its black rump and upper tail-coverts, and its white inner secondaries. In the winter plumage, in which the back is sooty black, there is a distinct tinge of purple, from which the bird gets its name. The summer plumage is very dull and has an admixture of rufous on the upper parts. The present species is found on rocky coasts and on the sea-shore, but it does not frequent mud-flats in the manner of a Dunlin. The nest is a depression in the moss, and the eggs are four in number, pear-shaped, like those of the Dunlin, but are larger, and measure about an inch-and-a-half in length.

THE CURLEW-
SANDPIPER.
(*Ancylochilus
subarquatus.*)

The tarsus in this species is longer, and exceeds the length of the middle toe. The bill is slightly curved downwards and is very slender. The Curlew Sandpiper is a regular autumn visitor to all our coasts, and on the return journey in spring a few red-plumaged birds also occur. Although found nearly all over the world in the winter season, the nesting-place of the Curlew Sandpiper remained a mystery until 1897, when Mr. H. L. Popham discovered the eggs at the mouth of the Yenesei. The nest was a depression in the ground and the eggs closely resembled those of the Purple Sandpiper. In its habits the present species is much like a Dunlin, from which it may be distinguished by its white rump and upper tail-coverts. Young birds, which are most frequently met with on our English coasts, have some buff-coloured edges to the feathers of the upper surface, and there is a tinge of buff on the fore-neck and breast.

THE CURLEW-SANDPIPER.

THE KNOT.
(*Tringa canutus.*)

Like the foregoing species, the Knot is rufous in summer, and white underneath in winter, and the young birds are freckled with white margins to the feathers of the upper surface. The bill in the Knot is straight and somewhat widened at the end, and the middle tail-feathers do not protrude beyond the others, so that the tail is square, not pointed as in the Dunlins. The breeding-home of the Knot is in the Arctic Regions, but, although nestlings were procured by Colonel Feilden in Grinnell Land, the eggs are still un-known, though there is one in the British Museum from Greenland, which seems to be fairly well authenticated. It is of an olive stone-colour, blotched and spotted with reddish brown, black and grey; the length is a little over an inch-and-a-half.

THE KNOT.

The Knot migrates in company, and is often associated with Dunlins on the mud-flats. It visits Africa and India, and even Australia in its winter migration, as well as South America, but many remain in more northern haunts and winter on the English coasts.

THE DUNLIN.
(*Pelidna alpina.*)

In these birds the bill is longer than the tarsus, and the tail is graduated and pointed, the centre feathers exceeding the others in length. In summer the Dunlin has a black breast, this being white in winter. It nests on the moors in the South-west and North of England, as also in Scotland and Ireland.

In autumn and winter it is very plentiful on the mud-flats and the shores of all our coasts. It also nests throughout Northern Europe and Northern Asia, as well as in North America, wintering as far south as the West Indies and California, and in the Old World visiting the Mediterranean countries, the Red Sea, and the coasts of India and China.

THE DUNLIN.

Of all our Wading-birds the Dunlin is the most common and easy to observe, and it may be noticed in large flocks on the mud-flats, or on the beach when the tide is full. The nest is a little depression in the ground, with a lining of grass, roots, or moss, and is generally well concealed by overhanging grass or heather. The eggs are four in number, and pear-shaped; they vary in colour from stone-grey or greenish-grey to chocolate, with the usual blotches and spots of reddish-brown, black and grey.

THE
BROAD-BILLED
SANDPIPER.
(*Limicola
platyrhyncha.*)

The peculiar bill of the present species is its best character for distinction, as it has the culmen broad and flat, tapering off into an awl-like tip, which is slightly decurved also; the bill too is rather long (1·3-inch) and exceeds the tarsus (0·8-inch) considerably in length. It is a darker bird than a Dunlin, being mottled with rufous in summer, and having the throat and

THE BROAD-BILLED SANDPIPER.

breast thickly marked with dusky blackish streaks; in winter the under surface of the body is white, with a few dusky streaks on the breast. So far as is known the species has not been noticed in Scotland, and has occurred only once in Ireland, but nearly a dozen specimens have been procured in the eastern and southern counties of England. It breeds in Northern Europe and Siberia, and is found in winter in China, India and in the Mediterranean countries. The nest is placed on a tuft of grass in a bog. The eggs are four in number, and are dark in colour, varying from pinkish-brown to stone or olive-grey, blotched and spotted with chocolate-brown and grey; their length is about an inch-and-a-quarter to nearly an inch-and-a-half.

THE
GREAT SNIPE.
(*Gallinago major.*)

The Snipes and the Woodcocks can be told by the position of the eye, which is placed so far back in the head that the opening of the ear is just below the hinder margin of the eye. Snipes may be distinguished from Woodcocks by the markings on the head being linear, and not transverse, and there are no bars on the primary quills.

The Great Snipe has the outer tail-coverts white, without bars, and the wing-coverts have conspicuous white tips. It has also sixteen tail-feathers instead of

THE COMMON SNIPE.   THE GREAT SNIPE.

fourteen, and has a shorter bill (two-and-a-half inches) than the Common Snipe, though it is a larger and heavier bird than the latter species. It has occurred in every part of the United Kingdom, and a few are shot every autumn. It nests in Northern Europe, as well as in Holland and Northern Germany, as far as the valley of the Yenesei in Siberia, and it winters in Africa. The males congregate in small parties during the nesting-season, like the Ruffs, and are not shy, feeding mostly in the evenings. The nest is a depression in a tuft of grass, with a little moss or dead grass for lining, and the eggs, four in number and pear-shaped, are stone-grey or clay-colour, with strongly marked black blotches, generally clustered round the larger end of the egg. The length varies from an inch-and-three-quarters to nearly two inches.

THE COMMON SNIPE. *(Gallinago gallinago.)* The Common Snipe has a long bill (2·8 inches) and may be recognised by the blackish bars on a rufescent ground on the outer tail-feathers. It nests everywhere in Great Britain in localities suited to its habits, and large numbers visit us in the autumn and winter. It also breeds in northern and temperate Europe, east to Central Asia, and winters in the Mediterranean and Red Seas, as well as in India, Burma, and China. In autumn and winter the Snipe, without being exactly gregarious, is found in considerable numbers in the same marsh, and instances are on record of flocks having been noticed. During the breeding-season the male has a curious habit of 'drumming' in the air, which seems to be a kind of love-song. The nest is a small depression lined with dead grass, and is placed in a tuft of grass or clump of sedge. The eggs are four in number, and are brownish clay-colour or stone-grey with blotches and spots of black, reddish-brown and purplish-grey; the length is about an inch-and-a-half to an inch-and-three-quarters.

SABINE'S SNIPE is only a dark form of the Common Snipe, and occurs not unfrequently.

THE JACK SNIPE *(Limnocryptes gallinula.)* This is a smaller species than the two foregoing ones, and has a blackish wedge-shaped tail, composed of only twelve feathers. The breast-bone is also remarkable for having two notches in its posterior border. The

THE JACK SNIPE. SABINE'S SNIPE.

colour is like that of the other Snipes, but the back is beautifully shot with green and purple. The Jack Snipe has never been found nesting in Great Britain, and is known only as a winter resident. It nests in the high north of Europe and Siberia, migrating to China, India and the Mediterranean countries. In habits it resembles the Common Snipe, but does not utter any note on rising, from which cause it has often been called the 'Dumb' Snipe. The nest is built in marshy bogs: the eggs are four in number, pear-shaped, marked like those of the Common Snipe, and measure from about an inch-and-three-eighths to an inch-and-three-quarters in length.

THE WOODCOCK.
(Scolopax rusticula.)

As already noticed, this species may be distinguished from the Snipes by the transverse markings on the head, and by the notches or bars on the inner web of the primary-quills, which only appear on the secondaries in the young birds. The tail-feathers have a grey band at the tip, which is silvery-whitish underneath.

The Woodcock nests in most of the wooded districts of England, Scotland and Ireland, and a large migration takes place every autumn and spring. It breeds throughout Central and Northern Europe and Asia, as well as in Japan and the Himalayas. The food of the Woodcock consists of worms, for which it probes with its long bill in the ground, feeding chiefly at night. Every evening in the mountains of Alfheim in Norway a Woodcock used to fly from the woods on one side of the lake to feed in a marsh on the other side, and he came each evening exactly at ten o'clock, nor during a whole month did I ever notice a couple

THE WOODCOCK.

of minutes difference in the time of his passing, so that he was as good as a clock to us on our fishing excursions on the lake.

The nest is a depression in the ground, lined with grass and dead leaves. The eggs are four in number, and are more rounded than those of the Snipes, though occasionally pear-shaped. The colour is a clay-brown with reddish-brown and purplish-grey spots. The length is from an inch-and-five-eighths to an inch-and-seven-eighths.

THE GREY PHALAROPE.

THE GREY
PHALAROPE.
(*Crymophilus
fulicarius.*)

The Phalaropes are peculiar little birds and are remarkable for their lobed toes, and for the serrated ridge on the hinder aspect of the tarsus, in both of which characters they resemble the Grebes. In the Grey Phalarope, which, it should be remarked, is only grey in winter and is rufous in summer, the bill is short and does not exceed the tarsus in length; it is somewhat flattened and slightly widened at the end. It is an inhabitant of the Arctic Regions of both Hemispheres, and only visits Great Britain on migration, but occurs sometimes in large numbers. In winter it has been found as far south as the coasts of Chile, the Indian Ocean, and even in the New Zealand seas. The female is a larger bird than the male and does all the courting, the male being left to hatch out the eggs. The nest is a depression in the ground, scantily lined with dry leaves, and the eggs are four in number, very much pointed, and of a dark clay-brown or chocolate, sometimes tinged with olive, and marked with dark brown or blackish spots, and grey underlying spots. They measure about one-and-three-sixteenths to one-and-three-eighths of an inch in length.

THE
RED-NECKED
PHALAROPE.
(*Phalaropus
hyperboreus.*)

The bill is longer in this species, and tapers to a point, while the tarsus exceeds the length of the middle toe and claw. The colour also is different from that of the Grey Phalarope, being slaty-grey above, including the head and hind-neck, with the lower throat bright rufous, as well as the sides of the neck. The Red-necked Phalarope nests in the Orkney and Shetland

THE RED-NECKED PHALAROPE.

Islands, as well as on the Outer Hebrides, but is diminishing in numbers. It also breeds in the north of Europe and Siberia as well as in North America, but does not extend quite so far north as the Grey Phalarope. In winter it is found along the Atlantic coast of America, and also occurs in the Indian Ocean and the Australian Seas. As in the latter species, the male is smaller than the female, and is not so brightly coloured as his mate, and takes her place in the incubation of the eggs and the rearing of the young. The nest is a depression in the ground, lined with fine grass, and is generally placed in the middle of a tuft of grass, close to water. The eggs are smaller than those of the Grey Phalarope and are darker, with blackish blotches all over the surface; the length is a little over an inch-and-a-quarter.

WILSON'S PHALAROPE.

WILSON'S
PHALAROPE.
(*Steganopus tricolor.*)

In this Phalarope the bill is very long and slender, and the tarsus is also long and equals the bill in length. The plumage is more variegated with grey and rufous than in the preceding species. It is an inhabitant of North America, migrating to South America in winter. A specimen is said to have been obtained in Leicestershire.

THE GULLS.—*Order LARIFORMES.*

At first sight a Gull would seem to be different from a Plover in no small degree, but anatomists have shewn that the two groups possess many characters in common, so that it is impossible to draw a wide distinction between them in the Natural System. However much they may be related, there is one character which at once distinguishes the Gulls from the Plovers and Snipes, and that is—the webbed feet of the former. The Gulls have two well-marked Families, viz., the *Laridæ* or Gulls and Terns, and the *Stercorariidæ* or Skuas. The former have no cere at the base of the bill, and have two notches in the hinder end of the breast-bone. The first Sub-family of *Laridæ* consists of the Terns or Sea-Swallows, and the latter differ in their more or less forked tail, and in the shape of the bill, which is usually slight and slender, with the two mandibles nearly equal in length. First of all we have the Marsh-Terns (*Hydrochelidon*), consisting of small species, of wide range in both Hemispheres.

THE BLACK TERN. (*Hydrochelidon nigra.*) This species has the upper surface slaty-grey, and the under surface leaden-black. In winter the under surface is white, as well as the forehead, the hinder crown and nape being black. It can always be distinguished from the other small Marsh-Terns which come to our shores, by the pale grey under wing-coverts, and in winter the rump and tail are grey like the back. The Black Tern formerly bred in the marshes of the eastern counties of England, but now only visits us on migration, many of the young birds being found along our rivers in autumn. It nests in the marshes of Central Europe, as far east as Central Asia, and winters off the coasts of Africa, resorting to the marsh-lands and nesting

THE BLACK TERN.
THE SOOTY TERN.

in colonies. The nest is made of decaying plants and weeds, the eggs being only three in number, varying from deep clay-colour to greenish-grey or buff, with black confluent blotches or spots, and grey underlying spots. The length is about an inch-and-a-half.

THE WHISKERED TERN.
(Hydrochelidon hybrida.)
See p. 195.

An accidental visitor to Great Britain, of which five examples have been recorded from England and one from Ireland. It is a South European species, but it also breeds in Africa and India. It is easily distinguished by its red bill, white chin and sides of face, and white under wing-coverts, as well as by the grey upper and under tail-coverts. In the winter plumage, when it resembles *H. nigra* more closely, it may be told by the deeper incision of the web on the foot. In habits it resembles the Black Tern, and breeds in colonies. The nests float on the water, and are merely platforms of reeds and rushes. The eggs are three in number, of a greenish-grey or clay-colour, with blackish blotches and scribblings; their length is from an inch-and-three-eighths to an inch-and-five-eighths.

THE WHITE-WINGED BLACK TERN.
(Hydrochelidon leucoptera.)

THE WHITE-WINGED BLACK TERN.

This species has the under surface of the body and the under wing-coverts black, and it is easily told by the white upper tail-coverts and tail, and by the patch of white along the carpal bend of the wing. In winter the white tail still distinguishes the species, but young birds are more difficult to tell, though they always show some white on the rump. It has occurred many times on the southern and eastern coasts of England, as well as in Ireland. It breeds throughout the marshes of Southern Europe and Central Asia, as well as in Africa. In habits, nest and eggs, the species resembles the other Marsh Terns.

THE GULL-BILLED TERN.
(Gelochelidon anglica.)

As will be gathered from its name, this Tern has a very stout bill, like that of a Gull. The tail is short, and decidedly forked, and the tarsus is long, exceeding the length of the middle toe and claw. The Gull-billed Tern is a common bird in Southern Europe and even nests as far north as Denmark, and it is also found breeding in China, Australia and North America. It has been taken in England on several occasions. It feeds on small fish and frogs, as well as on grasshoppers and other insects. The nest is a hollow in the sand, lined

THE WHISKERED TERN.   THE GULL-BILLED TERN.

with a little sea-weed or dead grass, and the eggs are two or three in number, pale stone-buff with a slight olive tinge, spotted all over with blackish and grey, but not so as to form blotches ; the length is from an inch-and-three-quarters to two-inches-and-a-half, so that there is great variation in the size of the eggs.

THE CASPIAN TERN. (*Hydroprogne caspia.*) This species measures nineteen inches in length, and is recognised by its large size and by its red bill. It has occurred several times off the southern and eastern coasts of England, and it breeds in the Island of Sylt and in the Mediterranean, as well as on the Indian and Australian coasts. It also nests in North America. This large species feeds almost entirely on fish, and is a bird of powerful flight, making a great demonstration in defence of its nest. The latter is only a depression in the sand, with a few shells or bents of grass for lining. The eggs are two or three in number, greyish-buff or stone-buff, with markings of chocolate-brown or blackish, not forming blotches. Their length is from two-and-a-quarter to two-and-a-half inches.

THE CASPIAN TERN.

THE
COMMON TERN.
(Sterna fluviatilis)

The members of the genus *Sterna* all have a very slender and pointed bill, and a long and forked tail. The tarsus is short, and is less than the length of the middle toe and claw. The Common Tern is of a pearl-grey colour above, white underneath, with a black cap; the bill is coral-red, tipped with black. In winter the head is white with the hinder crown more or less black. Young birds may be told by a dark grey band along the wing-coverts; otherwise they resemble the winter plumage of the adults. The species breeds as far north as the Isle of Skye on the west, and the Moray Firth on the east of Scotland, its place being taken to the northward by the Arctic Tern. It is also found nesting on the islands off most of the coasts of Ireland as well as on inland lakes in many of the counties. It nests in most parts

THE ARCTIC TERN.   THE COMMON TERN.

of Europe, both on the coast and on inland lakes, and is also found through Central Asia to Cashmere and Thibet. It also breeds throughout temperate North America as far south as Texas. In winter it is found in Brazil and on the coasts of Africa and India.

The food of this species consists principally of small fish, for which it hunts in company, continually dipping into the water with a graceful flight, which has gained for the birds the name of 'Sea-Swallows.' They also nest in company on the shingle, making a depression in the sand. The eggs are three in number, rarely four, varying from stone-colour to ochreous-buff or rufous brown, with black spots and markings, more or less distinct according to the light or dark colour of the egg: the length is an inch-and-a-half to an inch-and-three-quarters.

THE
ARCTIC TERN.
(Sterna macrura.)
See p. 196.

A slightly smaller species than the Common Tern, and having the bill entirely coral-red without any black tip. The tarsus is shorter than in the last-named species and does not exceed the length of the middle toe without the claw. The wings reach to the tip of the tail and the latter does not exceed them. The black cap is only assumed during summer, and the winter plumage resembles that of the Common Tern. It is a maritime species and is rather more northerly in its nesting-range than the Common Tern, and replaces that species in the north of Scotland; it also breeds in Ireland along with *S. fluviatilis.* It nests in the high north of both the Old and New Worlds, and in winter occurs on the coasts of South America and Africa.

In habits the Arctic Tern does not differ from its ally, and the nest is a depression in the shingle or moss, with a little dead grass for a lining in the latter situation. The eggs are very similar to those of the Common Tern, but are often more spotted; they measure one-inch-and-three-eighths to one-inch-and-three-quarters in length.

THE ROSEATE TERN.   THE SANDWICH TERN.

THE
ROSEATE TERN.
(Sterna dougalli.)

The slender and graceful form of this Sea-Swallow, with the black bill, orange only at the base of the mandible, and the rosy blush on the breast, distinguish the species from its allies. The inner webs of the primaries are also white up to the tips. The Roseate Tern used to breed in several localities in England and Ireland, but of late years its nesting places have become more restricted, though it occasionally nests on the Farnes and on the coast of Wales. It breeds in many parts of North America and in certain localities in Europe and in the Indian Ocean as well as in Northern Australia. It is also found in many of the southern seas in winter. In habits it resembles the other Terns and makes a similar depression in the sand for the reception of its eggs, which are only two in number; they are a little larger than those of the Common Tern, and measure from an inch-and-a-half to an inch-and-seven-eighths.

THE SANDWICH TERN.
(*Sterna cantiaca.*)

The present species is larger than the other species of *Sterna*, and is recognised by its black feet and bill, the latter having a yellow tip. The head is crested, the feathers being pointed and so forming a crest. The Sandwich Tern is a summer visitor to Great Britain, and still breeds in a few places where it is protected, but many of its old nesting-haunts are no longer frequented. It breeds throughout Southern Europe and the Caspian Sea, as well as in Eastern North America. In winter it is found along the African coasts and those of the Indian Ocean, as well as off Central America. The nest is a depression in the sand, and is sometimes lined with bents. The eggs are two, seldom three, in number, clay-coloured, and generally boldly blotched with black. They measure two to two-and-a-half inches in length.

THE SMALLER SOOTY TERN.

THE SMALLER SOOTY TERN.
(*Sterna anaestheta.*)

The upper surface in this species is sooty black, with a white forehead and a black streak through the lores; the mantle is somewhat more grey than the head or back. The young birds are quite different from those of other Terns, being of an uniform sooty colour with white or rufous tips to the feathers. The species inhabits the seas of the Tropics on both sides of the Atlantic, and is found also in the Indian and Pacific Oceans. One specimen is said to have been caught at the mouth of the Thames in September, 1875. This Tern lays its single egg in the fissure of a rock or in holes of the coral sandstone.

THE SOOTY TERN.
(*Sterna fuliginosa.*)
See p. 193.

This Tern is exactly like the foregoing, but is a larger bird, and has the web of the foot more fully developed and not so much excised as in that species. It is generally distributed over the southern oceans, and has occurred in England on three occasions. It nests in enormous numbers on Ascension Island and on other islands such as Laysan and also on the islands of Torres' Straits. The single egg is laid on the sand or among the fissures of volcanic or coral rocks.

THE LITTLE TERN.
(*Sterna minuta.*)

The small size and the yellow bill, tipped with black, serve to distinguish the Little Tern from its allies. It nests throughout the greater part of Europe and Central Asia, and is found along the coasts of the African and Indian Oceans in winter. It breeds in scattered colonies on most of the shores of the British Islands. The habits of the Little Tern resemble those of its larger brethren, and the nest is a depression in the sand, though in some places it is surrounded by a ring of shells. The eggs measure a little over an inch-and-a quarter, but never reach an inch-and-a-half in length. The eggs are two, seldom three, in number, of a light buff or clay-brown, with the blackish markings distributed over the egg and seldom forming blotches.

THE LITTLE TERN.

THE NODDY TERN.

THE
NODDY TERN.
(*Anous stolidus.*)

The uniform chocolate-brown colour and the grey crown render the Noddy easily recognisable. Two specimens have been obtained in Ireland, but the species inhabits the tropical seas, where it nests on many of the islands in large numbers, the nest being placed on the ground or on the top of a small bush: it is made of sea-weed and is nearly flat on the top. There is only one egg, similar to that of the Sooty Tern, but distinguished from the egg of that bird by the green colour inside when held up to the light; the length is from two inches to two-and-three-eighths.

SABINE'S
GULL.
(*Xema sabinii.*)

Sabine's Gull belongs to the group of fork-tailed Gulls. It is a beautiful little bird, of a grey colour above, which extends over the throat, and is separated from the white breast by a black

SABINE'S GULL.

British Birds.

collar; the bill is black with a yellow tip, and there is a ring of bright vermilion round the eye. The specimens of Sabine's Gull which occur off our coasts are mostly young birds, but at least two adult ones have also been secured. Its nesting-home is in the Arctic regions, and it breeds throughout North America, from Baffin Bay to Alaska, as well as in the high north of Eastern Siberia. The habits of this species are said to be very like those of a Tern, but it also frequents the beaches, and runs with great swiftness, so that it can be easily mistaken for a Wading-bird. It nests in company, and the two eggs are laid on the ground or on a few blades of grass. The colour of the eggs is unmistakable among those of the Gulls, being of a very dark olive-brown with indistinct spots and blotches of reddish-brown and grey; the length is from an inch-and-five-eighths to an inch-and-seven-eighths.

THE WEDGE-TAILED GULL. *(Rhodostethia rosea.)* In breeding plumage Ross's Gull, as this species is generally called, is of a light pearly grey, with the tail, underparts, and head and neck white, with a black collar round the latter. On the breast there is at first a lovely rosy blush, which

THE WEDGE-TAILED GULL.

fades in preserved specimens: it is less pronounced in winter, when the black collar is also absent. In young birds there is a black band at the end of the tail, and there is a black patch behind the eye.

Ross's Gull breeds in the Arctic regions, and Dr. Nansen found its nesting-haunts on some islands in Lat. 80° 38′ N, Long. 63 E. It has been noticed in Greenland and many other places in the high north, and has been seen abundantly on migration at Point Barrow in the autumn. A single specimen has been said to have been procured in Yorkshire. The nest has not yet been described, but an egg ascribed to this species is in the British Museum; it resembles that of Sabine's Gull, but is a little larger: length an inch-and-seven-eighths.

THE LITTLE GULL. *(Larus minutus.)* The small size of this pretty little Gull is the best character for its recognition, as it is only about ten-and-a-half inches in length. It has a black cap in summer, but in winter the head is white, with the hinder crown slaty-grey, and a blackish patch behind the eye. The young birds resemble the winter plumage of the adults, but have a black band at the end of the tail. The species

occasionally visits our shores in some
numbers, and occurs nearly every
autumn and winter. It breeds on the
lakes of Northern and Central Russia,
the nest being on the marshy ground,
and composed of leaves, grass and
sedge. The eggs are three or four
in number, and are like those of the
Common Tern: they measure from
an inch-and-a-half to an inch-and-
three-quarters in length.

THE LITTLE GULL.
BONAPARTE'S GULL.

**THE GREAT
BLACK-HEADED
GULL.**
(Larus ichthyaetus.)
See p. 202.

This large
Gull, which
measures about
two - and - a - half
feet in length, is
easily distin-
guished by its size from all the other
Hooded Gulls. It is an inhabitant
of South-eastern Russia and Central
Asia, and a summer-plumaged individual was shot near Exmouth in
May or June, 1859. The changes of
plumage are similar to those under-
gone by the smaller Hooded Gulls.

**THE
MEDITERRANEAN
BLACK-HEADED
GULL.**
(Larus melanocephalus.)
See p. 202.

The bright
coral-red bill
of this species, contrasting with the black head, distinguishes
it from the allied Hooded Gulls. The back is light pearly
grey. The young birds may be told by the black on
both sides of the shaft of the second and third primary.
The species inhabits the countries of the Mediterranean and
the Black Sea, and has twice been shot in England, once on Breydon Broad, near
Yarmouth, and once at Barking; both specimens occurred in winter.

**BONAPARTE'S
GULL.**
(Larus philadelphia.)

This North-American species has been noted about half a
dozen times in Great Britain, specimens having been shot in
Ireland and Scotland as well as in England. It has a black
bill, and the hood is of a leaden black, and in the young birds
there is no black on the inner margin of the shaft of the third primary, and very
little on the inner web of the first and second. Bonaparte's Gull breeds in colonies
on the lakes of the interior of North America and makes a nest of sticks in a tree.

The eggs are three or four in number, olive-brown or dark clay-brown, with markings of reddish brown and dusky-grey. Their length is from an inch-and-three-quarters to a little over two inches.

THE GREAT BLACK-HEADED GULL.

THE BLACK-HEADED GULL.
THE MEDITERRANEAN BLACK-HEADED GULL.

THE BLACK HEADED GULL.
(Larus ridibundus.)

This species has a dark brown hood in summer, but in winter the head is white, with the hinder crown greyish, while there is a dusky spot in front of the eye and another behind the ear-coverts. There is often a distinct rosy tinge on the white under surface of the body. The species nests in colonies in many parts of the United Kingdom, generally in marshy places, or on islands in lakes, very seldom on rocks or near the sea-shore. It is found nesting in similar localities throughout temperate Europe and Asia. In the autumn and winter these Gulls are found frequenting the coasts, and often ascend rivers. They are now quite a common object on the Thames and on the waters of the London parks. It is a tame species, and may often be seen, in the north of England, following the plough. The nests are built on the ground, but are often floating on the water or supported by water-plants. The eggs are two or three in number, and vary greatly in their colour, some being greenish-blue with scarcely any spots, while others are of such a dark brown that the blackish markings can scarcely be seen. The length is about two to two-and-a-quarter inches.

THE GREAT BLACK-BACKED GULL.

THE GREAT BLACK-BACKED GULL.
(Larus marinus.)

This is the largest species of British Gull, and is easily distinguished by its dimensions. The black back and white head, as well as the large white tip to the first primary are also characters by which it may be told, while the large size of the bill and the length of the wing (exceeding nineteen inches) will determine young birds in their brown plumage from those of any other British species. The Black-backed Gull breeds in certain parts of our southern and south-western coasts, but is more common in Scotland and Ireland. It is a very powerful bird, and a great destroyer of the eggs and young of other species. The nest is generally a rough structure of grass and sea-weed on the summit of a bare rock on an islet, but on the Smölen Islands in North Norway I found one in the midst of the moss and ling on the top of a green islet, and in this case the nest was rather more elaborately made. Eggs, two or three, measuring about three inches in length, of a clay-brown or stone-colour, with spots of reddish-brown or black, and underlying grey markings.

THE LESSER BLACK-BACKED GULL.
(Larus fuscus.)

This species has a black or greyish-black back, so that it resembles the Great Black-backed Gull in this respect, but it is a much smaller bird and has yellow, instead of flesh-coloured, feet. It is found in summer breeding locally throughout the British Islands, and at that season is also generally distributed on the coasts of Northern Europe, as far east as the Dwina and as far south as the Mediterranean, where it also breeds. In winter it visits West Africa, the Red Sea and the Persian Gulf. I have seen considerable migrations of this species off the coast of Norway, which it passes about the end of May, proceeding northward by day in flocks of from twenty to two hundred in number. The nest is like that of other Gulls, a rough structure of grass and sea-weed, and the eggs are three or four in number, of a darker tint than those of *L. marinus* : they measure about two-and-three-quarter inches in length.

THE ICELAND GULL.　　　　　　　THE LESSER BLACK-BACKED GULL.

THE HERRING-GULL.
(Larus argentatus.)

This beautiful Gull is nearly as large as *L. marinus*, but is recognised at once by its pearly-grey back. The bill is not nearly so large as that of the Great Black-backed Gull, and the dimensions will generally serve to identify the young birds in their brown plumage. It breeds in Northern Europe, west of the White Sea, and also in North America, and it is found nesting throughout Great Britain in places suited to its habits, but it is everywhere a marine species and does not nest inland. In winter it migrates south to the Mediterranean Sea and in America as far as the West Indies. Like the other big Gulls, the present species is a great robber of

THE HERRING GULL.

other birds' eggs, but it is sometimes seen inland feeding with other Gulls on worms and grain. The nest is placed on the rocks or on the slope of a cliff, often in company with those of *L. fuscus*, and the eggs are so similar to those of the latter species, as to be practically indistinguishable: they measure from a little over two-and-a-half to three inches in length.

THE COMMON GULL.
(*Larus canus.*)

This is a miniature of the Herring Gull, with a white head and a pearly-grey back, but it is much smaller than the latter species. The Common Gull nests in Scotland and Ireland, and it is found breeding in the North of Europe and Asia as far as Kamtchatka, migrating south in winter. In the islands of Northern Norway I have found this Gull very plentiful, and it is a beautiful sight to see the islets dotted with these snow-white birds, while the clamour which they make when any one lands on their domain is indescribable. Their cries are so varied that I found

THE COMMON GULL.

it impossible to make any attempt to express them in words. Some of the notes are quite musical, while others consist of a harsh scream. The nest is seldom placed at any height on the rocks, but generally at a low level, near the shore, a scanty collection of dead grass or sea-weed forming the nests in a little patch of grass between the low-lying rocks. Sometimes they are found on the shores of inland fresh-water lakes, and the Common Gull has been also known to utilize the deserted nest of a Crow or other bird in a tree. The eggs are three in number and vary considerably in ground-colour, but the markings are like those of other Gulls.

THE GLAUCOUS GULL.

THE GLAUCOUS GULL.
(*Larus hyperboreus.*)

This is a large species of Gull with a white head and tail, and is especially distinguished by its white primaries. It is a winter visitor to Great Britain and occurs mostly in the northern parts of our area. It is found in the Arctic regions of both Hemispheres during the breeding season, and migrates south in winter. In habits the species resembles the Great Black-backed Gull, and like that bird is a great robber, feeding on fish, crustacea and also on young birds, as well as on offal or anything it can pick up. The nest is a depression in the sand, lined with sea-weed, and the eggs, which are three in number, have no especial characteristic to distinguish them from the eggs of other Gulls, and they look like large editions of eggs of the Lesser Black-backed Gull. The length is about three inches.

THE ICELAND GULL.
(*Larus leucopterus.*)
See p. 204.

This species has white quills like the Glaucous Gull, but is smaller (wing 16·5 inches). It visits Great Britain in the winter, but occurs principally off the coasts of Scotland, occasionally in some numbers. It nests in Greenland, and wanders south in winter to Great Britain and the shores of Norway and the Baltic Sea. In its habits it is more like the Herring-Gull than the Great Black-backed Gull, and is not so active a bird as the latter. The nest is a depression in the

THE IVORY GULL.

ground or on a rock, and the eggs are two or three in number, rather smaller than those of the Glaucous Gull, and measuring two inches-and-a-quarter to nearly three inches in length.

THE IVORY GULL. (*Pagophila eburnea.*) This is a truly Arctic species and is clothed in snowy plumage throughout, in the adult birds, the young ones having some spots of greyish

black. It usually occurs in the British Islands in winter only, and thirty specimens have been captured, the greater number of which have been taken in Scotland. The Ivory Gull nests in the Arctic regions of both Hemispheres, and wanders south in winter as far as New Brunswick in America, and the coasts of Britain and France in Europe. Its flight is described as being more like that of a Tern than a Gull. In Franz Josef Land Mr. F. G. Jackson tells me that he found it breeding in crowds near Cape Mary Harmsworth, the nest being merely a depression in the moss. The eggs are greyish-brown with blackish spots, and do not exceed two in number. Their length is from two-and-one-fifth inches to two-and-two-fifths.

THE KITTIWAKE. (*Rissa tridactyla.*) It is easy to distinguish the Kittiwake from all the other British Gulls by the absence of its hind toe. It breeds in great numbers on many of the headlands of Great Britain: it also nests in the extreme Arctic Regions, and it appears to be distributed over the north of both the Old and the New Worlds. It wanders south in winter as far as the Mediterranean Sea, and down both the Atlantic and Pacific coasts of America. In the cold season it is often found in large numbers off

THE KITTIWAKE.

the coasts of Norway, but at a considerable distance out at sea. The nest is of turf or sea-weed and generally placed on the ledge of a cliff, but sometimes on the top of a rocky islet, and in America the birds are occasionally found not making any nest at all. The eggs vary considerably in ground-colour, from the ordinary Gull-like type to white or bluish, with dark spots and markings. The length is about two inches and a quarter.

RICHARDSON'S SKUA.   THE GREAT SKUA.

**THE
GREAT SKUA.**
*(Megalestris
catarrhactes.)*

The Skuas are Gulls of sombre coloration, and they are distinguished from the true *Laridæ* by having a 'cere' at the base of the bill, as in a Bird of Prey, while the claws are extremely sharp and curved, and resemble those of the last-named birds. This is a larger bird than any of the other Skuas which occur in Great Britain, and has a square tail instead of prolonged central tail-feathers.

Though formerly not so rare, the Great Skua has become almost extinct in Britain, and only two colonies now exist within our limits. These are in the Shetlands, where the birds are protected, so that we may hope that the species will still survive as an indigenous British bird. It also breeds on the Faeroes and in Iceland, and is occasionally found in winter as far south as the Mediterranean, but it is everywhere becoming a scarce bird, owing to the persecution which follows it on account of its predatory habits. It is very bold and fearless, defending its eggs and young with vigour. The nest is a hollow in the moss, and the eggs, which are never more than two in number, are dark chocolate or olive-brown, with reddish brown or black spots. Length from two-inches-and-a-half to nearly three inches.

The only difference of importance between the **Great Skua** and the three smaller species which follow consists in the elongation of the centre tail-feathers. The Pomatorhine Skua is the largest of the three, and the middle tail feathers project for about four inches beyond the others, and are vertically twisted. It is not so active a bird as Richardson's or Buffon's Skua, and

THE POMATORHINE SKUA.
(Stercorarius pomatorhinus)

is generally said to be less brave than those two birds. The present species breeds in the tundra of the Arctic Regions of both Hemispheres, and only visits Great Britain in winter. The nests are simply depressions in the moss, and the eggs are of the usual dark brown type of those of Skuas, being deep clay-brown or olive-brown, with reddish or blackish-brown spots. They measure about two inches-and-a-half to two inches-and-three-quarters in length.

THE POMATORHINE SKUA.

RICHARDSON'S SKUA.
(Stercorarius crepidatus.)

This species has the centre tail-feathers long and tapering, and projecting quite three inches beyond the others. It has two phases, which are white-breasted or sooty-breasted in colour, and the latter is generally considered to be a melanistic phase of the white-breasted form. In the high north the dark-coloured bird is scarcely known, but in parts of Norway and in the north of Scotland, both light and dark forms occur nearly in equal numbers, and often pair together. Richardson's Skua is a very active and agile bird, and harries the Terns and small Gulls to make them disgorge their prey. For this reason they are not loved by their relations, and are regarded with suspicion by other species, whose eggs they will try to carry off. I have seen the normally peaceful Oyster-catcher attack one of these Skuas and give it such a buffeting that it was glad at last to clear off. The nest is a depression in the moss on the summit of a low island, and the eggs, two in number, are dark chocolate, with brown or blackish spots, grey underlying spots being also distinct. The length is from two inches-and-a-quarter to two inches-and-a-half.

BUFFON'S SKUA.
(Stercorarius parasiticus.)

Very similar to the preceding species, but always much greyer in appearance, and further distinguished by the length of the centre tail-feathers which sometimes attain the length of nine inches: only the two outer primary quills have white shafts,

14

whereas all the primaries of *S. crepidatus* are white-shafted. Buffon's Skua breeds in the Arctic Regions of both Hemispheres, and migrates southward in winter, when it occurs at intervals on the coasts of Britain. The habits, as well as the nest and eggs, do not seem to vary from those of the preceding species. The eggs measure about two inches in length.

BUFFON'S SKUA.

THE AUKS.
Sub-Order
ALCÆ.

The Auks are inhabitants of the northern portions of the Old and New Worlds, but although very similar to the Gulls as regards their anatomy and osteology, they are quite different in external appearance, as well as in their method of nidification.

THE RAZOR-BILL.

THE RAZOR-BILL.
(*Alca torda.*)

This species is at once told by the white groove which ornaments its bill, and by its exposed nostrils. The general plumage is black in summer, and the throat is black with the rest of the under surface of the body white, as well as the tips of the secondary-quills and a small streak across the lores to the eye. In winter, the throat and sides of the face become white like the breast, and there is a line of black above the ear-coverts, while the bill still retains the white grooves. In the young birds, however, these are not seen in winter. The Razor-Bill is an inhabitant of the rocky coasts of Northern Europe and the Atlantic side of North America. It nests in suitable places throughout Britain, but is more plentiful in the north, and is principally found on our southern coasts in winter. It is a gregarious bird at all times of the year, and like the Puffins and Guillemots obtains its food by fishing. It lays but a single egg in a crevice of a rock, or on a bare shelf of the latter. The ground colour of the egg is white, and it is generally very handsomely blotched with rufous. It is not so pear-shaped as that of the Guillemot, and is rather smaller than the egg of the latter bird.

THE GREAT AUK.
(*Plautus impennis.*)

The Great Auk is no longer a British bird, as there can be no doubt that it is now entirely extinct. In form it was like a gigantic Razor-Bill, but had such small wings that it was not able to fly. It used to nest on St. Kilda, and some of the last examples recorded were found near the Orkneys, but in former times it must have extended further to the south, and also to Ireland, as is proved by the discovery of fossil remains. About seventy specimens of its eggs are preserved in different Museums of the world, and they go through the same extent of variation as those of the Razor-Bill, which they resemble in colour and markings, though they are, of course, much larger. The range of the Great Auk was never very extensive, as it seems to have occurred only from the north of Scotland to Iceland and the latitude of Newfoundland on the Atlantic coast of North America.

THE GREAT AUK.

THE COMMON GUILLEMOT. (*Uria troile.*) *See p. 212.*

Guillemots are distinguished from the Razor-bills by their long pointed bill, which has also no grooves. The colour is not so black as in the latter birds and is more of a smoky brown, but otherwise the species are very similar. It inhabits the seas of Northern and Western Europe and the Atlantic coast of America. In Great Britain it inhabits the same rocky districts as the Razor-Bill, but breeds in greater numbers than the latter bird, which it resembles in its habits. It is to a certain degree migratory, and disappears from its breeding-places as soon as the young are able to look after themselves. One pear-shaped egg only is laid on the bare rock, and the variation in colour is so great that there is no possibility of giving an exact description of the egg, as it may be white, green, buff, or bluish, with scanty markings or dense scribblings and blotches of black or rufous. The length is from three inches to three inches-and-a-half.

THE BRIDLED GUILLEMOT. (*Uria ringvia.*) *See p. 212.*

This bird only differs from the Common Guillemot in having a white eye-ring and a white line along the crease which skirts the upper edge of the ear-coverts. By many naturalists it is considered to be only a variety of the Common Guillemot, as both forms occur together. Its occurrence is too frequent, however, to make me think that this can be the case, though there is no difference in habits or nidification between the two forms, as far as is known.

14°

BRÜNNICH'S
GUILLEMOT.
(*Uria lomvia.*)

This species has quite a differently shaped bill from the Common Guillemot and might almost be generically separated: it is much stouter and has an enamelled appearance near the gape. The colour, too, is different from that of *U. troile*, as the throat and sides of the face and neck are of a chocolate-brown colour, which contrasts with the black of the upper surface   It is only an occasional winter visitor to Great Britain, being an inhabitant of the Arctic Regions, nesting in Spitsbergen and Greenland, as well as on the Pacific side of North America. The single egg is laid on the shelves of rock, and is subject to great variation in colour. In habits the species resembles the Common Guillemot.

1- The Common Guillemot.   2 The Bridled Guillemot.   3—Brünnich's Guillemot.
4 -The Black Guillemot.

THE BLACK
GUILLEMOT.
(*Cepphus grylle.*)

This is a much smaller bird than the preceding, and has a smaller bill. The summer and winter plumages are also very distinct, though it would appear that very old birds retain their black dress throughout the winter season. It can always be distinguished by its bright coral-red feet. Young birds are at first white-breasted, and when the black dress has been donned, they can always be told by the black ends to the wing coverts, these being always pure white in a fully adult bird. The Black Guillemot breeds in the north of Scotland and in Ireland, and is found on the coasts of Northern Europe, the Faeroes and Southern Greenland. It is generally seen in pairs, but occasionally small parties may be observed, even during the breeding-season. The eggs are two in number, and are generally placed in a narrow cleft of rock at some distance from the opening, so that they are by no means easy to reach. There is no nest, and the eggs, which measure from two to two-and-a-half-inches in length, are white with black spots and underlying purplish-grey blotches or spots.

THE
LITTLE AUK.
(*Alle alle.*)

The small size of the Little Auk is its most distinguishing character, as it does not exceed seven-and-a-half-inches in length. It is black, with a white breast, and with the flanks streaked with black, while the scapulars have white edgings and the secondaries white tips. It may probably breed on some of the Hebrides but is principally a winter visitor to Great Britain. Its home is in the Arctic Regions where it is a common bird, occurring in flocks of many thousands together. Unlike other Auks, it is a noisy species, and breeds in cliffs, laying a single egg, which is greenish-white without any markings, and measures about two inches in length.

THE PUFFIN.

THE LITTLE AUK.

THE PUFFIN.
(*Fratercula
artica.*)

This species is often called the 'Sea-Parrot' from its large, but not in any way Parrot-like, bill. The latter differs, however, remarkably from the long thin bill of the Guillemots, and is not only very deep and compressed, but in the breeding-season it has grooves arranged in a series of plates, and a blue wattle above the eye, all of which are shed or moulted in the autumn, just as an ordinary bird moults its feathers. On most of the rocky coasts of the United Kingdom the Puffin breeds, even on those of the south-west of England, where it is abundant on some of the islands. It is also found breeding on the Atlantic coast in North-eastern America, as well as in various localities in Western Europe down to the coast of Portugal. Its food consists of small fish, and the lancelet is a favourite prey. In some of its northern haunts it nests simply in thousands, but, unlike the Guillemot, the single egg is deposited in a burrow, or in the cleft of a rock. It is white, with a few spots of pale brown and grey: the latter are the underlying markings and are frequently more pronounced than the brown ones. The length is from two inches-and-a-quarter to two inches-and-a-half.

THE PETRELS.—*Order* PROCELLARIIFORMES.

PETRELS may always be distinguished from Gulls, which many of them resemble in appearance, by their tubular nostrils. The Order contains a number of species, mostly inhabitants of the southern or tropical seas. But few species breed in the north, and, therefore, most of our Petrels are rare or occasional visitors.

THE TRUE STORM-PETRELS. *Sub-family* PROCELLARIINÆ.

The members of this Sub-family are small black birds, and are distinguished by having the nostrils united above the ridge of the bill. The secondary quills are thirteen in number, and the claws are sharp and compressed.

THE STORM-PETREL. (*Procellaria pelagica.*)

The Storm-Petrel is recognised by its rounded or even tail. It is sooty-black, with the rump and upper tail-coverts white, the latter tipped with black. It breeds on the islands off the coasts of Wales and Scotland, as well as in similar localities in Ireland, where some large colonies are known to nest. The single white egg is laid in holes of rocks or burrows, with a few blades of grass for a nest, and many birds are found breeding in close proximity.

THE STORM-PETREL.

The Storm-Petrel does not venture forth from its burrow during the day-time, but is very active at night. The egg measures a little more than an inch in length, and is white, with a thin sprinkling of tiny reddish-brown spots, sometimes forming a zone round the larger end.

BULWER'S PETREL.   WILSON'S PETREL.   THE FORK-TAILED PETREL.

THE FORK-TAILED STORM-PETREL.
(Oceanodroma leucorrhoa.)

The distinguishing character of 'Leach's Petrel,' as this species is often called, is the forked tail. It is a larger bird than the Storm Petrel, and has a short tarsus, which is not so long as the middle toe and claw. It breeds on the islands off the west of Scotland, the outer Hebrides and St. Kilda, and has been known to nest in Ireland on the Blasquet Isles, off the coast of Kerry. Its range extends throughout the temperate seas of the Northern Hemisphere, and in winter it wanders southwards. On St. Kilda Leach's Petrel makes a slight nest of dry grass, and lays a single egg, which is white with a zone of minute lilac-coloured dots, and measures about an inch-and-a-half in length.

THE MADEIRA STORM-PETREL.
(Oceanodroma castro.)

This species, which is an inhabitant of the tropical seas, has been found on one occasion in England, a single specimen having been picked up dead on the beach at Littlestone, in Kent, in December, 1895. This specimen is now in the collection of Mr. Boyd Alexander. The species is not uncommon in Madeira and the neighbouring islands, and has been

THE WHITE-BELLIED STORM-PETREL.   THE MADEIRA STORM-PETREL.

found in St. Helena, and also on the Galápagos and Hawaiian Islands in the Pacific Ocean. It has a forked tail like Leach's Petrel, but is black, and the upper tail-coverts are tipped with black, while the outer tail-feathers are white at the base. The habits are doubtless similar to those of the other Storm-Petrels, and the single egg is laid in the crevice of a rock. It is white with a zone of reddish spots round the larger end.

THE FLAT-CLAWED STORM-PETRELS. *Sub-famile* OCEANITIDIN.E.

The secondaries in this group are only ten in number, and the claws are flattened instead of being sharp and compressed. But one species has been found in British waters, viz., Wilson's Petrel, *Oceanitis oceanicus*, which is easily recognised from the other small Black Petrels by the yellow webs between its toes. It occurs sometimes in considerable numbers off our south-western coasts, and its habitat extends over the greater portion of the southern seas, but it is not known from the American side of the Pacific Ocean. The single white egg, with the usual zone of reddish dots, is laid in the crevice of a rock or under a boulder; it measures about an inch-and-a-quarter in length.

THE WHITE-BELLIED STORM PETREL. *(Pelagodroma marina.)*

The White-bellied Storm-Petrel differs in its light coloration from the rest of the Storm-Petrels, and has the claws very broad and flattened. It has twice been found within our limits, once on the Lancashire coasts in November, and once in the island of Colonsay in January. It has a wide range in the tropical seas. Mr. Ogilvie Grant found it breeding in the Salvage Islands, and obtained several of the eggs, which were placed at the end of a burrow. No nest is made, and the single egg is white, with tiny spots of reddish or purplish-brown, either sprinkled all over the surface or collected in a zone round the larger end. The length is nearly an inch-and-a-half.

THE SHEARWATERS. *Family* PUFFINID.E.

The Shearwaters are larger birds than any of the foregoing species of Petrel, and differ from them in several well-marked osteological characters. The family consists of the Fulmars and Shearwaters, the former having distinct lamellæ on the sides of the palate. One species of true Fulmar is found in Great Britain.

THE FULMAR. *(Fulmarus glacialis.)*

In appearance the Fulmar very much resembles a grey Gull, but it can of course be easily distinguished by its tubular nostril, which shows that it is a Petrel. Although its grey and white coloration is that of a Gull, its yellow bill and bluish feet ought to make identification easy, in addition to the character of the nostrils noted above. Its nesting places in Great Britain are confined to the Shetlands and the Hebrides, the chief breeding place being apparently on St. Kilda. It also nests in Spitsbergen and the other northern islands, to Iceland, and Greenland. In its flight the Fulmar resembles a Gull, and it has also the Gull-like habit of following a steamer for

THE CAPPED PETREL.   THE FULMAR.

whatever scraps it can pick up, and it is thus a frequent attendant on whaling-ships. The single white egg is laid in a crevice or on the shelf of a rock, or sometimes in an excavation in the grassy turf. The egg is about two-and-three-quarter inches in length, or from that to three inches.

A single specimen of this tropical species has been recorded

THE CAPE FULMAR.
(Daption capensis.)

from Ireland, but it is said to have been captured on three occasions off the coast of France. It is principally known as an inhabitant of the Southern Ocean, where it is very common. It resorts to rocky islands to breed, and lays its egg on the ledges of cliffs, but the egg has not yet been described: it is doubtless white. The species is easily recognised by its black and white spotted plumage.

THE CAPE FULMAR.

THE GREAT SHEARWATER.
(Puffinus gravis.)

The Shearwaters show no lamellæ on the side of the palate, and they form a distinct Sub-family from the Fulmars, from which they also differ in their longer and more slender bills. The Great Shearwater is a brown bird with

THE GREAT SHEARWATER.   THE SOOTY SHEARWATER.

white tips to the long upper tail-coverts. It is white below, with a patch of sooty-brown in the centre of the abdomen. The length of the bird is over nineteen inches, and the wing twelve-and-a-half inches. The tail is short and rounded, and not wedge-shaped as in some of the other members of the genus. It is found throughout the greater part of the Atlantic Ocean, and visits Ireland and the western coasts of England and Scotland, sometimes in considerable numbers. It is generally seen in pairs, but sometimes in small flocks, and it will feed on almost anything, while it is also an expert diver. Authentic details of the nesting of the species are still wanting.

THE MANX SHEARWATER.
(*Puffinus puffinus.*)

This species belongs to the smaller section of the genus *Puffinus*, the general colour of whose upper surface is black, including the head and neck. The under surface is white, including the under tail-coverts, the latter having only a little black along their outer webs. The length is about fourteen-and-a-half inches, and that of the wing from nine to nine-and-a-half inches. Like the foregoing species, the Manx Shearwater is an inhabitant of the Atlantic Ocean, and it breeds in many parts of Ireland and on our western coasts from the Scilly Islands to the Hebrides, Orkney, and Shetland Islands, in suitable localities. Although it is occasionally seen during the day-time, the Manx Shearwater, like most Petrels, is a night-flying bird. It burrows into the peat or into the sandy-soil on a cliff, and lays its single white egg either on the bare soil or on a few scraps of grass, or dead leaves of plants, which serve as an apology for a nest.

THE DUSKY SHEARWATER.
THE MANX SHEARWATER.

THE LEVANTINE SHEARWATER.
(*Puffinus yelkouanus.*)

This southern representative of our Manx Shearwater differs in being slightly browner, and in having the lower flanks dusky-brown, as well as the under tail coverts. The tarsus seems to be a little longer than in *P. puffinus*, and the middle toe is 1·95 inch in length instead of 1·8 inch.

THE LEVANTINE SHEARWATER.

The home of this species is in the Mediterranean and Black Seas, but it occasionally wanders northward, as is shown by two specimens in the British Museum, one from Plymouth and the other from Torbay. Nothing has been recorded of its habits and nesting, but these are doubtless similar to those of our own Manx Shearwater.

THE DUSKY SHEARWATER.
(*Puffinus obscurus.*)

This is a smaller species than the Manx Shearwater, from which it is distinguished by its pure white axillaries, and the length of the wing, which does not exceed eight inches. A specimen of this species, which is found in the tropical and sub-tropical seas of the whole world, has been captured in England, near Bungay in Suffolk, in the Spring of 1858. Another specimen, said to have been procured in Devonshire, is in the British Museum. The single white egg is laid in the hole of a rock, and the nesting habitat of the species appears to be in the West Indian Islands.

THE ALLIED SHEARWATER.
(*Puffinus assimilis.*)

A specimen of a small Shearwater was obtained off Valentia Harbour, in Ireland, in May, 1853, and has always been referred to *Puffinus obscurus*. Recently, however, Mr. Howard Saunders re-examined the bird in question, and it turned out to belong to *P. assimilis*, a species very similar to *P. obscurus*, but smaller, and distinguished by the white shading to the inner webs of the primaries, the white under tail-coverts, and the more decided white line on each side of the neck. As the species breeds in the Canaries, Madeira, and the

THE ALLIED SHEARWATER.

Cape Verde Islands, there is nothing extraordinary in its occurrence in British waters. It has a very wide distribution over the seas of the tropics, and ranges from New Zealand and Australia through the Atlantic to the Madeira group.

THE SOOTY SHEARWATER.
(Puffinus griseus.)
See p. 218.

Several specimens of the Sooty Shearwater have been obtained on our coasts in summer and autumn, but it can only be considered to be an accidental visitor to Great Britain. It is a small species, about eighteen inches in length, with a wing of twelve inches, but it can easily be distinguished by the sooty-brown colour of both upper and under surface, and by its inner wing-coverts, which are white with dusky shafts to the feathers. It is almost cosmopolitan in its range, being found in both the Atlantic and Pacific Oceans, reaching to the Faeroe Islands in the former and to the Kurile group in the latter, while in the south its range extends to the Straits of Magellan, as well as to the Auckland Islands and New Zealand. It breeds in the small islands in the latter region, laying a single white egg in a burrow, which it excavates for itself in the peaty soil.

THE CAPPED PETREL.
(Œstrelata hæsitata.)
See p. 217.

The species of the genus Œstrelata, to which the Capped Petrel belongs, differ from the members of the genus Puffinus in having a rounded, instead of a compressed, tarsus, in the shorter bill, and in the smaller size of the hallux. The Capped Petrel is a very rare bird, and but few specimens have been obtained. Nothing is known of the place where it breeds, but its nesting habitat is believed to be in the mountains of some of the West Indian Islands, probably Haiti, Martinique, or Guadeloupe. From the latter island there are four specimens in the Paris Museum, and single examples have been obtained in Hungary, near Boulogne, in Eastern Florida, and on Long Island, New York. One British specimen was captured in Norfolk in the spring of 1850. In this species the back is sooty-brown and the head black, forming the cap from which the bird takes its name; the back of the neck is white, like the under surface and the upper tail-coverts.

THE WHITE-THROATED GREY PETREL.
(Œstrelata brevipes.)

As an instance of the way in which Petrels wander from their normal habitats, no better example could have been found than in the occurrence of *O. brevipes* in England. A single specimen was presented to the British Museum by Mr. Willis Bund; it was obtained near Aberystwith in the winter of 1889. The only habitat of the species previously known was in the Pacific Ocean, having been met with in the Fiji

THE WHITE-THROATED GREY PETREL.

Islands and the New Hebrides, where it is found in the mountains burrowing into the turf for a nesting place. The egg, however, has not yet been described. It is a small species, measuring only ten-and-a-half inches in length, with a wing of eight inches. It is slaty-grey in colour, both above and below, and the upper tail-coverts are of the same tint, but the throat is white as well as the forehead, and the cap is dusky-blackish.

BULWER'S
PETREL.
(*Bulweria bulweri.*)
See p. 215.

This species is distinguished by its sooty-black colour and its wedge-shaped tail. The nasal tubes are separate and directed forwards, and are flesh-coloured at the ends. One specimen is said to have been procured in Yorkshire. The species is an inhabitant of the Atlantic and Pacific Oceans, and it breeds in the Desertas Islands. The birds make no nest, but lay their single white egg in a hole or under a rock.

THE
BLACK-BROWED
ALBATROS.
(*Diomedea
melanophrys.*)

A single specimen of this Albatros was captured near Linton in Cambridgeshire, on the 9th of July, 1897. It is an inhabitant of the Southern Oceans, but occasionally strays into the North Atlantic, and has been observed near the Faeroe Islands, where a specimen was obtained in 1894.

THE BLACK-BROWED ALBATROS.

THE DIVERS.—*Order* COLYMBIFORMES.

THE external appearance of a Diver is sufficient for its recognition, and the only bird that it could possibly be mistaken for would be a Grebe, from which the Divers are at once distinguished by their larger size. In certain anatomical characters they closely resemble the Grebes, but they have the toes united by a web, and not scalloped as in the last-named birds. They are the most expert and powerful of divers, but they are almost helpless on land, as their feet appear to have no power whatever and lie stretched out behind the birds on each side. The usual upright position in which these birds are mounted in Museums is now generally admitted to be an impossible one.

THE GREAT
NORTHERN DIVER.
(*Colymbus glacialis.*)

This is one of the larger Divers, and has a wing of fourteen inches in length. In summer plumage it is distinguished by its purplish black head, while the sides of the fore part of the neck are purplish-blue or dark greenish-blue. In winter the upper parts are dark brown, the feathers margined with greyish ash-colour.

The present species may probably breed in the Shetlands, but no authentic eggs have been taken, though it nests in Iceland, Greenland and in Arctic America. To Great Britain it is chiefly known as a winter visitor, when specimens are noticed off all our coasts, its remarkable diving powers making it by no means an easy task to procure a specimen, as it is able to sink its body low in the water or dive at once, sometimes accomplishing a distance of a hundred yards or more before it reappears. The nest consists of only a few bits of dead grass or water-plants and is placed close to the edge of the water, so that the bird can shuffle down to the latter and escape by swimming, on the approach of danger. The eggs exceed three-and-a-half inches in length, and are two in number, of a dark olive or chocolate brown colour, with black spots and indistinct underlying spots of grey.

THE
WHITE-BILLED
DIVER.
(*Colymbus adamsi.*)

There is no difference in size between this and the foregoing species, but it can be told by its yellowish or whitish bill, which is also of a different shape from that of the Great Northern Diver, for it is nearly straight from the forehead to the tip, whereas in *C. glacialis* the culminal ridge is bent

THE RED-THROATED DIVER.　THE WHITE-BILLED DIVER.　THE GREAT NORTHERN DIVER.

downwards towards the tip, and there is scarcely any indication of an angle on the lower mandible, whereas in *C. adamsi* the angle of the genys is strongly marked. In the latter bird the colour of the throat and upper fore-neck is purplish instead of greenish-blue, and the white edgings to the feathers on the band which crosses the throat are broader and longer. In winter plumage the two species are alike, but the colour of the bill distinguishes them at this season of the year.

The White-billed Diver has occurred several times on our coasts, and is perhaps more common in winter than has been supposed. Its home is in the Arctic Regions of Europe and Siberia as well as North-west America. In habits it does not differ from *C. glacialis*, and the nest and eggs are similar.

THE BLACK-THROATED DIVER.
(Colymbus arcticus.)

This is a smaller bird than either of the foregoing, and has the head and neck of a dove-grey colour; the fore-neck is purplish black, with rows of white-striped feathers on either side of the neck. In winter it may be told by its smaller size, the wing being from eleven-and-a-half to thirteen inches in length: the upper surface of the body is dark ashy-brown and the wing-coverts are more or less spotted with white. The Black-throated Diver is found nesting in the North of Scotland, and occurs in winter on our coasts. It nests in Northern Europe and Asia as well as in North America, migrating southwards in winter, when it is found

THE BLACK-THROATED DIVER.

in the Mediterranean and in the United States. It is a bird of powerful flight, and often circles round in the air with a long sweep before settling down on the water of the loch where it has placed its nest. This is always to be found close to the water, and is sometimes built of grass and weeds in the water itself, but generally the two eggs are laid on the bare ground. The eggs are like those of the other Divers, and measure from three-and-a-quarter to three-and-a-half inches.

THE
RED - THROATED
DIVER.
(*Colymbus
septentrionalis.*)
See p. 223.

The red patch on the throat in summer plumage distinguishes this species, and in winter the upper parts are ashy-brown, with white spots. It is a small bird, like *C. arcticus*, and the wing does not exceed eleven inches in length. Like the latter species it nests in Scotland, and very locally in the north of Ireland. Its breeding range extends throughout the Arctic Regions in Europe, Asia and North America, and in winter it ranges to the southward, and is not uncommon at that season on the British Coasts. In habits it does not differ from other Divers, and breeds on inland lochs, laying two eggs on the bare ground not far from water. The eggs are dark olive or chocolate-brown, with black spots and faint underlying spots of grey, and are about three inches in length or a little less.

THE GREBES.—*Order* PODICIPEDIDIFORMES.

THESE birds are closely related to the Divers, but can be distinguished from them by their lobed toes, and by the apparent absence of a tail, which is represented by a little tuft of feathers scarcely to be dissociated from the feathers of the rump.

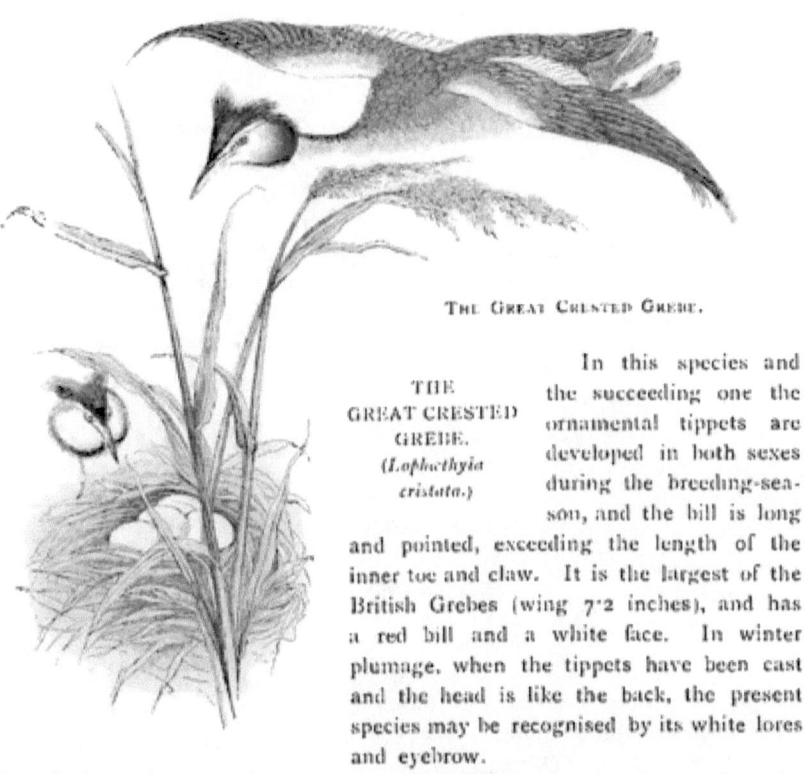

THE GREAT CRESTED GREBE.

THE GREAT CRESTED GREBE. (*Lophæthyia cristata.*)

In this species and the succeeding one the ornamental tippets are developed in both sexes during the breeding-season, and the bill is long and pointed, exceeding the length of the inner toe and claw. It is the largest of the British Grebes (wing 7·2 inches), and has a red bill and a white face. In winter plumage, when the tippets have been cast and the head is like the back, the present species may be recognised by its white lores and eyebrow.

This species is found nesting in many parts of England and as far north as the Clyde, as well as in several counties of Ireland. It occurs nearly everywhere in the

Old World and breeds throughout its range. In England the nest is generally found near the edges of the reeds or among the rubbish which accumulates on the side of a 'Broad' or lake, but in some places on the Continent of Europe the species breeds in colonies in the reed-beds, and Seebohm says that he found dozens of nests on the Garda Lake, about sixty miles west of the Gulf of Danzig. The nest is made of weeds and sedges; the three or four eggs are greenish-white, with a chalky covering, and are a little over two inches in length.

THE RED-NECKED GREBE.
(Lophethyia gristigena.)

The grey throat of this Grebe distinguishes it from *L. cristata* in summer plumage, and in winter both old and young birds want the white eyebrow which distinguishes the last-named species. The wing is over six inches in length, so that the Red-necked Grebe cannot be confounded with any of the succeeding species, which it resembles somewhat in winter plumage.

It is a rare bird in Great Britain, and only visits us in winter. Its breeding range extends from Southern Norway to the Baltic provinces, through Russia to Central Asia. It is very common in Northern Germany, where it arrives in April, and builds a floating nest of reeds and decayed water-plants: the eggs are three or four in number, and are greenish-white, with a chalky covering. They measure about two inches in length.

1—THE RED-NECKED GREBE.   2—THE SCLAVONIAN GREBE.   3—THE BLACK-NECKED GREBE.

THE SCLAVONIAN GREBE.
(Dytes auritus.)

In the genus *Dytes* the bill is shorter and stouter than in *Lophethyia*, and the form of the tippet is different, extending round the entire throat, while there is a distinct crest of rufous plumes on each side of the head above the tippet. The present species is a regular winter visitor to Great Britain, especially to the east coast of England. It nests in Iceland, and throughout Northern Europe and Siberia to North America. In winter it is found in the Mediterranean and also extends as far as the Bermudas. The nest is built, after the manner of all Grebes, in a fresh-water lake. The eggs are four or five in number, and are greenish-white with the usual chalky coating; the length is about an inch-and-three-quarters to nearly two inches.

THE
BLACK-NECKED
GREBE.
(*Proctopus
nigricollis.*)

The present species has a very thin bill, which is slightly upturned at the end and wider at the base than it is deep. In the summer plumage it is also distinguished by the black fore-neck and chest, and by the heavy tuft of ornamental plumes which spring from above the ear-coverts: these differ in character and appearance from the ornamental feathers of the Sclavonian Grebe. In winter the two birds are more alike, but the shorter wing (five inches, and the shape of the bill will serve to separate the species. The Black-necked Grebe is an occasional visitor to Britain, generally in the spring and summer. It nests in Central Europe and the Mediterranean countries and throughout temperate Asia, as well as in many parts of Eastern and Southern Africa. In winter it is found on the coasts of China and the Indian Ocean. The nest is made of moss and reeds, and the eggs are from three to five in number, of the usual greenish-white colour, and they measure from an inch-and-three-quarters to nearly two inches.

THE LITTLE GREBE.

THE
LITTLE GREBE.
(*Podicipes
fluviatilis.*)

This is the smallest and the commonest of the British Grebes, and is familiar to every one under its name of the ' Dab-chick.' In summer the upper and under surface of the bird are alike black, and the sides of the face and neck are chestnut, while the bill is black, with a yellow tip and a mark of greenish-yellow at the base. In winter the back is brown and the breast pure white. It is a resident species throughout the British Islands, and occurs also all over Europe to Northern Asia and Japan.

The Little Grebe is, like the rest of its family, a very expert diver, and can swim under water for a surprising distance. The birds will also take their young under their wing, and dive with them in this position, to escape danger. The nestlings are pretty little creatures, with the upper parts and the throat striped with black and rufous in zebra-like pattern. The nest is a mass of rotten reeds and water plants, floating on the top of the water at the edge of a lake or river, and as the bird covers her eggs on leaving the nest, the latter are generally quite invisible. The eggs are at first white, but gradually become discoloured to a buff or brown colour; they are five or six in number, and are about half-an-inch in length.

THE PIED-BILLED GREBE. (*Podilymbus podiceps.*) This is a widely distributed species in North and South America, and is said to have been captured on one occasion near Weymouth, in January, 1881. The Pied-billed Grebe has a very thick bill, of a milk-white colour, bluish at the tip, and crossed by a black band.

THE PIED-BILLED GREBE.

THE RAILS.—*Order RALLIFORMES.*

THE members of this Order are remarkable for their long and slender toes. The typical Rails have very slender bodies, and are inhabitants of the marshes. The Coots and Moorhens are birds of a stouter build, and are more often seen in the open water. All have black downy nestlings, very different in appearance from the old birds.

THE WATER-RAIL. (*Rallus aquaticus.*) Like all Rails, the present species is a bird of skulking and retiring habits and is not often seen. It has a longer bill than any of the other British species, and is of an olive-brown colour with black streaks on the head and back, while the throat and under-parts are slaty-grey, with black flanks barred with white : the under tail-coverts are also barred with black and white, and have buff tips.

THE WATER-RAIL.

The Water-Rail is found in marshy localities throughout the whole of Great Britain, but is somewhat rarer in Scotland. It is also an inhabitant of the rest of Europe, excepting the more northern portions, and extends to Central Asia. It is a shy bird, and takes to flight unwillingly, preferring to escape by running, which it does most deftly, threading its way like a rat through the mazes of the reed-bed. The nest is rather neatly made of sedge and leaves of reeds, and lined with slender reeds: it is built in a clump of rushes about a foot above the ground, and the eggs vary from five to eleven in number. They are of a creamy stone-colour, with rufous spots and grey underlying ones, and measure about an inch-and-a-half in length.

THE LAND-RAIL.
(*Crex crex.*)

This is one of the short-billed Rails, and is generally known as the 'Corn-Crake.' It is distinguished from the Water-Rail by its shorter bill and by the colour of the plumage, which is brown, streaked with black, while the wing-coverts and primary quills are bright chestnut: the ear-coverts, lower throat and chest are ashy-grey.

THE LAND-RAIL.

The Land-Rail is found throughout Great Britain in summer, and extends its range over the greater part of Europe to Central Asia and Siberia as far as the valley of the Lena. It occasionally straggles to Greenland and the Eastern States of North America, and visits South Africa in winter. Its nest is placed on the ground in hay-fields and corn-lands, and the eggs are from seven to ten in number, of a buffish clay-colour, with rufous and grey spots: they measure about an inch-and-a-half in length.

THE LITTLE CRAKE.
(*Zapornia parva.*)

The sexes in this species are different in colour, and the middle toe is longer than in the Land-Rail, the wing is more pointed, and the secondaries are much shorter than the primaries. The male is ochreous brown, with black streaks on the upper surface, and the lower parts of the body are ashy grey, with a few white bars on the flanks, while the under tail-coverts are white, tinged with ochre and barred with black. The female is browner, with the chest and throat white, and the rest of the under surface pale vinaceous isabelline. The length of the species is seven inches, and the wing four inches.

The Little Crake is only an occasional visitor to Great Britain in spring and autumn. It is an inhabitant of Central Europe, and is found in Russia and Central Asia. It winters in Equatorial Africa and North-western India. The habits

BAILLON'S CRAKE.   THE LITTLE CRAKE.   THE SPOTTED CRAKE.

are similar to those of other Rails, and it makes its nest in tussocks in the marshes. The eggs are seven or eight in number, of an oval shape and olive in colour with brown markings; they measure a little over an inch in length.

THE SPOTTED
CRAKE.
(Porzana porzana.)

In the Spotted Crake the sexes are alike in plumage and the secondaries are as long as the primaries, so that the wing is more rounded. It is an olive-brown bird with small white spots distributed among the black markings of the upper surface : the throat and breast are ashy, and the bill is yellow, inclining to orange-red at the base.

To Great Britain the present species is a summer visitor, but is everywhere very local in its distribution. It is distributed throughout the greater part of Europe in summer, and extends to Central Asia, wintering in the Indian Peninsula and North-eastern Africa. In habits it resembles the Water-Rail, and it makes a somewhat large nest of reeds and sedge on the ground in reed-beds. The eggs are from eight to a dozen in number, of the usual double spotted Ralline type, and measure about an inch-and-a-half in length.

THE CAROLINA
CRAKE.
(Porzana carolina.)

A single specimen of this North American species has been obtained near Newbury in Berkshire. It differs from the Spotted Crake in having the cheeks and centre of the throat black. It is a plentiful species in some of the United States, and wanders south in winter to Central and South America. In habits it resembles our Spotted Crake, but the eggs are slightly smaller.

THE CAROLINA CRAKE.

BAILLON'S CRAKE.
(Porzana intermedia.)

This is a smaller species than any of the foregoing, and has the wing about three-and-a-half-inches in length. It is brown, sparsely spotted with white on the back, and has the sides of face, throat and chest grey, but it can always be distinguished by its uniform brownish-grey axillaries, these being barred with white in the Spotted Crakes.

Baillon's Crake has been found in spring and autumn in Great Britain, but is very rare. It is, however, believed to nest occasionally in England. It is distributed over the greater part of Central and Southern Europe, and is found in winter on the Persian Gulf and in Africa. The nest is made of rushes, and the eggs, from six to eight in number, are olive brown with spots of reddish brown and dark grey: they measure a little over an inch in length.

THE MOOR-HEN.
(Gallinula chloropus.)

This is a well-known inhabitant of our rivers and marshes, and is a resident species in all parts of Great Britain. It is found all over Europe and Asia, and also occurs in Africa and Madagascar. The Moor-Hen is easily recognised from the other British Rails by its larger size, by the red shield on its forehead, and by the red band above the tarsal joint, both of which characters, as well as the white markings on the flanks, are plainly seen when the bird is swimming.

It is much less shy than the other species of Rails and is now to be seen in many of our London parks, where it is as tame as the other water-fowl. It is said to do some damage by eating the eggs of game-birds and ducks, but its principal food consists of worms and insects. The nest is a compactly built round structure of flags and

THE MOOR-HEN.

sedge among rushes or on a branch overhanging the water. The eggs are from seven to nine in number, and are of a stony-buff colour, with reddish brown or blackish spots and grey underlying ones. They measure from one-and-a-half to two-inches in length.

THE PURPLE GALLINULES.
Genus
PORPHYRIO.

Two species of these brilliantly coloured birds have been recorded as having been shot in England, viz.: the Purple Gallinule (*P. cœruleus*) of Southern Spain and the Green-backed Gallinule (*P. porphyrio*) of Africa. As, however, these ornamental birds, remarkable for their green or blue plumage and their bright red bill and legs, are often kept in aviaries, the specimens procured have doubtless been some that had escaped from confinement.

THE
COMMON COOT.
(*Falica atra.*)

Although of a blackish colour like the Moor-Hen, the Coot is a much larger bird, and has the webs of the toes scalloped, so as to form lobes, while the ivory-white frontal shield is also a plainly visible character when the bird is seen swimming about. It breeds on the lakes and rivers in every part of the British Islands, and occurs in some of our southern harbours in great numbers in winter. It inhabits the whole of Europe and Asia, but does not extend

THE COMMON COOT.

to Africa, nor beyond the Indo-Malayan Islands. The Coot is a shy bird during the breeding-season, but at other times it may often be seen swimming on any large inland water, where its white frontal shield renders it conspicuous. The nest is substantially built of flags and sedge and is generally found in shallow water among the rushes on the side of a lake. The eggs are seven or eight in number, of a pale clay-colour dotted with tiny blackish spots and grey underlying ones: the length is about two inches.

THE PIGEONS.—*Order COLUMBIFORMES.*

—

THE Pigeons are separated from the other Orders of Birds by several well-marked anatomical characters, especially in the arrangement of their plantar tendons. Their external aspect is too well-known to need further description, and in many points they resemble Game-birds, but they have a differently shaped bill, the nostrils being pierced in a soft skin near the base.

THE
WOOD PIGEON.
(Columba palumbus.)

This handsome bird is found in most parts of the British Islands, with the exception of the north of Scotland, whither, however, it is gradually extending its range. It is found throughout Europe, and as far east as Central Asia.

THE STOCK-DOVE.
THE WOOD-PIGEON.

In the country the Wood-Pigeon is one the shyest of birds, and it is only in the autumn and winter, when they feed on the beech-mast, that they are seen in any numbers together. The large size of the species and the white marks on the side of the neck and the wing easily distinguish this Pigeon in flight. The nest is a platform of crossed sticks placed in a tree or bush. The eggs are two in number, pure white, and measure an inch-and-a-half to an inch-and-three-quarters in length.

THE
STOCK-DOVE.
(Columba œnas.)

The range of the Stock-Dove is similar to that of the Wood-Pigeon, but it goes further to the eastward in Central Asia. It is found throughout the greater part of Great Britain, and is extending its range in Scotland and Ireland.

The Stock-Dove differs from the Wood-Pigeon in its smaller size, and in the absence of the white patches on the neck and on the bend of the wing. It has also four spots of black on the wing, caused by the black bases to some of the inner coverts and secondary quills : these spots are absent in the Wood-Pigeon. Unlike the latter bird, the Stock-Dove nests in the hole of a tree or cliff, as well as in rabbit burrows. The nest consists of a few sticks or roots, and sometimes there is no nest at all, the two white eggs being laid at the bottom of the hole : the eggs measure about an inch-and-a-half in length.

THE
ROCK-DOVE.
(Columba livia.)

This bird is easily recognised by its white lower back and by the black bands across the wings. It is found throughout Europe to Central Asia and North-western India, and frequently crosses with domestic Pigeons, of which it is the parent stock. In Great Britain it is a local bird and nests in the sea-cliffs of the north of England, as well as in Scotland and Ireland. The nest is built on a shelf of rock in a cave or on the ledge of a cliff, and is a flat roughly made structure of small sticks, sea-weed and grass-bents. The eggs are two in number, white, and measure about an inch-and-a-half in length.

THE ROCK-DOVE.

THE PASSENGER PIGEON.

THE PASSENGER PIGEON.
(Ectopistes migratoria.)

Although this Pigeon, which is found over the greater portion of North America, has been said to have occurred in Britain on five occasions, it is doubtful whether any of the birds were really wild ones. It may be recognised by its long and pointed tail, the feathers of which are grey with a cinnamon-coloured base and a good deal of white on all but the centre feathers, which are slaty black. The length of the bird is about sixteen inches.

THE TURTLE-DOVE.
(Turtur turtur)

A summer visitor to England, but not known to the northward of Southern Scotland, and of rare instance in Ireland, though Mr. Ussher believes that

THE TURTLE-DOVE.   THE ORIENTAL TURTLE-DOVE.

t may nest there more often than has been supposed. It is commonly distributed throughout Europe and extends, in a slightly paler form, to Central Asia.

It is easily recognised by the black spotting of the upper surface, which is of a ruddy brown colour, the greyish lower body and rump, the white tips to the tail-feathers, the vinous colour of the throat and breast, and the scaly patch of black and white feathers on the sides of the neck. The nest is a slight one of twigs, placed in an evergreen bush, or in a hedge, and well concealed. The eggs are two, creamy white, and measure about an inch-and-a-quarter in length.

THE ORIENTAL
TURTLE-DOVE.
(Turtur orientalis.)
This eastern species, which inhabits the Peninsula of India and Burma, as far north as Manchuria and Japan, has been met with on one occasion, when a specimen was procured near Scarborough on the 23rd of October, 1889.

It is a little larger than the common Turtle Dove, and has the colours rather darker, especially on the under surface, where the vinous colour of the breast overspreads the abdomen as well; the band at the end of the tail-feathers is bluish-grey instead of white.

THE SAND-GROUSE.—*Order* PTEROCLETES.

THESE birds have many anatomical characters which ally them to the Pigeons, but in appearance they are very like Game-birds, though they differ from the latter in their short legs and in the shape of the eggs, which are oval and distinctly double spotted.

PALLAS'
SAND-GROUSE.
(Syrrhaptes paradoxus.)
Only one species of Sand-Grouse has occurred in Great Britain, and this is a bird whose home is the steppes of Central Asia. Periodically, Pallas' Sand-Grouse comes

PALLAS' SAND-GROUSE.

westwards in large numbers, and on these occasions it has visited Great Britain. One great irruption took place in 1863, and another in 1888. On the last occasion some of the birds lingered on till the next summer and bred here. They make no nest, but the eggs are laid in a slight hole in the ground. The eggs are three or four in number, of an olive or brownish-buff colour, spotted with brown or pale olive, with underlying grey markings, and are unmistakable on account of their perfectly oval shape.

THE GAME-BIRDS.—*Order GALLIFORMES.*

THIS Order of Birds is too familiar to every one of my readers to need an elaborate description of its characteristics. Many anatomical features separate the Game-Birds from all the other Orders, but their external form is so well known that there is no need to characterize them in detail.

**THE
RED GROUSE.**
(*Lagopus scoticus.*)

The Grouse are distinguished from the other British Game-birds by their feathered nostrils and feathered toes. Our Red Grouse is perhaps the most characteristically ' British ' species which we pos-sess, for it is found nowhere else than in Great Britain. Considerable variation in the shade of its colour-ing is met with in different localities, and the male and female do not go through the same process of change of plumage, for whereas the male moults into an autumn dress and again into a winter one, he retains the latter through the breeding sea-son until the next autumn moult supervenes. The female moults in summer and autumn only, and has no distinct winter plumage, while the male has no distinct summer plumage.

THE RED GROUSE.

The Red Grouse is an inhabitant of the moors up to the limit of heather-growth, above which the Ptarmigan takes its place. The nest is a slight hollow in the ground, lined with moss or grass and hidden by some overhanging heather or ling. The eggs are sometimes as many as twelve in number, and are very richly coloured, having the ground-colour creamy buff, more or less concealed by the spots and blotches of dark reddish brown, which are scribbled all over the egg : their length is about an inch-and-three-quarters.

THE PTARMIGAN. (*Lagopus mutus.*)

The chief difference between the Ptarmigan and the Red Grouse lies in the fact that the former bird has a snow-white winter plumage, excepting for its black outer tail-feathers. The male has a black patch in front of the eye, which is absent in the

THE PTARMIGAN.

female. In summer the dress is much blacker, and in the autumn it is greyer, so that there are three distinct phases of plumage. The Ptarmigan is only found on the high mountains of Scotland, and it inhabits the same altitude in Scandinavia and the other high mountains of Europe to the Alps and the Pyrenees. Its plumage assimilates to its surroundings at the different seasons, and it turns white when the snow covers the mountains. Its nest and eggs resemble those of the Red Grouse.

THE BLACK GROUSE (*Lyrurus tetrix.*)

The coloration of this species is so

THE BLACK GROUSE.

well known that no detailed description is necessary: no other British Game-bird can be mistaken for it. The Black Grouse is found throughout the pine-woods and birch-woods, especially in the mountains, of Europe and Northern and Central Asia, and it inhabits the north of England and Scotland in the localities suited to its habits, being also found in the wilder districts of the west and south-west of England and Wales. It is a tree-frequenting species rather than a ground bird like the Red Grouse and Ptarmigan, and further differs from those birds in being polygamous. When the breeding-season comes round the males often indulge in furious combats, and go through all sorts of dancing manœuvres, but they disappear as soon as the females have begun to sit. The nest is a hollow in the ground, with scarcely any lining, and the eggs are from six to ten in number, of a buff colour, richly spotted with brown: they are about two inches in length.

THE CAPERCAILIE.

THE
CAPERCAILIE.
(*Tetrao urogallus.*)

This, the finest of our British Game-birds, is only found in certain districts of Scotland, where it has been re-introduced after having been exterminated. It is also an inhabitant of the pine-forests of Scandinavia and the rest of Europe as far east as Central Asia and the Baikal region.

Like the Black Grouse, the Capercailie is polygamous, and drives away all the younger males from its district as the nesting-season approaches, fighting furiously with any other old male bird that trespasses on its particular domain. It is often captured while performing its love-song or 'spel,' as it is called in Scandinavia, when the bird works itself up to a great pitch of excitement and can then be approached and shot by a skilful hunter, who understands its habits during the nesting-season. The female performs all the duties of incubation, for as soon as the hens commence to sit, the males take themselves off, and are no more seen that summer. The nest is placed on the ground, and resembles that of the Black Grouse, and the eggs, which measure a little over two inches in length, are large editions of those of the last-named species.

THE RED-LEGGED PARTRIDGE.
(Caccabis rufa.)

The Partridges differ from the Grouse in their unfeathered legs, and they are distinguished from the Pheasants by their short tail.

The Red-legged Partridge was introduced into England from the Continent during the last century, and is now a common bird in our eastern and midland counties. It is found in all the countries of western and south-western Europe, as well as Madeira, the Canaries, and the Azores. It is a beautiful bird with its white throat surrounded by a black collar, its rufous belly, and its banded flanks. It is more given to running than our Common Partridge, but when once started its flight is direct and swift: it is also a very pugnacious bird. The nest is a slight hollow in the ground under the shelter of some grass or hedge-row. The eggs are sometimes as many as eighteen in number, of a stone-colour or buff with numerous dots and spots of reddish brown.

THE COMMON PARTRIDGE.
THE RED-LEGGED PARTRIDGE.

THE COMMON PARTRIDGE.
(Perdix perdix.)

Like the other British Game-birds our Common Partridge is so well known that a description would be superfluous, but it should be noticed that a hen bird can be told at any age by the colour of the scapulars and the lesser and median wing-coverts, which are black with broad cross-barrings of buff, as well as by the central buff stripe down the centre of the feather. This is also seen in the male, but the coverts and scapulars are not barred, being black with a marking of chestnut on the inner web. Sometimes the old female has a chestnut horse-shoe mark on the breast, but this is generally small, and is sometimes absent. Young females, however, curiously enough, have a chestnut horse-shoe on the breast,

and the young of both sexes can always be told by their
pointed, instead of rounded, first primary, and by the
more yellowish colour of the feet.

The Partridge is found throughout Europe eastwards
to Persia and Central Asia, as far as the Altai mountains.
The nest is placed on the ground, in a sheltered position,
and the eggs are from ten to fifteen in number, of an
uniform pale olive brown : they are a little more than an
inch-and-a-quarter in length.

THE COMMON
QUAIL.
(*Coturnix coturnix.*)

This is a much smaller bird
than the Partridge, and is only a
summer visitor to certain parts of
Great Britain. It is found over
the greater portion of Europe and Northern Asia, and
migrates in enormous flocks to its winter home in Africa
and the Indian Peninsula.

THE COMMON QUAIL.
THE ANDALUSIAN HEMIPODE.

The nest consists of a hollow in the ground with a
scanty lining of grass. The eggs are unmistakable, being creamy buff or white, with
broad and conspicuous blotches and spots of rich brown : they are from eight to
twelve in number and measure nearly an inch-and-a-quarter in length.

THE COMMON
PHEASANT.
Phasianus colchicus.

Pheasants differ from Partridges and Quails in their long
tails. There is no necessity to dwell upon the coloration or
habits of this well-known game-bird. It is said still to exist
in a wild state in Asia Minor and the Caucasus, but in most
countries of Europe it has been introduced. The nest is a hollow in the ground,
with a lining of dead leaves, and is well concealed. The eggs are from eight to
twelve in number, of a brown or olive-brown colour, and sometimes bluish eggs are
found : they measure about an inch-and-three-quarters in length.

THE COMMON PHEASANT.

THE ANDALUSIAN
HEMIPODE.
(*Turnix sylvatia.*)

Three specimens of this bird are said to have been taken in England, but the general opinion is that these occurrences are not genuine. In appearance the species, which is an inhabitant of Southern Europe, is like a little Quail, but it can be distinguished from the latter by the absence of the hind toe. The female is larger and more brightly coloured than the male.

APPENDIX.

PAGE 28. *Add :—*

THE
CHESTNUT-BELLIED
WEAVER-FINCH.
(*Munia atricapilla.*)

On October 27th, 1898, I received from Mr. G. Hubert Woods a specimen of this Asiatic species which he had shot in Suffolk on the 26th of October, out of a flock of twelve individuals. Mr. Hartert has also seen a small flock of these Weaver-Finches in the reed-beds of Tring Reservoir. That the little birds had originally escaped from some aviary there can be no

THE CHESTNUT-BELLIED WEAVER-FINCH.

doubt, but they would appear to have nested in England, and it will be interesting to see whether the species succeeds in establishing itself as a British bird. It is to be hoped that protection will be afforded to it, as an English winter will be quite enough to test its powers of survival. That two flocks of these birds have been seen speaks well for the endurance of our tropical visitor, which is well-known as a dominant species in its eastern home. Introduced into Borneo, it has flourished exceedingly, and in some districts has exterminated the resident Weaver-Finch (*Munia fuscans*). Now it is face to face with our Sparrow and our Greenfinch, and we shall see whether it can survive the enmity of these skull-cracking Finches.

16

The Chestnut-bellied Weaver-Finch is an inhabitant of India, China, the Malayan Peninsula, and Indo-Malayan Islands. It is chestnut in colour, with a black head and neck, upper breast, abdomen and under tail-coverts: the upper tail-coverts and tail-feathers have a gloss of golden straw-colour. Length four-and-a-half inches.

PAGE 61. *Add:—*

THE WESTERN TREE WARBLER.— *Hypolais polyglotta.*

PAGE 61. *Add:—*

RADDE'S BUSH-WARBLER.
(Herbivocula schwarzi.)

At the meeting of the British Ornithologists' Club held on the 19th of October, 1898, Mr. G. H. Caton Haigh exhibited a specimen of this Siberian species, which he had himself shot at North Cotes, in Lincolnshire, on the 1st of October. He noticed the powerful note of the bird and had the hedge thoroughly beaten out to find the owner of so loud a voice, with the result that *Herbivocula schwarzi* was added to the Avifauna of Europe, for it has never been seen in any part of the continent.

Its breeding-home is in Siberia, and it winters in Southern China and the Burmese Provinces. In form *Herbivocula* is intermediate between the Reed-Warblers and the Willow-Warblers. Like the latter it has a nearly even tail, not graduated as in the *Acrocephali*, and the bill is black, short and stout. The colour of Radde's Bush-Warbler is very simple, being olive-brown above and tawny-buff below: it has a very distinct buff eyebrow and the under wing-coverts and axillaries are also buff. Length five-and-a-half inches, wing 2·45.

RADDE'S BUSH-WARBLER.

PAGE 87.   *Add :—*

THE
PURPLE MARTIN.
(*Progne purpurea.*)

This North American species is said to have been shot on one occasion near Kingstown in Ireland, in 1839 or 1840, and the specimen is in the Dublin Museum.

PAGE 129.   *Add :—*

THE AMERICAN DARTER.

THE
AMERICAN
DARTER.
(*Plotus anhinga.*)

Professor Newton ('Dic. tionary of Birds,' p. 882) calls attention to the fact that a Darter has been shot in England, though the occurrence has been omitted by most writers on British Ornithology, myself among the number. In the 'Zoologist' for 1852 (pp. 3601, 3654), the Rev. A. C. Smith states that a specimen of a Darter was shot near Poole, in Dorsetshire, in June, 1851, by a young man named Cripps. I quite agree with Professor Newton that the record of the capture of this American bird in British waters is quite as well-established as many other instances of occasional visitors.

The Darter is distinguished by its long neck and serrated bill, as well as by the curious ribbed tail.   It has otherwise the appearance of a Cormorant.

PAGE 137.   *Add :—*

THE
TRUMPETER SWAN.
(*Cygnus buccinator.*)

A young Swan was shot near Aldeburgh in October, 1866. It is believed to be an immature bird of the American Trumpeter Swan, and has been so identified by Professor Newton. As the species is often kept in confinement in

16*

this country, the individual in question may have been an escaped bird. The Trumpeter Swan belongs to the section of the genus *Cygnus* which has no knob on the base of the bill, and the trachea enters the hollow keel of the sternum. There is no yellow at the base of the bill, which is large and has the culmen nearly four inches in length.

PAGE 192. Add :—

THE ANTARCTIC SHEATHBILL.
(Chionis alba.)

A specimen of this curious species was killed at Carlingford Lighthouse, in Co. Down, in December, 1892. It was exhibited at a meeting of the Zoological Society on the 28th of February, 1893, by Mr. R. M. Barrington. The bird belongs to a purely Antarctic genus, and it must have escaped from confinement, though the condition of its plumage did not indicate that it had been recently kept in captivity. The species is pure white in plumage, with a yellow bill, ornamented with the curious ' sheath ' at the base of the mandible, whence the Sheath-bills take their name.

FINIS.

ALPHABETICAL INDEX.

BUTLER & TANNER,
THE SELWOOD PRINTING WORKS,
FROME, AND LONDON.

www.ingramcontent.com/pod-product-compliance
Lightning Source LLC
Chambersburg PA
CBHW030630030726
47497CB00006B/1713